# ICE AND SHADOW

# ANDRE NORTON

BAEN

ICE AND SHADOW

This is a work of fiction. All the characters and events portrayed in this book are fictional, and any resemblance to real people or incidents is purely coincidental.

Ice Crown copyright © 1993 by Andre Norton. Brother to Shadows copyright © 1999 by Andre Norton.

A Baen Books Original

Baen Publishing Enterprises
P.O. Box 1403
Riverdale, NY  10471
www.baen.com

ISBN: 978-1-4516-3913-1

Cover art by Stephen Hickman

First Baen mass market paperback printing, August 2013

Distributed by Simon & Schuster
1230 Avenue of the Americas
New York, NY  10020

Library of Congress Cataloging-in-Publication Data:
2012009330

Printed in the United States of America

10  9  8  7  6  5  4  3  2  1

# ☀ CONTENTS ☀

# *ICE*
# CROWN

# ✳ CHAPTER 1 ✳

**ROANE FOUGHT** against closing her eyes, tensed her slight body until it ached. One could argue intelligently (she could hear Uncle Offlas now with that odious patience which always colored his voice when making any explanation to her) that such discomfort was all mental. If you fastened your mind on something else, the sensation of being entombed alive while in the express bolt would disappear. But she lay now in the padded interior of the speeding bullet and tried to endure.

Though she did fight her fear—the thought of smothering here—Roane clenched her fists, bit hard on her under lip. The pain of that helped. According to Uncle Offlas you could overcome *anything* if you willed it. Unfortunately, she fell far below his standards. Now that she had a chance to prove she was worth something to his plans, she must not spoil it.

Why, even the department head at Cram-brief had envied her this chance. And it was only because she was Offlas Keil's niece that she had it. The expedition to Clio

would be a family affair—Project Director Keil, his son Sandar, and Roane. She tried to breathe evenly and slowly, to keep her eyes shut, forget where she was now, and think only of the goal before her.

Maybe once in a hundred, no, closer to a thousand times, did something like this happen. And she was so lucky to be a part of it. Only right now, even her brain felt tired. All that cramming! She—Well, it was like being an osbper sponge set in a pool and given the command to absorb. Only she could not swell the way those did; she had to pack it all behind bone and flesh which was not able to expand. By rights her head ought to be so heavy with all that the briefing computers had hammered into it that she could not hold it upright.

Clio was one of the sealed planets. Yet because of the circumstances Uncle Offlas had definite orders to land there, to stay as long as it would take them to locate the treasure. Treasure! The very word gave one a shiver— though this treasure was nothing that anyone but a member of the Service would want.

Real treasure—precious, beautiful things—would not interest Offlas Keil at all. He might glance over it to classify it by historical period, but to him such would be toys. However, knowledge of the Forerunners—that was something else. And this treasure had been pinpointed by a hint there, a clue here, stretching over years of sifting, to a single general area on Clio.

Because Clio was a sealed world, the final stages of their search must be conducted in complete secrecy, as quickly as possible, using Service devices. And the Project demanded as small a task force as was necessary. Which

had sent Roane to Cram-brief to learn as much of Clio as she might need to know.

She wondered what it would be like to live on a closed planet (not for the period of days they would set down there but for a lifetime). Of course, the whole theory which had established the closed planets was wrong; such manipulation of human beings broke the Four Laws. Clio had been settled two, maybe three hundred years ago when the Psychocrats dominated the Confederation, before the Overturn of 1404. It was the third such experimental planet rediscovered, though there were rumors that there had been more, no one knew how many. The blasting of the Forqual Center during the revolt of the Overturn had destroyed most records.

All those worlds had been chosen as sites for projects which were the particular interest of one of the Hierarchy of the Psychocrats. The original colonists, brain-cleared, given false implanted memories, were settled in communities which to their briefed minds seemed natural to their new worlds. They were then left to work out new types of civilization, or a lack of civilization—to be watched secretly at intervals.

When such inhabited test planets were now rediscovered, they were declared closed. For none of the authorities could be sure what the impact of the truth might do to their peoples. Less advanced they were, as well as mutated on at least one planet. But on Clio the inhabitants were entirely human, though they were living in an archaic way, much as Roane's ancestors had lived several hundred years before space flight.

What the Psychocrat who had established Clio had

been aiming for was now not certain. But the Service thought he had set up something akin to the old Europa plan known on Terra. The large eastern continent had been divided into an irregular pattern of small kingdoms. The two western continents had been otherwise "seeded" with "natives" at a far more primitive level of culture—wandering tribes of hunters. And then they had all been left to their own devices.

On the eastern continent a series of wars for territorial expansion had ended with the establishment of two large nations, fronting each other uneasily across a border of small buffer states which still possessed their freedom, mainly because the two great powers were as yet unready to strike at each other. Intrigues, minor skirmishes, the rise and fall of dynasties were all a part of life on Clio. It was, to an onlooker from the stars, a giant game, though one in which lives were lost by a badly managed stroke of play.

In the west the tribesmen, too, fought each other; but since they remained on a more primitive level, the cost in blood had not yet been so great. However, Roane need not consider them. It was on the eastern land mass that her party would make their secret landing, in one of those small buffer states between the great powers.

"Reveny," she said aloud now, "the Kingdom of Reveny."

It was a strange word and she had had difficulty at first in pronouncing it. But no stranger than a lot of other-world names, some of them so utterly alien they could not be shaped or voiced by human vocal cords.

She had viewed the tri-dees of the site where they would do their prospecting, often enough to make the countryside familiar. But this was an old duty, part of

her wandering life. Uncle Offlas had taken her along, sometimes like excess baggage, from world to world during his own wanderings as an expert on Forerunner archaeology.

Roane liked what she had been shown of Reveny. The district they must comb for their purposes was, luckily, sparsely settled, being mountainous and forested. Part was a hunting preserve for the royal family. The only settlement was one of verderers and keepers. The rest of the inhabitants were shepherds who moved their charges seasonally from range to range. If the off-worlders had luck and were cautious, as they must be, they would have no contact with any of these.

In the tri-dees it seemed a story tape come to life. There were actual castles with sky-pointing towers, colorful towns with crooked streets (so unlike the ordered dwelling blocks of her own people), and—But she must remember that it was very primitive. Wars were still fought across those fields. Roane shuddered, remembering a couple of tapes which had revolted both her mind and her queasy stomach.

The people of Reveny were, as far as could be determined, still under some type of conditioning process. Or else the initial training had been so complete as to repersonalize their descendants as well. She would undoubtedly find them as alien emotionally and mentally as they were akin to her bodily. That, if she had any meeting with them at all.

The sway of the bullet holding her slackened. She opened her eyes as it came to a stop. With a sigh of thanksgiving that that ordeal was behind her, Roane disembarked to look around.

"You're late—"

She turned eagerly, instinctively smoothing down the flare of her overtunic. Not that it would matter to Sandar whether she looked as rumpled as a wart skin, as she well knew. But it would be nice if he saw her, just once, as a girl and not an encumbrance.

"There was a delay at the Metro thrust," she said quickly and then felt provoked. Why was she always in the wrong with Sandar and his father? If there was any delay, any difficulty, it always involved her, never them.

She tried to put aside the need for apology as she looked at her cousin. He had not changed, not fallen from his normal superiority. Though why should he in a matter of only two months? There was no reason why he should have shrunk from the height he carried so well, grown irregular features in place of those almost-too-handsome ones, been denuded of the charm he was willing to exert for everyone but her. Sandar could wear the grimed coverall of a tubeman and still look like a tri-dee hero. In the Service tunic he was still Sandar the Great. She had heard him named that once by a girl she had met back on Varch. The fact that she was his cousin sometimes made her temporarily popular, just long enough for it to take other girls to learn how little influence she had with him.

"Come on!" He was already walking away and she had to trot to catch up. "We have just half an hour to reach the field before countdown."

He kept to that long stride and she had to hop-skip to match it. Resentment began to stir in her. When she was away from Sandar Roane always hoped they could be

friends. But when they were face to face again she knew how stupid that hope was.

"My kit—" she cried.

"It came through. I stashed it in a holder."

"But we have to get it. Which way—" He was heading for the outside door.

Now he reached out and his fingers closed firmly, and none too gently, about her arm above the elbow.

"We haven't time, I told you. If you're late you'll have to take the consequences. And you won't need what's in it. There are full supplies on board ship."

"But—" Roane wanted to dig in her heels, pull back from his highhandedness. Only she knew he was perfectly capable of dragging her along by force. She saw the set of his mouth—Sandar was in a rage about something and he would make her the target of that anger if she gave him a chance.

Her shoulders sagged. Once more she was caught in the old pattern. Her two months at Cram-brief had given her a false confidence in herself. Just how false she now realized. She would have to leave her kit locked somewhere in this hateful building.

That she would not be bereft of necessities she knew. Uncle Offlas traveled with the highest degree of comfort any project allowed. But there were personal things—some which had been a part of her for a long time. It was hateful of Sandar, a bad start for the trip.

She stood quietly, still captive in his hold, as he hailed a transport flitter. Captive, yes; resigned, no. Somehow she was going to get the better of Sandar—somehow, someday. She stared down at her hands as the flitter spiraled up with

them. They were small and brown; her skin was several shades darker than Sandar's. That both he and her uncle resented her mixed blood, she knew. Sometimes Sandar acted as if he did not even want to look at her.

The port was busy with four ships on the pads—one a stellar liner embarking a number of passengers. They swooped past its tall column to settle by a much smaller ship, which bore the insignia of Survey. Roane managed to avoid Sandar's hand and made for the ramp, trotting up it as she had so many times before.

She fed her ident into the port checker, saw the welcome light flash. A crewman stood a little beyond.

"Gentle Fem Hume." He consulted a ship map. "Third level, Cabin 6, ten minutes to countdown."

She made for the ladder hurriedly, wanting to reach the privacy of her own cabin with no more interference from Sandar. And she did, throwing herself on the bunk, although the warning bell had not yet sounded, snapping the protective take-off webbing into place.

The cabin was the standard one of a junior officer. There were cupboards in every possible section of wall space, plus a narrow slit of curtained door which must give on a cramped sliver of a stand-fresher. The bunk she lay on was comfortable enough, but the furnishings were all regulation. There was no sign of personal possessions about the dreary cell. If someone had been shifted for her, he had taken all his belongings with him.

Once more she wondered what it would be like to have a real, set-on-a-planet, immovable home where one dared accumulate things one fancied and enjoyed to look upon just because they were beautiful, or reminded one of some

happy time, or were fun to own. If Uncle Offlas had ever
had such desires, they were long since lost. And Sandar
seemed not to care.

She hoped what he had said of complete equipment on
board was true. Of course, on a dig one wore Service dress—
a one-piece coverall of material suited to the climate,
fashioned for hard use. And she had long known that any of
the luxuries of feminine life, such as scents or the cosmetics
that planet-rooted women dared to use, were not for her.

There was a warning clang overhead, the signal for last
countdown. Roane snuggled deeper into the bunk's
protective cocoon. Here they went again, for the—she was
not sure she could even reckon now the number of times
she had gone through the same procedure. Would there
ever be an end to such wayfaring for her?

It was a voyage like any other. As soon as they were in
hyper, Uncle Offlas sent for her to put her through a
searching examination of what she had learned. He did not
signify at the end any more than that she would do,
providing she kept her mind strictly on her work. He then
gave her a load of tapes and a reader and ordered her to
make the best use of space time she could. She dared not
protest, since she knew that sooner or later he would
demand an accounting from her.

The voyage was as dull as most. On a liner, where there
were many pastimes to amuse passengers, travel might be
fun. But certainly Uncle Offlas thought that such intervals
between jobs were for study only.

They made landfall at last—that is, their ship went into
orbit well above Clio, and they packed themselves and their
gear into an LB, the standard type of small life-saving craft,

which had been specially modified for a directed landing. It was twilight when their meticulously planned descent brought them to the surface of the planet.

All three of them hurried to unload the supplies and instruments, for the LB had a time setting to return it to the parent ship. And even that would then withdraw into a longer orbit. Though any sky watchers on Clio would not recognize a starship, yet there might be talk of any strange appearance in their sky.

The first thing Roane was aware of as she manhandled out the boxes and containers was the wonderful freshness of the air. After the stale, recirculated atmosphere of the ship this was like breathing a subtle scent. She drew it deeply into her lungs.

They had no time really to look about until the last of the equipment was out. Uncle Offlas slammed the hatch and jumped back as the LB bounded up. Even during the short time of the unloading, twilight had deepened into night. Roane sat back on a box and brought out from the inner pocket of her coveralls a pair of night lenses. With these on she looked around.

They were in a glade surrounded by tall trees. Several bushes had been squashed by the LB, splintered and flattened, and the boxes they had tumbled out had torn and gouged up chunks of moss.

Uncle Offlas had a small map and was glancing from it to the right and left as if he hunted landmarks. Meanwhile Sandar forced open one of the padded containers and brought out a box which he balanced on his knees, bending close to read the dials on its top. He set two of these, then reached for another twin box to do the same.

"Good enough. Put it about twelve—no, perhaps twenty paces in that direction." Uncle Offlas pointed left. "I'll do the same with this." He picked up the second box.

Once those distorts were working they could set up camp. The distorts would prevent any unauthorized invasion of either man or beast native to this planet. Each member of their own party wore, clipped to the front of his belt, the broadcast which would nullify the effect for him.

By midnight they were settled in. Under Uncle Offlas's expert handling a working laser had cut a pit as deep in the ground as Sandar was tall. Over this arose, for more than an arm's length, a weather dome, which in turn was concealed by greenery which had been stass-sprayed not to wither for days. Their equipment, moved within, formed narrow partitions for three small cubbies and one larger one. And they dared to turn on a camp-sized beamer there while each prowled in turn around the clearing to inspect for any betraying light.

For a time they must work by night, sleep by day. Roane was tired enough to yawn her way to sleep as soon as she was free to curl up in her own cubby. Nearby were the detects and as soon as it became dusk again she would take one in hand and begin her first sweep of the area. Sandar would go in the opposite direction, while his father was in charge of assembling the com, setting out the other tools they would need as soon as a detect gave them a lead. It was apparent that Offlas seemed very sure they would find what they sought. In the past his confidence had never been so high. It was as if he had complete assurance they would make their find shortly.

Such belief was infectious. Roane almost expected to be able to report success on her first scouting trip. But she did not; neither did Sandar. And the third night they ranged farther afield, guided back to camp by distort signals. While it was impossible to get lost, Roane found that venturing alone into the wilderness made her slightly uneasy. She had never been completely by herself before. On board ship there was the cramped feeling, even in a private cabin, of other lives close by, just as the lifeless air one breathed had, as one well knew, been recycled many times. But here—with the night lenses to give her clear vision, she began to feel at last oddly free.

Midway through the fourth night she climbed a ridge, swinging the detect on its strap over her shoulder, using both hands to pull herself up. It had rained earlier and the grass tufts and the branches which slapped at her were moisture-laden. But the waterproofing of her clothing kept her body dry, and she relished the feel of the droplets on her face and hands, even though they plastered her short hair lankly to her skull.

Roane had passed by a road earlier, in fact had tumbled into it when a sleek clay surface made her slip. It had been an odd hollow, boring through greenery which grew on grassy banks taller than her head, and it was overarched with a lacing of boughs which roofed it. Whether this had been done by purpose to make a tunnel hidden from sight or was merely the result of unchecked growth she did not know. But the surface was rutted and scored with hoof prints to tell her it was in good use. And she had hurried to climb out, using a broken branch to sweep away her own tracks there.

This ridge lay at right angles to that road and well above it. She did not get to her feet as she reached its crest, but squirmed along so that she would not be silhouetted against the sky. The moon was now well up and bright.

Thus her sight of what lay below was very plain. Roane substituted distance lenses for the night ones to study the scene carefully. For there was a village-sized collection of buildings.

Almost directly below was the major one. It consisted of two square towers about five stories high, connected by a building looking to be no more than one room wide but rising three stories. The towers and the roof of the smaller portion were all parapeted and there was a tall outer wall completely encircling the building. Two or three of the very narrow windows showed faint gleams of light, late as the hour was. The tower nearest her had a gate giving on a garden which ran to the very foot of the ridge.

The garden itself was cut by walks gleaming white-bright in the moonlight and there were beds of flowers formally arranged. But what kept Roane from withdrawing at once was that there were men busy in the garden. They worked in pairs, six in all, and the couples were setting up in the ground posts which supported large grotesque figures. Each one of these weird effigies bore on one forelimb an oval shield painted with a complicated sign, while the other forepaw, or claw, gripped the pole of a small banner.

These were being placed in line to face the lower story of the tower, and the work seemed to be no light task. The effigies were of animals or birds, or in one case a crowned and shrouded humanoid thing. But all were strange to

Roane and she wondered if they had some allegorical significance.

Why they must be put in place in the middle of the night was the puzzle, and she watched until the last was braced in place. Then the men disappeared toward the buildings along a single cobbled street running to the main gate in the wall. Outside the fortress-like wall there were two lines of houses built of the same stone as the keep, but they were much smaller, the largest only two stories high. Their roofs were slabs of stone slanting sharply from the peaks, the ends of those turning up to be carved into heads of beasts.

It was a keep, a village, in miniature. And though it looked different from the tri-dee she had been shown, she knew it for Hitherhow—the principal royal hunting lodge of Reveny.

Did the setting up of the figures mean that the King was coming? If so, what would such activity in the forest mean to her own party? Of course the distorts would protect them. But if there were many hunters abroad, they would have to hide until the chase was over, and Uncle Offlas was not going to take kindly to that loss of time.

# ✳ CHAPTER 2 ✳

**"WHAT DID THEY SAY IN BRIEFING?"** Uncle Offlas was pacing up and down, chewing at his thumbnail, an old sign of deep drought. Now he rounded on Roane with that question. "Who might be coming—the King?"

"King Niklas is an old man, judging by planet years—would he be hunting?"

"I am asking *you*. You saw the tri-dees the snooper robots brought in."

"They weren't sure about anything. If it isn't the King—" Roane thought of the possibilities. "His children are all dead. He has one granddaughter—Princess Ludorica—"

Sandar laughed. "Now that's a mouth filler! How do they think up such names?"

"Be quiet! A princess—who else?" Uncle Offlas demanded.

"Why does it matter?" His son refused to be subdued.

"It matters a great deal, you fool! The rank of the hunter can govern the number of followers he brings along."

Sandar flushed. Uncle Offlas was really upset or he

would never have been so short with his son. She hurried to tell the rest she knew.

"There's a Duke Reddick, a distant cousin of the King but a lot younger. That's all the snoops picked up."

"With all the preparations you saw"—Uncle Offlas fretted his lower lip with the nail he had been chewing on earlier—"it has to be one of the royal line. If it's the Princess we may be a fraction safer—she might be less keen on hunting. But I don't like such activity so close. It might be well to take day watches until we do know who comes. Time!" He balled his right hand into a fist and brought it down forcibly into the palm of the left. "We have to make the best time we can. The longer we remain planet-planted, the better chance of discovery—"

Sandar's head was up, he was sniffing the rising wind. "There'll be cover today; storm coming. But it won't be good to be out in it—"

His father had swung around in the same direction. The thin gray of dawn did seem to be more dusky than usual. And they could all see massing clouds.

"Several hours before that breaks. Roane," he said to her, "you take first watch, before the storm. Report in with this if it is needful." He handed her a wrist com. "And work your way in from the north; these foresters are trained trackers. Sandar, you set out the extra distorts. I didn't want to use up the charges so fast, but now there is a need. I'll put a repell as well as a distort into working order."

Roane sighed but not audibly. She did not relish crawling the long way back to the ridge. But in spite of being tired, and chancing discovery by storm, the thought of watching the pocket castle was exciting. And inwardly

she was surprised that Uncle Offlas had set her to it. Except that Sandar knew more about setting distorts.

She slipped inside the camp and crammed some of the sustaining, if tasteless, E-rations into her coverall. There was no reason to go hungry, and her stomach already felt empty.

Circling north brought her into new territory. She could waste no time in exploration, but she did all she could to wipe out traces of her passing, being careful to snap no branch and to smear out any boot track in the forest muck. This delayed her, so that the gray was lighter when she again reached the ridge. She had made one discovery during her travels, a second tower set in the woods, brush growing so high about it that it was almost masked. There was no door closing the opening in its side and the place had the appearance of long disuse. Perhaps it was an abandoned ruin. She would have liked to explore it and promised herself she would when she had the chance.

Now she watched both village and castle. There were lights in plenty at the windows. And she could see people moving about. The wooden figures were bright with color, and the flags they held snapped in the wind.

Roane was so intent on the scene that she was startled by a rising call, saw a man on the castle parapet wearing a brightly colored overtunic raise a horn to his lips to answer that. Riders were coming down into the village, led by a man who managed his reins with one hand while he blew a horn for a series of calls. Behind him rode another in the same fantastic clothing, the tunic overlaid on the breast in an intricate design.

There was a small troop of six then, riding in military

formation, wearing metal helmets and carrying bared swords in formal salute. Behind them came two riders, followed by a longer train of armed men. One of the riders was a woman, her long skirt flapping on either side of her mount as if it were slit. The skirt was of a deep forest-green, and her tight jacket was of the same shade, though it bore braiding of silver in spirals across the breast.

From this height Roane could not see her face, for she had the collar of a cloak turned up about her throat, though the rest of its folds had been pushed well back on her shoulders. And on her head was a broad-rimmed hat ornamented with a cockade of long yellow feathers.

Her companion was in the same green from the boots on his feet to the narrow-brimmed, high-crowned hat on his head. Roane could see little of his face either, though by his dress he must be of the high nobility.

The villagers had turned out to greet the company. Men waved their caps, women curtsied. And the woman rider raised one hand in salute. All the mounts were Astrian duocorns and thus the fact was brought home to Roane that this was indeed a settlers' culture, established at the whim of a mind half the galaxy away, with the resources of many planets to call upon. These beasts were smaller and lighter than those Roane had seen before. But there was no mistaking their curved sets of horns as they tossed their heads, even danced a little.

Roane watched the party enter the courtyard of the keep, the woman and the green-clad man dismounting before the main door. He bowed from the waist and offered her his wrist, she touching her fingers to it formally. It was like watching a living story tape and Roane was

enthralled. The brilliant colors, the people did not seem real, rather story-inspired, and she could not believe in them. It was one thing to have such reported on snooper tape, another to see it in action. She slipped away from her post reasonably sure of one thing, that it was the Princess Ludorica who had just arrived.

Who the man might be, Roane could not guess; any member of the Revenian nobility from Duke Reddick down. She held to caution in her retreat, knowing she must take the roundabout way back. And the time so spent brought the storm upon her.

Suddenly it was night-dark, so that if she had not had her night lenses she would have been lost. Wind caught the crowns of the trees with a fury which frightened her. Roane had been on many worlds; she had known storms of wind, of drenching rain, of whirling sand, wind-driven grit to scrape the skin raw. But then she had been in such cover as their camps afforded, sheltered from the full force of such gales.

Now, caught in the open, her nerve almost broke. She must find shelter. And for that there was only the ruined tower. With what strength she had left she headed for it.

Rain added to the hammer blows of the wind. Branches splintered and fell. Roane cowered away from one jagged club. The whip of lightning lashed across the dark, to be followed by a crack of deafening thunder. And the tree to which she now clung, thick and sturdy as it seemed, swayed under the pull of the gale.

She could not stay there, but dared she try to go on? There was another bolt of lightning, which found a target not too far away. Roane screamed, her voice swallowed by

the thunder, and tried to run, beating at the bushes to force a path. Then she saw ahead the mouthlike doorway of the tower.

Once she gained that, she held tight, panting and gasping. Her clothing, meant to be waterproof, had kept her body dry. But her hair was plastered to her head; water dribbled across her face and into her half-open mouth. For a moment or two out there she had felt as if the force of the storm had torn away her breath.

Now she recovered enough to move on in, and then dared to use the beamer, set on its lowest power, to inspect what lay about her.

To her surprise there was furniture here. But as she went closer she could see that its presence was probably due only to the fact that it could not have been moved except by the greatest of effort.

There was a table hewn from a single thick slab of dark-red stone which was veined with thin lines of gold that glittered even in the weak light when she smeared away a deposit of dust. Inset in the top of this was a series of squares, alternating red and white, perhaps to form a playing board for some game.

Facing each other across this slab, which was mounted on round balls of legs, were two chairs lacking legs at all, the seats being square boxes with the high backs and wide arms. Both arms and backs were carved, the gray dust filling the hollows of the patterns until they could hardly be distinguished.

Against one wall was a massive chest, also carved. And beyond it was a stair set against the wall, the outer edge unguarded by any rail, fashioned of the same stone as the

walls, not quite as red as that of the table, but a dull rust shade.

There were, in addition, two tall standards of rust-encrusted metal, the tops of which were level with Roane's shoulder. Each of these held a lamp, a bowl with a support for a wick.

A drift of leaves and soil spread inward from the doorless entrance. Roane went to the stair and began to climb, pointing the beamer to where the steps disappeared into a dark opening above. It was when she came out on the second level that she discovered that the tower, which had appeared three stories high from without, was really only two. If there had ever been a third floor above, it either had been wood and rotted away or had been removed. She flashed the beamer up there to see only stone and mighty beams.

This second room had furnishings also: two more of the lamp standards, plus a chest, and on a step dais a wide bed frame of the same wood which formed the massive chairs below. It was in the form of an oblong box, full of an evil-smelling layer of what might have been rotted fabric, perhaps the remains of bed linen left to molder away.

There were windows, narrow slits, without any protection against the wind and rain which now drove spears of damp across the floor. Another bolt of lightning made the whole room brilliant. And then followed such a burst of thunder that Roane dropped the beamer and cowered against the chest, her eyes squeezed shut, hands over her ears.

It seemed to her the thunder filled the tower, which shook from the blast. Even when it had gone she was too

weak with sheer terror to move. She had never known such natural fury before and it made her a prisoner.

How long that panic lasted—it could well have been more than one hour, even two—she never knew, but finally she began to think again. Uncle Offlas—Sandar—they were in the woods. Could the camp stand up to such a storm as this? What if the lightning hit—or a tree crashed down?

She fumbled with her wrist com, tried to tap a code call. But she listened in vain for any reply. The storm must be cutting off reception. If there was any longer a receiver—

Although the wind still moaned around the tower and now and then she heard a crash as if some branch or even tree fell, the very worst of the storm seemed spent. Roane brushed off the top of the chest, testing it gingerly lest it splinter under her weight, and then sat there, bringing out an E-ration tube and making a meal from its contents.

So heartened, she used the beamer once more and made a careful examination of the room. That the tower had ever been a dwelling place she doubted, in spite of the bed. Perhaps it had been intended for just the use she was now putting it to, a shelter for storm-stayed hunters.

The evil smell of the bed, which was growing stronger in the dank air, had kept her away from that portion of the room. But finally she ventured to approach it. The bed itself was like a box without a lid, the cavity holding the rotten stuffs. At the four corners stood carven posts, matched as well as tools could sculpture to the bark of trees, vines twined about in high relief, now much masked by thick spider webs which held dust and mummified insects to form a nasty draping.

But there was a small open space between the tall head (also much carven and possessing several niches in which were set miniatures of the bigger lamps) and the wall of the tower. The beamer there showed Roane something odd, a series of holes hollowed into the stone, as if they were a ladder by which one might mount to the rafters overhead. Turning the beamer on to full, she traced those as high as she could and found that they did lead to one of the great crossbeams. This had the suggestion of a secret way, which it would have been in truth had the walls been covered with any form of tapestry or hanging.

She was tempted to take that climb. But prudence argued that she had better be on her way again, ready to leave the tower as soon as the storm slackened a little more. And she knew she must go when the lightning, which she feared the most, ceased.

Only she was too late. Hovering at the door, watching the rain, debating whether or not she dared chance it, Roane saw a flash of color, heard the high nicker of a duocorn. Some hunters storm-stayed like herself? She jerked back, looked at the floor where the pattern of her tracks had been only a little blurred by her restless coming and going.

She jerked open the seal of her coverall and brought out a scarf mask. Using that as best she could, whisk-fashion, she retreated to the stair and the only hiding place she could think of—behind the head of the bed above.

Though she had snapped off the beamer at once, there was enough grayish light for her to grope aloft. And she reached the upper story none too soon. She was no more than into the bedroom when she heard voices, the

tramping of feet below. No more taking chances. She had already been far too reckless. Roane squeezed between the head of the bed and the cold of the wall, her hands covering her nose against the putrid scent of the bed stuffs.

She could not see now—the wood before her had no cracks. But she could hear. The newcomers did not speak Basic, of course. But her briefing had given her a working knowledge of the Reveny tongue. And now she began to pick up words. They were coming up the stairs, how many she could not tell, though she tried hard to distinguish voices and number of footsteps. Now and again there was a metallic clang as if something had struck the wall, followed by exclamations she could not translate but thought were curses.

They moved out into the chamber and she could hear their speech plainly now.

"—ride on in this? Are you empty between the ears?"

"—not like it—" The second voice was hardly above a mumble.

"Back of my hand to him then! I tell you, this is as safe a place to keep her as the underway at Keveldso. Dump her in the bed there, snap this leash on her, and we can wait out the rain below. Think you she can turn herself into a snake maybe to get out one of those windows? And with us sitting nice and easy down here she is not going to come tripping down the stairs and do a flit. Nor is she going to slip this here leash neither. That is made of good sword steel and the collar's made to hold one of His Grace's direhounds. Try it, go ahead, try it, man." There came the sound of metal clinking. "We snap this right around her throat, so. Now she cannot get away withouten this key,

and that goes right here on my belt latching. I weren't a hound help for nothing, not that I weren't glad to get away from those kennels neither!"

"He will not like—"

"Would he like it more if we was squashed into a jelly by some tree coming down on us? You saw what happened to Larkin. Made you sick, didn't it just? Maybe he has plans for this little bird, but those don't include having her smashed up—not just yet. He said to see she kept on breathing, and he said that firm, as you heard him."

"Yes—" But it seemed to Roane that agreement was made with reluctance. Once more she heard the clink of metal, then a laugh, and the first speaker continued:

"Nobody is going to break that. She's as well tethered as if she was half walled in this place. Come away and let her lie. Better do nothing to rouse her up; she is enough trouble limp. She was a fighting cor-cat before Larkin gave her that little love tap."

Tramp of feet, the sound of them on the stairway. Roane dared to breathe more deeply. The fetid odor of the bedding was worse, as the settling of the captive within its box had stirred up the nasty remains. How long would she have to hide? And could she stay where she was at all? That stench made her sick. She wished she had not eaten the E-ration in spite of her hunger.

There was no sound in the room, though any slight one would be covered by the rising wind. The dying of the storm seemed to have been only a lull. It was getting worse again. From the words of the men she was sure that whoever they left here was unconscious. And she must have more air or she would be sick. She could slip along

the wall, gain the open beyond the bed by one of the windows. It did not matter that rain was blowing in again; she must have the clean wind on her face.

But Roane moved with due caution, stopping every few inches to listen. And when she finally got from behind the headboard she froze to watch the head of the stair. There was a faint glow of light from below. They must have brought a lantern with them. But the room was dusky with thick shadows.

She took another step, heard the rattle of metal, tensed again, turning her head to look at the bed. A dark figure arose from the muck which filled it. And the smell aroused by that stirring brought a coughing, quickly muffled, as if the cougher was trying very hard to subdue those racking spasms.

Another flash of the revealing lightning burst. There was a girl in the bed, holding both hands over her mouth and nose, her shoulders shaking. And over those muffled hands her eyes were wide open, looking straight into Roane's.

# ✳ CHAPTER 3 ✳

**ROANE MOVED** without any conscious volition, at least afterward she could remember none. When she was thinking again she found herself face down in the stinking morass of the bed, a struggling body pinned under her. One of her hands was across the girl's mouth, and Roane was using her own weight to try to subdue the other's struggles.

There was a sharp pain in Roane's gagging hand and she snatched it away instinctively. The girl had bitten her. But the shrieks she feared might follow did not come. Instead the other spoke in a low voice:

"Why try to smother me, you dolt?"

Roane jerked away, nursing her bitten hand. She fumbled her beamer out of its belt loop, set it on low, and turned it on. And with her hand about it for a shield, she held it full upon the other.

The pale face caught in that light was streaked with black smears; dark hair tumbled about it. Below the determined chin was a broad metal collar, and from that a

chain stretched into the dark. The girl caught at the collar with both hands, worried at it, though she continued to stare straight at the light as if seeking Roane behind it.

"If you are not one with the offal below," she said in a whisper, "then who are you?"

"I came here to shelter from the storm," Roane said evasively, in a whisper even more constrained. "I heard them bringing you and I hid."

"Where?" The girl asked that eagerly as if the answer held some desperate meaning for her.

Roane switched the light so it touched the headboard as a pointer. "Behind that. There is space enough."

"But where you were does not tell me who you are," the girl returned sharply. "I am the Princess Ludorica!" And there was a note in her voice which canceled out the dirt streaks on her face, the clinging stench, the collar that confined her.

Roane looked at that collar, and in her a small spark of anger flared. By all the urging of her training she should leave here right now. She could use that niche ladder. By the strongest oaths known to her people she was pledged not to make any contacts. Revenian quarrels were no concern for off-worlders. The old laws on noninterference were strictly enforced. And yet—that collar—

"I am not of Reveny," she said, evading once again, striving to keep her answer as low as she could.

"Thus making this matter none of your affair?" the Princess snapped. "What are you then, a Vordainian spy? Or perhaps a smuggler from over-border? He who will not reveal his face nor speak his name cannot thereafter be troubled if we see him as a walking evil." She repeated the

last as if she quoted some saying. "Can you be bought? My offer will be very high—"

Roane wondered at the calm control of the Princess. Instead of sitting in this odorous box with a chain and collar making her fast, she might have been at ease in her own palace, save that she held her voice to a whisper. And now Roane saw that what she had first thought another smear of grime across the side of the girl's chin was the darkening of a large bruise. Now and then Ludorica did hesitate between one word and the next, as if she found speaking somewhat difficult.

"Who are those men below?" Roane had a question of her own. That they had so dared mishandle the heiress to Reveny's throne meant they were not common criminals. And the more she learned of what lay behind this, the better she could plan what to do. Though she already knew she could not turn her back on Ludorica.

"Since I had to play the swooning female, that they use me with less alertness, I did not see too much of them. They wear foresters' jerkins, I do not believe honestly. And how I came into their hands—" She shrugged and the chain tightened, the collar jerked, bringing a choking cough from her. "That I do not know. I went peacefully to sleep in my bed in Hitherhow. When I awoke I was lying in a bumping cart on a forest track with the rain pouring like to drown me. Doubtless that restored my wits. Then the storm struck us full, bringing down a tree. The cart took the brunt of that to the fore. I gather that he who drove it had no further interest in the matters of this world. They pulled me out and brought me here.

"I do not think you are a Vordainian," she said, changing

the subject abruptly. "If you are a smuggler, you will be given full pardon, with a good purse added to it. Get me loose of this"—she pulled at the collar again—"and guide me to the post at Yatton." She still stared ahead as if she could see Roane clearly.

When the off-world girl did not answer, the Princess set her lips tightly together for an instant and then added:

"It would seem you also have no reason to wish to be discovered by those below. Let this then be a case of your enemy is my enemy, so a truce between us for this one battle." Again she appeared to be quoting. "Your speech is strange, you are not of Reveny, and you have not the inflection of Vordain, nor the tongue clicks of Leichstan. Unless you are some mercenary from the north—No matter, get me free and you can rest easy on the gratitude of Reveny for your future, and that is no small thing!" There was pride in her voice, and once more Roane could forget where they were and that she fronted a prisoner and not one seated on a throne.

After all, what could some aid matter? She had already interfered, by merely being here and letting the Princess know it. If she left now, always supposing that she could climb to freedom by the wall way, the Princess, in anger at being abandoned, might call her captors, or Roane, trapped above in some manner, could be discovered. But if she were able to get the Princess away, she could contrive to lose her in the woods. Let the Princess then believe that she was a smuggler, too deeply involved in some criminal activity to be more than wary.

The Princess seemed to think her a man, perhaps

because she had glimpsed, by the lightning flash, Roane's coverall and cropped hair.

"All right." Roane gave grudging consent. "But that collar—" She leaned over to train the beamer first on the band around the Princess's throat, and then along the chain to where it had been fastened about one of the bedposts. There was a lock, but she could see no way of forcing it.

Which left the bedpost or the chain itself. Her hand went to a tool on her belt. To use that again went against all she had been trained and taught. It was odd, one part of her mind observed as she drew that rod out of its loop: the longer she stayed here, the more it seemed right and proper that she do as Ludorica wanted—as if the desire of the Princess awoke a companion response from her.

Roane hunched over, trying not to breathe in the fumes of the debris, held the rod out in the beamer's small gleam, thumbing the right setting. Then she touched the rod to the chain as far from the Princess as she could reach. There was a flash of light. Roane pushed the cutter back in her belt, gave the chain a quick jerk. It broke. She heard a small sound like a sigh from the Princess.

"You will have to wear the collar yet awhile," Roane whispered. "I dare not cut that so close to your neck."

"That I am free in so much is something to give thanks for. But there are still the men below. If you have a dagger—how do you—"

Ludorica had balled the chain up in one hand so it might make no noise as she moved. She reached the edge of the bed box, swung out to the floor, as Roane was doing on the opposite side. The Princess's white robe, or once-white robe, billowed around her. One of her braids of hair

had come undone and the long locks, tufted with debris from the bed, hung about her shoulders. She clawed out the filthy rags with a small shudder of disgust as Roane joined her.

The off-world girl surveyed the Princess's clothing doubtfully. The only way out was up that toe-and-finger-hold stair, and surely the Princess could not climb it wearing all those folds of cloth. Bringing her charge (for now Roane accepted the responsibility which followed her never-clearly-faced choice) around to the back of the bed, she flashed the beamer on the holes and explained their hope. But facing it now, she found the future more dubious.

"Lend me your dagger!" Ludorica whispered. "Oh"— she made a sound close to laughter—"I do not mean to fight my way free below. But I cannot climb in this." She gave an impatient tug to the robe.

"I do not have a dagger—" Roane returned.

"No dagger? But how then do you protect yourself?" the Princess asked wonderingly.

What Roane did produce was a belt knife, and the Princess seized upon it eagerly, slashing her full skirt front and back, cutting strips to bind the pieces to her legs in a grotesque copy of Roane's coverall. Before she returned the knife to its owner she tested its point on the ball of her thumb.

"This is like to a forester's skinning tool, yet different still," she commented. "You have not spoken your name— nor shown me your face—"

She caught Roane off guard as her hand shot out, her fingers closing around the wrist which supported the

beamer. The impetus of that attack worked. Before Roane could dodge, the other had focused that light to fully illuminate its owner.

Roane broke the other's grip, but too late. The Princess had had a good look at her, and being quick-witted as she was, she must have noted a lot. Roane was developing some awe of the other. A girl who had been dragged from her bed, brought to this place, chained up like a hound, assaulted by Roane herself, yet who managed to keep a level head, ask for aid, argue logically on her own behalf— Such was no common person, on Clio or off. And Roane wondered if under the same circumstances she would have done as well.

"You are not a man!" The beamer turned floorward between them, having done its work. "Yet your manner of dress—that I have not seen before. And your hair—so short. You are indeed strange. Perhaps the legends are true after all. If—if—" For the first time there was a tremor in the Princess's voice. "If you are one of the Guardians then answer me true—it is my right for I am of the Blood Royal, the next Queen Regnant of Reveny—if you are a Guardian, what has become of the Ice Crown?"

To Roane her plea was a mixture of command and petition, and it meant nothing. But a sound from below did. During their struggle on the bed and their escape from it, the storm had been dying; now they could hear the men moving below.

Roane caught at the Princess's hand as she switched off the beamer. If the men were coming for their captive, there was little they could do in their own defense. Back in camp were stunners; Roane longed for one now. But those

had not been unpacked, since they had no need to fear any forest animal with the distorts on. And those of the team were well aware they were not to be turned against any native here unless in the very last recourse. She had the knife—which the Princess still held—and the tool she had used to break the chain, nothing else.

Hand-linked, they stood very still to listen. The room had grown lighter. Perhaps they would not need the beamer. Roane drew the Princess to the head of the bed and behind it. The sooner they proved whether or not the holes led to freedom, the better.

"Climb!" She shoved Ludorica ahead of her and hoped the Princess could do just that. As the other faced the wall, raised her hands to the niches, Roane crouched so she could watch the top of the stair. It was too bad that they could not bar that way—say, shift the chest across it. But one good look at that told her that such a feat was impossible.

It seemed that the Princess's breathing, the faint scratching of her fingers and toes (for she was barefoot), were very loud. Roane strained to catch any answering sound from below.

The Princess was now well above the level of the headboard, straining to reach the shadowy crisscross of the upper beams. Roane started after her. It was, she decided, about equal to climbing a steep slope, save that she took each lift with the fear of at any moment being caught. Her breath rasped harshly in her own ears and she tried to control that fear, thinking not of what might happen but of what she must do in the next moment and the next.

"There is a place of flooring here," the Princess called

down in a whisper, "and, I think, a door. This must be an overreach—"

What the other might mean, Roane had no idea, but she was heartened to know that her companion seemed to recognize something well known to her. Then Roane's hand, reaching for the next niche, scraped a solid surface and she pulled herself out on a platform laid across the junction of two beams.

"There is a door to the roof. I have drawn its bolt," the Princess told her. "But it may take us both to hit it. It must be a very long time since this was last opened."

They crouched shoulder to shoulder on their knees, their four hands flat over their heads against a wooden surface. The dry dust they so raised sifted into Roane's face and hair, but she closed her eyes to it and said—

"Now!"

At first it seemed that that barrier had been firmly cemented by time. Then there was a giving which led to a greater exercise of strength. A crack of light grew wider as they strained. And, as if some further fastening gave way, the door lifted with a rush. Fresh, rain-wet air blew in upon them.

Roane drew herself up and out, turning to lend a hand to the Princess, who was making an effort to follow. They were on the roof of the tower in the full open. Around them ran a waist-high parapet. And it was day, though the rain clouds hung heavy above. Roane dropped the door into place. That they had bettered their case much was doubtful. Unless they could stay here in hiding until the men below left—which she thought was a very slim chance.

But the Princess was crawling on hands and knees

around the parapet, stopping now and then to run her hands over its surface, almost as if she were in search of something she was sure she would eventually find. Even as Roane watched she paused and her fingertips outlined a space first on the parapet and then on the surface under it.

"We are favored by fortune," she said. "There is indeed an overreach here."

Roane went to look over the parapet. Some distance away the edge of the cliff backing the tower jutted out. The girl tried to measure the distance between that and the tower. But it was too far to hope for a crossing—lacking a jump belt of her own civilization. Yet the Princess was now brushing at the roof, sweeping away the debris left by years of wind sowing.

"Ah—here!"

She had crawled some distance back from the parapet, and now she dug away at what seemed to Roane an ordinary crack between those slabs of stone which made up the roof. "Your knife—give it to me! This must be loosed."

Again Roane believed that Ludorica knew what she was about. She passed over the blade, nor did she voice the protest she felt when the Princess rammed its point into the crack.

Small rolls of black were gouged out, the Princess smearing them away with her hand. Now Roane could see that the break was much wider than it had first looked, so that a few minutes' work cleared a recess wide enough for Ludorica to get her fingers into. She motioned impatiently to Roane—

"Move back—over there. This may take some time; the

packing is very old. But these were meant for escape means
during the first Nimp invasions and I have never seen one
yet which would not answer. Though I must find the lock
stone."

She moved her hand back and forth, manifestly working
her fingers within the crack. Then, even as the trap door
had given, there was a thin grating sound and the stone
block moved, sliding as a drawer toward the parapet. A
whole section of that, as wide as the moving slab, sank out
and forward as if on invisible hinges.

"Help me—" the Princess panted.

Roane scrambled to the opposite side of the slab,
pushed at it. It slid on and on, passing out over the now
horizontally leveled section of parapet to form a narrow
bridge which did not quite touch that rocky spur beyond
but came close to closing the gap.

The Princess sat back on her heels, panting with effort,
her dirty face flushed. "We must be quick; these do not
hold long—"

Roane did not try to take that narrow path on her feet
but crawled on hands and knees, and was careful to keep
her eyes to the tongue of stone which she must traverse.
There was a giddy sensation in her head. She had never
been fond of heights, though she had fought that fear
through the wandering years of her life. This was the worst
test she had yet faced.

She reached the end of the slab. There was still open
space between its end and the ledge. She jumped, landing
heavily on the stone. Then she stood ready, holding out her
hands, to aid the Princess.

It was lucky that she did, for just as Roane took firm

grip of the wrists the other girl held out to her, the stone tongue trembled, moved, backed toward the tower. She was just in time to jerk Ludorica to safety. The slab rolled into place, the parapet arose, and their bridge was gone.

"Now—for Yatton—" The Princess was trying to order the remnants of her robe. She took a step and then gave a sharp exclamation, holding up a bare foot to brush at its sole.

Roane thought of her own plans—to aid the Princess and then fade away into the woods, leaving the other to go where she chose. Now she discovered that she could not desert her companion. The rain was chill and the Princess was barefoot. How long would it be before those men in the tower found their captive gone? And then—how long before they ran her down again?

"Where is this Yatton of yours?" Roane demanded impatiently. The only alternative would be to take the Princess back to camp, and she could foresee only outright disaster in that. Either way she was in deeper trouble with every passing moment.

"Two leagues—nearer three." The Princess raised her other foot to brush at it. "To speak the truth, I do not believe I can walk that without shoes. It would seem my feet are too tender for such wayfaring."

"We cannot be too far now from Hitherhow."

The Princess, having brushed her feet, was now busied in coiling the collar chain about her slender shoulders in a strange and ugly necklace. "I do not return to Hitherhow—not until I am sure—"

"Sure of what?"

"Of how I could be lifted from my bed there so easily

with no guard's hand raised to prevent it." She eyed Roane
bleakly, and then her eyes focused on the off-world girl far
more searchingly.

"You—you are surely not one of us. But a Guardian
would not have needed to climb that wall stair, cross a
safety bridge. A Guardian, by all the old tales, needs merely
to desire a thing and it becomes so. I do not know what you
are, and you will not tell me who—"

"I am Roane Hume." Roane had not meant to say that.
It was again an odd compulsion to tell the truth which
moved in her before she was aware. "I am not of Reveny,
but I think I have proved I mean you no harm."

"Roane Hume," the Princess repeated. "Your name,
too, is strange. But this is a time of many things which are
not as they once were." She had continued to eye Roane
closely, but now she smiled and held out her hand.

And when she did so Roane experienced a melting
inside her. It was as if no one had ever really smiled at her
before, asking her aid, not demanding it impatiently. And
her own well-tanned hand caught those whiter, if dirty,
fingers and squeezed them for an instant before she
remembered again that she, least of all on this world, had
any right to commit herself in friendship, or even in a
fleeting companionship.

"You pay no homage. In this you are like a Guardian,"
commented the other. "Is it that where you come from
there is no difference between those of the Blood Royal
and others?"

"Something of that sort," admitted Roane cautiously.

"I do not believe that one of Reveny could live easily in
such a strangely ordered place," the Princess began and

then laughed, put her fingers to her lips as if she would catch back those frank words. "I mean no disrespect to your customs, Roane Hume. It is only that, bred in one pattern, I find such a different one bewildering."

"We have no time to discuss it." Roane fought back her own desire to ask questions, to know more of Ludorica. "If you cannot return to Hitherhow, and it is impossible to reach Yatton, then where will you go?" *She* must be on her way, but still she could not abandon the Princess.

"You have come from somewhere." The Princess seized upon the very solution Roane dreaded. She had no idea what Uncle Offlas might do if she turned up at the camp with this bedraggled fugitive. That the end would be drastic, she could guess. But there did seem to be nothing else left to do.

"I will take you there then." Her voice sounded harsh and cold in her own ears. She tried to think of some other way. There was one feeble hope. She might discover a hiding place in the woods, leave Ludorica there, get supplies, clothing, footwear for her, and eventually start her off to her own people. A project in which there were as many chances for failure as she had fingers and toes. But there was nothing else—

Now she turned to study what she could see of the tower and the woods. That they would be tracked she had no doubt. Therefore she must leave as devious a trail as possible. At the same time she must give the Princess as good a chance of escape as she could.

"We must head that way—" She gestured north, away from the camp. The detour would buy them time.

They climbed down from the ledge and the Princess

must go slowly. Finally Roane took her supply bag, dumped its contents into the front of her coverall, slit it with the knife, and bound the halves about her companion's feet. That done, they were able to march at a better pace.

The rain continued to fall steadily, if not with the force of the storm, and the Princess was shivering. Roane had a new worry. Immunized as she was through the arts of her own civilization, she was aware that those without such medical protection must be highly susceptible to exposure. What if Ludorica became ill, what if—Their future was far too full of such ifs. Roane should lead her directly to camp. Only the stern conditioning of Uncle Offlas kept her intent on leaving a confused trail which might ward off disaster.

But, she realized at last, Ludorica could not stand much more. Though the Princess made no complaint, she lagged behind. Twice Roane returned, having missed her, to find her charge leaning against a tree, holding to the bole as if she were lost without support. And finally she must half carry her along.

It was then they came to one of the stony hills Roane recognized as a landmark. On its side was a raw new gash. And there was the smell of burnt, smoldering wood. Lightning must have struck and, in so striking, started a landslide.

Where that had passed now gaped a hole. The slide must have uncovered a cave, or at least a deep crevice. Here was shelter and Roane brought the Princess to it.

# ✳ CHAPTER 4 ✳

**THEY WERE NOT TOO FAR** from the camp, Roane knew. She could leave the Princess here, go for the supplies she needed and return. And she refused to think of all the difficulties which might face her during the performance of that plan. One step at a time was best.

Once they pushed into the raw opening in the cliff wall the rain no longer reached them. And though the opening itself was narrow, it widened out, stretching into the dark as if they had entered a place of considerable space. Lowering the Princess to the floor, Roane unlooped her beamer, turned it to full.

This was no natural cave. She was startled by the evidence the light made plain. It was the anteroom to a tunnel, one that she had enough knowledge of archaeology to know had not been formed by nature. In fact the walls were so smooth that she went to lay a hand on the nearest, finding that her finger tips slipped across it as they might on a sleek metal surface—though it still had the outward look of native stone.

44

Swiftly she triggered the control on her detect, heard the answering tick which told her she was right in her guess. Not only was this a nonnatural cut into the cliffside, but it bore a reading for ancient remains. By chance she had stumbled on the very site they had been prospecting for! Roane brought up her wrist, ready to try again to relay her news via com. But before she pressed the broadcast pin she remembered.

Bring Uncle Offlas and Sandar here—let them find the Princess—They would never allow any inhabitant of Clio to go free with the news of this discovery. If their cover was so broken, they would not only be under the ban of the Service; they could be planeted for all time wherever the authorities sent them. Uncle Offlas, Sandar, their careers blasted, blacklisted in the only field they knew—Their only alternative would be to silence the girl now sitting hunched on the stone, coughing and rubbing her hands across her flushed face. That silencing would not mean death, as it might have once. (Roane had heard the horror tales of the early days of space expansion.) But it might mean memory blocking, or even transportation off world into a limbo for Ludorica. Either way the innocent would suffer. All Roane could do was buy time and hope for some miracle to occur. Her head ached with her inability to see her way clear. She did not know what there was about the Princess that so enchained her sympathies. Perhaps she was being affected by a faint shadow of the original conditioning which had repatterned the settlers here when this unhappy test world had first been conceived.

As she stood there, caught in the net of the dilemma, a hand gripped her wrist, tightening above the com which

she must use if she were to be true to her people and her training.

"What is this place? It is no cave!"

She had believed the Princess too sunk in exhaustion to be fully aware of her surroundings. But Ludorica was now on her feet, staring into Roane's face, not accusingly, but as if she could not wholly believe she saw what her eyes reported.

"You have done it!" The Princess swayed as if it were hard to stand on her bruised feet. "You have brought us to Och's Hide! The Crown—give me back the Crown!"

"Please, I do not know what you are talking about— what crown? And Och's Hide—" Roane protested. Was it possible that a Forerunner find had already been made in Reveny, that they were too late? But the Service snoopers had picked up not the slightest hint of any such happening, one which would have caused stir enough to leave a deep imprint on public memory.

For a long moment the Princess stared into the eyes of the off-world girl, as if by the very force of her will she would get the truth from Roane, past any ambiguous or false answer. But whether she might have decided that her companion was lying Roane was not to know, for there was a dull roar from the mouth of the opening.

Roane whirled, the Princess clutching at her for support. Recklessly she turned the beamer on the opening to the outer world. But that door was no longer there. Instead the harsh glare of the beam showed a curtain of rocks and earth, with bits of splintered bough and torn leaf caught in it.

Crying out, Roane pushed aside the Princess, ran to

tear at the fall which had corked the entrance. She was able to scrape out some of the rain-slicked clay, pull at the branches in it. But underneath was a boulder she could not move. Though perhaps she could use the power of her tool to undercut it.

"Are—are we trapped?"

Roane had gone to her knees, was holding the beamer steady on the boulder. In one way her own problem was solved. For both their lives now depended upon help from outside—from the camp. Only the men there had the equipment to handle this easily.

"Yes. I do not have power enough to undercut this. I shall have to call for help." Should she warn the Princess of the results of that? Or continue to wait, always hoping that something might happen to make a hard choice easier?

"This could be Och's Hide. If we must wait for help, need we remain crouching here? For if it is the Hide and I can find the Crown—" She drew a deep breath. "For me, for Reveny, this could be the greatest day in a hundred years!"

"What crown do you seek?" Roane thought of the many forms that Forerunner discoveries had taken in the past. There *had* been a few times when such had consisted of objects which could come under the age-old designation of treasure—gems, weird art forms of precious metal, and the like. Though what were more important by far, and what they had come to seek here, were machines, records, and the clue to such a find had been enough to make them risk search on Clio.

"Our crown—the Ice Crown of Reveny." The Princess answered almost absently. She no longer watched Roane

but gazed into the shadowed passage. Then she did turn, and her face was stricken with a shadow of fear and her hands went to her mouth, covering her lips. When she spoke again it was in a very low and shaken voice.

"That is a great secret, Roane Hume, one that only two people know—my grandfather the King, and I. And I have sworn by that which is most sacred to our people not to speak of it. Now I am forsworn."

"But I am not of Reveny, and I shall swear as you wish to say nothing." Roane, made uncomfortable by the bleak look on the other's face, was quick to answer.

"If this is Och's Hide, then the harm is small, covered and forgotten in a greater good. But I *must* know! Come, use your light and let us look—"

If they stumbled on Forerunner remains and the Princess saw them—But what did that matter now? Roane had to do what she should have done long ago.

"Let me first call for help to free us." She fingered the com, moving its button in the camp call. Waited—and saw the answering code flash on the dial, demanding—But she interrupted with her own terse signal, of where she was and what she might have stumbled upon. Though she made no mention of the Princess.

The answering flash was a jubilant series of dashes, promising all speed. She had forethought enough to add then a warning of people in the forest, thinking of the searchers which might be combing there.

She half expected some question from Ludorica, but the Princess said nothing, only turned the beamer on the passage.

"Can you not tell me more of what you seek?" Roane

asked as they started on.

"Knowing a part, there is no reason now for you not to hear it all. The Ice Crown is the crown of Reveny, given by the Guardians at the far beginning. Just as the Flame Crown is for the rulers of Leichstan, the Gold Circlet worn in Thrisk—but surely all this is known to you. My grandfather, King Niklas, came to the throne while he was yet a boy and his stepmother-under-second-rights, Queen Olava, was regent in his name—though she was no true kin, not even of the Blood Royal, having been taken in a marriage on the left hand by my great-grandfather when he was well into his dotage. She was of the line of Jarrfar. They once held this hill country and tried twice to make a kingdom of their own. However, having no crown power from the Guardians, they of course failed.

"But it was in their blood to rule and they did not lose that desire, even when their lands dwindled and they held only a stead keep and two villages. Olava had great beauty, and it became the plan of her people that they might achieve by an ambitious marriage what they had not been able to do by force of arms. So they gathered their resources and brought her to court, humbly presenting her as a handmaiden.

"The King had long been a widower. Oh, he had had his ladies during those years, but they were only passing fancies, and he chose shrewdly such as would be easily satisfied with small favors and not beg for greater. But though Olava seemed of a like sort in the beginning, she was not! And—well, it is said she had had occasion, before she came to court, to visit a certain wise woman who dabbled in things better left alone. But then such is always

whispered of a woman who rises rapidly in the favor of a high-born man. As time passed she became first a wife of the left hand and minor law, and then the Queen—though she was not allowed to touch the Crown lawfully, for all her pleading and intrigues. My great-grandfather might be besotted with her, but he was royal born, and it is very true (though some today think this is also a legend) that the crowns choose who will wear them. And once they have so chosen, that king or queen cannot surrender them during his lifetime. It is a protection the Guardians set upon them. Though sometimes it has led to death for the proposed wearer, he being killed that another might present himself to the crown.

"So Olava had to bide her time until death reached for the King, hoping that before his son might confront the Crown for its choosing, her own candidate might take it. And he was her son—though the King would never let him drink from the kin-cup and thus acknowledge him as a true blood son before the Court, since he was not fully of the Blood.

"When the King died, they went to fetch the Ice Crown for the choosing. Though Olava tried to prevent my grandfather from standing before it, the choosing went as it has always done and he was proclaimed king. However, he was but a child and there were great lords enough favoring Olava to say that the old King had named her regent with them as a council to advise her.

"A common enough tale, one which has been told before. But what had not happened before is that when my grandfather came of an age to put on the Crown and thus assume all power, the Crown, brought from safekeeping

for the ceremony, disappeared immediately thereafter before it could be returned.

"For Olava dared what never had been dared before. She took the Crown, meaning thus to defeat my grandfather. And the power of the Crown blasted her as it always does those handling it unlawfully. But before she died, my grandfather finding her privately, she laughed and said that it had gone to Och's Hide and that only chance might now find it. Her clan, she said, would guard the way to it, and only when it accepted one of them would it appear again.

"Since then there has been this hidden darkness in Reveny. We dared not let any know of the loss. And since it has not yet been needed to hail a new king, the secret has been kept. My father died during a hunt in these very hills, but what he sought was no animal of the chase, but Och's Hide. Two of my uncles also died young. The third disappeared. And now—King Niklas is very old, and it has fallen on me to take up the search. For if I cannot stand before Reveny with the Ice Crown when death claims him—then our line comes to an end. And Reveny itself will be overrun by Leichstan or Vordain, where true wearers of crowns rule. A land without a crown is a land without name or being. So the Guardians decreed in the far beginning."

"Has it ever happened that a country did lose its crown?" asked Roane.

The Princess shivered, but with more than just the chill of the passage through which they walked now.

"Once, in Arothner. The crown—it was the Shell Crown, for Arothner was of the sea—was destroyed in a

tidal wave. And what followed was horrible. The people—
a madness fell upon them. They turned upon their own
lords, upon each other, so that all the nations on their
boundaries set up armies to keep them in their own torn
land. And thereafter it has been accursed and no one goes
there for fear the same mind-blasting force might strike
them. What was once a great nation with many ships, and
the trading city of Arth as its capital, is now only barren
waste, and if any still live there, they are no longer men—

"At least the Ice Crown has not been destroyed, for
then the same fate would have fallen on Reveny. And to
that hope we hold. But it must be found!"

"It would seem that there are those who also know the
secret and do not want this crown discovered—if your
father and the others died and this has happened to you."

"Yes." The Princess's lips tightened. "I guess and think
I guess rightly, though I have no proof, that it is Reddick's
doing. Though I never thought he would go so far as to
have me taken out of Hitherhow when it was well known I
was within those walls. There must be some desperate
need to bring him so into open action. It may be this
passage he would protect. Roane, does it seem warmer
here to you?"

Ludorica slowed, put out her hand as if to touch the
wall, but did not quite complete that gesture.

She was right! The chill which had closed about them in
the fore part of the passage was gone. This was like walking
under a gentle sun, just comfortingly warm. Roane touched
the wall. There was warmth there, more so than in the air
about them. And also something else, a faint vibration.

Excitement surged in her. A Forerunner installation

still alive? It had happened on other worlds—Limbo, Arzor. If that were possible then this would be one of the *big* finds, and anything—even breaking cover on a closed planet—would be forgiven the discoverers! This could be the answer to her problem.

"What is it?" Ludorica, watching her closely, must have read the elation on her face.

"I do not know—not yet—" Roane returned quickly and then asked: "Who is Reddick, and why would he want to hold the Crown?"

"Though the King would not claim Olava's son, he ennobled the boy and gave him command of Hitherhow in his lifetime, a right which must be renewed in each generation. Reddick is his grandson. But so might he have the secret of Och's Hide. If I can only find the Crown, Duke Reddick has no chance. Then he cannot lay hand to it before the King's death, or as long as I live—"

"As long as you live," Roane echoed her meaningfully.

"You mean—but of course! That is why—he had a double purpose." The Princess nodded. "Stop me from searching, or else make sure if I did chance upon it— Which also means—" Her face now mirrored not only determination and cold anger but also fear.

"Roane, I have not seen King Niklas for five days. It was he who told me I must make haste to find the Crown, gave into my hands all he had denied me for years, the clues he had tried to sift and follow, all that my father and uncles had when they went seeking. Perhaps he is more ill than he would have me know, or else has since grown worse. And Reddick knows this. If the King were himself, the Duke would never have dared to have me stolen from Hitherhow."

"Do you not have someone to depend on?"

"None sharing the Crown secret. But if I can now find that and reach Yatton or the border, I can cross over into Leichstan with the Crown and gain a breathing space in which to rally the loyal lords. My mother was a princess of Leichstan, though she died at my birthing and he who sits the throne there is but a distant cousin. Yet I can claim blood kin, and all must aid one who wears a crown!"

She flicked the beamer ahead. "Come! If it lies here— do you not see? I must have it, and soon!" Now she began to run.

But the beam had picked up something else, a change in the wall to their right. Roane pressed to that side and then halted at a slab of transparent material. Inside—an installation! It could be nothing else. Rows of machines with here and there a flashing point of colored light. She pressed her face to the glass, trying to see more of what lay there. But the light was too intermittent—she had only glimpses as one flash was echoed by another. Green, blue, red, orange, a multitude of colors and combinations. Yet those did not reflect into the passage where she stood.

"Come on!" The Princess was ahead, paying no attention to what held Roane fascinated. "Why do you stop?"

"The lights—this must be an installation. But what—"

Ludorica came back reluctantly. "What lights?" she demanded, flashing the beamer directly onto the panel, thus revealing two machines of pillar shape inside, spinning off flecks of color.

"What lights?" The Princess pulled at Roane's arm. "Why do you stand staring at bare wall and talking of lights?

Are you mind-twisted?" She dropped her hold, drew back a little.

"What do you see there, then?" Roane asked.

"Wall—just as there, and there, and there—" With a stabbing finger the Princess pointed ahead, to the side, behind them. "Nothing but wall."

Roane was shaken. But she *did* see a strange installation behind a transparent panel! She could not be mistaken or imagine that! There could be only one reason why the Princess did not see it too—conditioning!

And such conditioning could mean something else. Roane's thoughts took a leap into dark surmise. Perhaps what they had uncovered was not Forerunner remains, but rather something left by the Psychocrats who had decreed Clio's fate. While such a find might not have as much impact as the discovery of a genuine Forerunner installation, it could be important in another way. The Service knew little of the techniques of conditioning on the various closed worlds. To discover part of such an experiment might excite those in fields beyond that which Uncle Offlas represented. So she might have a bargaining point after all, some claim for consideration for the Princess.

"It is just bare wall!" Ludorica proclaimed again, still backing away from Roane, now eyeing the off-worlder as if she expected some dangerous outburst.

"A trick of the light." Roane thought that a feeble answer, but she knew that if the Princess was conditioned she would resist even the thought of what might lie there.

"Trick of the light?" repeated the Princess doubtfully. "Oh, perhaps Olava set her own safeguards against seekers.

I have heard of such tricks but they only work with some people." She now regarded Roane pityingly and put out her hand. "Let me guide you past. I cannot be so bemused, you know. None of the Blood Royal can be caught in a foreset mind-maze."

Ironic, Roane thought with wry amusement, a case of the blind leading the sighted. But if the Princess was willing to accept that explanation, she should be thankful. She did not look again at the panel.

Shortly thereafter the nature of the passage changed. The wider, smoothed walls gave way abruptly to a narrower way with rough rock on either side—as if those who had cut this path had used a natural break in the cliff for their purposes and this was the original cave unmarked by their improvements.

As the beamer caught the narrowing of those rough walls the Princess slackened pace, looked puzzled.

"Why should it change so?" she asked, more as if she questioned in her own mind than expected an answer from her companion.

"Do you still think this is Och's Hide?"

"What else could it be? There would be no other reason to cut a passage through rock. Yet—"

"Wait!" Roane lifted her free hand, held it before that crevice. "There is air—a current of it. Maybe there is another way out ahead."

They found the narrow passage a rough one. Twice walls closed in, so that they had to scrape through, and Roane had no idea how far they might be from the entrance. What if those from camp cleared the blockage there and did not find her? But at least they would have

her report and so go exploring. Of course, the men might run into difficulties raised by some hunting the Princess and thus be delayed.

As they emerged into a wider space Roane spoke: "I do not know about you, but I am hungry."

"Do not speak of food!" retorted Ludorica. "When one has nothing, it is better not to dwell on that lack. Let us get out of here—"

"But I have provisions of a sort," Roane countered. There was no use in trying to conceal such things as tubes of E-ration when so much else in the way of cover had been broken, and she was painfully hungry.

"Where? You carry no provision bag—" The Princess once more turned the beamer on Roane, who had already unsealed her coverall and brought out one of the tubes. There were only two left, and with their rescue still uncertain, it was better that they now divide one between them.

The Princess stared at the tube. "You carry food so? But there is not enough in that to make even a quarter of a meal if you hunger as I do."

"This is a special kind of food, made for travelers," Roane explained. "A small portion, say half of this tube, is equal to a full meal. It does not taste as the real food you know, that is true. But it is as good for the body, and it will give us strength. If you hesitate, I shall eat first." She measured off half the length of the tube, squeezed the contents bit by bit into her mouth without touching the edge to her lips.

Her companion watched her with deep interest. And when Roane had done and passed her the tube, Ludorica

put it to her mouth in turn. She made a slight face as she tasted the paste, swallowed.

"It has little flavor, as you warned. Truly I do not think I would relish many meals taken so. But when one hungers there need be little choice of dish; any food will do." She finished the tube quickly and gave it, empty, back to Roane.

From long training the off-worlder wadded it into a ball, which she hid under a loose stone. The princess had set the beamer upright as one might a candle, and its light reflected from the roof over their heads, showed them that the space in which they now stood was a true cave.

But it showed something else, too. Roane gave a start as she caught sight of it, snatching up the beamer to turn it full upon what lay there. That had been a man once. But she had seen ancient burials enough not to be squeamish. These bones lay half buried under a fall of rock which concealed the skeleton above the waist.

She heard an exclamation from the Princess as the light caught a spark of fire to one side of the crushed bones. Roane stooped to pick up a band of metal in which were set small gem stones. It was a fine piece of work, the stones making small flowers among raised leaves of the metal.

A moment later the circlet was snatched from her hand, the Princess turning it about in her own fingers.

"The arm ring of Olava! This is Och's Hide! And the Crown—the Crown!" She turned around, searching the walls of the cave as Roane swept the beamer. But the side wall opening which had once existed where the skeleton lay crushed was filled in past their exploration. There was now no opening at all that Roane could see.

# ✳ CHAPTER 5 ✳

**"IF IT WAS EVER HERE,"** Roane pointed out, "then it must now be buried under that fallen rock." Privately she thought the bracelet a very small clue.

"But it can be dug free!" Ludorica crowded as close to the mound as she could and still avoid the skeleton. "You say those you know will come to free us from the outer cave. They surely can aid here to find the Crown! Let me but rest my hands on it and Reveny has naught to fear, for then as long as I live no one else can claim it—"

"As long as *you* live. What then, if, once you have found the Crown, your enemies find you? How long will you continue to live?"

The Princess looked back at Roane, her eyes wide with what might be shock.

"But no common man can raise his hand against the wearer of the Crown; such are under the protection of the Guardians. Any such death must come *before* the Crown has rested on the chosen's head."

"But the Crown now would belong to your grandfather,

would it not? So long as he remains alive you will be in danger."

"True. But if what I fear is also true, and that is in a manner proved by the fact that Reddick moved against me so openly, then the King is very near to death. The Crown will know that; it has many strange powers. All the crowns do. They are the hearts of the countries possessing them and their lives are those of the nations—as was proved at Arothner. No, when your people come they must dig for the Crown. It still exists and I must find it!"

And that influence she was able to exert at times, which Roane recognized but somehow could not resist, brought Roane to half agreement now. Yet enough of her fought that compulsion so that she was able to persuade the Princess to return to the other end of the passage to meet their rescuers.

That Uncle Offlas would come she had no doubt, but how long he would take was another matter. Especially if he had to avoid searchers in the woods. And she said as much in warning to the Princess.

"But you can send a message—though why tapping on that ugly arm circlet carries a message—" Momentarily she was diverted. "I do not know who you truly are. But that you are not of Reveny, nor of any kingdom I know, I will swear to. Had you not brought me out of that tower, I would not—" Again she paused. "But I stand here and not in the hands of Reddick's men, so I have a measure of trust in you. Send another message to those you say will come to unseal us; tell them to use my name to the garrison at Yatton. There is there Colonel Nelis Imfry. He was of the palace wards before he took service with the March

Guards. Summoned in my name, he will come. You may tell your people, if those clicks really talk, to say to him—"

"No." Roane shook her head. "They will not go to Yatton nor any other place for your guard, no matter what message I send."

Perhaps she was wrong in being so definite about that. It might arouse Ludorica's suspicions even further. But she must make plain before the camp party arrived that they would not give the Princess any help in solving her complicated problems of dynastic inheritance.

"My people are sworn"—she tried to put the situation into words the Princess would understand—"by oaths, very tightly binding, to have naught to do with the affairs of others. I have already broken this oath by what I have done since we met. For this I shall have to pay. But you will find deaf ears if you ask for any aid from those who come."

They were passing the wall panel which the Princess could not see but which so fascinated Roane. The latter kept her eyes resolutely turned from temptation. And at that moment the com on her wrist flashed. She did not need the beamer light to read the sparked code.

Sandar! But no mention of Uncle Offlas. Only a sharp demand that she turn the call beam higher so that he would have a guide.

"They are here now!" She began to run along the smooth flooring, not caring whether the Princess followed or not.

Back in the entrance cave she again faced that plug of stone and clay, cautiously, since she did not know the force of the tool they would use to clear it. And she threw out an arm to hold the Princess to an equally safe distance.

The latter had given no vocal protest when Roane had denied her help. But she was smiling with anticipation. There was such an aura of confidence about her that Roane was uneasy. Perhaps she should have given her the whole truth in warning—not only that Ludorica could expect no aid, but that those who came might take her into another captivity, that her quest for the Crown might well come to an end here and now. Roane half opened her lips, was about to say what she must, when there was a shifting of earth about the plug. The stone which was its anchor disappeared.

Roane caught her breath. They were using *that* tool! Then indeed they were ready for desperate measures; such were unboxed only at times of extreme need.

She glanced at the Princess. What effect had that sudden disappearance of a very large and heavy rock had on her companion? But she could detect no sign of surprise, only a deepening of that confidence which was going to be so rudely shattered soon.

Fresh air bearing the damp of the rain blew in. Then Sandar, stooping a little, came through. He was alone, and in his hand—Roane gasped but she had no time to move, to warn. He had already pressed the button of the stunner. Beside her the Princess wilted to the rock floor. For the first time in her life Roane faced her cousin with open anger.

"Why did you do that? You did not even know what—"

His mouth had the same twist as Uncle Offlas's could wear upon occasion. But this time it did not daunt her as it might have in days only shortly past.

"You know the rules. I saw a stranger—" he said harshly. "Now—" He looked down at the detect he carried,

as if Ludorica were no more than the rock he had blasted out of existence. Then his face lost a little of its grim cast. "But you are right! There is a find here—"

Roane was on her knees by the Princess, lifting her limp body to lie against her shoulder. Ludorica would sleep it off, of course, but she must not remain here. The dampness of that inflow of air was already reaching her. Roane did not know how disease might develop on Clio, but she was certain that the inhabitants could not endure long exposure without suffering for it.

"Leave her—she'll keep!" Sandar came to her side. "What's inside?"

"An installation. You can see it through a plate in the wall down there." She made no move to guide him.

Nor did he wait for her, but switched on his own beamer and trotted away in the direction she pointed, while she was left with the problem of the unconscious Princess. Uncle Offlas and Sandar would be solidly united against any plan of freeing Ludorica; Roane had known that. But she determined that the Princess would have shelter and care even if she herself had to face such pressure of their wills as had always before frightened her.

She was still holding the girl against her for warmth, interposing her body between that of the Princess and the damp inflow of air, when Sandar returned.

"I don't know what it is. It may be Forerunner. But at least it is not of present-day Clio," he reported.

"Maybe something of the Psychocrats, to do with the settlers' conditioning."

"How do you—" he began and then shrugged. "Who knows before we take a closer look at what is in there?

Now—there are men searching the woods. I had Eight-fingered Dargon's own luck trying to dodge them. Father has had to extend the distorts to cover this area. Who are they after—her? If so, we give her a brainwash and dump her where they can pick her up. Then our troubles are over."

"No."

"No, what?" He stared at her, Roane thought (with wild laughter stirring far within her), as if she had suddenly grown horns or turned blue before his eyes.

"No brainwash, no dumping. This is the Princess Ludorica."

"I don't care if she's the Star Maiden of Raganork! You know the rules as well as I do. You've broken them already by being with her at all. How much else have you spilled?" He was twirling the setting on his stunner. Roane went cold with more than the wind.

She drew the small cutting tool from her belt. "You try brainwashing, Sandar, and I'll burn that stunner out of your hand. Drop it—now—or see how you like a seared finger! I mean exactly what I say!"

He eyed her with even greater astonishment. But he must have read the determination in her eyes. There had not been many times in the past when Roane had been faced by some major demand upon her will and courage, but twice that had occurred in Sandar's company and he must remember now her reaction.

"You know what you are doing?" His voice was very cold. He still held the stunner, but she noted, with a small sense of triumph, that his finger was now carefully away from the firing button.

"I know. Toss that over to me!" Her tool did not waver.

She might have used close to its full charge when she cut the Princess's chain, but there was enough left to give Sandar a burn and at that moment she would not hesitate to do just that. The captivity, her own feeling of inferiority and helplessness, to which the domination of the Keils, father and son, had sentenced her for so long was like the Princess's metal collar and chain.

That restless desire for freedom which had been born at Cram-brief was coming to a flowering here on Clio. Certainly she might know far less than her uncle and Sandar, be now under their orders, but she was also a person in her own right, not a robot they had programed.

Not that all this flowed coherently through her mind now. But she was determined to stand up to Sandar. His callous solution to the problem of Ludorica had acted on Roane like the cut of a whip—not to lash her into a slave line, but rather to awaken her resistance.

Sandar did not try to reason with her. Not that he ever had. He had given orders, she had meekly obeyed—until he and his father had had her wrapped in a cocoon of acceptance. But larvae develop in cocoons and in time they break free.

He tossed away his stunner. Roane steadied the Princess against her, held the cutter steady until she could reach out and close her fingers about that weapon.

"Are there any searchers near here now?"

"As long as the distorts are on they will keep their distance without knowing why—you ought to know that! But that will hold only for a short time. We shall have to move quickly."

"Good enough." Roane tucked the cutter back in the

belt loop, kept the stunner in her hand. "Now we'll go. You carry her."

"It won't do any good," he said. "You know that. Father has discretionary powers. He'll make the final decision and there will be no appeal. Also, you're finished with our team. I trust you understand that!"

Roane would consider that future when she had time. The here and now were more important—getting the Princess to shelter and seeing she stayed out of the hands of her enemies.

"You'll carry her," she repeated.

Carry her he did. Enough of Roane's training remained, even as she enjoyed the heady sensation of ordering Sandar around, to prompt her to use the last of the tool's powers to bring down another fall of earth as a mask for the hole. She hoped that would keep its secret. For what lay within and the fact that she had discovered it were all she had left to bargain with.

Though the distorts were on, Sandar took no chances, setting a fast pace, even thought he had the inert weight of the Princess draped over his shoulder. Roane walked behind, intent on concealing their back trail.

So they reached camp. At least Uncle Offlas was not there, and Roane ordered Sandar to put the Princess in her own private cubby. She set to work then, stripping off the soaked, mud-caked rags Ludorica wore, tugging loose the strips of cloth making her improvised leggings. And she had the Princess rolled into a heated sleeping bag when the chief of their party did tramp in.

He came straight to the cubby and looked at the Princess with no readable expression on his set face.

"Who is she?"

"The Princess Ludorica, heir to the throne of Reveny."

"And the story?"

He had a recorder ready, Roane noted bleakly. She was going to be condemned out of her own mouth. But there was nothing else she could have done. To her, Sandar's suggestion was unthinkable.

In the clear, terse manner of making a report which had been drilled into her, Roane began her story—the storm, her refuge in the tower—their flight, the cave—what she had found there—the Princess's tale of the Ice Crown, and all the rest.

Uncle Offlas listened without comment, though Sandar stirred now and then as if he wished to voice some derisive interruption. Yet he did not. And having concluded, Roane waited for the storm to break, knowing that verbal lightning could be as disastrous as the real.

"As for this girl," he said first, "we can attend to her when it is needful. But this find of yours—you saw it, Sandar?"

"Yes. What I could make out through the panel. It may not be Forerunner, but Psychocrat. It could have something to do with the experiment on Clio."

"Either way, it is apparently a find of importance. We can report that, along with this." He looked at the Princess as if she were not a human being at all, but some object which must be disposed of. "However, we have a matter of two days before the com can relay properly to the right orbit pickup, and by that time we should have much more information."

"What about the Princess?" his son demanded. "They

are going to keep hunting her, and we can't run the distorts on high for long. If we do as I wanted and brainwash her— then leave her where they can find her—"

Roane knew better than to voice another "No" right now. She had no weapon to back it up. That confidence which had supported her began to ebb. She might be able, for some moments of wrath, to stand up to Sandar. She had no defense against Uncle Offlas.

"For the moment they are hunting to the north. And I would like to know more about this crown she believes hidden in there. Once her memory is erased we can learn nothing. We haven't the equipment for being selective in such matters. We can wait—for a while. Now, I want to look at that installation.

"As for you"—he spoke to Roane—"you must realize what you have done. You are not a blind fool, just a fool. And I would suggest you think upon the future which you have just thrown away."

This was much milder than the blast expected. Though a moment later, after the men had left the camp shelter, she realized that considering a bleak future was a punishment in itself. The least she could hope for was to be planet-bound on some world the Service selected, forbidden ever again to use any skill she had learned. They might even demand that she be brain-censored also. She shivered and put her face in her hands, though she could not shut the dire pictures out of her mind.

Why *had* she done all this? Looking back now, she was certain she could have remained hidden in the tower, perhaps even made that climb into safe hiding above, without having dealings with the Princess. Such evasion

had been a part of Roane's training from the start. What flaw in herself had forced her out of the ways of prudence?

Again, she could have left the Princess once they were free of the tower. She might have done this—or that—But in every choice, she had made the one to condemn herself to Uncle Offlas's justice and she knew what she could expect from that.

She could not use her find as any bargaining point. Uncle Offlas would claim it had been made by chance alone. The only new information she had was that the Princess was conditioned not to see the panel—and any more Ludorica could supply about the Ice Crown.

Since they did not have the techniques here to drag information out of Ludorica against her will, perhaps she could be forewarned to bargain—But for that she must be conscious, and how long—

"What did they say about me?"

Roane was startled. The Princess could *not* be conscious—she had gone down at Sandar's stunner blast. But her eyes were open and watching Roane. The off-world girl had no idea how this miracle had come about—unless a difference in planetary inheritance was responsible. She had never known one to recover so quickly from a stun beam. But she must take advantage of it before the others returned, give the Princess warning.

"Listen!" Though there was no one in the shelter and she made sure the recorder was safely off, Roane leaned very close before she spoke. "They want to take away your memory, so you cannot remember us. And then—then they may give you to those hunting you."

She had expected some expression of disbelief from the

Princess. But though the other's eyes narrowed a little, she showed no surprise. Instead she asked: "And you believe that they can do this thing—take away my memory?"

"I have seen it done to others."

"I believe you believe it, yes. But whether it can be done to one who has the right to a crown—" Ludorica frowned. "If I could get the Crown—I must get the Crown!"

But Roane had a question of her own. "How long have you been awake? It is important for me to know."

"A memory which is useful, eh? Very well, this I remember clearly—a young man wearing clothes such as yours. Why is it with you, Roane, that men and women dress alike? Even our peasant girls delight in their bright skirts and would think your wear very ugly and drab. Yes, a young man. Then all is blackness as in a sleep without dreams. Until I lay here—wherever here may be—and you were taking from me those disgraceful rags to make me clean and warm. But I thought it well to learn what I could before those others knew I was awake.

"So they wish to take away my memory and give me to those who would like me best in the far deeper sleep of death. Why would they do this to a stranger who has worked them no harm?"

"They fear your knowing of their presence here."

"And what act of thievery, or worse, do they plan that they fear any knowledge of their presence may spoil?" There was a new sharpness in the Princess's voice. "It is the Crown! You seek the Crown! But it is the truth that I told you—for one not of the Blood to take it means a wasting death. Which one of our neighbors sent you to

destroy Reveny so? And are you so careless or dedicated
that you will kill yourselves to achieve your ends?"

It was no use. Roane could not explain without telling
all. But with a conditioned mind—would Ludorica accept
her explanation any quicker than she would believe in the
installation she had not been able to see?

"We came here to search for a treasure, but I will swear
to you by any power you wish to name that that was not
your crown! Until you told me of it, I did not know of its
existence. Nor would it mean anything to me. What we
seek is not of your time. Oh, I do not know if I can make
you understand. Before Reveny was a nation, before your
people came—at a time so distant we have never been able
to reckon it—there were others. They may not even have
been like us in form and they were gone before our form
of life came to be.

"But in some places they left things behind them,
hidden things. And from these our wise men try to learn
something of them. They had greater knowledge than we
possess. They were able to do things which we can hardly
believe are possible. Yet we know that they did them.

"And every such find we can discover adds to our small
store of knowledge, makes it more likely that someday we
can learn more of their secrets. My uncle and my cousin,
the young man you saw, are both trained to hunt down
such treasures. And I have been schooled to help them,
since I am of their family and supposed so to keep their
secrets." She was trying hard to set this within a framework
of planetary custom. "By revealing myself to you I have
broken a very strict law, and I shall have to pay for that.
But you are not at fault—"

"So you believe this is wrong, the taking of my memory?"

"Yes. And yet—"

"Yet you also have a way of life to uphold, even as we of the Blood," the Princess interrupted. "Yes, that I can understand. But I tell you, Roane, I do not propose to let them take my memory and give me to Reddick. Nor do I mean to lose the Crown when my hand may be only inches from it. I am treating you as one treats an honorable enemy. If it be war between us, let us say so, and from this moment the rules of war will hold."

"I do not want war. But my uncle, my cousin—"

"Yes. And what will happen to you, Roane? Will they also take away your memory as a punishment for aiding me?"

"They might, yes. Or they can send me to a place where I shall have to abide for the rest of my days."

"A prison? And you will let them do this to you?"

"You do not understand. They have powers you cannot conceive of. And there are others behind them more powerful still. They will do with me in the end just as they choose."

The Princess sat up. "I do not understand you. You are strong of body, quick of mind. This you have proved. Yet you will let them take you—you sit here and *wait* for them to take you!"

"*You* do not understand!" Roane thought of the devices they could use to hunt her down. Uncle Offlas might even call in Service aid. The Princess might be conditioned in one way, but, Roane saw now, she herself was conditioned in another, unable to break free without aid—

"Stay if you will," Ludorica said. "But I do not remain here to have them play with my mind."

"Where will you go?"

"To Yatton, if I can escape Reddick's net. He is a stubborn man and will not lightly let me out of his hands. And you—will you remain here waiting for prison?" There was a faint scorn in that.

But Ludorica could not know. To run was hopeless, ending in defeat. If Roane could persuade the Princess to bargain with Uncle Offlas—Only the time for bargaining might already be passed. Roane shook her head. Slowly she arose.

"If I help you to Yatton—" At least she might protect her from Reddick's men. If she could keep the Princess safe, there might be a little hope for a later bargain.

"If you help me to Yatton, I think there will be no more talk of memory stealing, nor prison, for either of us!"

# ✳ CHAPTER 6 ✳

**"FOOD FIRST."** Roane went to the stores, triggered the heat caps on those containers she thought held the most sustaining nourishment, brought back her selection.

There was clothing, too. Ludorica's collection of rags was useless. Roane could give her an extra coverall—it would, with its strange make and fabric, be one more thing to explain to any native, but there was no help for that. She had compromised her standing with the Service past repair. But there was no reason why the Princess should be surrendered to an alien "justice" which to her would be the rankest injustice.

As she hunted for clothing and boots she rubbed her forehead with her scratched fingers—not because of any ache there but because she could not wholly understand how she had been drawn into this tangle. Roane had wanted nothing but shelter from a frightening storm, and all this had come from that perfectly natural desire. Somehow it was as if all her training, all she had been drilled in as "right" or "wrong," had been overturned once she met the Princess.

With a sigh, she spread out the coverall, ready for Ludorica, who was sampling cautiously the contents of a container.

"But this is good!" commended the Princess. "It is much better than what you carried with you in the cave. How is it that you have it hot? For you did not take it from any stove—I saw you!"

"It is another of our ways," Roane told her wearily. She was very tired, wanting nothing more than to lie down in the warm and comfortable bed bag, to sleep. But instead she mouthed two sustain tablets, which would ease her fatigue. Then she ate her share of the meal.

The Princess finished first and was now fingering the coverall. She and Roane were much of a size and Roane did not think it would be an ill fit. She showed her how to work the inseal by merely running a fingertip along it, and the Princess gave an exclamation of surprise and pleasure.

"But what ease you have in dressing! Though there is a beauty to buckles and lacing. And"—she surveyed her slender figure, muffled now in the alien dress—"I do not think I would like to wear this for long. Wait until we reach Yatton, Roane. Then I shall exchange gifts with you—and I think"—she eyed the other critically—"you will look well in our dress. Though it is a pity about your hair. Perhaps it will grow in time. Ah, I know! You can wear a Charn bonnet, that will be proper. Wine yellow for your dress, and a bonnet with tyra ribbon for cording—"

Roane laughed. She felt as if she had slipped from the real world into fantasy. How could she, Roane Hume, be sitting in a Service camp listening to the Princess of Reveny describe a dress of high Clio fashion meant for her to wear?

Perhaps it was best to treat this venture as a dream, to drift along with the tide of events rather than trying to fight them. But for a wistful minute or two she wished it could be true, that once she *could* see herself as the Princess visualized her.

"Best hold a dress in your hands before you don it," she commented. "I know we are a long way from Yatton—*if* we ever make it."

Roane took what precautions she could against being traced. She unbuckled her work belt and laid it straight on the floor to study its cargo of tools. The beamer—yes, with fresh charges. Not the detect, nor her wrist com either; they were linked to devices in the camp. The cutter—no. Though she had betrayed the Service in some ways, she would draw the line with that. It could be lost—and, found by another, arouse too much speculation. A small medic kit and—

"Have you aught here to free me from this?"

Roane looked up at the clink of metal. The Princess was pulling at the collar, its chain dangling down over her shoulder.

"Come closer to the light and let me see."

The Princess stooped so that Roane could inspect the small lock hole, which had not been visible in the tower. The off-world girl brought a larger kit. She tried two of the tools it held, inserting their tips into the hole, prying with them. Then, with a click, the collar sprang open.

"Ah." Ludorica jerked it off to rub her throat where red marks showed. Roane reached for the medic kit, squeezed out a fingerload of soothing paste, and applied it carefully.

"Ahh—" The Princess sighed again. "That takes away

the soreness. Another of your many marvels. With your food in me, your clothing on my back, and now your paste of herbs, I feel as if I could front Reddick and be victor. Though I know well that is a belief I should not put to the proof."

Roane continued to choose supplies. Not a flamer, of course—but a stunner was another matter. In the first place, its inner workings would be instantly destroyed if handled by anyone who did not know its use. Service personnel had to be furnished with some form of protective weapon for other worlds, and this refinement was the ultimate result of much research. It could not kill, though on the highest voltage it could cause brain damage—as Sandar had proposed to use it.

She had refurnished her belt—beamer, stunner, the medic kit, a bag of rations, but nothing which would link her to the camp or the camp to her. When she was done and ready to go, she saw that the Princess had gathered up the collar and chain, winding the latter around the former for easier carrying.

"Why take that?"

"Why? Because it was put on me. There are those I shall show it to when I tell my tale, and they will be the hotter against Reddick. Women are not treated so in Reveny. Even more will it be resented that a Princess of the Blood was chained like an animal. I do not know how deep or wide Reddick has made his move against the throne, but that he has done this to me is a warning. There may be those who follow him without knowing what manner of lord he is. And to those such a symbol as this"— she shook the collar and the links clashed against one

another—"will lead to second thoughts. Let me but reach Nelis—"

Roane took a last look at the camp. It was no different from the ones she had known on half a dozen worlds. Yet now she had the feeling that once she walked away she was turning her back on everything which had always been. So, as she glanced from this to that, all had a slightly unfamiliar cast, as if they were already strange and she was one apart.

At least yesterday's rain had stopped, though there were still effects of the storm to be seen as they moved from the bubble half buried in the muddy earth. Out in the open Roane was wary, not only of Reddick's men, but of Uncle Offlas and Sandar. She quickened pace. And the Princess, her feet now protected by boots, matched her stride for stride.

That Yatton lay to the north was all Ludorica could tell Roane. The Princess was not used to traveling except by well-defined roads, and all that lay here were foresters' tracks. Nor had she any idea how far away from their goal they might now be.

"Sending Nelis there three months ago was perhaps another move of Reddick's," she commented. "All I know is that he is loyal only to the true line. Ahh—though these boots are better to tramp in than bare feet, I wish for a duocorn. My good, fleet Zarpher—or even Batlas, though I have named her slug-crawler in the past!"

She paused, one palm against a tree trunk for support. Her face was drawn and there were dark shadows, almost matching her bruises, beneath her eyes.

It had been well into afternoon when they had left the camp, though the cloudy sky made it dusk in the thicker

parts of the woods. Although they had borne north as steadily as they could, there had been many detours forced by the rough country, so they could not have covered too much distance. The only hopeful note was that they had seen no searchers.

Roane, to her surprise, discovered that the Princess had an acuteness of sight and hearing besting hers, often pointing out some trace of bird or animal Roane missed. She smiled at Roane's comments, saying that Hitherhow had been her favorite place when she was a child and that she had often gone with the foresters.

"But that was when Duke Reddick was still a palace squire in Thrisk. And would that he had remained there! He was sent to Thrisk in exchange for the second son of the Duke of Zeiter. I think all hoped he would make a marriage of merit. What did happen"—she shook her head—"not even I know. Though the King was told. And after, he sent Reddick for two years to Tulstead. Which is a place to make a man think twice before he wishes to settle therein. Reddick came back much altered—for the better, my grandfather thought. Though he might have known that the blood of Olava was not to be so purified. Anyway, the Duke's actions thereafter were such that he could not be denied his rights to Hitherhow. That beautiful place! To be so tainted! But let me get the Crown—"

"And what of your grandfather?"

"We are blood kin," Ludorica answered slowly. "He is an old man and to him I am merely a means of preserving our House. He wanted a prince; he must take me. So for the years since my Uncle Wulver's disappearance, I have not been a person—myself—but a tool in his hand. That

he is right makes it no more easy for me. If he dies I shall be a little sorry, for in his way he is a good man, and has always done his best for Reveny. But it will not be true heart-sorrow. I have none close enough to me to strike that deep." She spoke as if stating a fact she had long faced.

"And with the Crown you rule Reveny?"

"I do! Then Reddick shall learn what it means to reach for what is not his. I have already made plans—since I do not know how far he has flung his net, nor in what places it lies to entangle me. I shall get Nelis and his men to escort me, and ride to Leichstan, crossing the border where one may slip over with no eyes upon one. Then we shall go to Gastonhow where the High Court summers. As blood kin I can treat with King Gostar—" She hesitated and the chain of the collar rang as she turned it.

"He has sons, two still unmarried. One such would be an acceptable prince consort for Reveny, and such a marriage would pacify that border at least. So he will be ready to listen to me. Then—with a chance to gather loyal forces—I shall find the Crown and ride to Urkermark City. If I enter with the Crown and with border peace secured, Reddick will have no one left to guard his back. The ambassador at Gastonhow is Imbert Rehling, who was cup-brother to my father in their youth. He will arrange it all once I get to him. Yatton, the border, Gastonhow—it is all a straight move."

It might seem a straight move to the Princess, but Roane thought she could see a good many places where trouble lay. However, that was none of her concern. She would get Ludorica to Yatton, if she could. What happened

thereafter would be the result of the Princess's actions, while Roane returned to camp to take what would be waiting for her there. All she would have to offer in her defense was that the future Queen of Reveny would be in her debt—always supposing Ludorica did become Queen.

"And how do you get the Crown?"

"We know now where it lies. Once I have support behind me I can find it. But those to go there with me to loose it from the rocks must be carefully chosen. This is a story which must not spread. Nelis I can count on to the death and beyond. He will know others that I can trust."

Roane wondered if she was as confident as she sounded. But the off-world girl was not prepared to question it. She was too intent now on the fact that night was coming. The night lenses—she had forgotten those. How could she have been so stupid? The effect of the sustain tablets she had taken was wearing off, too. And it was very apparent that, for all her push and courage, the Princess was in an even worse state. They would have to rest, eat, and perhaps spend a portion of the night in whatever shelter they could find.

That in the end proved to be in the lee of the trunks of two trees brought down in the storm, their broken limbs still flying rags of withering leaves. The girls tramped the smaller branches and leaves into an untidy nest and hunkered in together. Roane brought out E-rations and they ate. By the time they had finished it was dark.

The Princess slipped into an exhausted sleep, lying in a tight curl, her head pillowed on a tree limb. But they would have to keep watch! Roane battled her own deep fatigue as the long minutes slipped by.

Sharp pain in her shoulder—Sandar was prodding her with a Gamelean longsword. He wanted her to get up—march—show him a crown of ice. If he took that into his hands he would be a ruler—He drew back the sword, to turn the point on her again—

Roane opened her eyes.

"Up!" The command came out of deep dusk, was enforced by a prod in her ribs. Not Sandar—

One of Reddick's men! Roane's sleep-rooted daze cleared a little. She moved her hand toward her head, only to meet with a sharp blow on her wrist, delivered by the man standing over her.

"Keep your hands in sight—try nothing. And on your feet!" His orders were terse, and she could see he held a weapon ready to enforce them.

So they had been captured in their sleep. But Roane was still too tired to know more than a remote dismay.

"What do you do, Sergeant?" That demand came from the Princess.

"My duty. You are on Royal land without a warrant. You shall so answer to the Captain."

"That is right, Sergeant," the Princess replied briskly. "But you will act with more courtesy, or *you* shall answer to the Captain, and that answering will not be pleasant. Touch us not again!"

Perhaps the imperiousness of that command had its effect, for he withdrew a pace or two. There was pale sunlight about them. And in the full light stood three men. They wore a uniform of boots, tight breeches, and tunics which were latched from throat to waist with metal, the skirts cut to flare out over the hips to mid-thigh. These

coats were of a rust brown, and each bore on the right breast a complicated symbol worked in purple and green, the same colors appearing in a small tight crest of feathers jutting from the bands of their high-crowned, narrow-brimmed headgear.

Each wore a sword slung in a shoulder baldric, and their leader had drawn his weapon in threat. But in addition they had other weapons Roane recognized as being the most lethal on Clio, hand arms which fired a solid projectile.

"You are of the Jontar Cavalry," Ludorica said. She faced the Sergeant and he stared at her, plainly puzzled. "Your Colonel is Nelis Imfry. Him I would see and speedily."

"You will see the Captain." The Sergeant might have been momentarily disconcerted by her attitude but he had regained his composure. "March."

March they did, through a tangle of brush into a road which was a trail of beaten earth. And there waited four duocorns, another man holding their reins. Roane found herself uncomfortably mounted behind one of the men, the Princess behind another. This was not, the off-world girl decided, an easy way to travel. But it did bring them to another tower, or rather a set of towers, not too unlike the one in which Roane's adventure had begun. Only these were in use, and they formed the pillars of a gate with a threatening portcullis, through which the forest track went to join a much better road.

The Sergeant had spurred ahead, and by the time the rest arrived, there was an officer awaiting them. The insignia on his collar was in the same purple and green and his cockade of feathers had an extra metal embellishment.

He looked curiously at Roane, but when his glance went to the Princess his eyes widened and his astonishment was plain. He moved swiftly to the side of that mount and held out his hand to aid her down.

"Your Highness!" Then he turned upon the Sergeant. "Off with you to the Colonel; tell him we have found the Princess!"

The Sergeant took a second look and climbed back into the saddle. Under his spurs the duocorn leaped under the gate arch, thudded out into the road beyond.

Roane was aided from her own perch far more gently than she had been bestowed there. And she followed the Princess up to the second floor of the left-hand tower, where chairs were hurriedly brought, the second having been summoned by a hand wave from the Princess for Roane's accommodation.

"Your Highness, we have been out hunting for you. When the word came by courier bird last night that you had disappeared from Hitherhow, the Colonel dispatched three companies in search—led the first one himself. But how—" He had glanced several times at her coverall, and at Roane, as if he wanted explanations he dared not ask for openly.

"I was taken from Hitherhow," Ludorica answered, "from my very bed. By the grace of the Guardians, and the good will of the Lady Roane Hume here, I escaped whatever fate was intended for me. For the rest—it is not to be discussed openly. But you I have seen before. You accompanied Colonel Imfry to Urkermark on the occasion of the last birthday review of His Majesty. You are Captain Buris Mykop, and you come from the stead of Benedu."

"Your Highness, but only once did I have the pleasure of being presented to you—and you remember!"

She smiled. "Does anyone forget those who serve them faithfully? It is not strange to do so. Rather it would be unfitting and strange if one did not."

She leaned forward suddenly and tossed the collar wound with the chain onto the top of a nearby table.

"You see there, Captain, a small keepsake of my adventure. That collar was fitted to my throat for a space, the chain was well anchored to hold me at another's pleasure."

The Captain looked from the Princess to the chain. He put out one hand to touch the collar. When he turned, his face was grimly expressionless.

"And who did this, Your Highness?"

"I do not know—yet. But doubtless all shall be made clear in time. It suffices for now that that did *not* hold me as was meant. And for that, thank my Lady Roane." She nodded to her companion, and the Captain gazed at the off-world girl as if he would impress the sight of her on his memory for all time.

"What day is this? We have been turning night into day for our traveling. I can no longer reckon clearly."

"It is the fourth day of Lackameande, Your Highness."

"And it was on the second that I rode to Hitherhow," she said. "There has been no word of weight out of Urkermark?"

"None, Your Highness. By all accounts the King rests comfortably with no change in his condition."

Ludorica relaxed a little. But that she did not altogether rely on that report was proven when she asked: "The

Leichstan border is within two leagues of here, is it not? This is the Westergate?"

"That is true, Your Highness."

"And what—" But what she might have asked was lost in sounds below. A moment later another man came into the room with a rush which halted when he saw Ludorica. He was tall and young, but there were already lines of responsibility on his face.

Beside Sandar's finely cut features his would seem blunted, plain, of a coarser mold. Yet Roane found she was staring at him as the Captain had earlier done with her; she wanted to fix his face in her mind. Though why, she could not have told.

His hair was close to the shade of his tunic, a rusty red-brown, but his eyebrows were as black as the Princess's, and one had an upward tilt which gave him a slightly cynical look.

The way he eyed Ludorica now made Roane a little uncomfortable, as if to be witness was taking an unfair advantage. Then that expression was gone as he crossed the room, took the hand Ludorica held out to him, and raised it to his lips, bowing before her with a grace Roane would not have credited him with had she not seen it for herself.

"Good greeting, my Princess!"

"Good indeed, kinsman." It seemed to Roane that the Princess stressed that last word deliberately. It might have been a private code, or a warning. "I hear you have been searching for me."

"Did you believe we would not?" He spoke with a drawl, and he smiled as if inviting her to share some small

joke. "But as always, my Princess, you have managed to prove yourself a worthy daughter of kings and have not needed our efforts after all. Captain," he said to his subordinate, "we might well all enjoy a glass of lasquer, and—have you yet lunched, my Princess?"

"Lunched?" She laughed. "Kinsman, we have not yet breakfasted. Though we did sup—by my Lady Roane's good will." She nodded to Roane. "Roane, this is my good kinsman and dear friend, Colonel Nelis Imfry, of whom I have already told you."

The Colonel bowed, perhaps not quite as low as he had to Ludorica, but with that same amazing grace. Somehow Roane found her tongue—though as she was not quite sure of the formal terms of address in Reveny she fell back on those of her own civilization.

"I am honored, Colonel—"

"The delight is mine, my lady."

"It is by her hands alone I am found again, kinsman. And now—Captain Mykop says there is no ill news."

The Captain himself had disappeared.

"You expected some?" the Colonel asked.

"Because of my adventure, yes. Nelis, he would not have dared such a move had he not had some private news which led him to believe the King was near his end."

"But I will wager nothing can be proved against your charming cousin," the Colonel returned, the adjective in that speech made an epithet by his tone.

"Naturally not. But, Nelis, there is something else—a secret. You must hear it, and perhaps also others, those you can well trust. May we speak openly here?"

"Yes. Let them bring refreshment. Then you can talk. It

cannot be so immediate that you must go fasting to tell me, can it?"

But the Princess did not echo his smile. "It may be, Nelis, it may just be."

He frowned. But just then the Captain entered, behind him a soldier with a laden tray, the burden of which he set out on the table while the Colonel poured yellow liquid from the bottle the Captain had produced.

"You also, Nelis, and Captain Mykop." Ludorica motioned to the waiting goblets.

"I give you a toast," said the Princess when they each held one of those, "and that is the King's good health!"

Roane let the slightly tart, refreshing liquid fill her mouth. She read meaning into what might be a conventional toast. Ludorica indeed had need for the continued health of her grandfather, unless she could gain her long-lost crown.

# ✳ CHAPTER 7 ✳

**ROANE GLANCED** from the Princess to the Colonel and back again, wondering what lay between the two, who seemed to have forgotten her existence. Though the Princess made an obvious point of addressing him with warmth, yet he in return appeared to set some barrier of formality between them. They faced each other now across the table where the remains of the best meal Roane had yet had on Clio still lay.

Ludorica had told her story in terse language—of the loss of the Crown, of where she now believed that it lay. And when she finished, the Colonel made no comment, but instead looked to Roane.

"And how does the Lady Roane come into the matter, beyond the fact that she has been of great service to Reveny in her actions toward Your Highness?"

Since the Princess made no answer, Roane spoke for herself. Again she must say more than she wished to. Always she plunged deeper and deeper into disaster for an off-worlder.

She told the edited story she had given Ludorica—of the hunt for ancient remains which had brought her people here. But when she had done the Colonel looked far from satisfied.

"You do not, Lady, say from whence you come, you and these other treasure seekers—"

Roane hesitated a long moment. "Colonel, have you never served under orders given to you in confidence, which you cannot disclose to others? Or, if you have not done this, are not such cases known to you?"

"That is true. Though I have not, until this hour, dealt with aught which is not common knowledge."

"Then accept that I must be silent. But I swear to you that those I serve mean nothing ill to Reveny. In fact before we came here, we were pledged to do nothing to bring us to the knowledge of your countrymen, nor to influence affairs here. In this I have erred, and I shall have to pay for that."

"They can make her lose her memory—or put her in prison—" broke in the Princess.

"She told you that?" The Colonel's eyes were cold now.

"Yes," Roane returned baldly. It was plain he doubted her. "They can do this—whether you believe it or not!" Her chin went up a fraction of an inch as she met disbelief with defiance. "And now," she said to the Princess, "I promised to bring you to your friends. This I have done. So I shall go—"

"Not so!" The Colonel's words came sharp and swift. And Ludorica put out her hand, caught Roane's wrist where it rested on the table, as if to hold her prisoner.

"Whether you wish it or not," the Colonel continued,

"you have chosen your path, my lady, and you must continue to follow it until the Princess is out of danger. Your Highness, let this lady remain with you. It is fitting that you have a companion when you cross the border. And it would seem fortune favors you with one who dares not betray secrets lest she betray herself even more."

Roane flushed. Did he jeer at her now, or issue a challenge to prove she was as she said? She was a little afraid, for she did not doubt he meant what he said— evidence that he was prudent, for the wise thing for him was to keep her close. That she had not foreseen this simple end to the action puzzled her. It was all a part of that muzzy thinking which she had done ever since she met Ludorica. Almost as if she were conditioned—

Conditioned! What if the Service techs had been wrong and their off-world guards did not hold? Or at least not entirely, so that subtly she had been taken over by the force which existed to make Clio a closed world? A new spark of fear was born in her. She was she, Roane Hume, who could perfectly remember a life beyond the stars. She was not a subject of a ruler on this forgotten, living museum of a world! And that thought she must hold to.

"You are set on this plan then, Your Highness—to go to Leichstan for aid?" The Colonel, having delivered his order, seemed to have forgotten Roane again.

"There is the Crown. I do not think that, even if Reddick knows where it lies, he quite dares to reach for it while I live. But with my death, he believes—or I would in his place—that the Crown will acknowledge him. For unrecorded though his descent may be, there is a trace of the Blood in him. He may have taken me only to make sure

I was under his control when the word he expects comes. But that he ever meant I live on past that hour—" She pointed to the chain and collar. "That is good evidence he did not. And Leichstan can prove a refuge until we are sure of what we do face now."

She seemed to accept very calmly the fact that she was the target of her cousin's intrigues. But perhaps such intrigues were so common on Clio that they were a part of daily experience. Maybe one held one's position here through a series of struggles in a deadly game.

"Reddick must still be at Hitherhow. We can take him there!" The Colonel's brown hand twitched as if the fingers wished to hold some weapon.

"Not knowing how far his plans extend or what support he can summon? That would be folly. But if I go to Leichstan I can claim aid, and I have put myself beyond Reddick's reach, given us time to find the Crown and learn the true state of the King."

"Leichstan is ambitious," the Colonel returned slowly.

"So is Vordain to the north. If we must ally ourselves— which? I wish this no more than you do, kinsman. But if one must choose between alliance and alliance, Leichstan through friendship is better than Vordain by force."

The Colonel looked down at the cup he held as he turned it around and around. He might be reading some message in its depths.

"There is a price for such alliances," he observed in a very level voice.

"That I know also," the Princess returned. "But to everything on this earth there is a price, kinsman. And to me Reveny comes first, its safety and future. I am what I

am by reason of birth, of much training. Were there another of my House to carry sword in battle, perhaps I could turn my thoughts from what must be done. But there is not. And I believe that this lack is also of Reddick's doing. Before the Crown falls into his grasping hands I will do much. And the way lies through Leichstan—though I must go there without any of the trumpeting of a royal progress. You have wandered the border long enough to know its secrets. Nelis, there must be some hidden way across, and not far from here—"

"Smugglers' ways are rough going."

The Princess laughed. "None can be worse than that I have lately used. Though this"—she looked down at the coverall—"is very durable clothing for such work, I think it would be better if I entered Leichstan wearing something less noticeable. I know that I cannot expect an army post to produce clothing for a lady, but can such be obtained for us both?"

Nelis Imfry smiled, as if the Princess's request had a somewhat lighter note.

"We do not have much provision for ladies, that is certain. If you are willing I can send to Fittsdale for peasant clothing."

"Well enough. That they be fit for riding is all that is necessary. And you have an escort for us who knows these smugglers' ways?"

Now the Colonel laughed. "Indeed I do, Your Highness. We have held these hills so long that we know the four sides of every rock. And since the smugglers in question are bound for Leichstan and not for our side of the border, we have no ill will to fear."

But when he had left, Roane made one last attempt to break free from this current carrying her farther and farther into danger.

"I must go back!"

Ludorica shook her head, a smile on her lips. "But, my dear Roane, indeed you must not! If what you said is true, that they will treat you ill for what you have done on my behalf, then all the greater reason not to. Also, suppose you are taken by Reddick's men—do not think that he will not use harsh means to learn all you can tell him. The mere fact that you are found in a Royal forest after my escape will make you suspect. You wear such clothing as is strange, carry mysterious tools and weapons—Yes, you would make a puzzle Reddick would work hard to solve, and the solving would not be to your comfort. We ride for Leichstan. And when the Crown is in my hands, then shall we in turn treat with your people. Never go to a bargaining, Roane, unless you have that on your side which is a mighty aid."

The Captain came to show them to his quarters in the third story of the tower, and there Ludorica announced they had better get what rest they could, since no one could guess how long the journey across the border might last. That she was as close a prisoner as if she now wore the collar and chain, Roane knew. There would be no slipping away from this place, unless she used her stunner freely. And then the chaos she would leave behind—She shook her head. She could do nothing but hope for the future.

She slept, and it was twilight when the Princess aroused her with a gentle shaking. On the floor sat a very large tub, into which Ludorica now poured steaming water.

"As a bath," the Princess remarked, "this is a primitive

affair. But we are undoubtedly lucky in this time and place to have one at all."

She shed her clothing and stepped carefully into the tub, kneeling to splash its meager contents over her, rubbing with a bunch of rough fibers which left foaming streaks on her smooth skin.

"If you will pour the rest now—" Ludorica indicated another jug and Roane obeyed. The Princess arose and made good use of the towel her companion handed her.

"Now—if we empty this into that other—"

The Princess anchored the towel more firmly about her as they dumped the water into an outsize bucket and refilled the basin for Roane. Though this was far different from the more efficient freshers she had always known, she found it good. The soapy substance oozing from the matted fibers of the scrubber had a fresh, herbal odor she liked.

Ludorica sorted a pile of clothing, holding up one garment and then another to measure against her body. She laughed.

"Nelis has the name of being one who does not notice women too closely. But this is proof his cold reputation is not deserved. These are a good fit. We shall go reasonably well clad. Now—the brown for you, and I will take the blue."

Roane dressed in the unfamiliar clothes. They were clean, if creased, and to them, too, a good herb scent clung. There were no mirrors, but she thought the Princess right. These fitted well. The skirt was full, ankle length, and its folds felt odd against her legs so long used to coveralls. In contrast the bodice was tight, laced from belt to just under her throat with silken red strings. Embroidery of the same

shade of red bordered those lacings. The dress itself was a pleasant yellow-brown. There was also a hooded cloak lined with red, and a close-fitting cap with a turned-back border, embroidered all over with small, very skillfully fashioned red feathers.

The Princess wore dark blue, her trimming a vivid green but otherwise differing none from Roane's. There was no cap for her. Instead she combed and braided her long hair, allowing the braids to lie free on her shoulders.

"Very good." She looked from Roane down along her own person, then back to Roane. "We eat now and then we ride. At least it is a clear night. Nelis thinks it will remain so, and he knows this country well enough to speak with authority."

They descended to the lower room, where the table was once more set with food, rounds of cold meat, bread, and fruit. The man who rose to greet them was not in uniform but wore a dusty gray suit, with a close-fitting cap which allowed only his face free, for it had a lower frill lapped about his neck, fastening under the chin.

"Nelis!" Ludorica seated herself in the chair he drew out for her. "You?"

He laughed. "Did I not tell you that I knew these hills well? Do you think I would let you ride them alone, Your Highness?" Then he became serious. "You will have your escort of picked men, men from my own stead. They own me overlord as well as field commander."

"But if Reddick learns you are gone, he may suspect—"

"We have worked out a scheme for that. Remember, you are lost out of Hitherhow. I am searching for you with a flying column and am thus hard to reach, very hard. As far

as this company is concerned—though we can answer for
their loyalty—they will march within the hour to patrol
west of Granpabar, which is territory I do not think the
Duke dares invade as yet—seeing as how the lord there has
good reason to dislike him."

"Trust you, Nelis—" The Princess laughed, too.

"I hope you can, Your Highness," he cut in, still sober.
"I hope you can! I understand your reasoning, and it was
ever the way of your House to play boldly at need. But
there are many ways this play can go wrong. Do not be too
confident—"

"Which urging I have had from you many times in the
past! No, there is something now which gives me
confidence, Nelis. Reddick could not have foreseen the
arrival of Roane to spoil his plan. So far every throw of the
wish sticks has turned up in my favor. Oh"—she held up
her hand when he would have spoken—"I cannot count on
such fair fortune's continuing. But while it is with me, let
us make the most of it, just as we shall now make the most
of this most excellent food."

They were not, Roane discovered to her silent relief,
expected to ride duocorns alone. She had never guided
such a mount in her life, and to begin riding lessons now—
there was no time.

To keep their cover of peasant women, who did not
usually ride alone, she and the Princess must ride pillion,
the Princess with the Colonel, Roane behind one of the
other men. All wore the drab civilian dress. And under the
cloak she still had her belt, which she determined to cling
to. Possession of that gave her the feeling that she was still
Roane Hume, not a stranger to herself also.

By dawn, after threading a maze of dusky valleys and scrambling up hillsides where they must dismount to walk their animals, they reached a pass through which the wind blew cruelly cold. Roane was glad of the cloak. Twice they had halted to let the third man of the party scout ahead. But there had been no alarms. And now the Colonel pointed down the slope before them.

"Leichstan, but Gastonhow lies a good eight leagues on. We shall have to rest and change mounts before we reach there."

"We cannot go to any inn," the Princess protested.

"Neither can we go far on worn-out duocorns," Imfry returned. "With those clothes you are of Reveny right enough, but many border families have kin on either side. There may well be a wedding to which we have been bid—"

"Not so! A wedding would have been far-cried. These people will know what chances even from hamlet to hamlet. It had better be a birthing, perhaps in a head homestead. We can pick straw for a babe garland as we go."

"It never ceases to amaze me, Your Highness, how you know all customs—"

"But it should not, kinsman. Of what use is any ruler to her people unless she understands their ways? Oh, I know that there is in some countries the odd belief that there is no common meeting point between king and subject. But that is not so with my House and never has been."

"A point which has kept your line safely enthroned."

"Until now! And then that dark shadow comes not from my own people but from kin. And kin quarrels are always the most bitter."

But it seemed that the Princess's plan was not to be put into practice, for their scout returned with the news that a party was traveling the main road to the nearest inn and that he had recognized one face among the travelers.

"Kaspard Fancher!" the Princess repeated.

"I fear"—the Colonel had dropped his voice a little—"that our period of favoring fortune is over. Fancher is—"

"I know well what he is," Ludorica interrupted. "Which means that Reddick has given me credit for trying to reach King Gostar. But he also knows that I am not altogether stupid, however much he wishes that so. Very well. Fancher may be riding with all the support the Duke can raise for him, but Reddick is not yet King of Reveny, nor even close to the throne. I am the Princess, and Imbert Rehling was my father's good friend. He will smooth my path to Gostar, and Reddick cannot prevent that."

"If we reach Rehling—"

"The Court is at Gastonhow, so all ambassadors will follow. It is early in the season for such a move, but King Gostar cherishes this young second queen of his. The rumor has it that she may present him soon with a princeling—so he has brought her to drink the waters of the Faithwell."

"Superstition!"

"Perhaps—but then again perhaps not. There was a Guardian at the Faithwell; that has been attested to beyond any doubt. And also there have been many cases of women in difficult childbirth being soothed by its waters. Why, Gastonhow was built by Queen Marget because she feared to lose her fourth child, having three others die as she still lay in bed from the bearing of them. She stayed there

during the major part of her time of carrying and thereafter bore five sons and three daughters with no ills."

"History! What does it matter now about Queen Marget? If the court is at Gastonhow and Fancher goes here we must be very sure of our ground. Best send a messenger—"

"But why should we not just push on the faster to Gastonhow ourselves?"

"Not until I am sure what awaits us there."

"Sure of what? That Fancher is here to make what trouble he can? We know that. Lord Imbert will prevent him from seeing the King, and he cannot work mischief with Imbert himself. But—perhaps—Perhaps you are right, Nelis. It is better not to spoil our plans now for the want of a little caution. And I shall give the messenger that which will get him speedy speech with Lord Imbert." The Princess pulled at one of her long braids, breaking loose five hairs, which she counted carefully before she knotted them together. "Now a resuah leaf—"

"Games?" asked the Colonel.

"Games—with a purpose. But a game Lord Imbert will remember, for I shared it with him. It was when he came to me after my father was newly dead. He had taken me to his Lady Ansla—she who was High Lady of Kross in her own right—for the King would have me away from the Court as he ailed. Lord Imbert liked the old tales. He has ordered many of them collected from the Tork singers and copied out that they may not be forgotten. And one was of the Lost Lady of Innace. The geas which was laid on that lady was broken by leaf and hair. Yes, he will remember and listen to your man."

The Princess had been searching through the vegetation around and now made a swift pounce, catching up, earth-covered root and all, a plant with long narrow leaves. The largest of these leaves she twisted free, wrapping her knotted hair about it.

After their messenger departed, mounted on the duocorn Imfry judged their best, they headed on at a much-curtailed pace. Here, close to the heights where they had crossed the border, the country was wooded, so that they had to turn into one of those overhung, branch-roofed lanes. And this brought them to a bridge which was more ornate and even wider than the road they had come, as if the latter had once been a more important thoroughfare than it now was. On the opposite side of that arch was a small single-story tower, built in the form of a triangle firmly wedded to the bridge. Even the two very narrow windows in it were wedge-shaped.

"Have you any way money?" Ludorica asked the Colonel. "I see this is a vow bridge."

"An old one. The vow must have long since been fulfilled."

"How can we know that? Have you money for the alms slit?"

He brought a small bag from the front of his tunic, passed it back to the Princess.

"Be sparing with that, Your Highness. I had no time to gather a fortune before we left."

She loosened the drawstring, felt within the bag, and pulled out a round of metal.

"A plume will suffice. We travel with clean hands and no malice at heart."

As they came to the three-cornered building, the Princess leaned from her pillion and tossed the coin into the open window near to hand.

"For the good of him who built the way, for the good of those who walk the way, for the good of the journey, and the good, surely, of its final ending," she intoned as if speaking some formula.

"His name"—she moved her forefinger through the air, tracing the curves and angles of some weather-worn carving on the wall—"was Niklas and he was lord of—The stead seal is too badly worn to read. But it is a good omen that we ride by one Niklas's favor!"

The road ahead was not concealed by drooping tree branches, but rather edged with hedge walls. It was wider, also, and the dust of its surface was slotted with wheel ruts and hoof prints, as if the road which joined from upriver brought more traffic.

No longer could the duocorns be kept to a steady trot. When their riders stopped urging them, they fell into an amble. The morning they had met in the pass was now well advanced. They had broken their fast in the hills but Roane was hungry again. And it seemed to her stiff body that they had been riding or walking for half a lifetime. Those with whom she traveled seemed to need little rest.

Suddenly Imfry reined in his mount, held up his hand. One of the duocorns blew and then was silent. Far off Roane heard it now—the sound of a horn, clear and carrying.

# ✳ CHAPTER 8 ✳

**ROANE STOOD AT THE WINDOW.** Between her fingers she held caressingly the soft folds of the heavy curtain. She loved the feel of that, the strange luxury of the room behind her—it was like coming out of the cold to the warmth of a welcoming fire. As yet it was early morning, and no one seemed to stir in the great house. But there was life in the street before its tall courtyard gates.

A boy had come out of a shop, sprinkling down the cobbles before the door from a holed can which he sloshed back and forth without care, nearly sending its spray on the wide skirts of a passing woman. Those skirts were gray, with scarlet flowers bordering them, to match in vivid color the bodice of her dress. She walked with a free, swinging step, one hand raised to balance a basket on her head, its contents hidden by a covering of leaves.

She was only the first of a small procession of such wayfarers, their gray and scarlet almost a uniform, each with a basket aloft. The boy with the sprinkler cried out something and they turned smiling faces to him. It was all like watching a live tri-dee.

Roane remembered her impression of the house as they had come to it the night before. It was large, three stories high at least, all of stone, the windows on the lowest level being very narrow. There was no growing thing to break the drabness of the courtyard pavement, and the only spot of color was the symbol on the house face—she could see an edge of it from here—facing the gate, representing the might of Reveny.

She had not met the ambassador on whom Ludorica relied so much. In fact she had not even seen the Princess since they had entered a side door and been shown almost furtively through dark hallways by a single servant. Though she could not complain about the room in which she stood, nor the willing serving maid she had sent early away. Only—Roane felt uneasy as well as somehow charmed by her surroundings.

All of it had a dreamlike quality. Though in the beginning it had been more of a nightmare when that horn blast had sent them into quick hiding. There had been a troop of horsemen, and the identity of two of the riders had disturbed the Princess and the Colonel, though neither had explained why to Roane. Instead of pressing on themselves after that other party had passed, they had waited until nightfall. Then they had ridden hard, across fields many times, to reach a crossroads. There they were overtaken by a carriage, curtained at the windows, with four of the large draft duocorns to draw it.

Their messenger rode on the box beside the driver, and the letter he delivered to the Princess banished the shadow from her face. She waved it triumphantly before the Colonel.

"Did I not say so? Lord Imbert gives us good welcome—and certainly softer travel. Ah, I feel as old as the hills with every bone in my body aching to tell me so!"

The interior of the carriage was dark, but no one raised its curtains. Roane found it hardly more comfortable than riding, in spite of Ludorica's words. The swaying of the body on a sling of straps—which took the place of any springs—made her queasy. But her companions settled back against the cushions as if this were the height of comfort, and the Princess went to sleep, her head against Roane's shoulder.

Twice they stopped for fresh animals, and the second time a basket of cold but good food was handed in. Only Roane, hungry as she might have been under other circumstances, could but nibble and wish herself back in normal life.

They had come to Gastonhow in the middle of the night. And she had fallen half-dazed into the great curtained bed behind her. But for all her fatigue she had awakened early, as if she had been alerted by some inner alarm.

Now she turned from the window to view the room again, seeing much more than the limited lamplight had shown her.

The bed, which dominated the room, was extremely large, almost a quarter the size of a camp bubble. Having most of her life fitted into very narrow spaces, in camp, on board ship, she was not used to such freedom. It stood on a two-step dais and had four posts carved with flowers and leaves to support a canopy with curtains that Roane had not suffered the maid to draw about her, tent-fashion, the

night before. Both the curtains and the cover on the bed were fancifully patterned by needlework.

All the colors were bright, almost too strident for her taste. The walls were boldly painted with designs in the same shades. There was a table with a wide mirror, a backless stool set before it, to her left. On her right stood a tall cupboard with double doors. And there were chairs, stools, and a smaller table or two scattered around.

She moved before the mirror to gaze at her reflection. The white folds of just such a night robe as the captive Princess had worn hung about her slim body. Against that her weathered hands and face looked very dark and brown. Her short hair had grown enough since she had left Crambrief to form a fluff on her forehead and behind her ears. And that too was odd against her deep tan, for the locks were a pale yellow-brown which sometimes held a hint of red when the sun touched them.

By the standards of her own civilization Roane had no beauty and had early learned to accept that. And, since her roving life had taken her into the wilderness of unknown worlds, she practiced none of the cosmetic arts used by the women of the inner planets. Beside the Princess she was certainly very insignificant. How much so, she had not realized until now.

There was an array of pots and bottles on the table. Roane sat down eyeing them, wondering who had supplied these, what they held. Then, emboldened, she investigated. The first was a small yellow pot, very smooth to her fingers, lidded by a stopper fashioned as a half-opened flower. It contained a paste with a sweet smell. She ran a fingertip tentatively over it but had no idea what might be its use. As

her explorations continued she made many guesses. There were smaller pots of red which perhaps colored lips or cheeks, though she had not seen anyone wearing the elaborate designs painted on forehead, cheek, or chin which were in high favor on some worlds. There was one narrow box of black stuff flanked by a tiny brush—and more beautifully shaped bottles and flagons, each of which held a sweet scent.

"My lady?"

Roane started and nearly dropped a delicate transparent bottle. Over her shoulder in the mirror she saw the maid carrying a tray on which rested a covered bowl and a cup.

Roane gave the morning greeting of Reveny. "Sun and a fair wind rising—"

"With thanks to you, Lady. Will you morn-sup now?"

There were berries in the bowl, intermixed with what seemed cooked grain, sweet contrasting with tart. The mug contained a thick, hot drink she could not identify. She was sipping at that when the door opened again and she faced the Princess.

Now Roane saw her in clothing becoming her station— the full-skirted dress of a deep green, with wide lace flecked with threads of silver turned back in cuffs, a collar of the same dew-and-cobweb material lying on her shoulders. The hair which had swung in braids during their journeying was now piled and pinned into an imposing structure on her head. There was about her such an air of consequence that Roane arose to pay her tribute.

"Roane." Ludorica did not move with a stately gait but sped across the room to catch the off-world girl's hands in hers. "We are safe here. And my good Lord Imbert has

gone to speak to the King. Fortune has favored us. And once we see King Gostar—" She laughed. "Oh, Roane, you will enjoy it here! There will doubtless be a ball—did I not say he had sons to be settled, and what better way can a gallant display than at a ball? And we will ride in the Brogwall in an open carriage as is the fashion and—and—and—"

The Princess could be any girl from one of the inner planets thirsting for pleasure. But Roane found she could not match the other's high spirits. And Ludorica must have quickly sensed her lack of response, for she lost some of her sparkle as she asked:

"What is it, Roane? Truly we are safe here, perhaps more so than in Reveny, until the full of Reddick's schemes be known. And you—you do not have to fear losing your memory or being shut in a prison. This is a day for a light heart, not a sober face. Or perhaps yours merely looks sober because you are still wearing a night robe. White is *not* a color which becomes you! But that is speedily remedied."

She pulled upon a bell rope and the maid returned, to scurry about under a rain of orders so quickly delivered, Roane was not sure of their number or kind.

It was later, when she sat once again looking into the mirror, that the dream seemed even stronger. There were drugs, forbidden drugs, which could do this to one, produce an alternate life for their user, so entrancing a life that he or she clung to the fantasy, fought return to reality. She had not used those and yet she was enmeshed—surely that reflection was not of any Roane Hume she knew.

The soft fabric of her gown was a shade of yellow, but

woven in such a way that each fold as she moved was overcast by a hint of rose. Lace, not as wide or as ornate as that which bedecked the Princess, but still finer than any other she had ever seen, ruffled about her brown wrists, rose a little behind her head to make a fragile frame for her thin neck. Not for her the piling of hair, but rather a lace cap curving to a point over her forehead, from which folded back two wired wings, as if an alien bird had settled there.

And her face—they could not take away the browning that years of exposure had painted on her, but they had made knowing use of the contents of many pots and bottles. So that brown was enhanced, and she was vividly alive as she had never seen herself before. Viewing herself so, she gained the courage natural to her sex, the armor a woman dons by knowing she looks her best.

Ludorica clapped her hands and laughed. "My Lady Roane, but this is how you were always meant to look! Not to go in that ugly dress like a man. Why do you desire to look so plain when it is not necessary? Do you not know, dear Roane, that it is the true duty of any woman to look the best she can, no matter how the Guardians may have designed her face at birth? Come now, you must learn to walk properly in skirts, my dear-like-a-man-that-was!"

Exiling her doubts to the back of her mind, Roane followed the Princess. They came out into a wide hall, one side of which was hung with panels of needlework between other strips painted in the same bright colors which had lightened the bedroom. The other wall had windows, four of them set out in bays. And those windows were checkerboarded with clear and colored glass, the colored

being wrought in complicated patterns. Overhead the ceiling was molded in balls and leaves in high relief, those also painted. And at the far end was a large fireplace, while at intervals down the length of the hall were braziers of metal on tripod legs, from several of which curled scented smoke.

There was no one in that hall, neither servant nor master. But when they went through the door at the far end and came to a staircase a man did appear, to stand at the foot of the stair awaiting them.

He uncovered his head (for he had been wearing a soft flat hat of colorful stuff with a big ornament of gold) as the Princess descended, and bowed. His clothing was richly trimmed with metallic embroidery and he fitted well with his surroundings.

"Your Highness—"

He was middle-aged and had allowed his facial hair to grow, a custom new to Roane, who knew only spacers, who went with smooth cheeks and sometimes even totally denuded heads so that space helmets would fit the better. But the lower part of his face was masked by wiry gray hair.

"My dear lord." The Princess held out her hand. "You must meet my good companion, the Lady Roane Hume. Roane, this is Lord Imbert, who gives us shelter in our troubles."

He bent his head to kiss the Princess's hand. Then he turned a searching glance on Roane, one she found disturbing though she met him eye to eye.

"I am honored, my lord." Gathering up the full folds of her skirt with either hand, she essayed what she hoped was

a passable curtsy. She was not too graceful. And those eyes watching her had in them that which daunted her confidence.

"We have much to be grateful to you for, my lady, we of Reveny." Unlike his stern and rather colorless outward appearance, his voice was warm and rich. Roane's first estimate of him changed. When he spoke it was as if another person awoke behind the mask he presented to the world. "We have our Princess safe, and all who serve her now are very welcome."

He bowed again with a smile. But when she watched him without listening to his voice, Roane felt a chill in his manner. Words could provide screens for thoughts. Though the Princess valued Lord Imbert Rehling so highly, Roane did not feel for him that trust the Colonel inspired in her.

"You are very kind." Her words sounded feeble. The stately language of Reveny was so foreign to the clipped Basic of her own people that Roane found it difficult to use it readily.

"We are going to view your garden, my lord." Ludorica smiled at him with a sparkle in her eyes. "What I have seen from the window of my bedchamber promises well—"

"Your Highness"—his voice took on a deeper timbre—"such a faring would not be wise at this time."

"A walk in the garden not wise? But why?"

"Your Highness, as you know, Fancher is in the city. And the Soothspeaker Shambry as well. You yourself saw them both traveling hither."

"But this is Gastonhow and the Embassy of Reveny under the mastership of my best of friends, Lord Imbert

Rehling himself," she countered. "What have we to fear from Fancher, a man without any lord here in Leichstan? As for the Soothspeaker, yes, we saw him. But what has he to do with us, or Reveny?"

"It would seem something," Lord Imbert began and then glanced at Roane, as if he willed her withdrawal. Perhaps that was the fashion of the court, but she did not pretend to be more than she was, a stranger caught up by chance in their ways. She stood where she was and the Princess said impatiently:

"Do you speak openly—the Lady Roane knows all."

He shrugged and continued. "Very well, Your Highness. The Soothspeaker has foretold King Niklas's death to the exact hour."

She sobered instantly. "How much value can we put to his words? No, I will not ask you that, my lord. We all have our own opinions of such gifts or talents. And Shambry has foretold with remarkable success on several occasions. Though I have heard—less loudly—that he has also had his failures. To foresay the King's death, however—he must be very sure to do that. But why comes he out of Reveny into Leichstan? Unless—"

Ludorica looked down at her own hands as if she held there something very precious the others could not see. "Unless he would be out of Reveny before his foreseeing can be proved. What excuse does he give for coming?"

"That he has matters of great moment for King Gostar which will affect the future of his House, and that he was bidden by his gift to come."

"By his gift! Then he is very sure—"

"Just so," cut in Lord Imbert. "And it is against all

custom for him to be so persistent. He has lately been at Ichor, and the Lady of Ichor—"

"Was once Reddick's very dear friend. But surely here, well guarded in your house, my lord, I need not fear any web to entangle my feet. Why, you yourself said to Nelis that he could leave us here and go with a free mind. Why, if you had these reservations, did you say that?"

"For the simple reason, Your Highness, that this news had not yet come to my ears when the Colonel rode forth. And it is best also that he return to his command, for if your journey has not yet been discovered, his return will help to keep it secret."

"A secret? I did not think that here—" She hesitated and then continued. "But let me see King Gostar and all will move as we wish."

"There, too, you must practice patience, Your Highness. The Queen is not in good health and King Gostar is much concerned about her. He is never at the best an easy man to deal with. Rather is he sometimes prey to odd whims and sudden changes of mind, so that no one can predict what he will do. For the past three months, since he learned the Queen is carrying a child, he has not even been to the secret sanctuary of the Flame Crown for guidance.

"He will receive no delegations from the council and has refused his ministers' audiences. Even to reach him with a message may take some time."

"And time we may have in scant supply!"

"I understand, Your Highness. But I am being frank with you. We shall have to approach the King with care. An incautious move on our part may arouse him to refusal

before we even state the case. He has done such many times, more times even than his people have general knowledge of. Now—you will note, Your Highness, that you have seen few servants in this wing of the house. That, too, is on purpose. The fewer who know that you are here, until I have some understanding with the King, the better. For we have not only to fear his changeable tempers, but also interference, perhaps directly from Fancher, indirectly from Shambry—or so I suspect.

"The Queen is much taken with foreseeing and there is good reason to believe that once she knows Shambry is here she will have him summoned to read for her. Once gaining her attention, he could defeat us with ease. For he is a subtle man with more to him than the usual Soothspeaker. He already tells the day and hour of His Majesty's death with confidence. What if he adds to that some direful word concerning yourself? Could you then get a fair hearing for your plea? Ill luck is too real a thing to most kings and lords."

"What hour and day—no, I do not want to know lest I begin to believe it too. So I can do nothing but wait?"

"Hard as it seems, Your Highness, that is so. And not only wait with good grace, but also stay within these walls and let none have a chance to see you. You thought yourself safe at Hitherhow, and what happened? I have guards here, but how can I swear that all of them, and of my servants, are true to the old loyalty and that none of them secretly supports Reddick?"

"It is hard to believe," Ludorica said slowly. "I feel, as one trying to cross the Bog of Snelmark, that any step may be the wrong one. But suppose the King—" She turned a

little away. "Very well—tell me, how long does this smooth-tongued Soothspeaker give him yet?"

"Four days—until high noon."

"Four days! And he would not dare to make such a prophecy if he were not sure it would be proved true. Four days, and if I am not back to Urkermark by then with the Crown—I must consider this carefully, Lord Imbert."

"Do so, Your Highness. In the meantime, for your own sake, keep within these walls and out of sight. What I can do to reach King Gostar, and there are several ways that can be tried, that I shall do."

He left them with another bow and the Princess turned to Roane. "It would seem that we cannot enjoy the garden except through a window. But that we can do in the gallery. Come aloft again."

They returned to the long upper chamber and Ludorica brought Roane to the middle bay so they could look out. There were few flowers below, rather hedges and shrubs trimmed and clipped into fanciful shapes, many resembling the statues which had been set out at Hitherhow before the Princess's arrival.

"It is very well kept," commented Ludorica. "One has the feeling that were even a single leaf misplaced such would be instantly noted. Lord Imbert has a liking for such formality. There is a large garden such as this about his stead keep in Reveny. The Lady Ansla never cared much for it. She had her own place and the sweetest-smelling flowers grew there. Also a pond with an erand nesting, and the bird used to stand so still in the water one would believe her a statue—"

"The Lady Ansla—she is here?"

"She is gone." The Princess did not look away from the window. "It was the frost fever. I did not even get to put the fareforth candle in her hand—though she had been so good to me. When I came she was already closed away. I think that when I was small she was the only one who cared for me, Ludorica, and not because I was the Princess."

Though they could not go out into that stiff garden, nor even out of the section of rooms which had been made over to them, they found enough to occupy their time. Ludorica amused herself and Roane (to the latter's mild astonishment) by coaching her temporary lady-in-waiting in the duties of her position and furnishing her with the current gossip of the Court of Reveny—though due to the King's age and illness Court life had shrunk to a few shadowy functions and those only observed through necessity. Roane absorbed it even as she had the learning at Cram-brief, but found it more interesting. The Princess's description of the nobles and courtiers, their backgrounds and motives, were so detailed that the off-world girl thought she would know each when she met him—*if* she ever met him.

Deep in Roane herself something began to grow. She would smooth the soft flow of her skirts, glance now and then into a mirror, finger some cushion glowing with beautiful needlework or an ornament. All this was far different from the treasures of her own civilization, yet surrounded by such she was not ill at ease nor unhappy, but rather relaxed. If she was dreaming, she wished less and less to awake. At least, as she reflected with dry humor, if she ever got back to her own people she could supply enough data on this Psychocrat experiment from the point of view of those caught in it to amaze the Service.

On their second night at Gastonhow she was sitting in front of the mirror about to unpin the birdlike bonnet when Ludorica slipped into the room, a long, fur-lined cloak over her arm, her eyes alight with excitement.

"Imbert has done it! I am to go to King Gostar secretly. But not alone, Roane—Lord Imbert thinks you should be with me, that you can bear witness about the tower and your testimony will carry force. Hurry—there is a coach waiting. Where is a cloak?"

She opened the wardrobe and rummaged among its contents. Roane hurried to the bed, to her private hiding place. She felt under the wide pillow and drew out her belt with its off-world equipment. Even temporarily she was not going to be separated from that.

# ✳ CHAPTER 9 ✳

**THE COACH AWAITING THEM** in the dark courtyard was like the one which had fetched them to Gastonhow. As then, heavy curtains hung in place across the windows, and in the light of a single lantern the interior looked very dark. Lord Imbert himself stood to hand them in, and he murmured something in a very low voice to the Princess before putting out his hand to Roane as she tried to manage the folds of her skirts on the small step.

There was no Colonel to share their ride this time, but the cushions were softer than those of the equipage which had brought them to Gastonhow. The door closed and they were in the total dark, for there was no riding lantern.

"No light!" Apparently the Princess found this strange, but then she added, "I suppose Imbert wishes us to be as inconspicuous as possible."

"Where do we go?" Roane pulled her cloak about her. The evening was chill and there was a cold which seemed part of the coach itself, as if the vehicle had not been recently in use.

"To Gastonhigh. It is a stead used by the royal family—by Immer Lake. I suppose the Queen wishes more quiet."

A swing of the coach sent Roane against the Princess and she heard Ludorica laugh.

"My dear Roane, feel along the wall and you shall find a hold strap. It is best to make use of those when the pace is swift."

Roane groped for the anchor, running her hand over the side she could not see, though now and then came a faint glimmer of light around the edge of the curtain, as if they drove by some well-lighted site. She found the loop and took firm hold on it, but she wished they could raise the curtains, just so she did not have the impression that they were imprisoned in a jiggling, swaying cage. And once more her stomach rebelled against this form of travel.

"My mother was King Gostar's cousin," the Princess said. "I wish I knew on what terms they were. It might strengthen my appeal if they had parted in friendship when she went to Reveny to wed. If he had kind memories of her—"

"Is there any reason why he would not?" Roane asked.

"There are feuds not only among the stead lords, but also in the royal Houses. Am I not so caught with Reddick? And the House of Hillaroy, which is King Gostar's, have been noted for their quick tempers and many strange actions, even as Imbert has warned us about Gostar. It would seem that since the Guardians cut communication with men there have been many changes in the course of history. Only when we hold the crowns can we be sure of surviving such changes. I must get the Crown! At least Nelis will do what he can to further the search."

"You sent the Colonel to hunt the Crown?" Roane tensed. What would that mean for Uncle Offlas and Sandar? If a large party of Revenian troops showed up to prospect along the cliffs and so meet the men from the camp—She could see such trouble as had never disgraced a Service operation before. Why, they might even have to lift off!

"He knows the country, and him I can trust. If he moves in boldly, Reddick cannot face him, since I do not believe that until the King is dead the Duke will dare to come into the open."

"But the Crown—I thought you wanted to keep others from knowing it was hidden."

"No one shall. For Nelis will wait for me to take it up. None *can* touch the Crown save me. Nelis is only to find the way to it."

But what of her own people? Roane thought of them and clung to her strap anchor as the coach rocked on. They must now be traveling at the fastest pace this vehicle was capable of maintaining.

"King Gostar must be impatient," she commented. "It would seem that he wants us in a hurry, or is this the usual speed of a royal coach?"

The pace grew even faster. In spite of that anchor loop she was shaken back and forth, and she gulped and swallowed with grim determination not to yield to the queasiness of her much-abused interior.

"This—is—too—fast—" The Princess's words came in little gasps as if shaken out of her. "What can they be—"

There came still another burst of speed and the swing of the coach was such that Roane was sure she could not

stand it long before disgracing herself by being thoroughly sick. She held her free hand over her mouth and fought for control.

"What—" The Princess's voice rose a note. "Roane!" And now her cry was a danger alert. "Feel along the edge of the window if you can. Are you able to raise the curtain?"

Roane tried, but found it difficult. Finally her groping hand did touch what she judged was the edge of the curtain. But that did not yield to her tug. It was rather as if it had been nailed or otherwise sealed in place.

"It is the same on this side! The curtains are fastened down. Now, Roane, can you lean forward, find the latch of the door?"

It seemed perilous to try that. Roane feared that if she loosed her finger-cramping grip of the anchor strap, she might be thrown against the narrow seat facing her. But she stretched and, between more and worse jolts which sent her back and forth, ran her other hand over the inner surface of what she was sure was the door. There was no latch, nothing but a smooth surface. And her fear of a trap added to her sickness until she longed to scream for them to stop. Then came another spell of really violent rocking.

"I—cannot—find—It—is all—smooth!" she gasped.

"Nor—can—I—on—this—side—"

"But why—" Roane began when Ludorica answered her.

"Why? Because we are prisoners. But of whom? Lord Imbert? No—unless he feels he must manage me for some reason he has not told me. But I can guess, Roane, that we are not now bound for Gastonhigh."

"Where—" Roane was thrown back by a particularly heavy jolt and cried out at a sharp pain in her side.

"What is it?"

"My—but how stupid! I have a light." The belt she had brought with her, how had she come to forget it? That lapse of memory was another symptom of the fuzzy thinking which had bothered her for days. It was almost as if she did not want to, or could not, remember the familiar things which had been a part of her off-world life. With one hand she worked the beamer out of its loop and turned it on low.

"The doors!"

But she did not need that direction; she had already turned the light on the one through which they had entered. And her exploration by touch had told the truth. There was no sign of a latch. When she moved the beam up to the windows they could see the strips of wood which sealed the curtains down.

"We are prisoners until we arrive and they—whoever they may be—are willing to let us out. But our future hangs on who is behind this—"

"Reddick?"

"Not with Imbert aiding—unless there had come a message purporting to be from the King. Or a substitution of coaches, or—We could offer as many reasons as we have fingers and perhaps still skip the real one. It suffices that we are prisoners, and the reason is less important now than the fact. What other tools or weapons have you that may get us out of here?" As usual she went directly to the most important matter.

"I have this beamer, and a medic kit, and a weapon."

Roane thought of the stunner. "It does not wound, only puts to sleep the one caught in its ray—"

"Such a weapon as your cousin used on me in the cave? But how clever of you to have brought that, Roane! We need only wait until they let us out and then you can put them to sleep and—"

"I shall do what I can," Roane said slowly. What she did not want to admit was that disturbance which came upon her when she had to make a choice between off-world and Clio matters, and which she now felt. She had used the beamer without really thinking, but to handle the stunner so was a different matter—Never before had she experienced anything like this. Or had she? Conditioning! She had gone through conditioning on numerous occasions—mainly to prepare body and mind to resist some planetary stress hostile to her species. But once that was done she had never been consciously aware of its effects upon her. Now it was as if her mind, when turned in certain directions, worked more slowly, and she shrank from off-world weapons—weapons fashioned to repel aliens from their use.

To prove this point to herself, she held out the beamer to the Princess. "If you will hold this—"

Then Roane laid her hand upon the butt of the stunner, although she did not draw it. And she had to force herself to that move. Her fingers shrank from touching the smooth metal. By the Tongue of Truth, what had happened to her? The cover which kept such a weapon inviolate on another world was operating against *her!* She was frightened as she had never been before in her life. Ludorica must have read that emotion in her expression, for she asked quickly:

"What is it? What is the matter?"

"It is nothing," Roane said quickly. The Princess was entirely too sharp-eyed, and she must not let her suspect— the more so when she did not know the truth herself. "The rocking—it makes me sick."

Ludorica grimaced. "I have traveled often by coach, though it is better to ride mounted, but never at such a wild pace. I, too, would like to—"

What she might have said was never uttered, for the gallop began to abate and the swing became less violent. They slowed and came to a halt.

"Be ready," the Princess ordered. She still held the beamer, training it on the door to shine full in the face of whoever opened it. Roane forced herself to ready the stunner.

But nothing happened. They listened closely and could hear, very muffled by the walls, a faint jangling. Only the door did not open.

"I think we are changing duocorns!" the Princess said. "A fresh team, which means a longer journey. Already we are far past the distance to Gastonhigh."

She must have been right, for only moments later there was a shudder through the coach and they were on the move again, first easily and then back to the rocking run which shook them so. Roane stowed away both stunner and beamer, not wanting to exhaust the charge in the latter. She was battered, sore, as if she had been beaten and bumped. But mercifully that second pounding did not last long. Once more they slowed to what was hardly more than a walking pace. The coach body tilted at an angle which suggested that they climbed. The Princess spoke again:

"We return to Reveny."

"How can you tell?"

"This is hill country and the only hills close to Gastonhow are those of the border. Now there are only two possibilities as to who will meet us—some representative of the King, or Reddick!"

"But you think the latter."

"Imbert must have been tricked. Yes, it will be best for us to expect the worst. I was foolish indeed—"

Either the dark which had held them for so long was lightening a little or else their eyes had adjusted. Roane could now make out the outline of her companion braced beside her on the seat.

"Fancher and the Soothspeaker—and how many others, some planted certainly in Imbert's own household as he suspected. But even he could not have thought how deep their plans ran. Nelis—we can depend upon Nelis. Perhaps we shall have a chance after all. It rests now on where they take us."

The Princess was quiet and Roane believed she must be weighing one chance against another. She had respect for Ludorica's courage, endurance, and wits. But even those three in combination could not bring her safely out of some kinds of disaster.

It was time, surely it was time, for Roane to begin to think of herself. She had the stunner, against which on Clio there was no defense, and with it she could break free from any party ready to greet their arrival. Then, back to camp— if camp still existed and Uncle Offlas had not gone off-world.

The toiling of the coach became even more labored,

and then its climbing slant leveled and it stopped. Again no one came to the door. There was a wait, during which they became fully aware of all their aches and bruises. When they started on, it was plain that they were now going downhill—luckily at a very slow pace or they would have been flung forward against the other seat. The slope of the road they followed must be steep. It did level out later, so that they rode in more comfort, and the light seeping in around the curtains grew stronger.

"It is full day. And we must cross the border soon. If we pass a gatehouse—" Then Ludorica shook her head. "No, they would not risk such passage unless they have good reason to believe this carriage will not be inspected. Yet this must be the main highway. A coach could not travel a lesser road. They must have a good plan—" She stopped so short that Roane turned to look at her.

The furred hood of the Princess's cloak had fallen back, her head was a little forward, and she was staring at the coach wall directly ahead. Roane followed the direction of that survey.

From some crack there puffed a thread of white vapor. Roane caught the taint of a new odor against the musty closeness of the atmosphere.

"They—they drug us! That is upus smoke!"

Ludorica dropped her hold on the anchor strap, threw herself at the wall, holding a fold of her cape over the inflow of white. But it was little use—there were two more spirals at opposite sides. They could not hope to stop them all. Roane's own move was not to try to hold out the menace but to force her belt into as small a package as she could.

Squirming about, she got up the heavy folds of her skirt and fastened the belt under it, though her fingers worked slower and slower and her head spun so that she had to fight to finish that job. Her last view of the Princess was of Ludorica sliding down the wall of the coach, away from the vent she had tried to cover, to lie upon the seat. And a moment or two later Roane followed her into the same unconsciousness.

She was warm, too warm. This was like lying under the desert sun of Cappadella. Roane stirred, brought up a hand to shield her face, her eyes, from the bite of the sun. But she did not lie on sand. Fabric of some kind drew and wrinkled under her as she moved. She opened her eyes.

Above her was dark wood, while across her face a bar of sunshine nearly blinded her. She turned her head fretfully. Her mouth was dry; her lips stuck together, and she parted them with difficulty. She wanted water, more than she ever had in her life, even in the desert country the sun reminded her of.

In the rays of the sun, on a small bench not too far away, stood a flagon. The shape of it promised what she needed so badly. Roane pulled herself up. Movement was a trial of strength, for she needed all the force of her will to make her body obey. She braced herself on stiff arms, her attention all for the flagon which might hold water.

Swinging her feet to the floor was an exhausting effort. She did not even dare to try to stand, but instead fell to her hands and knees and crawled toward that bench. She raised her dead-weight hands and somehow forced the fingers to

close upon the sides of the flagon, pulling it toward her, tipping it so that its contents did splash, not only into her gaping mouth, but across her chin and down the front of her dress. The moisture in her mouth brought her farther out of the daze. She sat on the floor, the flagon still between her hands, and looked about.

The room was small with a single window, across which was a screen of bars. The walls were stone. The bed from which she had crawled lacked any ornament and beside it, on another bed, lay Ludorica.

The Princess's cloak trailed half off her, her face was flushed, and she breathed with a puffing sound, clear to hear now that Roane had time to note it. Even as the off-world girl watched, she stirred, flinging out her arm as if to ward off some danger in a none-too-pleasant dream. And she murmured words Roane could not distinguish.

The small beds and the bench on which the flagon had stood were the only furnishings. There was a door opposite the beds. It had metal banding across it and a lock plate as large as Roane's palm. She had no doubts that if she managed to reach it she would find it securely fastened. There was no question that they were prisoners. But of whom and where?

Carefully she put the flagon back on the bench and struggled to her feet. Her head swam and she closed her eyes, fighting vertigo. From the bench she lurched in the direction of the window, bringing up against that opening. But at least she kept her feet.

What she saw below was a courtyard with a wall around it, a solid gate fastened by a bar. Beyond that wall showed the green tops of trees, and yet farther away were

rises of heights not unlike those about Hitherhow. Hope
glimmered in her. If they were in that country she could
find her way back to camp.

"Hot—thirsty—" The murmur from the bed brought
Roane around, holding to the wall for support as she
moved.

The Princess struggled up. She was pulling at the lacing
of her bodice as if to loosen it. The delicate lace of her
collar was crumpled and her fine dress smeared with dust
and badly creased.

Roane preserved her balance as best she could, made
for the bench, and then to the bedside with the flagon. She
held it with both hands for the Princess to drink.

Ludorica drank, sucking with the same desperate need
Roane had known. And when she signified she had had
enough, there was very little left.

Now the Princess surveyed the room. Her eyes fixed
upon the window and she wriggled off the bed, wavered to
the wall, and inched her way to that opening, catching the
bars with her hands. Roane joined her.

"Do you know where we are?"

Ludorica did not look around as she answered.

"As to where we are exactly I cannot say. But that
peak"—she loosed her right hand to point—"I know. It is
within a half league of Hitherhow. And I think we must be
on some minor stead—perhaps Famslaw—so it is Reddick
after all."

"You mean this is his land?"

"Land of close kin. But how—" Then she gave a little
gasp. "Look there!"

At one side of the courtyard very close to the wall was

a coach with a brilliant device painted on its door. It had carefully curtained windows, and although there were no harnessed duocorns and no coachman, Roane was certain it was the one which had brought them here.

"The coach—" she began.

"Of course! But that symbol—on its door—"

Roane could not understand the importance of that but the Princess was continuing:

"That is Lord Imbert's own! No coach with that on it would be stopped at the border. That was how they got us across."

"Wait—" Roane's memory stirred. She thought back to the dusky courtyard at Gastonhow, when Lord Imbert had handed them into what was to become a prison. She had seen the door in the lantern light; there had been no design then—or else it had been covered in some manner. "That was not on the door before."

"What does it matter? It served its purpose."

From somewhere over their heads there was a sharp call, which was answered by a horn note. And that fanfare was answered in turn by activity. Men appeared in the courtyard. They wore green or gray and fell into two lines at attention while two of their number ran to draw the gate bar.

"How dare he?" demanded Ludorica.

"What is it?"

The Princess turned a flushed face to Roane. Her eyes were wide and there was about her such an aura of barely leashed anger that Roane was glad it was not she who had aroused that emotion in her companion.

"That is the royal call! No one but those of the Blood

dare use it. It is my call—*mine*—by birth alone. I am heiress to Reveny—there is no other!"

The gates opened and once more the call sounded close and loud, as the trumpeter himself rode through. Over his tunic he wore a loose-sleeved coat stiff with metallic lacing, one half red, one yellow. Behind him came a second rider wearing a yellow uniform tunic, his hat hiding his face. But the breath came out of the Princess in a furious hiss.

"Reddick! And he rides behind the heir's own herald! Treachery, black treachery!" Her hands closed and wrung upon the bars as if she would pluck them out of their stone setting and hurl them spear-fashion at her cousin.

# ✳ CHAPTER 10 ✳

**ROANE PRESSED AGAINST** the iron-barred door, her ear laid to its surface, but she heard only the pounding of her own heart. She longed for one of the snoop devices of stellar civilization. Even time she could not measure, but she thought it had been a long interval since they had come for the Princess, leaving her here alone.

Ludorica had gone willingly, apparently only too eager to face her kinsman-jailer, as if that royal trumpet had carried her in flaming anger over the border of caution. Roane had been startled by that response, since she had looked upon the Princess as able to keep a cool head.

Only this was no quarrel of hers. Since Ludorica had left, Roane was able to see the whole situation in proper proportion. She had only one duty, to get out of this strongbox and back to camp. And the Princess had given her that mountain as a guide.

However, there was escape from this room, the keep itself, to negotiate first. Without any tools but a stunner and a beamer, how could she do it? For a second time she knelt

on the floor to examine the lock. This type was archaically simple, of course. She could force it if she had proper tools. But there was nothing useful in her precious belt, nothing in this masquerade on her back (the clothes she had enjoyed so much when she put them on, now crumpled and soiled, made her impatient for her coverall). Her cloak and the Princess's lay on the bed. Roane went back to run her hands over fur and fabric—and so discovered that Ludorica's hood had a stiff support to hold the fur in place.

Roane picked at the seam, finally, with her teeth, breaking the threads at one end. She pushed and pulled until she held a length of wire. With this in hand she returned to the door.

The sun which had awakened her was gone from this side of the keep, and the hills were throwing long, dusky shadows out to clutch at the walls. Her jailers had brought her a plate of bread and dried meat when they had taken away the Princess, and she had eaten all of that. They had not been near her since.

Roane crouched, listening. Sounds at last. But not from beyond the door—rather in the courtyard. She ran to the window. Duocorns saddled and ready. Four men—seven mounts. Lanterns were lit to banish the dusk.

Out of a portal immediately below her issued a party of three. One was Reddick, by his uniform, and he came with one hand around the Princess's wrist, though she moved without a struggle toward the waiting mounts. The other man was dressed in dark colors and had a cloak collar up about his throat, a peaked hood pulled over his head.

He held his hands at breast level stiffly before him and between them something glinted in the lantern light.

When they came to the duocorns, he swung around to face the Princess. What he held so carefully he raised to eye level before her. And at the same time Roane caught faintly his voice intoning words she could not distinguish.

Reddick boosted the Princess into the saddle, where she sat quietly. But the reins of her duocorn he kept in his own hand. And as the gate bar was withdrawn and they rode out he continued to lead the Princess's mount. Then the gate closed behind them.

Roane could only guess at the meaning of what she had seen. It was apparent that they had the Princess under some kind of control. She had seen too many like scenes in the past. But how they had achieved that (save that it must have something to do with the object the man held) she did not know. At any rate, their going left Roane on her own, to make her break for freedom.

Waiting was always hard. She kicked and pulled at her hampering skirts as she paced back and forth. These would be a hazard to her. Perhaps somewhere in this pile of stone she could find more suitable clothing.

She had no lamp and as soon as the dusk was thick enough, she knelt again at the door to begin her delicate manipulation with the wire. A job such as this needed patience. She had to keep her mind and hands under control as she worked. But at last there was a click and she edged the barrier open a little at a time, relieved to see there was no show of light on the other side. She slipped through and shut the heavy door carefully behind her. This was a narrow hall with two other doors. Beyond was a stairhead. Even as she stood listening, able now to hear

muted noises made by other inhabitants, the click of approaching footsteps rang an alarm in her mind.

Roane crossed to the doorway nearly facing that from which she had come. To her great relief, that yielded under her push so she could step within. A flash of the beamer showed her a room like that she had quitted. She turned to watch the hallway through a narrow crack.

The newcomer had reached the head of the stair, a man wearing the uniform of those who had ridden with Reddick. He carried in one hand a small tray on which rested a dish and another water flagon. A lantern swung in his other hand.

As he came to the door of her late prison, he put down the lantern, fumbled at his belt for a thong on which were strung several large keys. Roane aimed the stunner at his head and pressed the button. He crumpled to his knees without a cry, then slid forward on the floor.

Kicking angrily at her skirts, she ran to him. He was not too large to handle and she dragged him into the room. The flagon had fallen on the floor, most of its contents leaking into a pool, but she drank what was left and scooped up from the dish a round of coarse bread and meat, chewing as she went out, set the dishes inside, locked the door.

Then she sped back to the other room, where she had seen a promising heap of clothes, untidy on a chest. To get rid of these skirts and be able to move with ease again! The fit was bad; the owner of her new wardrobe was a much larger and heavier person. But she drew the jerkin tight about her with her precious belt inside, rolled up the sleeves, stuffed material torn from an underskirt in the toes of the boots to make them fit. There was one of those hood

caps which let only her face show, and she pinned its laps under her chin. Her discarded clothing she thrust within the chest.

The lantern still stood beside the other door and she was vexed that she had forgotten it. Perhaps it would be wise to take it along. With stunner at the ready and the lantern in her other hand, Roane sped to the stairs and looked down. There was another hall below with dim lighting. And she could hear the sound of voices and smell cooking, though that odor was none too appetizing. Her good fortune had held so far. She could only gamble it would continue.

For all her efforts her boots sounded on the steps and she was alert to any movement below. If she had to leave by the huge barred gate—But surely there were easier ways than that! She would even dare the wall if she had to.

The lower hall led to an open archway. To her right there was a door, firmly closed, which she hoped opened on the courtyard. Roane blew out the lantern, set it on the floor, and went to that closed portal. With infinite care she slid the locking bar out of its hooks, fearing at any moment that some one of those in the room ahead beyond the arch would notice her.

Five men sat at a table eating, while another moved back and forth bringing fresh supplies of food and drink. Roane balanced the bar against her for a moment, then set it carefully against the wall and tugged at the door.

The fresh air of night met her, dispelling much of the fugginess of the hall. It took only a minute to slip through and close the door behind her. Now—She lingered in the

shadow to survey the courtyard. That coach was still pulled close to the wall at her left. Beyond were stables—she could both smell them and hear the stamp of duocorns.

Though she studied the top of the wall and the tower behind her, she could not spot any watchman. But she dared not count that such a one did not exist. Her attention kept going back to the coach. If it were as close to the wall as it seemed, could she use it as a ladder to reach the top? But to get down the other side—She would need a rope. Harness—such as was still draped over the carriage shafts? She darted over to those.

To climb into the driver's seat was easy enough. Roane hunkered on that, watching for any sentry on the walls. The bulk of the tower showed several faintly glowing windows, but the evening gloom was thick enough to hide the carriage roof.

Once more she slid to the ground and fingered the harness. The buckles were easy enough to loosen and reclasp, and by careful work (she made herself go slowly, to test the strength of what she did and for fear of noise) she had at last a length tougher than rope, which she thought would support her weight. With this coiled about her shoulder she again sought the seat of the carriage.

There was still a space to climb and the smooth wall offered no holds. For a moment Roane was baffled, and then she investigated the uses of her present perch. There was the cushioned seat, which could be upended to lean out against the wall. But, could she balance on the upper end of that?

The wall above—but of course! There was a standard-pole there, one of a pair, the other on the far side of the

gate. No banner flew now, but it would provide anchorage if she could just throw—

Roane stood on the denuded seat of the carriage by the unsteady bridge of the cushion. She whirled the weighted end of the strap rope around her head and sent it flying. Up and out it went, to clang against the wall with a sound which, to Roane, was like a thunderclap. But it did dangle there, and it had encircled the pole above.

She must move fast, reach that dangling end before the cushion bridge could turn under her feet. She poised and leaped, one end of the strap in her left hand, her right reaching for the other.

She had been correct in fearing the instability of the bridge; it gave way. But not before she had grasped the other end of the strap to which she clung. Fortunately, the cushion sank only a little, not so much that she was left hanging with her full weight on her outstretched arms. Bringing both ends of the strap together, Roane climbed, struggling over the edge, hardly believing she managed it without disaster.

To slide down the far side was much easier. And when a flick of her wrist brought the strap down to her, Roane coiled it around her body. She could still make out in the dusk the peak the Princess had said was a landmark. There was a road running in that direction, not one of the tree-and-brush-hidden lanes, but a clear cut through the forest. Her best move would be to keep to that, ready to take to cover if she met any other traveler.

The route was not too deeply rutted and the footing was secure enough. She set out with a ground-covering pace she had learned long ago. Now that she was out of that

prison, she must plan ahead. To get back to camp, if the camp was still there, was, of course, the first step. If Uncle Offlas could learn what would happen—that the seekers of the Crown would be close to their find—

Roane's thoughts veered. The Princess—where had she gone with Reddick and for what purpose? Surely Ludorica had been under some compulsion, though she had walked to her mount and had ridden out docilely enough.

Ludorica had her problems, but Roane had hers also. These were no longer the same. Again Roane was puzzled. Why had it been so important all the time she was with the Princess that Ludorica be helped in any manner Roane could devise? And now—why did she feel as if released from some tie?

Had all the imprudent and ill-considered (from the point of view of the Service) actions of the last few days come from the fact that she had been the Princess's companion? And why, when that companionship had been broken had the strange influence of Reveny's heiress gone? Was it something in her own temperament which made her more receptive to suggestion?

Roane had had enough training in forms of communication, briefing, and controls, as practiced by both men and machines, to know that such an influence might exist and that it could be part of the mystery of Clio. In some very old civilizations, even in the dim past of her own before it had left its native planet to pioneer a thousand other worlds, there had been ages when kings were also priests credited with divine powers by descent.

Suppose those who had set up the experiment on Clio had made use of such memories, giving the families they

had selected to rule a mystique which bound their subjects to them? But then how could Reddick or other rebels find any followers, or dare themselves to go against such influences?

Those who had made Clio a testing ground for their theories would not want a stagnant society. Perhaps the influences would not affect those of equal rank, or would only hold for periods of time—say when a monarch was in dire danger. Or—she could supply a multitude of plausible answers.

But could she in turn use such suggestions to counter the accusations made against her by Uncle Offlas and the Service? Admittedly they would be glad to learn all they could about Clio. And if there was such an influence, a psycho-tech could verify that. But she would have to reach camp—and hope that native activity around it had not led Uncle Offlas to order withdrawal.

Roane now regretted most of all not bringing her com. Why had she not? Why, her thinking *must* have been influenced! To have been so afraid of being traced by her own people!

She shook her head. With every passing moment she was more and more unable to understand her own actions. The answer was, of course, that they must avoid the Clio natives in order to escape this influence set up to prove theories for men long dead.

The road she followed took a turn and then another. But never did it veer too far from her landmark and Roane kept to it. It did not seem to be traveled by night; at least she heard no sounds such as might be made by men, only those of wildlife, a crashing in the brush as if something

ran from her. A full moon was rising and its silver light lay along the road.

Roane reached a place where there was a turn away from her landmark as the road angled sharply north, crossing a stream. But the running water could now be her guide. Perhaps at some seasons it was a full river, but at present it had shrunk so that sweeps of gravel and sand edged it on both sides. And she used the nearer bank for her new path. Twice she disturbed animals which had come to drink, one a quite large but seemingly timid beast which let out a mournful hooting cry as it plunged away. She kept her stunner ready in the event she met something more belligerent.

Shortly thereafter the moonlight revealed deep prints in the soil, hoof slots. Duocorns, she was certain, a number of them. And there was a broken branch or two here and there to suggest passage had been forced by a mounted party. They were heading in the same direction she had taken. And though she had little training in woodcraft, Roane suspected the prints were fresh.

The party with Ludorica? If so, all the more reason for Roane to reach camp with her warning. They could be kept away from the actual site by the distorts. But too much use of those not only would exhaust their charges, but might awaken dim wonder in men who had been more than once subconsciously thrown off trail.

She need fear only one thing really—seeing the Princess again. Because in her own mind Roane had come to accept her idea that Ludorica could demand her aid as a fact. Also Uncle Offlas and Sandar must be warned of the same danger, though they had not succumbed to it when

the Princess had been in their hands earlier. But then she had been under the effects of the stunner.

In the moonlight the night was very white and black—shadows had sharp edges. Suddenly Roane paused and put her hand to her head. The first small touch of discomfort. She knew it for what it was—the first warning of a distort. Then she realized what she might have to face. She was not wearing her counter beam—the distort would have the same effect on her as it did on those it was designed to discourage. She could only hope that she might use the warn-off as a guide and force herself on into what she was most reluctant to approach.

Not far away the trail of the riders turned, leaving traces in the brush of their passing which suggested a quick retreat. That, too, had been caused by the distort. But Roane kept on course, though not much farther. The attack came without warning. Out of the night snaked a loop to encircle her chest-high, jerk tight before she knew what was happening to her. She had no time to use her weapon, for her arms were pinned to her sides, and then a body crashed against her, bearing her to the ground.

The weight was withdrawn but she was held in a grip which all her struggles could not break. She was pulled to her feet, turned to face a party of three, though a fourth must stand behind her holding her.

In the moonlight she recognized the leader of her captors and as she gasped breath back into her lungs, she managed to get out his name:

"Colonel Imfry!"

"Who are you?" He came closer, peered into her face. She saw his expression of surprise.

"Lady Roane! But what—where is the Princess? Free her instantly!" Question and command followed fast on one another. The grasp on her shoulders loosened, and with a twitch the rope circlet fell to her feet.

"Where is the Princess?" the Colonel asked again as he put out a hand to steady her.

"She rode out of the tower with Reddick."

"What tower—where—" She thought his grasp tightened as if he would shake the truth out of her.

"Let me get my breath." Roane determined not to be again swept in involvement.

"Of course." His grip loosened. "I pray pardon, Lady. But with Her Highness in Reddick's hold—"

She made her story as terse as she could. Though she was not able to name the prison from which she had escaped, save to give the Princess's name of Famslaw, the rest she reported up to the time she had seen the Princess ride away.

"They used a mind-globe on her," the Colonel interrupted. "And that coach with Rehling's symbol—I am sure he played a double game for all her belief in him. There is only one place they could be heading for now—to find the Crown! And you, Lady, know where that is. You can take us there. There is something strange—We have been wandering for two days unable to come near the landmarks the Princess gave me. But we must reach there now, or Reddick will use the Princess to claim the throne and then do with her as he wishes—"

"No!" Roane jerked out of his light hold.

"No? What do you mean?" He was startled, looking at her now as if she were a person and not merely a way to aid Ludorica.

"No, I will not go with you!" She had the stunner still. With it she sprayed him and the two men behind him as she pivoted to bring it also on the one a pace or two behind her.

They staggered, but they did not go down. However, she believed the blast enough to keep them unsteady until she could get away. She plunged straight ahead, into the full force of the distort, wavering herself under that mind-dazing blast, but enough the mistress of her body to keep staggering on in a direction she did not believe any of them would follow. And she did not waste time looking behind to see.

Brush whipped about her. She flung up her arm to shield her face from the sting of lashing branches. Always she was buffeted by those distort rays meant to bewilder. She tried to blank those as best she could, to reach the safe zone beyond the barrier. Let Ludorica and her henchmen find their own way out of their troubles; she was not again going to be drawn into their games.

# ✳ CHAPTER 11 ✳

**THE WAVES OF THE DISTORT** *were* less effective—she must be close to the edge of the protection zone. Roane plunged on, not trying to pick any path, merely attempting to get free of the influence. Then—she was in the clear!

Before her was the glade of the camp. She expected some challenge and threw back her hood so they could see her if they had picked up her image on tri-dee com. But there was no sign of life. Nobody here—but then where?

Roane half expected that the entrance might have been set on a new code, not answering to her thumb identification. But it opened as readily as if she had left it only moments earlier. So they had not yet exiled her.

There was no one within any of the small cubicles. But in the one that had housed their work tools were significantly empty racks and niches. They were at work somewhere, and she thought it could only be in the cave.

Roane went to the com. She could call from here—warn them. But even as that thought crossed her mind, she

saw that the planetside hookup had been detached. In its place was the off-world call ready for use. Either they had already arranged for lift-off, or else they expected that they must do so at a moment's notice.

She snapped down the replay level. Immediately the tape replied in code.

"So that is how it is," she said aloud. They had reported, and had received orders that they must make any investigations in three planet days' reckoning, be ready then for lift-off. As to when that deadline had been set, she had no idea.

There was one thing she could do now. It might not in any way mitigate her eventual punishment, but it would prevent Uncle Offlas from censoring anything she said.

Roane found a clear report tape and fitted it into the case which, once sealed and numbered, must be produced and could only be opened on the Service ship. She sat by the table, took up the mike, but thought out carefully what she would say before she thumbed it to *Go*. A simple story of what had happened was best. Thus she dictated the course of events which had followed from her first meeting with the Princess.

She added as concisely as she could the conclusions she had drawn concerning the Crown, the conditioning, all she had herself experienced. This might well be disallowed by the authorities, but the experts would have access to it. When she had done Roane pressed her thumb to the sign slot with relief. There was nothing Uncle Offlas could do to alter that.

Now she was so very tired that her bones ached. The fight against the distort had left her so exhausted she could

hardly get to her feet. But she dared not sleep now, give way to the ache in her back, the weakness in her legs! She had to warn Uncle Offlas and Sandar. They might stumble upon some party prospecting for the Crown.

Colonel Imfry—the stunner blast had been low; he and his men would not be incapacitated for long. But with the distorts holding they could not trail her.

Roane pulled at the unfamiliar clothing she wore, dragged it off piece by piece. She pawed through her now very meager wardrobe. One more suit—or would that be the right choice? If she went to the cave perhaps the Clio clothing would be less noticeable. But—her mind must be more clear—

Somehow she got to the small fresher, forcing her tired mind to focus on dialing. This ought to jolt her awake. Moisture gathered on her body as a haze rose about her. She buried her face in it eagerly, drew breaths of it into her lungs. It was like coming out of a dire murk into clear, fresh water. But she must be careful; not enough and her fatigue would return, too much and it would induce euphoria, which could lead her into some overconfident, disastrous move. This was a device to be used only when some danger demanded stimulation of mind and body, and then sparingly.

The fog cleared, she climbed out and rubbed down her damp body, no longer aware of aches and pains. With a bed robe wrapped around her, she went back to the control room.

No warn light on the off-world com. She was alert enough now to read the other dials. At one she paused, frowning. Surely the distort was not so limited as that!

There was a small map on the screen, red pinpoints marking the broadcast boxes. But the gauge showed a waning of power. Hurriedly she checked further.

So that was it—they needed recharging. But that was something Uncle Offlas would have been very careful about before he left. Which might mean he had been gone longer than he intended. And even as Roane watched, one of the red points flickered—disappeared. A distort had ended its sentry duty. Roane was faced with a new decision. She could visit each of those settings, replace the charges. Or she could make speed to the cave with her warning—

To visit the distorts might be a waste of precious time, could expose her once more to Imfry and his men. No—it was best to go to the cave. Once they all returned here and shut off the outlying distorts, they could turn on a central energy beam which would fortify the whole clearing until lift-off.

Back in her cubicle Roane once more pulled on the native clothing and then checked her belt, adding a freshly charged beamer, a new charge in the stunner, a detect, and a counter beam which would free her from those emanations.

It was morning when she left the camp. And it was going to be a fair day; there were no clouds overhead. She reached the cliff of the cave without picking up any trace of Imfry's party. But as she approached the narrow entrance to the underground ways, she dodged quickly into cover, her heart pounding. Not Imfry's men—but there was someone there in ambush. Only the detect she carried had warned her in time.

Roane studied the terrain. There was no way of

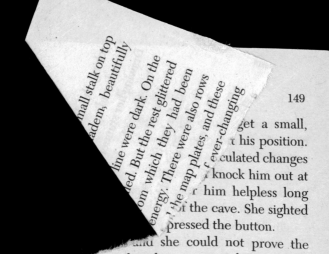

...get a small,
...t his position.
...culated changes
...knock him out at
...r him helpless long
...t the cave. She sighted
...pressed the button.
...and she could not prove the
...her attack without exposing herself. With
...shrug, she got up and walked forward, though that stretch
of earth and rock seemed the longest she had ever
traveled—on any world.

There came no attack, no challenge from the bush. She
ran past the cover, loose stones and gravel rolling under
her feet, and reached the cave mouth. There she dared to
look around. A booted leg protruded from the brush. It
moved feebly, gouging up the sandy soil, but that was all.
She used the beam again to make sure her victim was well
under.

She went on into the passage. Where before that way
had been silent, now there was a continuous murmur of
sound. Straining her ears, Roane tried to make out the rise
and fall of voices. But this was rather a mechanical clicking.
And it grew louder as she advanced. There was a glimmer
of light as she came to the transparent plate. Only the panel
was now gone, to leave a doorway from which issued the
sounds. Roane stepped into the chamber beyond.

She stood at one end of a double line of tall columns.
Each was fitted with a fore panel, lighted, on which were
maplike outlines. And cresting each was something else,
alien in form to the plain solidity of the pillars.

For each was literally crowned. On a s
of each pillar rested a miniature di
wrought, sparking with gems.

Two of the pillars in the double
nearer the crown was lifeless, dul
as if the metal and jewels f
fashioned now coursed with
of small lights above and around
flashed on and off with brilliant sparks o
colors.

Roane was sure now that these were no Forerunner
remains. They must be connected with the experiment of
Clio's settlement. But she had only a minute or two to
watch before her uncle moved out into the aisle between
the pillars.

She had not come unprepared for such an encounter,
fearing that she might even be rayed down by a stunner
before she could protest. So her weapon was ready. Nor
had she been wrong in her wariness, for Offlas also had his
stunner aimed.

"Roane!" He did not speak loudly, yet his voice vibrated
through the chamber, filling it, just above the muttering of
the machines. He moved closer. Warned by his speech, she
kept her voice even lower:

"The distorts are failing." She gave him what she felt to
be a needful warning.

"They don't run forever." His whispering voice was
harsh, just as Basic sounded curt and hard after the softer
inflections of the Clio tongue. "You—where did you come
from?"

"I escaped from a keep, back in the hills. But that is not

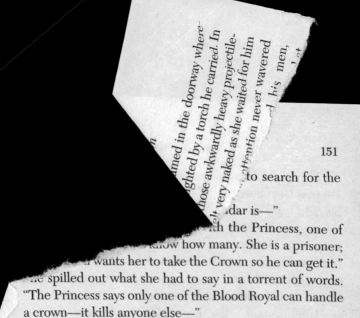

...med in the doorway where-
...ghted by a torch he carried. In
...hose awkwardly heavy projectile-
...very naked as she waited for him
...attention never wavered
...d his men,

to search for the

...dar is—"

...th the Princess, one of
...know how many. She is a prisoner;
...wants her to take the Crown so he can get it."
...he spilled out what she had to say in a torrent of words.
"The Princess says only one of the Blood Royal can handle
a crown—it kills anyone else—"

Her uncle had turned to face one of the machines and
now Roane, moving closer, was able to trace on its pillar
the outline of a map she knew—Reveny! The crown set
above that was a vision of ice. She could not have named
the metal of its forming—it might even be pure crystal. It
was a circlet composed of a series of points which inclined
toward the center, where four of them united at the apex.
Those in turn supported a star set with flashing white gems.
If the miniature was so impressive, what a glory the real
crown must be!

"Sandar went to hunt it," her uncle said. "He has not
returned."

He hurried to the end of the aisle, returned with a
portable tri-dee recorder in his hands. "Bring that—" He
indicated another instrument, set to one side.

Roane scooped it up. But just as they reached the door
there came the unmistakable sound of feet in the passage.
More than one person walked there. It could not be Sandar.

Should they take cover behind the pillars? But her
uncle did not move, seemed so sure of himself that Roane
stayed where she was. Could it be Imfry—or the Princess
and her captors?

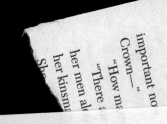

Then the Colonel stood fr[...]
the panel had been, clearly l[...]
his right hand was one of [...]
firing weapons. Roane f[...]
to turn and look at her. But his a[...]
from the way ahead. Behind him move[...]
seemingly alert for trouble, yet none of them glanced a[...]
the doorway or the room beyond it.

"Conditioned," she heard her uncle mutter. "An excellent example of top conditioning—additional proof, if any were needed."

They went on. What if they met Sandar up ahead? He would have his stunner. But the Princess and Reddick— what if they were already there? Her uncle was listening, and she ventured a question:

"What if they meet Sandar?"

He glared as if her whisper had been a shout, making no answer, a tactic which formerly would have silenced her. But Uncle Offlas was just a man, not some superpower. He might be able to force a dark future on her, but she could also fight back. And she was inwardly amazed at her own surge of confidence now.

Seemingly he was undecided. They could follow the Colonel's party, use their own stunners to clear the way. Roane wondered why her uncle did not take that course. But he was prevented from doing whatever he might have done by a change in the chamber of the pillars.

A sharp crackling drew her attention back to the machines—to the column supporting the Ice Crown. There was a wild flurry of the lights on its front—while the glitter of the miniature crown flared into a flame she could

not look at. There was another loud note and the pattern of small lights steadied.

Her uncle was staring at the display and now he aimed the tri-dee recorder at it. But even the flare of the crown had speedily subsided.

Roane knew what had happened as well as if she had viewed the act. The Ice Crown had been found. But had it been claimed by the Princess? Or had Sandar taken it—or Imfry?

More sounds, loud and echoing, but not from any one of the pillars—these came from the passage. She thought she heard a shout or two also. A fight between Reddick's party and Imfry's men?

"What—" She appealed to her uncle.

But he was totally absorbed in taking a recording of the pillar.

"Changes." He was talking to himself. "At least five major pattern changes! A totally new course of events!"

A new pattern! The Princess, or Reddick? But Roane was not going to be involved again—she was not!

Telling herself that, Roane went to the door. As she stepped into the passage, she dropped the equipment her uncle had ordered her to take and began to run. One half of her mind, the sane half which was Roane Hume, was in open battle with that buried part which she thought she had had under control. She did not want to go, but that inner compulsion made her.

Roane reached the end of the passage. Now she smelled an acrid odor. With her stunner at the ready she squeezed through the rough passageway, listening for any sound. She heard a muffled clamor of voices and then saw

the glow of torchlight. She crept to a point from which she could view the cave of the skeleton.

There was a raw hole where earth and rock had been dug away to make an opening to the outside. Some daylight showed there, but the torches were being used to light a second tear in the wall where the crushed skeleton had lain.

In that second opening stood Ludorica. She had her hands out before her, the fingers outspread to their furthest extent, as if she would protect with her flesh what she held. It was a copy of the Ice Crown on the pillar, save that it was of a size to fit a human head.

By the torchlight it blazed fire. And the expression on the Princess's face as she gazed upon it, entranced, was one Roane had never seen before. Greed—no—but some emotion which was alien to the Ludorica she had known— an expression which repelled, not drew as the Princess had been able to draw her into an alliance even against her own desires.

It seemed that Ludorica was aware only of what she held, not of those around her. She was flanked by a man in black who eyed her with almost as deep a fascination as she used for the Crown. On her other side was Reddick. He held one of those massive hand weapons and from its barrel still rose a thread of smoke fume.

Two of Imfry's followers lay still against the wall near where Roane crouched. And the Colonel himself—Roane's hand went to her mouth—his back was to the rock as if he needed support. One arm hung limp and there was a dark stain spreading on his shoulder. But he was being roughly bound by two of Reddick's men, while two more stood with hand weapons trained on Imfry's remaining men.

"The King is dead—long live the Queen," Reddick intoned. Then he added, touching Ludorica's arm, "My Queen, what would you have us do with these who came to seek the great treasure of Reveny?"

She did not raise her head or look away from what she held. When she answered her voice was thin and lacking in warmth, as if she spoke from a far distance of things which mattered little.

"Since I am Queen, as all can see, let them be served as traitors, for they reached for the Crown!"

Reddick smiled. But on the faces of the Colonel and of his remaining men there was shock, as if they could not believe what they had heard.

"The King being dead, our Queen has spoken," Reddick said. There was a solemnity to his words, as if he were some official of a court of justice relaying a lawful verdict. "Let them be dealt with as traitors. My Queen"— he turned again to Ludorica—"this is no fit place for you. Let us ride to show your people that you are truly their crowned one."

There was a hint of another emotion on Ludorica's face as that mask which so repelled Roane changed a little. "Yes"—now her voice was more human, eager—"let me do so! This is the Ice Crown; I hold it, I wear it, for Reveny!"

Looking neither right nor left, and certainly not at the men she had so summarily condemned, she went to the newly cut opening, the man in black beside her putting out a steadying hand now and then. For she paid no attention to her footing, only to what she held. But Reddick lingered, watching his men bind the rest of Imfry's force. When that was finished he spoke directly to the Colonel.

"The Crown has spoken, as it always does, my brave Colonel. I think that there is certainly a new day dawning for Reveny, but I do not believe it will be greatly to your taste. So perhaps it is best that you will leave us soon. Her Majesty will give the final word as to the hour and the manner of your going. But do not, I beg you, place any hope in old friendships. It is well known that the crowns always change those who wear them. It will be most interesting to see what changes will ensue once our liege lady is firmly on her throne."

"Mind-globe cannot hold her forever." Some of the stupefaction had gone from the Colonel now.

"Mind-globe? Ah, we might have used such a key to bring her here—since she alone could handle the Crown. But I assure you, my brave and interfering Colonel, what has passed since then is born of the Crown alone. To rule and reign is very different from living as an heiress to such glories. I think we shall find the Princess is no longer as you have always known her, but now a Queen! We must be riding. Bring these along—but intact," he ordered his men. "It will doubtless please Her Majesty to make an excellent example of them."

Roane had been so startled by the abrupt reversal of Ludorica's attitude toward the Colonel that she had watched the scene without any thought of taking a hand in the action. But now, as Reddick's men prepared to drag their prisoners away, she readied her stunner. She might not be any longer a part of Imfry's efforts on behalf of one who had so strangely repudiated him, but neither could she see Reddick take him to his death.

But as she raised her weapon she was seized from

behind, held in a viselike grip which did not allow her the slightest movement. And she heard the softest of whispers close to her ear:

"Not this time, you fool! This is no game for our playing."

Sandar! How he had got there—or why—Roane writhed but was unable to move any more than he allowed her. Using his superior strength, he forced her backward, so she could no longer see the cave of the Crown.

She continued to fight his hold until they reached a wider stretch of passage. There he slammed her against the wall, holding her pinned by his weight against her. There was no light, but she could hear the cold menace in his voice.

"Do you want to be stun-rayed and dragged back? I will do it if necessary. You've played the fool and worse. But you're through now with such tricks. What happens to these puppets is no concern of yours. They *are* puppets, we've seen enough to know that. They are programed just like Adrianian androids to do exactly what the machines back in that chamber tell them to do. What does it matter what games puppets play? We've learned a lot from those installations—"

"They are not puppets!" Roane denied in a burst of real rage. "Any more than we are when we are Cram-briefed. If they did not have the crowns—if those machines weren't running—they would be free—They are human!"

"But they are not." He continued to hold her in that bruising grip which hurt her. "They are acting out the lives the machines decide for them. And it is none of our concern. If the Service decides later to interfere, when they

have our report, that is another matter. But it is not for us to worry about. Now—are you going to walk—or do I stun and drag you?"

y I don't think

# CHAPTER 12 *

**THERE WAS NO STRUGGLING** with Sandar. She knew he would do exactly as he threatened.

"I will come," she said dully.

He did not release his hold on her right shoulder, and so linked, they returned to the wider passage, where they were caught in the ray of a beamer. She heard her uncle give a sigh of relief.

"Hurry!" He did not ask where Sandar had been, nor what Roane had done. The beamer swung around, pointed their way to the entrance. Her cousin gave her a savage push.

As they emerged into the open a haze of mist lay in clots of shadow beneath the trees, seeping out over the country. Neither of the men hesitated, but struck a direct path back to camp, passing without note the man Roane had stunned, Sandar still holding her as if he expected her to break for freedom.

"Distorts out—all except one." Sandar had taken a reading on his belt instrument.

"To be expected. They have not been recharged," her uncle replied tersely. "The sooner we get off-world the better. I don't know how much of an impression your stupid actions have made here." He favored Roane with one of those icy stares which he had used to subdue her for so long. "We can only hope that we can lift without fully blowing cover—"

"What about the installation?" For the first time she could remember, Roane dared to ask a question in the face of his quelling. "Are we going to—will the Service—just leave it running? Sandar says that all the people here are tied to it, that it makes them puppets. That's against the Prime Four ruling—"

"Closed planets, as you well know, do not come under the Prime Rules. What the Service chooses to do once our report is in is none of our concern."

He spoke as if that was the final word on the subject, and Roane knew the folly of further argument. But her cold fear of the installation stayed with her.

The Psychocrats had once forced men on unknown worlds into experiments. And when their horrible reign had been finally broken, their mind-slaves freed, the results of both the meddling and the liberation had been, for two generations now, a dire warning to all humankind. Even if she had not known Ludorica or the Colonel, had not been herself sucked into the web which enmeshed Clio, Roane would still have been aroused to anger by this discovery. Just as the people of Clio were conditioned to obey the machines their enslavers had set up generations ago, so was she armed to fight such influences. Sandar might name them puppets, which perhaps technically they were, but

Roane had lived with them. And they were real people, far warmer of nature than the two now hustling her along.

Leave all major decisions to the Service—the safe, sane cry. But if this was left to the deliberation of men half the galaxy away, how soon would they interfere, if at all? Certainly not in time to save the Colonel! She had no doubts that Reddick would do exactly as he promised and make very sure Nelis Imfry was removed.

And the Princess with the Crown—she had been a changed person, almost evil. Ludorica deserved better than such slavery. Roane's thoughts circled round and round the same cheerless path as she trotted along. She did not believe that she was now under that curious influence the Princess had exerted on her. But neither could she turn aside from the probable dark future of Reveny and the new Queen.

Sandar pushed her into the shelter on his father's heels and then went to gather up the distorts. Uncle Offlas paid no attention to her, but went straight to the com to look for any messages recorded during their absence. He put out a finger to flick across the top of the machine, as if that gesture could summon an answer. Roane guessed that nothing had been received.

Uncle Offlas sat down and drew out the recorder. He was about to plunge in the button when he had a clear view of the reading. Then, for the first time since they had left the cave, he turned to look at her.

"There has been a recording made." Though that was a statement rather than a question, she answered him:

"I made it, when I returned here." And Roane knew a very small flash of triumph. He could not erase what she

had done, for that tape was locked with the sequence of others.

But he was not frowning. In fact there was a trace of interest in his expression, almost as if she had as much value as some small find.

"And what did you record—your meddling?" Still no coldness in his tone. It was as if he honestly wanted to know. Her spirits rose a little. It could well be that what she had fed into the records might have some influence on the momentous future decision. Though that could not possibly help what was passing now. She moved restlessly—the thought of Imfry as she had last seen him, wounded, bound, very much in the power of his enemy, was a constant prod to action. But how, when, and where?

"What happened to me," she replied. Then she gathered what courage she had recently gained—to stand against a lifetime of domination—and made her plea a second time:

"They—the Duke Reddick—is going to have the Colonel killed. The Princess is under controls. It is all like the tales of the story tapes, the ones about evil spells. The Colonel is her friend, but she ordered him executed. Only she could not mean it—it was that machine! We can't let her do it—"

She expected him to dismiss her summarily. Instead he continued to watch her with deepening interest. But what had been at first encouraging no longer seemed so. It was as if *she* were a part of the installation and he was fascinated by her reactions. And at that moment she was convinced that if anything could be done to break the black pattern now being woven, she alone must do it.

"You like these people, feel a certain kinship to them?"

"Yes."

"Well, you *had* recently come from intensive briefing. That might explain why you would be more susceptible to the influence of a strong conditioning broadcast, even if it were alien. There is good evidence that the installation here maintains Basic as well as special directional broadcasts. I think, Roane, that perhaps once you are debriefed, you will find the Service will accept such an explanation for your extraordinary conduct. In fact"—he was warming to this disagreeable train of thought—"you could well provide them with an additional check here. But as for any more interference on our part—you must understand that that is completely out of the question.

"In the first place, to stop—if we could find a method of doing so—any of those machines would disrupt the patterns they have been weaving for a couple of centuries, and the people of Clio may be so tied to their influence that failure of control would be fatal. Have you thought of that?"

Roane blinked. That the control could be so far-reaching, no, she had not thought of that. On the other hand, it was a dire possibility. They knew something of what the Psychocrats had done to manipulate their human material, but they did not know all. Patient reprograming was one thing; sudden and complete cutoff was another. Clio might be brought out of her fog by degrees, but the cutoffs—Roane remembered Ludorica's tale of the country whose crown had been destroyed.

"Arothner—"

"What?"

"There was a seacoast country—" She outlined the story as the Princess had told it.

Uncle Offlas nodded. "You see, the crowns control the rulers directly, and perhaps indirectly most of the ruled. Destroy the crown and the people are as Sorfalan puppets when their motive power fails. This 'Ice Crown' had been lost for a couple of generations—but it was still in existence. The pattern broadcast by the machine had been interrupted. It could be that when the Princess found the Crown there was a sharp change to compensate and bring the country back into a determined future. This abrupt about-face could be the result of some such need—"

"Need!" Roane interrupted him. "To let *Reddick* dictate—and she was changed—evil—You may not believe me, but she was! And as for pattern—wasn't it true that the closed worlds were supposed to be given a basic background and then allowed to work out their destinies from that? That the whole purpose of these experiments was to watch such maturing?"

"That was our conception, up until we made the discovery here. But it would seem that we were wrong. We came here for Forerunner relics, but we may have found something of equal value. There is every reason to believe that this is not a basic control but a self-continuing experiment."

He turned to the recorder. "I must tape what we have learned. Remember, no more interference. If it is necessary"—his voice was once more cold—"we can put you in stass until we are back on the ship. No more action apart from what is necessary for the carrying out of our

mission. Leave your belt here—" He pointed to the table before him.

So he would take from her the means of any independent action. Roane pressed open the catch. As she laid it before him he added:

"You had better break out provisions. Double rations."

Sluggishly she went to obey. The lift which the session in the fresher had given her was wearing off. Even if she managed by some now unforeseen chance to get away from ~~~~~~~~ would not have the strength to reach ~~~~~erhow. And without even a stunner, what good would revolt do her?

Roane brought out tubes and containers. Double rations? For a moment her thoughts lifted from the narrow rut of her troubles. She heard Sandar come in. And having loaded a tray with her choices, she returned to the com.

"I do not understand their silence. No reply to our urgent signal. Surely they cannot have broken orbit! Or if some such crisis arose, they would have beamed a warning." Uncle Offlas was again tapping the com.

"One distort with about a quarter power left." Sandar was piling boxes on the floor. "The rest are gone. There is a drain, there must be! To need full recharging so soon—"

"We have no idea about that installation. It may well be that it can pull from any power source in the neighborhood."

"But if that is so," Sandar said eagerly, "such an effect might be reversed. We could tap from it, maybe build up a real force wall to hold until the retire signal comes."

"Too risky." His father shook his head. "But your

thought leads to something else. We cannot recharge the distorts now without endangering our com broadcast. And to remain in this unprotected camp—I don't like the thought of that."

"Strike this shelter—move into better hiding?" Sandar suggested.

"It might be well. Unless we get an answer soon."

"So far the forest seems clear around here," Sandar reported. "We could go back to the cave, set up a repeller at the mouth. They have their crown no~~~~
they'll come back."

Roane divided the food containers, took her share. With a tube and two small boxes she went to her own quarters. Sleep was so heavy upon her that she had to force her eyelids open, keep doggedly chewing and swallowing. But before she had finished she lost the battle and was asleep.

Dreams were not uncommon. One often dreamed. Roane had wandered so in many strange places, some of them far stranger than the alien worlds she had seen with waking eyes. But this was the most vivid and "real" dream she had ever known, though in it she was only a spectator.

It was as if she had walked through the curtain of sleep into such a room as she had seen in the ambassador's mansion in Gastonhow. There were chairs with tall, much-carved backs, portions of that carving touched with insets of metal, or with time-dulled paint, to make fantastic scenes. Behind them much of the wall was covered with a stretch of tapestry on which men mounted on duocorns hunted some quarry lost from sight in thread-formed trees. This, too, had the look of something faded by many years' passing.

Yet it was as sharply clear to Roane's eyes as if she stood there in body. Before her was a long table of rich red stone which bore on its surface a mottling of twisting green lines. And set out on this was a plate of gold. By that lay a set of knife, two-tined fork, and spoon, all fashioned of crystal ringed and banded with gold in which small green gems were set.

At a good, almost awkward distance away from this setting was a second. But here the plate was of silver, the eating implements of the same material, with handles of red. All had a richness of color which warmed Roane as had her surroundings in Gastonhow—though it was far removed from the more sophisticated trappings of her own civilization.

The room lacked occupants, but there was a kind of expectancy. Roane was keenly aware that she waited with rising excitement for some action of importance.

A man wearing a richly embroidered tabard backed in, bowing low at every step to the person he ushered through the portal. He had a staff in one hand and he brought the butt of that sharply down on the floor at intervals. If his action was some signal Roane heard no sound, nor, she was suddenly aware, had she heard any since her eyes had opened on this.

She whom the usher had so heralded entered, her full skirts skimming in graceful folds which she adjusted now and then with small movements of one hand. In the other she carried a flat fan of purple feathers mounted on a jeweled handle.

The skirts, with tight bodice, cut low enough to reveal much of her shoulders, were of a deep purple shade, the

lacings of the bodice black interwoven with silver. And the wide necklace of many drops, the earrings her elaborately dressed hair allowed to show, were of shining black stones. There was even a small circlet of them in her hair. There was no mistaking who walked thus—the Queen Ludorica.

Two ladies followed her, their dresses of a like cut, but of gray with laces of unrelieved black. They had ribbons of the same hue tied around their throats, and their heads were covered with lacy black veils. The whole effect was one of calculated somberness.

One stationed herself at the table to face the Queen, while the other remained by the door—though not so as to obstruct the entrance of the fifth member of the party—Duke Reddick.

His clothing was also purple, a duller shade than worn by the Queen. He passed around the table, drew out her chair and seated her with ceremony before he took that place at some distance from her.

A tray was handed in from beyond the door to the waiting lady, who brought it to her companion at the table. From it the latter took two fantastic cups wrought in the form of those grotesque animals Roane had first seen being set up in the garden at Hitherhow. Having filled them from a flagon, she set them on the table with care, touched each lightly on the side. Straightway the metal feet moved and the cups started on a stately march, one to Ludorica, one to the Duke.

A second tray with food was brought in and the Queen and then Reddick were served with great ceremony. They ate and drank. Roane saw their lips move and knew that they talked, but for her the scene was played out in utter

silence. Twice their walking cups were sent back to be refilled.

Then the plates were cleared and the Queen and he whom she had considered her greatest enemy sat in apparent amity. From the front of his tunic Reddick brought forth a scroll which he spread flat on the table before him. While Roane could not read the words written there, she could see the black lettering, and ribbons of scarlet and black at the foot of the sheet, affixed by an irregular blob of purple of the hue of Ludorica's gown.

—— back in her chair, fanned herself —— purple feathers. All the vivacity, those quick changes of expression which Roane had seen on her face in the past, had vanished. Her face was a mask under the piles and rolls of her hair. Even her eyes were half closed as if the lids and the long lashes acted to conceal what she thought or felt.

Reddick's lips moved. He must be reading aloud what was written on the scroll. He glanced up at last, looking straight at Ludorica. And it seemed to Roane that he did so searchingly, as if he expected some protest, or at least some comment from her.

But if he did so, he was disappointed. She gestured with the fan, and the usher who had led her in came out of the shadows, took the scroll from the Duke, brought it to place before the Queen.

She let it remain rolled. To all appearances she was not interested in what it contained, nor in what Reddick wanted from her. Perhaps he grew impatient, for Roane saw his lips move again.

For the first time Ludorica answered him. No show of

emotion troubled her mask. Instead a faint flush arose on the Duke's cheeks. If that was caused by anger he suppressed all other signs of resentment valiantly.

But, having perhaps rebuked her kinsman, the Queen laid down her fan, spread out the scroll with both hands. Perhaps she reread what was written there. At least she sat so for several long moments.

Then she spoke again. One of the waiting ladies brought forward a small tray on which was a box which she opened before presenting it. The contents seemed a solid black block. Ludorica raised her right hand, firmly against the block, and then to the paper clear print. She then dipped her hand in a small basin the lady was quick to offer and washed her thumb clean.

She still held the scroll in her left hand, but allowed it to reroll as Reddick moved to draw back her chair. As she arose she left it lying.

Passing her kinsman as if he had become invisible, Ludorica left the room. The Duke caught up the scroll and tucked it once more within the security of his tunic before he followed her.

Roane stirred, or tried to stir. She had watched a very real scene which carried with it the conviction that by some weird chance she had been projected into Ludorica's palace and there been witness to some dire action. But why—and how—

The room was gone suddenly. Instead she faced, for perhaps the length of one breath out of a lifetime, a single face. And that was going to haunt her—

"Roane!"

She was being shaken with increasing roughness,

roused out of that state which did not seem wholly akin to normal sleep.

"Nelis!" Did she call that aloud? There was danger—

Roane opened her eyes. She was being drawn out of her bed roll by Sandar, and he was doing that shaking. But Sandar was not a part of—

"Roane! Wake up, can't you? Wake *up!*" His last shake was hard enough to make her head roll on her shoulders. And she at last accepted that she was back from that strange far place. She lay in her cubicle at camp, and her cousin was using impatiently harsh means to acquaint her of that fact.

"Haabacca jet us to the Cloud!" he exclaimed. "Sniff this so you can see straight!" With one hand he pushed her head forward, with the other made a balled fist and then opened it under her nose, where the capsule he had so crushed could spend its fumes directly into her lungs. Sniffing those fumes cleared her head.

"What is the matter?" she asked sulkily. For all the ominous shadows which clung about that dream, she wanted to hold it—especially the very last—for a dream once gone is sometimes gone forever.

"We're moving out." He stood up. "Father let you sleep as long as he could. But we're ready to collapse shelter now. Store your gear and do it fast!"

She crawled out of the sleeping bag, rolled it with the ease of long practice into a packet which fitted into a pocket in the wall. For the rest there had been a clean sweep here. All the possessions allowed her in this Spartan life had vanished. They must have been hard at work while she slept, slept and dreamed.

And out of that dream she carried the conviction that she had witnessed a true happening. Nelis Imfry—that was who it had concerned the most. The scroll that Reddick had produced and that the Queen had signed—and that last glimpse of a lean brown face before Sandar had shaken her awake—they were strung together as might be a necklace of view-pearls.

View-pearls? Roane paused in her sealing of the pocket. She had not the slightest esper rating. Had not Uncle Offlas had her tested long ago? An esper was invaluable to an archaeologist. Retrogressive hypnotherapy could be used by a sensitive to locate digging sites. There were those who could hold a circlet of view-pearls in their hands and read the authentic past. But she was not one of them. Then how did she *know* that she had done so now? And how had she been so empowered? Was it part of the same subtle influence which had drawn her to the Princess at their first meeting, forced her to serve Ludorica? But why should that influence now switch her concern to another?

Roane's hand went to shield her eyes. She tried to think normally, to argue against this new compulsion. No—she was not going to—She was *not!* The installation was not going to use her, too. But it could not be that! The installation moved the Queen now and what she was doing was directly against her former will.

Could she herself now be a puppet—but whose?

"Roane, come on!" Sandar stood there. "What's the matter, do you need another waking inhalation?"

"No!" She needed nothing except some quiet, a calm mind, and a chance to think. But when she would get all three she was not sure.

# ✳ CHAPTER 13 ✳

**THE SHELTER** had been collapsed around the packed core of equipment. Unless someone stumbled upon it bodily, it was so well concealed that the camp could not be sighted by any forest traveler. With packs of emergency supplies the three withdrew to the cave passage.

There the elder Keil set a repell beamer working at the entrance, locked it on his thumb set so that no one else might turn it off. As long as he had Roane's belt she would be a prisoner here, as safely captive as if she were chained by a collar, since without its force she could not go out as others could not enter.

Saying that there was no reason to waste time during their enforced stay in hiding, he and Sandar went back to the installation chamber. They had left a call beam at the dismantled camp to provide direction for their off-world rescuers.

Roane trailed the two men, but to watch those crowned pillars disturbed her. Was it true that the destruction of those inhuman controls might devastate Clio, bring about planetwide chaos and death to peoples conditioned for

generations as puppets? Or—but one could not be sure without careful study made by those trained to deal with such cases. And such study could take planet years.

In the meantime, Roane leaned her head against the wall and closed her eyes. She discovered she could pull from memory every vivid detail of that dream, if dream it was—from the gleam of the colors, the metals, the gowns, the high ceremony of the meal, to the expressions or lack of expression on the faces of those who had played out the scene.

Time. Her scratched hands balled into small fists which she wished she could use to batter her way out of here. Time was going to defeat her. She need only glance down that aisle of pillars to Uncle Offlas, wearing her belt draped over one shoulder. She had no plan—

Her head ached and the constant mutter of the machines seemed to match it throb for throb, until she could stand it no longer. The men were both intent upon what they were doing, studying the play of lights across those pillar surfaces. She gave a sigh and returned to the cave entrance where they had stacked their survivor kits.

There was that other entrance to the cave passages, where Reddick's men had broken through. But Uncle Offlas had set a double broadcast to operate a second barrier a little beyond the installation chamber. No—Roane knew it was hopeless. Yet she found herself pulling at the pack seals, lying out on the floor, in the light of a small beamer, their contents.

Food—plenty of E-rations—a well-stocked medic kit, spare chargers for beamers and stunners—Nothing of service to her.

She piled all she had taken from Uncle Offlas's kit back into it. And she already knew all that was in hers. There remained Sandar's and she turned it out, without any real hope.

Another beamer—or—Roane turned the tube around in her hands, brought it closer to the light with a small thrill of excitement. Not a regulation beamer, and not the forbidden blaster, but an archaeologist's hand tool which had some limited properties of both. She studied the setting dial on the butt and then unsealed the charge-holding stem. If—oh, if only—

Roane hastily emptied out again all three kits, dumping their contents on the stone. In a short time she had three sets of charges lined up—those for stunners, those for two sizes of beamers. And—three of the latter fitted! One of those would not give her the highest force this tool could use, but perhaps enough. Only it would be slow in working—and she could not face either man were he armed.

She sat back on her heels. There was the repeller. Roane swung up the beamer to touch the ceiling of the cave at the point above where the machine sat. What she tried was such a gamble that the promise of failure far outweighed that of success, but she could see nothing else. And it would take time—

Holding the beamer on the spot she had selected, Roane thumbed on the tool, aiming its energy broadcast at that section, moving it with precision to cut the outline of a circle in the rock.

It did slice—but so slowly! And she could tell from the vibration of the tube in her hand that the operation was

using far too much power. The charge might well be exhausted long before her purpose was accomplished. But she kept at it.

A rain of small bits of stone, gnawed away by the ray, fell toward the repeller. Heartened, Roane grew reckless, bearing down on the button to send the highest intensity of beam into that cracking surface.

Back and forth she swept, weaving a maze of cracks and cuts. The powdery fall was thicker, and larger bits of rock came. The repeller had its own protective casing. She might not be able to bring down a piece large enough to crack that, but she was forcing the broadcast to use some of its energy to protect itself. And Uncle Offlas had already set it on high. He had had to, to produce the two force walls, here and down the passage.

Sweep, sweep. Pebbles fell now. Roane used the beamer to read the dial on the repeller. What she saw there was heartening. The needle was a fraction into the red-zone warning of overload. Then a larger fragment, perhaps the size of her own doubled fist, came clanging down.

A flash from the repeller, an acrid breath of odor. Shorted! She had shorted the shield!

Until that moment she had been moved only by hope. Hope, and the desperate need to be on the move which had come from that dream. Roane unscrewed the tube, recharged the tool.

That done, she stowed it in the front of her tunic and set about making up a small pack—food, a medic kit, the third charge for her weapon-tool, a beamer, a pair of night lenses. She knotted all together in a plasta sack before she allowed herself to think seriously of what she would do.

Roane stood a moment in the dark of the cave, listening. To her alert ears the murmur of sound from the installation was steady. She picked up no hint that either of the others might be returning. But—if she left here now she was making a final choice. All because of a dream? She did not know. Perhaps it was that influence which hung here on Clio, warping her reasoning powers.

She could even see clearly what she should have considered good sense, the only right pattern of living for an off-worlder. Only—Roane shook her head. She could not put name to the emotions which had shaken her out of the life she had always known, just as she could not withstand their present pull.

Taking up the sack, putting on the night lenses, Roane stepped over the repeller and walked out of the cave into a new life which she felt had been chosen for her, whether or not she consciously willed it.

Only, now that she was free, where should she go? Hitherhow was her lone point of reference. Wearing these native clothes (she had lacked another change of clothing in camp), she might be able to get into the village, learn something. That was Reddick's holding. Surely he would send his prisoners there. Though would they still be in the keep now?

Half the night later, as she had days earlier, Roane crouched on the hilltop to watch keep and village. There were one or two lighted lanterns along the street leading from the keep's massive gate to the highway. But the houses were all dark. She hesitated, certain of the folly of her vague plans, but just as sure she must do something.

As she lingered, she heard a sound that was not one of

the night noises, a pounding in regular beat, growing louder—until two duocorns, ridden at a steady, ground-covering pace, came into view from the west, the clatter of their passing awakening louder echoes as they reached the cobbled pavement of the short village street. They were brought to a stop before the gate of the keep.

A horn sounded, one of the riders holding it to his lips, blowing a series of notes with certainly no respect for the slumbers of any in village or keep, for the harsh peal shattered the peace of the night. Men spilled into the courtyard, two of them tugging at the gate bar. Then the riders were in, one coming out of his saddle to head at a hasty trot for the near tower.

The men in the courtyard scattered, leading away the puffing, foam-bespattered duocorns. Roane rolled over on her back, pulled off the night lenses to stare up at the sky. There was a paling there. It must be later than she had first thought. And she had accomplished nothing as yet. Better get down to the village. When she looked there again there were lights in some of the house windows. The horn had done its duty to awaken the inhabitants.

Then—lights in the keep—more stirring there. From the main tower came a blast of sound greater than that other horn, one that echoed from the cluster of heights ringing Hitherhow. Men formed lines on the courtyard pavement. More and more lights appeared in the village houses.

Roane pulled the Revenian hood up over her head, drawing it about her face as best she could. It was the only anonymity she had as she went down into the village. A second blast of sound which was a summoning spurred her on.

By the time she reached the short street the people were already coming out of the houses, many of them carrying lanterns, moving toward the keep. There the courtyard doors had been flung open, a line of guardsmen on either side. And from the snatches of conversation Roane overheard as she edged into the crowd, she learned that the peal from the tower was a summons which had not been sounded in years; the reason for it none about her could guess.

"War! Those Vordainians—they have always looked jealously in our direction—"

"No, we have most danger at the west—Leichstan, they have never been friendly since their king re-wed."

"It may only be some proclamation from the Queen. She is only new come to the throne and—"

"A proclamation would be delivered at a decent hour, not when a body is jerked out of a warm bed in the night. This must be something more weighty—"

Roane fastened the bag of supplies to her belt. The night lenses she had tucked into the front of her tunic. And now her fingers sweated on the smooth tube of the tool, her only weapon. If she had to use that, it would require skill.

The crowd tightened more about her as they pushed through the gate, between the ranks of the guardsmen, to stand facing the main door of the keep. Then the horn sounded for the third time and the murmur of questioning voices died away. Three men appeared so suddenly they might have materialized out of space. They wore uniforms such as Reddick's men had, with the addition of those badges and lacings which denoted officers. Two were

colonels if she read those signs aright, but the man in the center must be of even higher rank.

A riding cloak hung from his shoulders and he tossed it back impatiently as he unrolled a strip of writing. Roane bit hard upon her lower lip. As well as if she stood at his hand to see it, she knew what that was. She had seen it last in her dream.

"Know you all who swear allegiance to the Ice Crown of Reveny"—the officer had a carrying voice and read slowly and clearly as if there was need that not a single word of this escape those listening to him—"on this day of Martle passed, in the three hundred and fiftieth year of the Guardians, in the reign of Queen Ludorica of the High House of Setcher, Regnant Lady of Reveny in her own right by Blood and Crown, it is decreed that one Nelis Imfry, of the House of Imfry-Manholm, be stripped of his rank as Colonel in the Command of Reveny, of his place in the House of Manholm, and of all privileges granted him by our late gracious lord, King Niklas, whom the Guardians have seen fit to take into their everlasting Peace.

"The said Nelis Imfry, being no longer of the Court, of any House, or of those who stand to arms for Reveny, shall suffer in addition the death accorded to traitors to the Crown, since diverse acts of foul treason have been proved on him.

"And this sentence is to be carried out forthwith at the keep of Hitherhow where the said Nelis Imfry lies in the keeping of our well-beloved cousin and gracious lord, Duke Reddick. Given by seal and hand, under the wish of the Crown, by Blood Right of rule, ours alone on this day— Ludorica, Queen Regnant of Reveny."

The officer allowed the scroll to snap shut again, handed it to one of his companions. He then raised his hand to touch fingers to the badge so prominently displayed on the breast of his tunic.

"So says the Queen! Let it be thus done!"

There was a somewhat ragged assent from those about Roane, repeating the officer's words, but slowly, as if those who gave lip service to the sentiment he expressed were either astounded or not pleased. And Roane heard again questioning, though this time in the most subdued whispering, a faint hissing. She was working her way to the left and the edge of the gathering, striving to do so in the least noticeable manner.

What she could do to alter the future, she did not know. But the feeling that she must hold the key to the situation had been growing stronger by the moment. She was at the fringe of the crowd now, close to the line of sentries. They might have been set there to discourage any sympathy for the condemned, but Roane saw nothing to suggest a demonstration in the Colonel's favor. The people were very sober, and even the whispers had died. Once before Roane had felt such an aura of fear—on another planet when a crowd of cowed worshipers had watched a ritual killing. This was contagious; she knew the same chill.

They were bringing out the prisoner. His arm hung in a sling, and in the lantern light his face was worn, older seeming, the bones showing more clearly beneath the drawn skin, as if in the few hours since she had seen him last a number of years has passed. But he walked firmly, looking neither right nor left, until they brought him to the

wall. There were guards moving along the parapet above, towing a bulky contraption which rasped and jangled, until they pushed it over, to be lowered on chains until it thudded to the pavement.

By lantern light it could be seen clearly, a cylinder of metal hoops and netting, not as tall as the man they were shoving to it, so when they forced him inside, he was able neither to stand erect nor to move in relief from a torturous cramping. Once they slammed the opening shut, the bolts were made fast.

Then came the scrape of metal against stone as it was raised to the top of the wall, turned about so its occupant faced out to the dawn sky, there wedged fast. Those on the parapet drew back, almost as if they wanted no bodily contact with the cage.

But they left a guard on duty not too far away as the rest tramped off. There was a sigh from the villagers as they filed out through the gate toward their own homes.

And none of them, Roane noted, raised their eyes to the cage. It was as if they did not want to think of its occupant.

Roane hesitated. Should she leave with the villagers? She had no idea if more was planned for Nelis, or if he was simply to be so exposed until he died of hunger and thirst. Her briefing in the customs of Reveny had not gone into the details of local punishments. It was plain that he was now considered safely pent, so that a single guard was all that was necessary. In those few seconds she made her choice.

Drawing the tool, she aimed at the one target which might cause a diversion. The officers who were in the

doorway of the tower had not yet moved and over their heads a plaque of metal in the form of one of the royal symbols was bolted to the stone. Recklessly she used the cutting ray full force.

A glow appeared along the upper edge of the plaque. Her luck was better than she had reason to hope, for it swung down as if held now by a weaker fastening. She shouted, pointed to the shuddering metal. The plaque fell. There were cries, a crash. It had beaten down the man who had read the scroll. Guards ran toward him.

Roane sped along the wall, into the dark well of the stair leading to the parapet. She expected any second to be brought down by a projectile fired from one of those archaic weapons. But her luck continued to hold. She did not waste time looking back at the melee in the courtyard, where cries of help rang from the heart of the confusion, but took the steps at the best speed she could.

The sentry faced inward, leaning forward to watch what was going on below. Roane ran forward, slashing out at his neck in one of the unarmed-defense blows she had learned from Sandar. He made no sound, nor did he fall, for she steadied him against the wall, only hoping he would lean there until she was done. Then she used the tool at the lanterns blazing on either side of the cage. Their sides melted.

As she raced forward the explosive sounds of shooting came at last. Roane threw herself low, reached the foot of the cage, pressing the end of the tube to the fastenings of its door.

Metal glowed. She had to be careful in that cutting so that the raw energy would not reach the prisoner. And she

could so control it only by direct contact. Now she must expose herself, clawing up the length of the bars. It seemed to Roane that those moments when she clung there, pressing the tool to the iron, were the longest she had ever known.

"Can you get out?"

He had made no sound during her work. She was not even sure he was conscious. Perhaps the rough handling they had used to push him into that small space had worsened his wound. If that were so she did not know what she could do. It all depended on his mobility.

She pressed the tube to the last fastening. But this time there was no response. She had exhausted the charge, never mean for such demand. But to take time to reload—

"I cannot cut this!" She gave him the truth. To fail—

He spoke for the first time. "Pull—now!" His order was so incisive that she obeyed, jerking the opening toward her, aware he was pushing in turn with what strength he could summon.

"It will not give!" She raised the tool, brought it down hammerwise on the reluctant fastening. Perhaps their efforts had loosened it, for a second blow made it yield. He crumpled forward and for a second she was afraid that one of the projectiles being fired at them from the courtyard had struck home. A form lunged at them, missed Imfry, but sent the girl hard against the outer wall of the parapet, driving most of the breath out of her lungs as arms encircled her. Then her assailant reeled back, was drawn tight against Nelis's body, for the Colonel's arm was about his throat. The guardsman twisted and tore at the

bar of flesh holding him so. Roane staggered forward, used the tool to strike the head held against the Colonel's good shoulder.

Imfry crouched over the body he had lowered to the stone. He straightened up holding one of the hand weapons.

"Loose that—" He motioned to the wedging about the base of the cage. Roane saw what he meant and began to fight at it bare-handed. "I will cover."

He stayed behind the parapet, watching the head of the stair up which she had come. She was able to loose the wedges at last. Imfry glanced over his shoulder.

"Can you push it over—that way—here—" He joined her, set his good shoulder against the bulk of the cage and shoved, she lending her weight to his.

The heavy mass of metal swayed, inclined forward, toppled to slam against the outer parapet, and then overbalanced, to fall. There was a clanging crash. The wall under them vibrated as it caught at the end of the chain length. Roane divined his purpose. They had now a way down outside, if, one-handed, he could take it. And it seemed he would try. For he edged his arm well free of the sling.

"Down!" he ordered.

She fingered the chain nearest her, drawn taut by the weight of the cage, though it swayed. The links were large. She thought she could fit fingers into them. But could it be descended one-handed?

"Can you—"

"Get down!" he repeated.

There was movement at the head of the stair. He had

brought out the weapon, shot at that shadow, to be answered by a cry.

Roane waited no longer. She started down that improvised ladder, and later her feet struck the cage, so that she must climb over it. When there were no more holds, she dropped, using her space training for the best landing she could make.

It was not a light one. She would bear away more than one bruise. She turned. Surely some one of the garrison would be waiting here. But while there was a milling about, shouts and shots around the angle of the wall (the gate being hidden from sight here), as yet there were no soldiers.

"'Ware—I am going to drop—" She heard Imfry overhead, saw him holding to the cage, his feet moving as if he were trying to kick away from the wall. Then he let go.

She ran toward him as he made no move. Stunned? Broken bones? The ordeal of that descent with a wound might have been enough to—She pulled at his body, trying to roll him over, knowing they must get away.

Men were coming—out of the village. That weapon— did Imfry still have it? She tore at the front of his tunic, trying to find it. But there was nothing and the strangers were upon them.

She aimed a blow, had her hand caught in a tight grip. "Friends!"

The man who had her arm pulled her up and away from the Colonel. Two others were at the side of the fallen man, lifting him between them. Then Roane's guide drew her along at a half-running pace, while the two carrying Imfry matched that as well as they could. They were past the

houses, into a clot of shadowed shrubbery before she fairly caught her breath. She heard the stamp of duocorn hoofs against the turf and they came into a clearing where four men were mounted, holding on checking reins animals manifestly fresh and ready for the trail.

"Ride!" ordered the man with Roane.

The duocorns wheeled under spurring, pounded off to the south. But the men in her party pushed back into the shadows.

"Haffner knows these trails. He will lead them a good chase," commented one of Imfry's bearers with satisfaction.

"He had better," said his fellow. "We shall need all the time we can win. Help with the Colonel, he's bleeding bad. Needs looking to as soon as we can get him hid."

# ✳ CHAPTER 14 ✳

**THE MEDIC KIT!** There was the slim chance that its drugs might not aid one born on Clio. But if they could—

"Please." Roane moved in the grip of the man who had pulled her into this temporary safety. "I have that which will aid him. Let me—"

"Well enough. But we cannot remain here. There is a chance they may not be misled by that false trail. To the hound hut, Mattine."

Dawn was well upon them, but it appeared that these men knew what they were about. Even burdened with the Colonel they melted into the brush with fluid ease, while Roane's guide drew her through openings she herself could not distinguish.

This was not quite one of those hidden brush-and-tree-walled roads, rather a slot in the earth along which they trotted. Roane could hear the heavy breathing of the two carrying Imfry as she followed on their heels and the other man served as a rear guard.

That journey seemed very long, though it could not have been so in either time or distance. Then the bearers halted, and the man behind Roane wriggled through what again appeared a thick wall of brush. Roane tried to get a good look at Imfry.

His head lay against one of his bearers, and his eyes were closed. There was a sticky patch on his shirt.

"Let me—I can help him—" She tried to edge closer, but the man who supported Imfry hunched his shoulder as a barrier.

"Not yet!" His whisper was fierce. "Quiet!"

She huddled, listening. There were sounds. Noises which came, she thought, more from animal than human throats. Then she did catch a voice.

"Ha, Brighttooth, Rampage, Roarer—down—sit! And you, Shrew, Surenose—quiet! Eat, drink, and be quiet!"

The brush screen trembled as their guide returned. All three men wore their hoods pulled well about their faces, so Roane saw little of them save the thrust of their chins. But there was an air of authority in this man.

"Take these." He had some strips of material in his hands.

From them—Roane's nose wrinkled in disgust— steamed a nauseating stench. The last thing she wanted to do was touch those rags. But she was given no choice. One of the men supporting Imfry accepted three of the strips, hung one about his own neck and draped one on his fellow and one over the Colonel, while the fourth was thrown in her direction. Reluctantly, her hand shrinking from contamination as she took it, she picked it up.

"Our key to the kennels. I do not think we shall be

disturbed there. At least not for a while. Now—before they cast in this direction, let us move!"

They pushed out into a cleared space. There stood a tall fence made of stakes set firmly in the ground, tops sharpened into points. Tall as those were, Roane caught sight of a roof pitch beyond. There was a gate not too far away and their guide went directly to it, drawing a bar which was weighty enough to lock a keep.

Those carrying Imfry crossed the open at a shambling run, as if they were putting forth their best effort to get their burden quickly into hiding, and Roane trailed them. The gate slammed behind her and she heard the bar thud into place, so fastened by the man who had led them. But her eyes were for what lay within.

Direhounds! Like the duocorns, they were not native to Clio but had been imported. And she did not know any planet, save perhaps one of the inner worlds supporting an exotic zoo, which allowed the import of Loki direhounds. Deceptively they were not large, nor ferocious to look at, though the odor given off by their spotted hides could choke one. Their maned heads were down as they tore at chunks of meat.

As the human party moved toward the hut in the center of the pen, two swung around, making no sound, their black lips wrinkling back to bare the double rows of green-scummed fangs. And there was a hot and terrible hate in their eyes.

One took a step and then a second, moving to intercept the men, who had halted, visibly bracing themselves. Then those fringed ears, which had been flattened to narrow skulls as the creatures sniffed the air, went up as if they had

caught a familiar sound or their noses some usual scent. Roane held closer to her that rag she had so disdained. It was indeed a key here.

The leading direhound gave a last sniff, turned away to a clay-smeared chunk of meat, its companion copying its action. The men moved on, though it was very hard for Roane not to turn and walk backward as they passed among the gorging animals, the sensation that they would be attacked from the rear so weighed on her.

"The door—open the door—" one of Imfry's supporters ordered.

She edged past the men, still watching the direhounds with small, distrustful side glances, to push. The door opened readily and they entered into darkness and the stench of the animals, even worse in these confined quarters. Involuntarily she snapped on the beamer.

Along one side of the small room hung joints of meat, blackened and evil-smelling. Above those was a series of narrow shelves on which crowded stoppered containers. From spikes driven into the other walls dangled whips, leashes, collars, and muzzles massive enough to imprison a direhound's fangs.

To their right stood bales of straw trussed with rope. One had been cut open and half its contents taken. Roane laid down the beamer to attack that, spreading out the rest for a rough bed on the floor as fast as she could.

As they laid Imfry on that she brought out the medic kit. No time to test her remedies. The more she saw the gray-white of that face, the less she liked it. Now it was her turn to give orders.

"Room!" Her hands—she looked at her dirty, scratched

fingers. "Here—" She picked up a spray tube. "You—" She held it out to the nearest man. "Press this down, carefully now—it must not be wasted."

Roane bathed her hands in the antiseptic vapor. "Enough!" She held them away from any touch which would infect them again. "Ease his shirt away from that wound. No—use the spray first—on this—" She pointed to another tube to be prepared.

Then, taking it, she carefully dribbled a few drops of its contents over that stain. With the tips of her fingers she urged the fabric gently away from the flesh to which it had been glued.

"Now—tear it!"

As the contaminated cloth came away from an angry-looking wound, where blood still oozed sluggishly, Roane went to work with all the skill she had, spraying—twice with antibiotics, and then with Swiftheal—before applying a final sealing of plasta-flesh with double care, since it might be put to unusual tests before this journey was finished.

She sat back then to consider the remaining contents of her kit. Examination had assured her that the fall had not brought broken bones. It was the extra strain upon his wound which had sent him into the present state of unconsciousness. Certainly the longer he could rest, the better chance the plasta-flesh had for a firm closing. She thought it best not to try to arouse him.

The air of the hut was thick with the stench of the direhounds and the decaying meat. Roane was so hot she pulled off her hood, loosened the lacing on her tunic. For the first time she had a chance to inspect her comrades in

hiding. Both men had now relaxed against the bales of straw.

One was familiar—the other strange. But she put name to the one who had supported Imfry's head during that escape.

"You are Sergeant Wuldon. You went with us to Gastonhow."

He was older than the Colonel, it seemed to her, though it was difficult to judge ages on alien worlds. But his brown hair had a wide strip of silver over each ear. His face was as weathered as Imfry's had been before the sickly gray tint had overlaid that healthier hue. And there was a small puckered dot in the flesh of his chin, slightly to one side, like a misplaced cleft.

"Ysor Wuldon, yes, m'lady."

"You came to save him." She made that a statement rather than a question. Wuldon nodded.

"We had hopes. There were a few in Hitherhow ready to give us some aid. The Duke is not greatly loved. But they would not promise too much—and we would have failed, m'lady, without you."

Roane leaned back against one of the bales, raised her hands to brush straying hair out of her eyes. The smell, the heat made her feel ill, and again she wondered at her actions, as if that part of her which was the old Roane now stirred from captivity to view with dismay what had happened. This odd sense of being two persons added to her growing state of misery. She gulped, trying to subdue nausea, and feared that soon she would lose control.

The other man stirred restlessly. "This stink—" he muttered.

"No garden of turl lilies," agreed Wuldon. "But out there—" he jerked a thumb to indicate the enclosure of the direhounds—"we have about the best sentries we could wish for."

Roane swallowed again. "How long—" She found she could not complete that, but Wuldon had no trouble in understanding. Only he could not be reassuring with his answer.

"Who knows? Until nightfall, if we are lucky and they follow that false trail. If they can be drawn into the hunting preserve our men can lead them astray and lose them. Then we can move out. But with the Colonel as he is—" He shook his head.

"How is he, Lady?" the other man asked. "You have him fixed good enough to ride if we can move out? We cannot go far if we have to lug him."

There was a dissenting growl from the Sergeant, but the other man faced him squarely. "That is the truth and you know it. Me, I am liege man to m'lord. My own mother's sister fostered him when his lady mother died. Do you think I would say no to getting him free? Did I when you and Haus came asking? But we cannot carry him. He has to be able to ride. It is a long way to the hills."

"They will outlaw-horn him," the Sergeant said slowly. "Then how much help can he claim anywhere in Reveny? Best over the border. He would not be the first good man driven to that; and he has a sword worth selling—if not in Leichstan, the Isles of Marduk welcome mercenaries—"

"Thank you for the testimony, Wuldon." The voice was low, strained, and it startled them.

The Colonel's eyes were open. There was even a little color in his sunken cheeks.

"What a smell!" He sniffed. "Direhound! But where in Reveny—" He moved as if to rise but the Sergeant had clamped a big, gentle hand down on his uninjured shoulder, holding him where he was.

"Haus's idea, sir. We are in the hound hut at Hitherhow."

"The hound hut!" Imfry repeated. "Out of one cage, into another. But I must say that for all the smells, I find this one easier than the last. But—how did you plan—this—"

"Well, we did not—not together, sir. I saw them bring you out of that hole in the ground and Spetik and I split up ⌐d went to where we thought we could get help. He came ⌐litherhow and talked to Mattine and Haus. There were ⌐me men in the village who were willing to risk a little. ⌐hough they were not going too far, being a bit mindful of ⌐heir necks."

"For which you cannot blame them, Wuldon. Treason is not a crime one wants to aid. Spetik, and Mattine here—Haus, and you—Then what else did you do?"

"Well, I went back to the post. There were four or five of the men ready to see what we could do. So—we left—"

The Colonel frowned. "Deserted?" he demanded.

Sergeant Wuldon grinned. "Better say 'detached duty'—serving with our commanding officer. No man had named you different then. Nor have we been personally told so since."

Imfry's frown disappeared. "You heard it loud and clear in Hitherhow."

"No, sir. Ever since I was caught in that rock fall last year, sir—when you dropped down on a rope and pulled me free—well, I have not heard too clear at times. I did not hear anything about your not being my commanding officer."

"Impaired hearing can take you out of the service, Sergeant."

"It has, Colonel. If anything is said to Reddick—it has."

Imfry laughed, but sobered quickly. "If we are taken, no such flimsy arguments will get you out of a hanging—or worse."

"Then we shall take care we are not caught, sir. But we did come here, me, Haffner, Spetik, Rinwald, Fleech. They got duocorns, best mounts in the stables, and stood ready to either ride or set a false trail. But we did not know just how we could get to you. She did that in the end." He nodded at Roane.

"You were a part of this?" Imfry asked.

"Of their plans, no. I came—I came because I had to. It was my interference which began everything. I could not let it end so because of my meddling. But we could not have made it without your men."

"It is very strange." The Colonel's eyes rested steadily upon her. "From the first I knew that you held some fate in your hands, though that it was mine, I did not guess. I thought it was the Princess's."

He stirred again. "Odd, all the pain is gone." He looked at his wound, where the plasta-flesh had taken on the hue of the skin around it.

"What did you do to me, anyway?" he asked Wuldon.

"The lady did it, from her own supplies."

"She seems good at a great many things," commented the Colonel. "Wuldon, you would not have such a thing as a saddle bottle of water about you?"

"Sorry—"

"That is all right."

Roane forced herself to move. The fetid air and heat made her weak. But she found one of the E-ration tubes, turned the twist cap and held it out to him.

"Suck this," she said. "It is about half moisture, so it ought to help." She brought out two more, offered them to the men. They examined them curiously.

"How about you, m'lady?" the Sergeant asked.

Roane made a hard business of swallowing. "I cannot— it makes me sick. If you will—Please, Sergeant"—her voice became more urgent—"the kit—push it to me."

She thought that she would not be able to make it in time, but she hunted with one hand among the containers, came up with a capsule she broke between her palms, bending her head to sniff and sniff again of the reviving fumes. But she had too few of those to waste them. If they were here long, how could she stand it? Conditioned she might be to withstand alien worlds, alien odors, alien foods—there were some strains which her body could not take and it seemed she was meeting them now in this prison-like hut.

"I will have to go soon." She raised her head when the vertigo subsided a little and she was temporarily the mistress of her body. "They do not know me here—I ought to go safely."

"Do not believe that, m'lady," Wuldon returned. "With the Colonel free they will look thrice at any stranger. You

leave this place and the first one to see you will call for the guard. Every man, woman, and child in Hitherhow will be glad to help run down a stranger—if only to turn the Duke's men away from sniffing at their own doors."

"Exactly right." The Colonel's voice was stronger, had back that sure note which had once troubled her with its assumption that his way was the only right one. "And where would you go? Or will your people come looking for you?"

She shook her head, and then wished that she had not made that gesture, for it left her dizzy. "That is the last thing they would do. I broke orders to come here. They will believe anything that happens to me is richly deserved."

"What kind of talk is that?" the Sergeant asked. "No one would turn his back on a lady who had come to help—"

"There must be a good reason," Imfry cut in. "Sometime, Lady Roane, I would like to hear it. Now—I will admit that to stay here any longer than is absolutely necessary is something we all cannot do. Have you any plans, Sergeant?"

"Haus may have. He brought us here to wait. And he knows Hitherhow. Also—they know *him*, well enough not to go throwing any trouble in his way. It is good to be the only man who can really handle direhounds; keeps everyone on his toes seeing as how Haus stays happy and in good health. Of course, they could shoot them all to get to us. Maybe the Duke might do just that if he knew we were here. But the belief would be that those devil animals would not let us inside the gate, which would be the truth if Haus had not given us a key through their power of scent."

"Listen!" Imfry ordered.

Once more Roane could hear the loud grunting of the hounds.

"Someone's coming!" Sergeant Wuldon, weapon in hand, crossed with a silent tread Roane would have believed impossible for such a powerful man, to stand at the door of the hut. He hunched a little, apparently finding a crack through which he could see something of the outside.

"Haus!" The name was a hiss of whisper and then Wuldon added, "alone." But he did not reholster his weapon and Mattine moved, if not as noiselessly, to the other side of the door frame. Roane watched from the apathy of her discomfort.

"Soooooo." The voice of the man outside rang on a crooning note. "Good boy—brave—brave—Easy, girl, there is enough for all—mind your manners."

If she had not known what sort of beasts did roam without, Roane would have believed them the gentlest and most agreeable of pets. People did have odd tastes, as who should know better than she, who had been exposed to a variety of worlds and customs—but to find a man who dealt unreservedly with direhounds!

"It takes many kinds of men, m'lady, to make a nation." The Colonel might have read her thoughts, if not her expression. "There is"—his voice dropped to a whisper she could barely hear—"much to be said between the two of us. I know not why you came—but to you my—"

"Wait until you are free. Ill luck can come from too early thanksgiving." She had never been superstitious before, but now, uneasy as she was inwardly, she could

understand primitive natives who feared to invoke wrong powers, tempt retaliation from ill luck.

"Until another time, then. But, believe me, we shall have you forth as soon as we can—"

She looked at him steadily, a dull wonder in her. He spoke now as if she were the one to be concerned about, when *he* was the hunted man.

The door opened and the man who had led them here entered, dropping a heavy sack, which added another sickening odor of dog meat, on the floor with a thud.

"How is he—" he was beginning, when the Colonel spoke up.

"Come see for yourself, man! Your pets have played guard well."

"M'lord." Haus crossed the small room in a couple of strides, knelt, and laid his hand palm down on the one the Colonel held out to him, bowing his head for a moment as if the gesture was a small but solemn ceremony.

"It has been a long time, Haus."

"One can forget the toll of years, m'lord, when there is good reason. Now"—he sat back on his haunches so that his face was more or less on a level with that of the man he spoke to—"there is a plan, desperate, but the best which can be done for now. They have sent to Urkermark for *his* orders. Luck has so far served us in two ways. First, when the badge of Hitherhow fell in the courtyard, it brought down the Marshal of the West. He still lies unconscious and they do not know when, or if, he will come to his senses. Colonel Scharn got a broken collar bone and a bad scrape on the head, so he's not been much use in leading any hunt.

"While the other—this Colonel Onglas—has been fluttering around without much more wits than the least of my pack out there. He put most of the guard to searching the village, routing folks out of their homes to ask questions and seek for traitors.

"Two hours ago he demanded the direhounds. Some of the patrolmen found the tracks and he wanted to set the hounds to those."

Roane heard the men around her exclaim over that. "Yes." Haus nodded. "I told you he had the wits of a peckfowl! I told him how a coursing such as that would end. Even I could not hold them to any set trail which was not that of a spaybuck or a roffer. So—he ordered me to make identification scent."

"He is plain mad!" burst out the Sergeant. "Using what?"

"He has straw out of the cell they kept you in, m'lord, and some of the rags they used on your arm when they brought you in. It would be enough, and he will see that I do it. He is sending down guards to watch."

"Here? Then what—" Wuldon began.

"They will not come in, never fear. But I told him the truth, that even direhounds cannot pick up a hunted man's trail if he is mounted. So he is having a duocorn killed and the carcass brought here, too."

"A duocorn! Let your pets sniff that and they will turn on any like beast—even those of the hunters," Imfry observed. "He is truly insane."

"He is fear-mad, I think, m'lord. He does not dare face the Duke with no better news than he has now. But I told him straight facts, and others listened, if he did not. Never

mind about the straw and rags. I can doctor those. But it goes against my liking to make a duocorn into bait. The hounds could head straight for the stables. And why should innocent beasts suffer? Only there are those with him, lesser officers, who have their heads screwed on. One of them is going to Colonel Scharn right now, sure he can get that order countermanded. But—this is what I rightfully want to say, Colonel—that dead duocorn they are bringing down—I think that will get you out of here."

"Keep talking, Haus. This is beginning to interest me."

Haus nodded. "Like the old days along the border when the Nimps were raiding. Yes, m'lord, I thought you would remember. They deliver this duocorn, but none of them is going to risk his neck to push the cart inside that gate. So I fetch it in, with Sergeant Wuldon here—"

"Me!" The Sergeant jerked back a fraction of an inch. "But everybody knows that you are the only one who dares come inside—"

"I already told them I have a forester to help with the bait and the coursing—said you were wearing a treated coat to keep the hounds off, but it was mine and I only had the one. I also told them that you had helped on other hound hunts. The Duke did turn up some men he wanted trained, but none of them lasted long." He laughed. "All right, we drag the duocorn carcass into this hut to work on. In spite of all Onglas's raving, none of them is going to get up nerve enough to push in to watch. Then—we take out the Colonel, only he'll be wrapped up in the skin. We put him in the cart. Down comes Scharn's officer to say there has been enough of such foolishness. I say we have to get the bait out and bury it before the hounds go wild. I tell

you, these men know nothing of the nature of the beasts. They are ready to believe anything one babbles about them. We take the cart back into the woods and I have a little show ready waiting to cover us out there."

"And what about m'lady here and Mattine?"

"They go out now, to lay low in my place. I make a big to-do later about needing help with the cart, and bring them along. That's the best I can offer, Colonel."

"It is clever, Haus. But I do not want m'lady and Mattine to run a risk."

Roane found her voice. "I run a greater staying here. I tell you, it will sicken me and I have no remedies which will help."

He looked at her, searching, but she knew she spoke the truth.

"They will have protection, m'lord. I am taking the she hound Surenose up to my house. She is near whelping and I always take such to snugger quarters. With her loose in the inner yard, no one is going to stick nose through the gate."

"A lot of things can go wrong," Sergeant Wuldon observed. "What if this Scharn does not speak up in time and Onglas makes you take the bait to the hounds?"

"I can spend a long time making it. I tell you he knows nothing about direhounds, and he is not one to come and see what goes on here. I will get the guards to protest, and, if necessary, he will find he cannot force a hunting party into the chase. Sure it is risky, but so is any game you are going to play to get the Colonel out. And I cannot promise better."

"He is right," Imfry said. "There is no way I am going

to get out of here without taking more risk than I care to think about. And this game sounds as if it does have possibilities."

# ✳ CHAPTER 15 ✳

**ROANE,** her hood once more well over her face, slouched along in the wake of a bobbing cart. She was no actress and now was the time when the slightest error might arouse the suspicions of those following them on this faintest of tracks away from the village and into the forest. At least Haus had been able to prolong his bait preparations until midafternoon, and it was close to evening when they had been ordered by Scharn, come to his senses enough to take charge, to do away with the carcass. She gave silent thanks that at least there had been no further message from Duke Reddick.

The cart creaked and bumped. She would hate to lie therein, wrapped in a bloody skin which already attracted a trail of insects, as Imfry had to do. The Sergeant and Mattine pulled the shaft of that crude transport. No duocorn could be brought near the smelly cargo. Which was why the rear guard went dismounted. And how Haus, who walked by her side, proposed to get rid of those guards she could not imagine.

Thus far his plan had worked, and Roane could not quarrel with anything which brought them into the clean air, farther and farther from Hitherhow. At least she had slept away some of that period she and Mattine had been in Haus's house, so she felt more alert. Though as long as she knew of that installation, the machines clicking away to regulate the lives of those who could not imagine they were so governed, she would be ill at ease.

Roane plodded along, trying to act the sullen role of one pressed into unwilling service. She hoped to be ready for Haus's move, or one from Imfry.

"You—Haus!" A voice rang out from the rear. "How far do you expect to travel before you bury that carrion? We are not going to tramp all over this forest—"

"Neither do I want to worry about the hounds taking to our trail and getting a taste for duocorn the first time they are uncoupled in chase," Haus replied. "I do not fancy having to explain something like dead mounts to the Duke."

She heard grumbling, but no open protests. A moment later Haus's shoulder brushed hers and he said harshly:

"Can you not even walk straight, boy? By the Arms of the Guardians, what help are you? Get up ahead there and lend a hand to pulling or we are going to be half the night going a quarter league!"

Roane pushed between the cart and encroaching brush and saplings, reaching the Sergeant, to lay hand to the shaft beside him.

"Not long now, m'lady," he whispered. "Be ready to jump to the right when I give the word."

Jump right—She glanced in that direction. There was a

tumbling pile of stones, a trail of them, as if a wall had once
stood there. But in that were frequent gaps which were
filled with rank grass and matted vines. Also there were
brush and trees. It was a gray day, without sun, and there
was a damp feeling of coming rain in the air. Jump right—
she ran her tongue over very dry lips.

The track they followed, if track it really was, took a
sharp angle left. And they had the cart half around the
bend when out of the brush fronting them arose a grunting
which could only be a direhound! The Sergeant shouted,
gave a swift jerk to the pull, and the cart trembled. Mattine
pushed as if in panic and the small transport began to tip
toward Roane.

"Now!"

Once more the direhound sounded. Behind men yelled
warnings while Haus bellowed confused orders. Roane
took the chance that Wuldon knew exactly what he was
doing. She leaped for the cover of the tumbled stones,
plunging on away from the track. As she went she heard
the crash of the cart hitting on its side.

"Run, you lack-witted fools!" That was Haus. "They
must have broken out the gate, are circling for a kill. Get
away or face them!"

Roane slammed against a tree, held to it, her heart
pounding. It could not be as the hound master said because
Wuldon had been expecting something. But this was her
chance to be free of the whole action.

She gave a sob, would have stumbled blindly on, when
she heard a crashing behind her. So she backed around,
the tree against her spine, half fearing to face death on
four feet. What came was the Sergeant supporting a

bloodstained, half-clothed man—Imfry! He must have been able to claw out of his reeking cover as soon as the cart overturned.

"Come on!" The Sergeant and his superior officer passed, Roane followed.

Though she could see no guide through this wilderness, the men before her went with as much confidence as if they were following one of those off-world homing devices. But they had not gone too far before Mattine came into view also. He was laughing.

"That Haus! He has stampeded the whole squad! They are hearing twice as many hound calls as he sends, and they are racing back to the keep, doubtless to report we have all been eaten alive. M'lord, he is better than half a regiment by himself."

"He had better be! Were Reddick to suspect him—"

"Would not do the Duke any good. With those pets of his Haus has a better bodyguard than any king." Mattine lost none of his cheer.

"They are mortal; a few well-placed bullets—I hope he has a tight tale for Reddick when he comes."

"You think the Duke will come, sir?" asked the Sergeant.

"I do not flatter myself, Wuldon, that I am any great prize for myself alone. As you suggested, he will undoubtedly have me horned as an outlaw. After that"— Imfry shrugged—"I shall be meat for the shooting with a reward to top the fun of the chase. But Reddick knows that as long as I live I shall not rest until I know what spell he has set on the Queen!" There was such cold determination in that, Roane shivered.

"He had her under mind-globe back there in the cave—but this goes deeper than anything Shambry can devise, holds longer and tighter. You heard the proclamation, the earlier one, that she is going to wed Reddick. It will follow that she will raise him to Prince Consort, and then—how long will it be before he rules Reveny? If she wakes from that spell with his creatures around her, what chance will she have? I tell you, she is as much a prisoner now as I was at Hitherhow. Though she may not yet realize it."

"Sir." Mattine was serious now. "I always heard it told that mind-globe spells cannot make anyone do what is against his inner nature."

"I will not believe," Imfry said slowly, looking at Mattine, a set, hard line to his jaw, his eyes cold, "that the Princess—the Queen—would have signed my death warrant of her own free will. Nor can anyone who knows her well. Ask you the Lady Roane. She had been much with her."

They looked to her now. And she gave them the truth. "She is under a spell."

Mattine and the Sergeant looked disturbed, but Imfry nodded, and some of that hardness left his face.

"You see? The Queen needs our aid. Can we deny her aught we can do?"

"Sir, we can raise no army. If we hide out in the Reserve and send the word about we can muster men, yes, that much I grant you. But an army large enough to go up against those Reddick can easily put in the field, no. And if the Soothspeaker Shambry is so powerful that he can hold the Queen in thrall against her nature, then it may be possible he can do likewise with even us, if he can find

a way. Sir—if you will only go over the border—to Leichstan or—"

"And would any neighbor give me refuge? The Queen went to Leichstan and was met by treachery. Could we hope to fare better? We cannot let Reddick drive us out now or there will be no return at all."

"Well, we need not set off today, sir. We had better think about saving our hides or Reddick will have them skinned off our aching backs," returned the Sergeant.

"Right you are," Imfry answered. "This lay-up Haus told you of, is it far?"

"Far enough to keep us moving well for a while, sir. You feeling it now?" Mattine cut in.

"Less than I thought that I would, thanks to the Lady Roane and those miracles she carries in her jars and tubes. And you, m'lady, do you go with us now?"

He was giving her a choice. But as he spoke she discovered she had already made it—long ago. He wanted an answer to the change in Ludorica, she was sure she had it. Facing Reddick bravely would do no good, not so long as those installations kept clicking away. They would control all—maybe they did even now. And the Service would not move in time to aid, even if Uncle Offlas managed to bring down the LB and return to the mother ship out in orbit.

"Yes," Roane answered simply.

If she expected any encouraging comment from him, she did not get it. Mattine fell into step with her.

"It is still a far piece, m'lady. But at least we can lay up there snug and tight, and watch our back trail without worry. It is one of the old war camps of the Karoff

rebellion. The enemy did not take it by storm when it fell, but by treachery. Since we have no traitors we do not have to fear that, now do we?"

Moonrise came, had the moon been able to penetrate thoroughly the drifting clouds, before they reached their destination. Roane never discovered what guides the Sergeant and Mattine used to bring them through the forest to a stony rise and up that by a very wandering and narrow way to a plateau.

There were walls here, crumbling. But, while they had not been built with mortar, they were still intact enough to afford shelter. And that Roane was glad to have. She was breathing hard as she sank down in a corner niche and sat, her feet stretched out before her. They had not pressed on as hard during that journey as she had imagined they might, probably because her companions had wanted to spare Imfry. But the Colonel had regained some of his old endurance, for which she thanked her medical supplies. His shoulder seemed to give him much less trouble. Even during their last climb he had not favored it much.

Where they were in reference to the off-world camp or the hidden installation, Roane did not know, but that Imfry might be able to find his way to the latter she hoped. The question remained as to whether he would do it if he knew of the danger Uncle Offlas had prophesied. On the other hand, she was as sure as if she had definite knowledge that there was no hope of freeing Ludorica except via the defeat of the machines.

"Now, sir." Wuldon had made a circuit of the ancient fortifications, returned to stand before his officer as if on duty and making a formal report. "We got you here safe

and sound. Our boys who laid that false trail should have been free long ago and ought now to be waiting at the Twisted Sword. We will all breathe easier when we get together. So, with your permission, I will jog on to pick them up. And Mattine—he has to reach Pin Crossing to see about fresh mounts—"

"Sounds as if you have made a lot of plans, Wuldon." Was there a hint of surprise in Imfry's voice?

"Best we could, sir. Not knowing that you would be more yourself—as you are. If you want to change them."

"Why? I can be sure that they are the best under the circumstances. Good luck—Guardian's Fortune—to you both."

"We will whistle the old call, sir, when we come back. There is a good deadfall over the high path in, one of those traps we used to set in the Nimp times. Pull the lock rock and it will close off the path—take a full company a day to clear it. Guardian's Fortune to you, too, sir, and to m'lady!"

He gave a salute which Mattine echoed, and they were gone, lost in shadows before Roane could blink. In this dark she could only be sure she still had a companion when he moved. Fingers touched her arm, slid down until they closed, warm, alive about her wrist, where her own hand lay limp on her knee.

"Why did you come?"

Enmeshed as she was in a tangle of thoughts she was too tired to bring into order, she answered with the real truth:

"Because of the dream—"

"Dream?"

Somehow it was easier to talk when there was only that

quiet question out of the dark, that loose clasp about her wrist. And there was relief in speech, as if she were ridding herself of a long-carried burden. Whether he would believe her or not, Roane did not at that moment care. It was enough to put it all into words.

She began with the dream, trying to make it live for him as it had for her, bringing every detail to mind—the room, the dishes on the table, Ludorica's ceremonial entrance behind the usher, her ladies-in-waiting, the presence of Reddick—

"I could not hear what they said, I only saw their lips move. It was like watching a defective tri-dee in which the sound track had been cut away. But it was alive—it was!" She lost herself in remembering. There was a need to make him understand how she had seen it all. "I have dreamed before, who does not? But never like this."

"A true sending." His words reached her out of the dark. Now she realized also that his grasp on her wrist had tightened until it hurt by its pressure, and she pulled, trying to free herself.

"A sending?" She made of that a question.

"You have far sight—"

"No," she objected. "I was tested—I have no esper power. It was a dream."

"Of the small chamber in Urkermark High Keep, of the Queen wearing Court mourning, of the signing of the warrant which may mean my death. When were you last in Urkermark High Keep, Lady Roane?"

"I was never there."

"The time has come"—his words were even, measured—"for us to speak frankly. If truth does not lie

between us now, it never will—and we must have truth! Do you understand that?"

The last choice of all. And she saw in the dark, as well as if she did indeed face it, that row of clicking machines, each with its crown, its slaves. And she saw the Ludorica she did not know, the stranger she feared, who held a crown in her hands.

"Who are you," he continued, "or what?"

Roane drew a deep breath. "I am—a woman," she said, answering his last question first. "Also I am Roane Hume. But I am not of this world—"

Having taken the plunge, she dared not think, but struck out into the current of truth, which not only might sweep her away but could end everything she had been schooled to believe in.

She told him of the Service, of why they had come to Clio, of her chance meeting with the Princess, of the installation, and of what that meant to him and his people. When she had done she was drained, emptied, glad of that warm encirclement of her wrist which linked her to a living world.

"This is a tale beyond belief," he began and she tried to jerk away from his hold, chilled—frightened that he could not believe. Immediately his hold on her tightened. "Yet," he continued, "I know that it is true. You say you have no ability to foresee. Perhaps by the reckoning of your people, you do not. But my own House—we have that talent in part. We have also a strange tradition which has been a closely guarded secret for generations.

"It is one I would not ordinarily speak of to any, be he even close brother-kin, unless he knew it by right of birth.

But because it is akin to what you have told me, I will speak of it now. The Guardians—we worship them after a fashion, and to most they are supernatural beings. But in my House there is a tale that he who founded our line was a direct servant of Guardians—who were *not* immortals as all believe, but had flesh and substance. And he did certain tasks for them in that far beginning which were connected with the ordering of Reveny life.

"When men awoke here at the Guardians' bidding and set about living, my forefather retained hazy memories of another time and place. These he kept to himself, speaking of them only to his son, and so it passed through my line. We have in addition other things. There have been soothspeakers of our name. That is how I am sure that the Queen was not what she seemed when she found the Crown and ordered my death.

"Now you make plain she was not being moved by the control of any mind-globe, but that she, the Duke, all of us, are game pieces moved about to fulfill some plan made by men long dead, ones who had no right to set our forefathers into such patterns. But you fear that to destroy these controls would be to destroy us also."

"My uncle feared that. He wants to bring in the experts of the Service. They would study the installation, make sure—if they came at all."

"*If* they came at all!" That was bitter. "Then they would have chosen, had you not broken *their* pattern, to let us live forever under the domination of chattering metal things! What right have they to allow such slavery? Or are they themselves slaves to other patterns? Is it so from star to star, with no one really free?"

He was now echoing one of her own recent thoughts.

"And these men of your Service, *if* they come, would take time, maybe years, to study before they moved. Is that not so?"

"Yes."

"And all that while we would continue to be secretly ruled. Ludorica, who is good, would do evil. Reddick, who wishes to bring war and worse upon Reveny, who would slay even the Queen if by her death he could take the Crown, would continue in power. I—I shall do what I can against him. But if these machines will otherwise, I am defeated before I begin!"

"The installation can be destroyed."

"There was Arothner, which lost its crown—"

"The Princess told me that story," Roane admitted.

"Then you know what chanced there. To risk that—for Reveny—for all the world!"

"The result may not be the same. A lost crown could differ in effect from a silenced machine."

"But the risk—it is too great!"

"The choice is yours." She had done what she could. If he said now that Clio must remain in slavery, let it be so.

She turned her wrist again and this time his grasp loosened and fell away. With its going she felt as alone as if he had arisen and walked from her. There was no road back. She was locked in a prison she had built herself stone by stone. Yet she was unable to regret what lay behind.

Roane settled her shoulders against the harsh stone of the wall, raised her knees, and folded her arms across them as a pillow for her head. That emptiness she had earlier welcomed now became a billowing fog of fatigue. She did

not care if morning, light, or the need to take up the
burden of living ever came again.

But tired as she was, sleep did not come. Instead her
thoughts twisted and turned as an insomniac might twist
and turn upon a bed during a wakeful night. She walked
again on other worlds, relived this small fragment of the
past and that. It seemed to her that she had always been
part of a set pattern, also, imposed upon her by Uncle
Offlas, by the life he introduced her to. Was it true as Nelis
had said, that even from star to star there was no freedom?
Yet the rules of the Service called for no interference, no
meddling even for good in the destiny of a troubled world.

Pattern upon pattern, tie and bond upon tie and bond,
no freedom. Roane stirred and then once more that hand
out of the dark reached her, slipping across her shoulders
to draw her to rest close to the warmth, the safe anchorage
of another body, human, alive, no longer exiled alone in
the dark.

"What is it, Roane? Why do you cry?" His voice was a
breath warm against her cheek. And she knew then that
tears did wet her face and that she wept as she could not
ever remember having done since she was a small and
lonesome child.

"I think it is because I am alone." She tried to put that
desolation into words.

"But that you are not! Is it because you come from the
stars and here find no kin? Would you return to your
people? I promise I shall take you to them—"

"They will not want me now."

"Do not think that others believe in that fashion." The
grasp about her shoulders was very comforting. "I have

been wondering—why was it, do you think, that you saw the Queen and Reddick in this dream? You were not reaching as a Soothspeaker does to read some peril or fact needful to your life. Yet you saw that which brought you to Hitherhow, to aid in my escape. And such visions are not ordinary. From whence came this one?"

Perhaps he was kindly trying to make her think of something else. But there was certainly a strangeness to that dream.

"I do not know. But I am sure I have no esper powers. My people understand these things, they checked me. It was important that they make sure."

"Yet you have also said that you have done things on this world which were counter to all your training, to what you were taught was lawful. And I do not believe that you are one who has ever deliberately chosen to break rules and flout authority before. Is that not so?"

"I do not know why, but when I first saw the Princess, in that tower, I had to help her. Uncle Offlas said you were all conditioned. Perhaps when I had left the safeguards of our camp that also influenced me."

"Yet you could see these machines. The Princess could not. So if there was conditioning, for you it was not complete."

"What difference does it make now? I broke the Service rules, I—perhaps it was I who started the whole tangle. The Princess would not have known of the Crown had she not gone to the cave. And if she had not found the Crown—"

"Roane, Roane, do not take on yourself guilt for a whole country!"

Fingers touched her cheek gently, exploring, though that arm was still a barrier between her and dark loneliness.

"You are crying once more! I tell you, this is not of your doing! You have brought good, not evil. Had you not taken the Princess from Reddick's men then, you might have left her to her death. And had you not come to Hitherhow—I might have died, too, and been a long time in doing it."

"There was the Sergeant, Mattine, the others—"

"Who could well have thrown *their* lives away and to no avail. Nor would we ever have known of these machines. For had you not taken the Princess there for shelter, would you ever have found them?"

"Perhaps."

"And perhaps not. Nor without the knowledge you have gained from us would you have known what they were. No—there is a meaning to be read in all you have done, if we can see it."

"I do not understand."

"Neither do I. I can only sense it is there, a reason to move you to aid the Princess, and later to do all else. You say that those we know as the Guardians are long dead, have been judged evil by those beyond the stars. They used men as tools and it did not last. Now your people fear to upset what they have done. But—why have you told this story to the one man in Reveny who could believe it, because his far-off ancestor escaped the full blight sent on Clio?"

"Chance—fortune—I do not know—"

"Neither do I. Save that it is making me think. Roane, can you find this cave again?"

"Do you mean you wish to free the Crown?"

"I do not know. I think that I shall not be sure until I stand there and know what such slavery means. But that I must do; I know it now. Can you take me there?"

"If we dare go back. It lies near Hitherhow."

"Dare we not now?" he countered.

"The LB may have come. If not, they—Uncle Offlas, Sandar—they will try to keep us away and they have weapons—"

"Did you not use one such on me? Yes, I have tasted the power of those strange arms of yours. But that we must chance also. And I think time is fast running out."

"You mean we go now? Before the Sergeant and Mattine return?"

"I think for what we may have to do we should have as little company as possible. But let us wait for dawn before we take the trail. Sleep if you can, Roane."

He did not release her, so that Roane's head slipped down to rest against him as indeed she found now she could sleep.

# ✳ CHAPTER 16 ✳

**ROANE AWOKE** as if summoned by some imperative call, though there was silence as she roused. The light of dawn lay outside their small corner of refuge. Imfry's arm was still about her. They had huddled together in the night. Turning her head with care, she saw he still slept, or at least his eyes were closed.

There was a stubble of dark beard on his jaw, yet in sleep he looked much younger, unguarded, that rigidity of feature which usually masked him gone. There were lines perhaps born of pain, or the burden of decisions, but now they were faint. Studying him so, Roane thought of the one part of her dream she had not told him—the face she had seen at its ending.

For that had not been Ludorica's, nor Reddick's, and yet it had stung her into action.

Had Nelis been right in his theory that some force had moved her to play the part she had since she had landed on Clio? Superstition, common on a backward world, Uncle Offlas would term that, note it as a native trait on his tapes put aside for the anthropologists to study.

Many worlds had their strong faiths in powers greater than human, clung to beliefs in purposes beyond the comprehension of man. She had watched worshipers in temples, been moved once or twice by ceremonies which seemed to give those who took part an inner security and peace. But there were many gods, goddesses, nameless spirits and powers—unless each and every one was a small splinter of something greater toward which her species yearned and groped blindly. A something they must *have* to believe in, or be vanquished.

All her training balanced against the thought that she was moved now by any such influence! But if she could so think—Roane envied those with the faith, even those who looked upon Guardians here as beings to whom they could appeal in times of stress.

If they destroyed the installation would they in a way also be destroying the spirit which was Clio? What might enter in thereafter to fill the void?

Roane shook her head—fancies. She had been too often in the past ordered to restrain such imaginings. And if she had ever betrayed such irresponsible speculation before the Service she might even have been considered a suitable candidate for mental reschooling.

She shuddered at that thought, gazed out over the tumbled walls of the fort. There was already a tinge of red-gold in the sky—sunrise.

"Nelis—" She spoke his name softly, moved out of the hold he had kept on her during the dark hours, though his arm tightened even as she put it aside. Then his eyes opened, squinted in the light.

"Dawn," Roane told him, thinking he might still be in the lingering backwash of a dream.

"Dawn—" he repeated as if the word had little meaning. Then the lines of his face tightened once more, alert intelligence and awareness flooded back. He straightened up with a grunt, as if stiff and sore, and stretched.

"Your medicines do well by one." He flexed his arms again and then gently touched the plasta-skin covering over his wound before he picked up the jacket the Sergeant had left behind. "Have you any more of that strange food?"

"Enough." She knelt to open her bag. The night lenses—how had she come to forget that she had those? They could have started last night with their aid. And there was the tool—she could put the last charge in that now.

"Another of your strange weapons?"

"Not quite so. But it was what freed you from that cage. It can be used as a cutter or a digger—breaking stone, melting metal. But I have not the proper energy charges for it, only one of these left, and they are meant to power a beamer." She screwed the butt back on and laid it to one side. He picked it up.

"This is not what you used on me in the forest—"

"No. That was taken from me."

"But that is your best weapon?"

"It merely stuns. There are others more forceful, but we are forbidden to carry them on sealed worlds. There is a blaster which slays with fire, other devices. But those are employed only in the last resort."

He held the projectile thrower he termed a "gun" in one hand, the tool in the other, comparing them. "Your

people work in metal in a way we cannot begin to equal. Just as we ride duocorns, you visit stars. What is it like to stride from world to world, m'lady?"

"It is like being always before a constantly changing picture. Sometimes it is good, sometimes"—she remembered and shivered—"it can be very bad."

"As this world has been for you?"

"No! That is not so! Here—" She had found the ration tubes, twisted the cap of the first and handed it to him, taking up another for herself, using all, as they needed the strength. The warm semiliquid did not seem to taste as it always had, but even flatter, less appetizing.

She finished it quickly, squeezed the tube flat, put it under a stone before she reclosed her pack. The sky was now afire with sunrise. Had Imfry changed his mind during the night, or did he still want to go to the installation? She glanced up to where he stood, his head half turned from her, looking toward the blue-shadowed roll of the heights beyond.

"We head west." He pointed. "There are Thunderbolt and Lhang's Beard—"

So he was picking out landmarks. But once they were down in the forest cover, how could those guide them? She asked as much.

"We are not so helpless as you would believe, m'lady." He pressed the wide buckle on his belt, showed her a small dial within. "This is a device which works as effectively for path finding for us as your off-world trappings do for you. Now—" He surveyed the ground closely, knelt at a smooth stretch of earth, and there began to set up a tight circle of bits of rock, the center left bare while he flattened and

smoothed it. With his fingertip he gouged a series of lines and dashes there, digging them in as deeply as he could.

"For Wuldon and the others," he told her. "This will let them know the direction in which we have gone and that we appoint a meeting place for later."

The warmth of the sun was on the rocks as they started on the down trail. Roane, looking about her, and then hastily averting her eyes from anything but the path, thought it had been well she had come up in the dark. It would have been difficult for her to make that climb otherwise. The zigzag of the trail brought them to the bottom, where Imfry consulted his belt disk and struck out briskly.

There was no straight trail, of course. They detoured, lost time, came back. But if any hunt for them was in progress, it had not spread so far. There were birds and once or twice short glimpses of animals, but no sign men had ever walked this way.

They traveled in silence for the most part, and Imfry moved with an energy which suggested his wound no longer gave him any trouble. Roane refused to think of what lay ahead. It was enough to savor this one day which lay as a safe haven between the past and the future. She made no complaint at the steady pace her companion set, though now and again he did pause, suggest they rest. It was then he talked, though nothing of what they did, or had done, or would do—almost as if to speak of what concerned them most was to summon ill fortune.

Rather he painted for her the Reveny, the Clio, that he knew. And Roane listened as to a tale told in the Markets of Thoth, where, as all know, the most skillful of story

spinners compete. He spread before her his homestead of Imfry-Manholm, which lay in mountain country where they raised the long-fleeced corbs, and grew, on small terraces bitten out of the steep slopes, vines which bore those berries from which the sharp-tanged winter wines were pressed.

"My brother is lord there, being the younger son. Though his mother ruled in his name during his childhood—she being my father's second lady. He came to take liege oath at Urkermark last year. He is a good lad, steady. And he is already ring-promised to the daughter of Hormford Stead across the valley."

Imfry dug his boot heel into the soft earth as they sat side by side on the moss-cushioned trunk of a fallen tree.

"The younger son inherits? On most worlds it is the eldest."

"But this is the sensible way. A man's older sons are usually well grown, settled in lives of their own, at his death hour. But the youngest may still be unable to make his way in the world. Therefore it is only just that he be so provided for. I was a court fosterling, because of my mother—" He paused for a long moment and stared down at the hole he was excavating. "My father had good reason to believe my rise in the world would be favored. My sister was ringed young to the son of his best friend—Ward Marshal Ereck. But what of your life, m'lady?"

"There is little to tell. I am without parents, raised in a Service créche where my Uncle sought me out. I tested well for memory work and in certain learning arts, so he knew I could be a useful member of a team. So has it been."

"And you are perhaps ringed to this cousin of yours?"

"Sandar?" For a moment the speaking of his name evoked a sharp picture of him in her mind. Perhaps once, in the very beginning, she had nursed a few small colorless dreams. But those had been quickly quenched by working with Sandar—with whom her role had been that of a kind of dull-witted servant—and Roane found the memory of them embarrassing now.

"Certainly not Sandar!" she repeated firmly.

"But some other—on one of your star worlds?" he persisted.

"There is no time in the Service, or at least as Uncle Offlas plans one's life, for such things. He does not even think of me as a woman. I am another pair of hands, often clumsy ones, to his mind. He takes me with him because, as I am his kin, he is allowed to use me on sealed worlds, where a stranger might cause trouble." Suddenly Roane laughed. "But this time he was not fortunate—I have done just as he has always feared someone would do. And do you know, Nelis—I think—I hope—I no longer care!"

For that was true! Last night when she had told him her story a burden *had* rolled away. Uncle Offlas—she did not *have* to be his puppet. Let him blacken her to the Service—she had a world before her here. They could not hunt her down, or at least she thought they would not dare.

"Strange ways—" Imfry's comment did not seem to be exactly an apt answer, but he did not enlarge upon it, only got to his feet as a signal to push on.

That odd lightheartedness with which she had begun this march, that feeling of being apart from the past and the future, being in the safe present, faded as they went.

She had thought, for a few moments, that she did not have to fear Uncle Offlas. Perhaps she did not, if she kept away from where he was to be found. But she was heading right back there. Why?

"Please." She slipped around a bush to match pace with Imfry. "We must take care. You cannot guess what they can do. If the LB has come there will be more—"

"But you have said that the crown machine is the control—that we must destroy it. Was that not what you urged on me?"

"Yes. But I forgot—" To her vast surprise and self-disgust, she felt tears rising again. What *was* the matter with her? She had never done this in her life. She was no longer herself. Desperately she fought for control. "Yes. I am sorry—it is the only thing to be done." She fell behind, intent on restraining her troubling emotions. "I only urge caution. They have instruments which can detect us at a distance."

He shrugged. "We can only do our best and hope for the continuing favor of fortune. We are"—he consulted his guide disk—"not too far from the cave. And we shall approach it from the side where Reddick's men broke in."

Now she was able to watch a master woodsman at work. It seemed to Roane he melted into the brush, able to become invisible at will, while she sweated over her own efforts, which now appeared infinitely clumsy, to follow his example. But she applauded the caution he brought to the advance. If there were no repellers or detects—

They looked out on a slope of raw earth eroded by rain, flanking the hole Reddick's men had made. Imfry spoke so

low Roane had almost to read the words from his lips as he shaped them: "Is there any warning set here?"

"I do not think so. Unless they have a new one. I burned out the repeller."

His body was as tense as a runner's waiting at the mark. "Get in, as quick as you can!" And he was off in a dash to cover the stretch of open ground, disappear between mounds of earth and rock. Roane followed, to stand where Ludorica had held the crown in her hands.

"Wait!" She held up her hand in swift warning. From her former experience with the distort Roane knew she could feel that were it present. As Imfry's skill had been their guide in the woods, maybe she could serve equally well here.

Roane slipped into the rough passage, heard him move in her wake. So far, there was no trace of the protective measures she feared. But she could hear, every time she paused to listen, the faint pulsations of the installation.

They came to the smoothed portion of corridor. There was a faint glow from the machine chamber. Roane touched his arm, put her lips close to his ear.

"What do you see—right there?" She indicated the faint light.

"Nothing."

"You hear?" she persisted.

"Nothing. It may be that I cannot. The Princess could not, you said."

If that were true—had she failed before they had begun? Would he take on faith what she might describe to him? She slipped her hand down to lace his fingers with hers.

"Come!" Hand in hand, linked as children on their way

to some day of play, they crept along, edging warily toward the open panel.

Sandar? Uncle Offlas? If they were still within—Roane had no way of making sure. However, if she and Imfry were not spotted at the door, then there were places of concealment inside. Even the crowned pillars were tall enough to provide temporary cover.

At the panel Roane loosed her hold, pushed a step across the threshold. The mutter of noise, those lights which seemed so bright since she had been moving in the dark. But she could see no one there.

"Now!"

Roane could not see the expression on his face, but he caught her hand, held it in bruising pressure.

"You—went—into—the—wall!" He spaced his words as if he were struggling for some control.

"Through an opening. Close your eyes, do not try to see—but come—" Roane had a sudden inspiration. Perhaps conditioning existed only at the panel, and once inside, he could see.

She led and he followed. "Raise your feet, there is a step barrier—"

His eyes were closed, his hand out as if to feel the wall his confused senses said was there. Then she caught his fingers, drew him on until he was in.

"Look!"

He opened his eyes. A spasm crossed his face. "Dark— blind dark!"

"Hush!" Roane searched for any stir among the pillars. But it would seem that their luck held. The chamber appeared empty.

"It is all dark." He had himself under tight control again. "I see nothing—"

"Close your eyes once more." If he could be more sure of touch than sight—

Roane drew him to the first of the pillars.

"There is a column here." She made the description as simple as she could. "It has a wide plate set in the surface facing you. Around that are rows of lights which flash on and off constantly in patterns of color. At the top is a small crown about the size of your fist. It is in the form of—I think you might best term them flames—and these are brilliantly red, glowing as if actually afire—"

"The Flame Crown of Leichstan!" he cried.

"Now—give me your hands." She had to move very close to do this, press against his back, reach around his waist to direct his fingers to the surface of the map and the lights, making him trace across and around.

"Do you feel?" She waited anxiously for the answer on which so much depended.

"Yes! These then are the lights? And the crown?"

"It is too far above to be touched."

"And where is the crown of Reveny?" he demanded eagerly.

"Here—" She led him along to stand before the proper pillar and described it in patient detail.

"Tell me now of the others!"

Roane did, guiding him to each in turn, though he only touched a pillar now and then to reassure himself they were there. At last she came to the dead one, and since it had no light of its own she trained the beamer on it.

The diadem of fluted shells had turned an unpleasant green color which hinted of decay.

"The crown of Arothner in truth," he admitted. "You have marked each nation that I know—Are these all?"

"Yes."

"And *these* you believe can govern our thoughts, raise a kingdom high, smash it low—"

"We think so." Again after some space of time she allied herself with the Service. "Though the records of the Psychocrat hierarchy were largely destroyed in the blasting of their command station, some pieces of information have been fitted together. We ourselves have extensions of computers which are akin to these in general formation. There must be a broadcast linkage between pillar and crown."

"Which explains much," he said as if to himself. "There have been puzzles a many in the past—why some kings seemed to reverse themselves. Roane"—Imfry swung around, his eyes open, searching for her though she stood there directly before him—"you are very right. This is evil, the blackest kind of evil! And it is better to face chaos than such slavery. I have seen it work with the Queen before my eyes. She became someone else when she held the crown. The person—the *thing* this wanted her to be! There must be an end!"

His voice rose but that did not distract Roane's own warning system. A distort! Somewhere within these burrows a distort had begun to broadcast.

"Quick!" She pulled at him, forcing him around the edge of the pillar which stood farthest from the door. The sensation was growing stronger.

"There is something—I feel the need to get away," he said.

"I know. That is a distort, a protective device. If they set it here—" Perhaps she could break out, as she had before. But Roane seriously doubted Imfry could.

Movement at the panel—Sandar! He slipped through with supple agility, took cover in the dark behind the pillars. So he must suspect their presence. Roane did not doubt he was armed with a stunner. He need only use that, spray at will, to render them helpless. Unless he was afraid of unguarded use of any ray around these pillars.

She pressed Imfry's arm in warning, felt him tense. Had his sight been equal to hers, they might have chanced skulking behind this row of pillars, opposite to those behind which Sandar had gone to ground. But if there was a distort at the door to bottle them in, even reaching it would do no good. For the present Roane could think of nothing but to remain in silent hiding.

Imfry had his "gun," she the tool, but neither was any defense against a stunner. Could the tool take out the distort, unseal the doorway as it had finished off the repeller? Perhaps, but Roane could not lead Imfry through hide-and-seek. And to leave him here would expose him, helpless, to Sandar.

That her cousin was on the move she had no doubt, though she could hear nothing but the click-click of the machines. And so engrossed was she in listening for some betraying sound that she was almost startled into betrayal when a voice called:

"Roane, I know you are here—" The words were in

Basic and the loud tone echoed so she could not be sure of the direction from which they came.

"The LB is coming in," Sandar continued. "When it lands you know what to expect—stass. If you surrender, you'll escape that. The more you give evidence of abnormal behavior the worse it is going to be for you when the inspectors arrive."

He was trying to frighten her, and Roane had to admit he was succeeding in part. If the landing party had been warned about her, they would have no mercy at all—the quickest method of dealing with her would be used. They need only bring in a stass projector and spray, and she and Imfry would be locked in a prison as tight as the cage of Hitherhow. Her eventual fate would be no less now than complete mental re-education. Which meant that she must—*they* must escape before that happened.

"You can't get out." Sandar's voice continued to echo. But she must wait no longer. And one chance was as good as another. This duel was between them. He would be concentrating on her, not Imfry.

She took the chance of a whisper—"Stay here!"

His hand brushed her shoulder with reassuring touch, letting her know he understood. Roane slipped to the next pillar. She was more used to the echoing now and she thought that Sandar was still close to the door.

If she could create a diversion—there was the ruined crown of Arothner. Roane stood out and took aim on that discolored crest with the tool.

A flash of brilliance and the crown was gone, melted into fiery droplets. At the same time she saw Sandar begin a leap from one pillar to the next. In turn she took a

desperate chance, swinging the tool around, aiming for the rock ahead of him. He cried out as footing disappeared, stumbled—But his stunner was coming up, he had not dropped it. Roane rayed again, trying to nick that. The edge of the beam did touch it, but the full force she released cut across the pillar which held Reveny's Ice Crown.

# ✳ CHAPTER 17 ✳

**ROANE** cowered as the world split apart in incandescent flame. Under her the rock floor was as unstable as bog scum. It swayed, buckled. The pillar which had taken part of the tool's energy was now a torch, its brilliance blinding. And from that leaped tentacles of yellow-white to touch its fellows, so they also blazed.

Imfry—he could not see and he was behind one of those pillars. He might be caught in the holocaust sweeping from one column to the next. Only now she was as blind as he—

Roane began to crawl, feeling her way. A torrent of sound deafened her, even as the blaze sealed her eyes. That mutter arose to a shriek, as if the pillars had life and were now in torment. There was such a wave of heat that she could hardly breathe.

She never knew how she reached Imfry. Only by fortune she ran against his body. She clawed her way up to her feet, using him as a support, and then forced him back with her until they crashed against the far wall of the chamber. From there, there was no escape, not with them

236

both as blind and far from the door as they were. They could only endure and hope that they would not be utterly consumed in the fury which raged, sending out sound and stifling heat.

Sandar! For the first time Roane thought of him and winced. Had he been in the direct line of that blast? If so— it was by her doing he was dead. She had not wanted that. She had not intended him any harm, only to knock out the stunner, give them a chance—

The roar was dying—or else her ears were becoming dulled. And the heat—surely that was not so great. Roane fought to see, moisture welling in her smarting eyes, trickling down her cheeks, where she impatiently smeared it away with one hand while with the other she kept her hold on Imfry. But all she could make out was a blood-scarlet curtain against the world.

There was no measurement of the time that devastation raged. It could have lasted an hour, a day—for it seemed endless. But at last Roane was certain that it was nearing the end, for the heat was gone now, the sound. They were trapped in a dark which was complete, where it was hard to breathe. Her gasps matched the ragged breaths of her companion.

"Get—out—"

Feel their way along the wall to the door? It was their only chance. She tugged at Imfry, but he was already on the move. Roane was not even sure of the direction, though she thought they must go left, their guide being one hand against the warm stone, while they linked fingers lest they lose contact. Roane's eyes continued to tear and smart. In her a new fear was born. Had her sight been blasted? Then,

for the first time, Imfry spoke: "Where—where are we?"
There was an uncertainty in his voice which she had never
heard before. He might have been one who had suddenly
awakened from a deep sleep in a strange place.

"In the installation. No—stay with me!" For the hand
she held fought against her, and he gave a sudden lunge as
if to break her grip, but she held tight and pushed him on.

"Who are you?" Again that dull wonder. "What—what
am I doing here? Where is this?"

"Hold—keep hold or we cannot get out!" She
summoned what small authority she had to impress that
need on him. "We cannot see. But if we keep to the wall we
can find the door."

"Who are you?" He no longer struggled, but he stopped
short so she bumped against him.

"I am Roane—Roane Hume—" What had happened to
him she did not know, and her fear grew. What if—But she
would not allow herself to think of that. "Come—you must
go on—we must get out!" Her control wavered and her
voice rose shrilly.

"Out—where?" He took another step forward as if her
urgency as well as her strong push had activated him.

"Out into the open! Please, we must go. Oh, please—
Move, you must, you must!"

At least she had him on his way again. And a moment
later, when he halted once again, she dared to beat one fist
again the shoulder touching hers.

"On!"

"There is no way. It is all solid."

For a second or two she was caught in panic and then a
small measure of reason triumphed. Of course, they must

have reached a corner! They had found the wall in which the door panel was set.

"Right—turn right—" Roane tugged and pulled at him. Perhaps "left," "right," had no meaning for him. Somehow she got him around, started in the new direction. And then—blessedly—cool air and an opening!

"Through here! Be careful, there is a step up—"

Somehow she got him through. The distort—But the blast must have rendered that harmless. They were safe in the passage, breathing untainted air. Roane leaned against the wall, drawing that reviving coolness into her laboring lungs.

The scarlet curtain before her eyes had faded. There was one thing she might try. She fumbled at the supply bag, brought out the night lenses, was almost afraid to look as she got them on.

Her eyes still smarted, burned, felt as if hot sand had been poured into their corners, under their lids. But—she could see! Though it was as if she peered through a haze. She drew close to Imfry, surveying him searchingly. He leaned against the wall as she had done, his hands raised to his head where he pawed feebly, as if trying to rub away something clinging to his face. But she could see no sign of burn or injury.

By so much they had escaped. *They* had—but what of Sandar? She looked back. There was no radiance within the chamber now—and dead silence. Dead—She hesitated. It could well be that the shock of what had happened here could be detected by the crew of the LB. Against them she and Imfry were defenseless. Yet she could not take even the first step toward safety.

Roane caught Imfry's hands, held them tight, trying to get his unfocused eyes to meet hers as she spoke. "You must stay here until I return." She accented each word with force.

"Stay—return—" he repeated. His mouth hung slackly open. She had never seen anything as empty as his face.

Horror fed her fear. She dared not think about his condition.

She fled back through the panel, making herself concentrate on Sandar. Dim as her sight was, the lenses were an aid to show what had been wrought here. Where the pillars had stood, there were now rent and blackened stubs, the crowns gone. Bitter fumes made her cough, rasped her throat.

Where had Sandar been? Without the crowns to guide her she could no longer be certain. Roane stumbled on, not sure she would even find evidence of his being, a sour bile rising in her mouth so that she had to keep swallowing to fight it. Then she saw the huddle of body and flung herself down beside it.

The horror of a fire death did not face her. But when she pulled at his shoulder, he rolled heavily limp. If he still lived she must get him out of this poisonous atmosphere. Somehow she was able to grasp him under the armpits, scramble backward, dragging him.

She bumped him across the panel barrier, letting him sprawl out into the corridor. Once more she rolled him over, her hand seeking a heartbeat. And she found that flutter just as the ground under her shook. Roane cried out—was the whole tunnel about to collapse around them?

Sandar coughed feebly, his head turned from side to side, his hands tried to dig into the rock as if he would lift himself. The tunnel—

Then Roane understood. Memories from the old life which might have been lived by another person reassured her. That had been the shock of deter rockets. The LB had landed.

A clear warning to move out. She arose. Her cousin was not dead, and he would soon be in the hands of his own people. If she and Imfry would escape, they must do it now. Nelis still stood against the wall, but now his arms were out, braced against the smoothed stone, his head strained forward as if he listened for what he could not see. As she moved, his face turned quickly to her.

"Who is there?" There was a new crispness in his demand. His voice was not dazed as it had been earlier.

"Roane. We must go now."

When she touched him his tense body was iron-hard. He raised a hand, struck out blindly, as if to ward her off.

"Go where?" he demanded.

"Out of here. And quickly. They will come seeking Sandar, to see the installation—they must not find us here."

"Who must not find us here?" He was impervious to her urging, stubborn in his rigidity of body.

"Uncle Offlas—those from the LB. We must go!"

"You mean that. You are afraid," he answered her. "I can feel your fear. Who are you?"

"Roane! I am Roane." She was close to tears. His voice was clearer, his face no longer had that slack, mindless look. But that he did not know her—there was something very wrong.

"Roane," he repeated. "And who am I?"

She was trembling. Her worst fear was being dragged into fact. "You are Colonel Nelis Imfry. Do you remember nothing—nothing at all?"

He made her no direct answer. Rather he seemed to wish to avoid that. "You are afraid for yourself?"

"For myself, yes," she answered honestly. "And for you. They will have good reason to wish us both under their hands. Please, we must go." She reached for him again, fearing that he might strike her, yet determined to start him in flight. But when his hand came this time, it was not balled into a fist, but open, stretched to welcome hers. She seized it eagerly.

"Come!"

Again she pulled him along the passage at as swift a pace as she could urge on him. Then at last they were able to grope out into the open. She had hoped that, once free of the installation room, Imfry would regain his sight. But he still depended upon her guidance even as they walked into the night.

The wind, untainted by corrosive stench, was sweet and cold around them. Roane saw him lift his face into it. Then he said without visible emotion:

"I can see now."

She gave a cry of relief, dropping his hand. Her own sight was dimmed. Even the lenses could not give things clear-cut outlines. That that impairment might be permanent she dared not consider.

"It is very strange," Imfry continued. He might have been thinking aloud rather than speaking to her. "There is a kind of emptiness—"

Then more forcibly, as if he were uttering some necessary formula to establish a fact:

"I am Nelis Imfry, of the House of Imfry-Manholm. I am a Colonel in the service of Her Majesty, Queen Ludorica of Reveny. I am me—Nelis Imfry!"

He was quiet then, his eyes seeking the stars where the wind-tossed branches alternately revealed and hid their glitter. A waning moon was rising, its sickle of silver cutting the cloudless sky.

"I remember, but it is as if those memories have dimmed. Yet I am Nelis Imfry, and the rest of it is true."

"Yes," she told him.

Her agreement appeared to startle him out of that trancelike state. He turned swiftly as if he feared to face an enemy. Gazing full at her he stood silently, as one might study a landmark which was altered from what he thought it had been.

"Tell me," he ordered, "what has chanced. While I was in darkness."

"When I tried to stop Sandar the energy ray lanced across one of the pillars. It set off a chain reaction—all the installation was destroyed—the crowns are gone." Would he understand?

His dark brows drew together in a frown. "Crowns? Pillars?"

"The installation left by the Psychocrats to rule this world—"

His mouth set firmly. "The *Queen* rules Reveny."

"Now she does," assented Roane, wondering if that were indeed the truth, or if the destruction of the crowns had pulled down upon Reveny the fate of Arothner.

"You speak of facts you believe in, but it is not clear to me. Make me understand!" He advanced as if he intended to shake it out of her.

She was afraid again. This haggard stranger was not Nelis Imfry. Was this what the destruction of the crowns meant? For there was as noticeable a change in him as there had been in Ludorica when she held the Ice Crown.

"It is a long story," she said helplessly.

"That does not matter. Tell it!"

So once more she went over the familiar tale. Only this time she had no relief in the telling, only a cold feeling born not of the chill wind about them, but rather of a great loneliness.

He listened intently, though little change of expression was apparent on his lean face. He might have been some judge presiding over a trial where she was the accused.

Imfry did not interrupt her with any questions, but heard her through to that end which was the unplanned destruction of the installation. And when she was done Roane wavered. The pain in her eyes was worse, spreading back into her head, so that she was more aware of that than her surroundings.

"You understand the danger if those of the Service find us. They must not!" She put all the energy she had left into that last warning. Her eyes—her head—she could not stand it any longer. She remembered swaying, the sound of a cry, and then pain, a great sea of fire, engulfed her.

Coolness, blessed coolness—dark and cool. To hide in this dark, cool place and never venture forth again. Sensation rather than thought. Cool and wet—the fire

going. She did not want to move, yet she was moving. Roane tried to protest, discovered she had not the energy to form words. She heard dimly a moaning sound.

"Roane—" A ripple through the cool dark. No—let her alone—just let her alone!

"Roane!"

Dimly she knew that for a summons. She would not answer. Let her be! She was moving, though not on her own two feet. And the jar set her head hurting, so she made a great effort and thought she begged to be let alone. But if they heard her they did not heed. She escaped once again into the cool dark.

But the second time she was drawn out of that refuge she could not slip back. She lay on a surface which was not soft, though there was that under her which cushioned it a little. Her face was wet, as if she had been out in a storm, but that came from a soaked cloth laid across her forehead and eyes. At least she lay still, no moving racking her body.

". . . tall as a keep, I swear to you, sir. Nothing like it I have ever seen. And I counted five men come out of it. They went in and out by ladder, taking stuff back in. But a couple more went into that cave. Seeing that thing, you have to believe the whole story. But men traveling to the *stars?* You have to have proof of a tale such as that. And with one feeling like his head was empty—well, I could say this was a dream—or some Soothspeaker trick. Are you sure, sir, it is not? I mean, if Shambry was strong enough to hold the Queen in thrall that way, maybe he could be working on us now—even at a distance."

"A man cannot make you see what he does not know exists. That star ship has no match here."

"True enough. But this queer feeling in one's head—though that is wearing off now, sir. But I tell you it was really bad when it first hit. Mattine ran around in a circle for a space, actually yelling he was a Nimp scout or some such nonsense. At least I thought I heard him say that. Hunlow had to lay him out when he drew steel. And the rest of us, we did not even know our own names for a while. If it was like that for us here, just think of what might have happened in a town with all the people going dazed or crazy. Some seem to take longer to get over it. Fleech did. We had to lug him along for quite a march and tell him over and over who he was and where we were. Nasty experience. Worse than facing a Nimp charge."

Wuldon. Roane's sluggish mind matched a name to that voice. Who else was with him? They—or Wuldon—must have seen the LB. But what if its crew was now hunting them? She must warn—

It required such an effort to force her hand up to her face, to tug at the fold of wet cloth blindfolding her.

"Nelis—" Hers was a ghost voice, a thread of whisper.

But it brought quick response. "Roane!" And her hand was stayed in its effort to sweep aside the cloth, put down to lie once more at her side. So he knew—understood again?

"Let that be for a while yet. Your eyes are badly inflamed. Do you know who I am?"

Did he think *she* was the one who had been out of her head? "Nelis Imfry," she answered with a spurt of indignation. "And Wuldon is here, too. But—" She remembered that other urgency. "Nelis—the ship—they must not find us!"

"I assure you they shall not. We have a range of hills between us, and scouts out. I have all the respect for their powers you wish me to show. We take no chances. And at the first sign of any hunt we shall be on the trail again. Now"—a strong arm was slipped under her head, she was raised a little—"drink this!"

Cool metal against her lips. She sipped and then choked and coughed, for the liquid had a spicy warmth.

"No—" She found his hold was such she could not avoid what he offered. "More—it is what you need now."

After the first mouthful or two she discovered it was not bad. So she obediently drank until the cup was taken away.

"My bag—the medicines—"

"Here, m'lady!" That was Wuldon.

"Look for a white tube." With the spicy drink downed, Roane was regaining both strength and the ability to think for herself again. "It holds a green liquid—drops for the eyes."

"Got it!" Then Imfry added, "How many?"

"Two each—for now."

He settled her back on the thin bedding pad and the wet cloth was pulled away. Light dazzled and hurt, but she forced herself to lie still as the moisture dripped in. That burned, but with none of the pain she had known earlier. She held her lids tightly closed. If there would be any relief it would come quickly.

Slowly she counted to a hundred, but not aloud, hearing small sounds as if they were repacking her bag. Then she opened her eyes. The light hurt, but she could see—and more clearly than she had since the chain reaction.

Nelis, the stubble beard longer and darker, a tousled

lock of hair sticking to his forehead as if plastered there—the Sergeant at an angle.

"I can see," Roane said, more to assure herself then to inform them. "Let me look—please, let me look." For suddenly she must reassure herself of this recovery.

Once more Nelis raised her before she could struggle up on her own. They were in a clearing and she thought it must be midmorning. Men moved or sat some distance away. Behind them a rope was strung between two trees, a tie place for the reins of saddled duocorns, who stamped or wrinkled their hides to drive off insects.

Some of the men were in uniform. Others wore civilian clothes or the green of foresters. Their small band of fugitives had doubled many times.

"Could you eat, m'lady? We have nothing but field rations—or there is one of those tubes of your own food left."

"Get that," Nelis ordered and the Sergeant moved out of her line of sight.

"How are your eyes?"

"I can see!" And she knew by her very joy how deep-reaching had been her fear. "Do the others know what has happened?" she asked.

"Not the whole of it. It is not the kind of story to be widely told. To know one has lived in slavery to a machine—" There was a hot undercurrent in his voice. "And how far that domination has gone—"

"Ludorica and the crown." Her thought followed his. "If it has so affected all of you who had no direct contact with it, what will it do to those who hold the crowns?"

He was looking beyond her, as if he did not want her to see what lay in his eyes.

"That we must learn. The destruction seems to have affected people in various ways. So far all these men have come out of it. But with some the daze was longer, deeper. And they are all relatively far removed from influence. As you say—what has happened close to the crowns—"

"Here, m'lady." The Sergeant was back with the E-ration. Roane sucked at the semiliquid avidly, for she discovered that her hunger had awakened.

Her recovery seemed to be the signal for which they had been waiting. Sergeant Wuldon went to the picket line, and men began to ride out, in twos and threes, each saluting Imfry as he passed. In the end only Wuldon, Mattine, and two others were left.

"We had best be on the move," Nelis said. "I know you are not strong enough to ride alone, but we have a mount that will carry double, and that we can share."

So it was that after Imfry had mounted, Wuldon lifted her as if she had no weight at all, passing her up to his superior.

"Where do we go?" Roane asked as the trees arched over them, shutting out the sun.

"Skulking. Until we know more of what chances. We shall follow the river road. The men are scouting in a wide sweep to see what they can pick up. If there is an open path we shall head for Urkermark."

"The Queen?"

"The Queen—if she is still Queen." His voice was remote, cool. "We do not know what we shall find, we can only ride to find it."

"You had no part in this." She tried to guess his line of thought. "It was my hand—and chance—which did it."

"I told you, I do not believe that chance alone ruled this," was his reply. And he did not add to that as they jogged ahead.

# ✳ CHAPTER 18 ✳

**THE ROOM WAS WARM** in spite of its size, almost too warm; But the light from the two lamps on the table and on the hearth did not reach the corners, where shadows crouched. Roane looked about her with an interest fatigue did not quite dull. This was the first time she been in any house on Clio save a forester's and the border keeps, with their rough frontier interiors, and the magnificent mansion in Gastenhow.

This was an upper private room of the Inn of Three Wayfarers, within a half day's ride of Urkermark. Their steaming cloaks lay across a bench pulled close to the fire, for outside came the steady beat of rain. And it was under that cover they had ridden so far into the land.

Three days—Roane counted them off. The first been much of a blur for her. They had spent that night in the forester's cabin. And there the first reports had come.

Reveny was in a state of chaos. And the dislocation had been the greater in the upper reaches of authority. The yeoman farmers, the "little" men and women, made better

recoveries from the initial state of bewilderment. But in turn they had been alarmed by the erratic actions of their leaders.

Some appeared to go insane, either sinking into a state of idiocy to give no coherent orders at all, or mouthing such irresponsible ones that their own servants and followers refused to obey. Fighting had broken out, stopped as the men engaged suddenly asked themselves what they were fighting for. There were bands of raiders taking advantage of the misfortunes of others.

The closer their own party came to Urkermark—and now they traveled openly, having little to fear during this confusion—the wilder became the stories of what chanced there. Imfry grew bleak of expression, curt of tongue, with every succeeding report from his scouts. That there was dire trouble was certain. Three times they had met parties of refugees spurring away from the city. And each time those riders, men guarding women, some of whom had children in their arms, had refused any contact, twice shooting to warn off Imfry's men. There had been wounded among them. And seeing those bandaged bodies, Roane was deeply unhappy. Chance or not, she felt that each of those hurts had come from her hand.

Imfry's company had grown. The scouts who had spread to gain news brought, or directed, back to him more and more guardsmen, foresters, even stragglers from the private guards of stead nobles. He interviewed each newcomer himself, trying to sift from their stories a clearer picture. He was doing so now, sitting at the table, listening to the rambling story of a man in uniform.

There were few officers among these so far, and the one

or two who did appear were all of lower rank, though some of them still held together a nucleus of their former commands.

". . . the incall came," the newcomer was saying. "And Major Emmick talked to this other officer in the guardroom. We heard a shot. When we broke down the door the Major was dead—took it right through the head. This strange Colonel—he started to say that the Major was a traitor, which we did not believe, then he grabbed at his head and ran straight at the wall and smashed against it, knocked himself right out. Well, we did not know what to do. The Captain, he was still dazed like, lay on his bed and just laughed when the Sergeant asked for orders. So Sergeant Quantil, he said up with the gates and not to let anyone else in, not until we got some news that made sense. And he sent three of us out—Mangron, he was to ride to the Westergate, Afran up to Balsay, and me, I was to try to reach our own Colonel in Urkermark. Only the gates were up there, too. They will not let anyone in. And I think there is a fight going on inside—there are fires blazing, anyway. Then I met up with your man, sir, and what he told me made a lot more sense than anything I heard since Major Emmick was killed, so I came here."

"And this man who brought the incall, this Colonel—you did not know him?"

"Never saw him before, sir. He had a new royal badge, too—a black forfal head, with the mouth open and a forked tongue out, nasty-looking thing. The Sergeant searched him for papers afterward. Nothing but the warrant on the table. It was all written up like a real one but it did not have the Queen's name. It just said 'in the King's name'—and

King Niklas has been dead for days now! It was just some more craziness!"

"'In the King's name,'" repeated Imfry. And then he shot another question. "What king?"

The man stared at Imfry and then hurriedly pushed away from the table, glancing from side to side as if seeking some escape. Roane guessed his suspicions. He must think that Imfry was mad now.

"No, guardsman, I am not crazy. But there is good reason to believe that there is one near the Queen who might try to seize power in a time of trouble. If he has done so—"

The man swallowed. "Oh," he said eagerly, "that could explain—I cannot remember any name signed. There was the thumb seal on the warrant proper enough—but no name! Maybe that was what made Sergeant Quantil think it so queer. It was a warrant telling the Major to hand over command, but no proper name signed. But, sir, where—where is the Queen?"

"In Urkermark, or should be!" Imfry said with the emphasis of one taking an oath. "You say the city is closed?"

"Every gate sealed up as tight, sir, as it was the time the Nimps got down within siege distance in the old days. It would take the biggest siege guns to force those."

"The outer gates, yes, but there are other ways. Guardsman, how long will it take you to get a message back to your post?"

"If I have a fresh mount, I can make it by midnight, sir."

"Well enough. You know what you have seen. Report it to your Sergeant. And take him this message from me."

Imfry drew toward him a writing sheet, the small ink holder, and the pen. As he had before at the conclusion of such interviews, he wrote a few lines, dipped his finger tip in ink to impress beneath his signature.

"Mattine!" he called and as the forester appeared in the doorway, "a fresh mount for this guardsman."

"To be sure, m'lord."

When the man was gone, Imfry stared into the fire. Roane stirred, unable any longer to bear the silence in the room, the circling of her own thoughts.

"You say there is a way into Urkermark besides the gates?"

"It was meant to be a bolthole out. Our history has never been without its wars and alarms, dynastic struggles. The games in which we were the pieces have often been bloody ones. I wonder who took satisfaction from that? The machines could not. But were the results somehow known to those devils who fostered them upon us?" He looked at her as if he wanted an answer.

"At first they must have been. There would be no other reason for experimenting. But the Psychocrats have been dead a long time."

"The machines have only been dead for days and look what is upon us now. I wish I knew why it seems to affect some more than others. At any rate, the Queen is our first concern. It could well be that Reddick has set himself up as king. Which leaves two possible fates for Ludorica— either she died with the destruction of the crown, or else she is held captive to back Reddick's intrigues. In either case he must not be allowed to—" Imfry fell silent again, his face repelling Roane. That there was a strong bond

between him and the Queen, Roane had known from the first. And if the Queen was dead—

She gave a sigh, wondering if she herself would ever be free of her burden of guilt. It seemed that as soft as that sound was, it was enough to arouse him from his dire thoughts, and when he turned to her there was a faint relaxation about his mouth.

"Rest, m'lady, while you can." He nodded at a door to an inner chamber. "We may have precious little time in which to do so."

Yet it was morning when the inn maid drew aside the curtains to let in a pale sunshine.

"M'lady." She curtsied when she saw Roane watching her sleepily. "The Colonel says you must be on your way soon. But there is hot water for washing, and these also." She pointed to folded clothing on a chair. "They are not what a fine lady wears, being of my own seaming, but the Colonel says they will do."

"But I cannot take your clothes," Roane objected, even though she shrank from drawing on again the stained and sweated garments in which she had lived for days.

"Oh, m'lady, the Colonel has given me that which will buy me twice what he selected from those I showed him. And much finer! But these are new, and there is a rain cloak to wear."

Roane bathed, thankful for the water and the soap, which smelled of sweet herbs. She put on one of the divided riding skirts and the tight bodice jacket, both of green-blue, but lacking the bright braid and embroidery she had seen before. There was a gray cloak, lined in green-blue, with an

attached hood. Roane tried to order her hair. It had grown from the close crop and had now reached a length difficult to keep in order, straying about her face. She was still tugging at it as she went out into the other room, where the maid was putting a platter of food on the table.

"Please, m'lady, the Colonel asks that you make what speed you can."

"Surely." Roane found that for the first time in days she was really hungry. Though she ate as fast as she could, she left a well-cleaned plate behind her.

The maid ushered Roane down the stairs. There were many men in the common room, most of them eating in a hurried fashion, calling for refills of tankards. Most of their faces were strange but Mattine waved to her from the doorway and they quickly made room for her to pass.

Imfry stood by a duocorn, critically surveying a second mount. As Roane came up he gave her a quick greeting and then indicated that animal.

"She is warranted sound and steady-going, and we shall not have to use her for long, but she is a sorry-looking beast."

The mare was, Roane had to admit, a scrawny being, with a very ragged, rough mane at the root of her stubbed horns and only a wisp of a tail. Also she bawled a protest as the Colonel swung Roane into the saddle on her bony back, where she held on with a grim determination to last out the trip.

They rode out at the head of a troop which had been even further augmented during the night hours.

"We make for Urkermark?" Roane asked.

"Yes, but by the hidden way."

So they turned aside from the highway onto the second lane feeding into it. And a little farther on they leaped their mounts over the way hedges, and crossed open fields, where hoofs cut into crop planting, trampling half-ripened grain. It seemed that Imfry was taking the straightest line possible to his goal.

They veered to the west, seeming to Roane's mind to be heading directly away from their goal. But that brought them at about noon to the bank of a river and along that they angled back east, following the course of the flow as a guide. Not far along they came to one of those bridges with a small triangular tower as a part of its structure.

There they dismounted. Imfry and the Sergeant, plus two guardsmen, went to the tower. The men produced iron bars and set to work pounding in and breaking loose the blocks below the offering slit.

A block of masonry crumbled only too readily under that assault and they dragged the stones out of the way. With the same bars they swept the floor within. Coins spun into the air, fell into the grass, but the workers paid no attention.

Now the sun shone on the dusty floor, making plain a groove in the stone. Sergeant Wuldon worked the tip of a lever into the depression, under a small bar of stone set across it. He put his full strength on the lever, the men and the Colonel joining in his effort. There was a harsh grating, and the stone moved complainingly. Once it was up the two blocks on either side were released and drawn out in turn.

A short time later Roane found herself descending a steep ladder of stone, lit by the glow of lanterns held by

those who went before. Then she faced a long passage walled and buttressed with stone slabs.

The way was dark and there was an unpleasant smell of damp. But also there was now and then a very welcome whiff of fresher air, as if a ventilating system existed. There was only room for two to walk abreast, so their company was strung out, Imfry and Mattine at the head, Roane with the Sergeant, and the remainder of the troop behind.

For the most part their path was level and Roane thought that the making of such a way had been a formidable task. She was beginning to wonder if it did run for leagues clear to Urkermark when they were faced by a new series of steep steps, down which they went to a yet deeper level. Here there were no signs of man's building, but rather a series of cuts and caves, opening one into another, some large beyond the reach of lantern light.

Imfry went boldly on as if he knew the way well, though by all indications it must have been a long time since any had passed on this hidden road. He paused at last to consult his direction disk.

"Turn right here—" He signaled with the lantern. They were in one of the wider caves and the men were bunching up behind them.

Imfry went more slowly now, he and Mattine holding higher the lanterns they carried. And at length these revealed another stair, down which moisture dripped from where it gathered in great beads on the stone.

Roane climbed warily, fearing the slipperiness of the stone and the steepness of the steps. They ended in a stone passage fronting a fourth flight of stairs. The steps were enclosed on one side with wooden paneling, hung with

thick spider webs heavy with the dust of years. Up and up, though Imfry went slowly, and apparently counting as he went, as if some tally of the steps was a key he needed.

He signaled by hand wave and the Sergeant edged around Roane, touching her shoulder lightly as he went.

"Pass that back, m'lady."

She did, the signal halting the line of men.

Now, handing his lantern to Mattine, who held both lights closer to the wall, the Colonel felt across the wooden surface. His shoulders hunched as if he were exerting pressure on some stubborn fastening. Then a portion of the paneling swung open to make a door.

When it came Roane's turn to step through she found herself in a room as richly furnished as had been that dining hall of her dream. The same kind of massive, heavily carved furniture stood about; the same colorful, if time-faded, tapestries ringed the walls.

She stepped to one side as the men following her fanned out. Imfry was at another door of the room, the Sergeant flanking him, both with those guns in their hands. The Colonel edged open that barrier, looked beyond, and then waved them on.

So they came into the heart of Urkermark High Keep. And it was through its rooms Imfry led them. Twice Roane waited with a beating heart, listening to the sound of shots loud in these echoing rooms. And once she hurried by a body lying face down, from under which runneled a thin red stream.

But there was no unified resistance to their passage and they went swiftly. Here and there small squads of the company broke off under low-voiced orders. So that when

they reached another door, before which the Colonel again paused, there were only ten of them, counting Roane, left.

Imfry tried the latch carefully before he gave a quick, sharp pull, at the same time moving to face whoever might be within, gun ready.

"Drop it!"

There was a queer sound like broken laughter. The Colonel was already inside, the rest crowding behind him, so Roane was the last to enter. She did not find a battle about to begin, but rather a strange scene, as if the actors had been frozen in place by their entrance.

On a couch lay Ludorica, her eyes closed, her dress disordered, even torn, with draggled trails of black lace hanging from the bodice. Her hair was loose, matted in tangles.

Beyond her was a chair in which sat Shambry. He held both hands breast-high before him, and on them rested a glowing ball of rippling light. His mouth was slackly open, a thread of spittle drooling from one corner. But as he looked at Imfry his lips wrinkled in a hideous grin.

"Quiet, sir, the Queen sleeps. She sleeps, she dreams, dreams of us, and if she wakes, why, we shall all cease to be. Because we are her dream creatures. Only I, Shambry, can keep her dreaming so, and us alive!"

The men moved uneasily, edged a little away. Only Imfry continued to front the Soothspeaker. Then he went into action before Shambry could dodge, plucked the ball from the other's hold.

With a cry of pure terror, Shambry flung himself at Imfry, his crooked fingers reaching for the ball, or perhaps the Colonel's throat. But Wuldon interposed, hurling the

man, now mouthing curses, back into his chair with such force that it went over, spilling Shambry to the floor.

Roane was already at the Princess's side. Ludorica's face was very pale, worn, but it had lost that shadow of evil the crown had laid upon it. Her skin was hot and dry as if she burned with fever, her lips cracked and peeling. But she still lived, and her breathing was the even rise and fall of one who slept.

Wuldon had his hands hooked in the collar of the Soothspeaker's black cloak, was pulling the groveling Shambry to his feet. He shook the man, who now hung limply in his grasp, and looked to Imfry.

"He is really over the edge, sir. You will not get any sense out of him now. What has he done to the Queen?"

Imfry moved to the couch, took one of Ludorica's hands between his.

"She is under mind-globe, I think. If so, there is one drastic remedy for that." He turned and caught up the ball, which had spun away to the floor. Raising it high, he deliberately smashed it. Shambry gave a wild beast's cry, fought with such a frenzy that Wuldon could not hold him alone. Two of the men came to his aid.

Ludorica's head turned on the pillow. Then her eyes opened. But there was no recognition in them.

"See to her," Imfry told Roane. "There is one lacking from this company who must be found."

He strode across the chamber to the second door, setting his shoulder to burst it open by force. Beyond, Roane saw part of a pillared hall, most of which swept beyond her range of vision. But what the door framed was undoubtedly a throne on a dais, yet set low enough for her

to see that it was occupied. He who sat there wore a crown which was a glitter of icy splendor. And he did not turn his head to view Imfry's abrupt entrance.

Neither was he alone. But those who companied him were not standing to attention in their king's presence, but rather sprawled on the floor before him, so that when the Colonel, gun still at ready, went to confront the usurper, he had to step over and around their bodies.

"Reddick!"

There was no sign that the Duke either heard or saw Imfry. He sat so still he might have been frozen by the ice of the Crown. The Colonel studied him, and then went swiftly up to the throne and laid a hand on his enemy's shoulder.

He started back with a quickly suppressed cry, for his touch broke the dream in the form of a man. There was a chime of sound; the Crown shattered, fell in a rain of splinters about the head and shoulders of him who wore it. Then Reddick shriveled, blackened, turned into something Roane could not bear to look upon. She cried out and hid her face in her hands.

Lamplight showed the richness of the heavily embroidered cover on the daised bed. Though that radiance was far less than what Roane had been used to, it was enough to fully illumine Ludorica's face. They had propped her up on a backing of pillows and Roane fed her bite by bite, giving her many sips of watered wine.

The Queen did not lift her hands, seemed unable to help herself. She smiled now and then, once murmured Imfry's name when he came to look upon her. And in that

much they were assured she had some measure of consciousness. Only she was very weak.

Roane tried with caution two of the remedies from her kit. But neither seemed to give any strengthening to this slender girl who was now a helpless child in her care.

Perhaps they would never know what had happened in the High Keep before their coming. It could be that Reddick had already taken the Ice Crown to wear before that fateful moment when the distant controls had blazed into nothingness. That could well explain his gruesome death on the throne, the ending of those committed to his rule—for all in that chamber were dead. Shambry was insane, retreating into a catatonic state they could not break.

Roane watched the Queen. She was now afraid that Ludorica might be beyond the aid of untrained help, though they could cling to the hope that she would gradually awaken fully. But Roane had told Imfry the truth, that it would be well to seek the aid they needed elsewhere. And his messengers had already ridden to ask it.

Meanwhile the keep was coming to life. That town which had been in the iron grip of Reddick's traitors was freed. Some of the lawful councilors had been killed, one or two had disappeared, but four had been found, brought back. The servants were returning, other help had been recruited from the city, and the guards were all Imfry's men and so trustworthy. Roane knew this was in progress, but her own field of battle remained this bedroom.

She had two of the Princess's maids with her. They had been discovered locked in their chambers and freed by Imfry's searchers. They had at first been jealous of Roane,

but then were worried enough about the state of their mistress to welcome the stranger's aid. At night Roane herself rested on a divan at the other end of the room, ready for any summons.

Imfry had not returned since she had begged him to send a messenger to contact her own people. If the LB was still there, and the off-worlders were willing, now that the installation was gone and Clio was no longer slave to the past, they could have better help than any she thought native to Clio. But it could be they were too late in seeking it.

The Queen opened her eyes. She fell asleep during these hours in the blink of an eyelid and roused as quickly. Roane took those two inert hands into hers.

"Ludorica!" she called softly as a summons.

It seemed that this time those blue eyes did indeed focus on her and hold steady—as if she were a recognized person and not a part of the room. The cracked lips Roane had soothed with salve parted and the faintest ghost of a whisper reached her:

"Roane?"

"Yes, oh, yes!" The off-world girl tightened her grip eagerly. "I am Roane!" That the other knew her was a great leap forward out of that shadow land.

"Stay—"

Roane understood that as a question.

"Yes, I shall stay." But she could not be sure she had replied in time for the other to understand, for the heavy lids had fallen again and once more the Queen slept— though this time Roane watched with a lighter heart. She thought Ludorica's sleep more natural, not just a giving way

to a blanking unconsciousness. At last she laid down the hands she held and at that moment one of the maids came into the circle of lamplight and beckoned, slipping into Roane's place as she arose.

The chamber door was ajar and she went to it. Imfry was in the room beyond. He was wearing full uniform, and his thin face was shaven. He had been, she was aware, on his self-imposed duties to bring order out of chaos.

"Your star ship was gone." He broke it to her abruptly.

For a moment all she thought of was the lost opportunity to aid the Queen. Then the true meaning struck home. They had gone, leaving her behind, marooned it might well be for life if the Service decided against any further contact. Roane put out her hand for support, suddenly feeling a little dizzy, reaching for a chair back. But her hand was caught as he came to her, steadied her.

"I am sorry," he said and that crispness of command, much in his voice these past few days, was softened. "I should not have told you so."

"No, it does not matter." She shook her head. "I could not have expected otherwise. They knew we had been discovered, and they would not wait to find me. They may never come again. But Nelis, listen—the Queen— Ludorica—a short time ago she knew me! Perhaps we can hope she will come back to us. We might not need their help after all."

"You are sure—she is on the mend?" Something in his eagerness, the way he turned his head to look at the door into the bedchamber made Roane want to move away. She tried to pull her hand from his, but he would not loose it.

"I have a duty." He spoke slowly, almost as if what he said now was painful. "You have heard her call me 'kinsman'—"

Because, thought Roane with a wry inner hurt, Ludorica wished perhaps an even closer relationship with her Colonel.

"You see, there is in truth a bond between us—"

This she did not want to hear. If the bleak truth was not put into words, if she did not have to hear it just yet—And to have *him* say it! But she was not able to protest, and he was continuing:

"I took an oath long ago at my father's wishes—and it has ruled my life. Our rulers marry for reasons of state, the well-being of their countries. But often such unions are no more than formal alliances, though they are required for the begetting of true heirs.

"Our King Niklas accepted the royal bride from Vordain, as his advisers made plain was his duty. But his heart had already been given elsewhere. And such affairs can lead not only to pain but to cankers like Reddick's ambition—which was in part my father's fear after my birth.

"My mother was the King's daughter, but no princess. She wanted nothing from her father; in fact she refused all he would have gladly given her. And when she wed with my father she was pleased to leave the court.

"By her wish I was to claim nothing from the King, and this was my father's desire also. I was not to be 'kinsman' though I could easily have been so. To me Ludorica will always be the Queen whom I serve and honor. Beyond the service I owe her thus, I go my way, and she that which

destiny points for her. Do you understand what I would have you believe?"

Roane could not answer save with a nod. She was unable to sort out her emotions. For that she needed time and quiet and a chance to face a new self, a very new self which she must learn to know.

"What of you? Your people have left you—"

"Yes."

"But that is only as you think; the truth is otherwise!" There was hot emotion in his voice which she was too bewildered even to try to read. "*Those* have gone, your people are here! You are of Reveny, as much as if you were born among her hills, schooled in some stead hall. Believe that, Roane, believe it! For it is true!"

She was not just imagining what he said—it was the truth now. And with the tone of one wholeheartedly swearing allegiance she found voice enough to answer: "I do—Nelis, I do!"

# BROTHER
*TO*
# SHADOWS

# ✳ CHAPTER 1 ✳

**THE CHILL FINGERS** of the dawn wind clawed. Behind the spires of the Listeners the sky was the color of a well-honed throwing knife. There was not any answer to time's passing in Ho-Le-Far Lair.

Brothers stood in the courtyard as they had since twilight, keeping the Face-the-great-storm position with a purpose that rose above any cramping of limb or protest of body. Only their eyes were apprehensive and what they watched was that oval set at the crown of the arch which marked the door of the Master's great hall. What should have showed a glow of light was lifeless, as dull as the stone in which it was set.

Now through that door, which gaped like a skull's lipless jaws at the top of a flight of stairs, came the long awaited figure muffled in robes the hue of dried blood—The Shagga Priest.

He spoke and his voice, though low-pitched, carried as it had been trained to do.

"The Master has fulfilled his issha vow."

No one in those lines below wavered, though this was an ending to all the life they had known.

Those two to the fore of the waiting company raised hands in Sky-draw-down gestures. Then they strode forward with matching steps while the priest descended further to meet them. He stopped, still above their level, so they must look up to meet his eyes. In the growing light their Shadow garments were a steel to match the lowering sky.

TarrHos, Right Hand to the Master, crossed his hands at breast level, drawing with action too quick for the eye to truly follow, slender daggers.

"It is permitted?" he asked of the priest, his voice as hard as the weapons he displayed.

"It is permitted—by the Issha of this Brotherhood it is so." The priest nodded his shaven head and his own hands advanced, like predators on the prowl, from the shadows of his wide sleeves to sketch certain age-old gestures.

TarrHos went to his knees. Three times he bowed, not to the priest but to that lifeless stone above. It was a blinded eye now; that force which it had contained had fled, no brother or priest could tell why or how. It had been, it was not, and with it went the life of this Lair.

TarrHos's weapons swept in the ritual gesture. There was no sound from the man who crumpled forward, only the moaning of the wind. Red spattered upward, not quite reaching the perch of the priest.

LasStir, Left Hand of the Master, took another step forward. He did not look at his dead fellow.

"It is permitted?" His voice, rendered harsh by an old throat wound, outrode the wind.

"It is permitted—the issha holds."

With the same dexterity of weapons LasStir joined his colieutenant in death.

The Shagga descended the last two steps, making no effort to draw back the hem of his robe from the spreading pools of blood coming to join as one.

Ten more made up that assembly left below, younger men, some near boys. Their short cloaks were black, the sign of those who had not made at least ten forays for the honor of the Lair. One in that line dared to speak to the Shagga.

"It is permitted?" His voice was a little too high, too shrill.

"It is not permitted!" The priest silenced him. "A Lair dies when its heart is no longer fed by the will of its Master. The unblooded and half-sworn do not take up the issha.

"Rather you shall serve in other Lairs still as is demanded of you. Ho-Le-Far has ceased to be." He made the Descent-of-Darkest-Night wave with his left hand—so setting an end to all which had existed here, erasing a long and valiant history. "Here no longer is there a Post of Shadows."

For the first time there was a slight movement in that assembly. This was a thing of disaster, almost of terror, and it was an evil fate to be caught in it.

The Shagga moved along the line slowly, stopping to eye each one, and to address that one alone:

"HasGan and CarFur," he singled out the first two on the left. "Draw supplies and weapons, go to the Lair of Tig-Nor-Tu. DisNov and YasWar, you will do likewise, but go over mountain to Ou-Quar-Nin."

So it went until the priest reached the last in that line. He had to look up to meet eye to eye with the waiting novice and now that it was fully light it was plain to see the sparks of malice in his sunken eyes, the vicious twist of his lips as he shaped words which he had long savored and held ready for this moment.

"Outlander—misborn—no-blood—Out with you to where you will—you are not of the Oath and by the Will of TransGar you never shall be. You are an abomination, a stain. No doubt the Master's force death has come through you. You will take no weapons—for those are of the Brotherhood, and henceforth you will go your own way!"

The hooded listener refused the Shagga the satisfaction of seeing how deep that thrust went. He had long known that the priest hated him, looked upon his being there as a blot on the honor of the Lair. Since the force stone had started to fail he had foreseen this and tried to plan beyond it. But so much of his life was tied here that it was hard to break the bonds of discipline, to think of himself as moving without orders on a wayward path which had no real goal

Within the Lair only the Master had ever shown him any concern. He had been told why only three moon speds ago. The Brothers to Shadows, trained assassins, spies, bodyguards, had been in service on Asborgan for centuries. Rulers employed their services knowing well that, once oathed, they were absolutely loyal to their employer for the agreed-upon length of their bond. However, recently there had been a rumor that their particular talents were in demand off-world also and that was a new source of income for the Lairs. To employ one of off-world blood off-world

would be setting that Lair to the fore of the new idea and the Master had been a forward-looking man—which was, Jofre thought, a hidden point of disagreement between him and the custom-bound Shagga.

Jofre was the Master's own find, a literal find, for the Master, on one of his scout training missions, had come upon the wreck of an escape craft, one of those which sometimes could make a perilous rescue from a spacer in dire trouble. Jofre had been the only living thing in that tiny vessel, a child so young he could remember only a few scraps of scenes of his life before he had been taken into the Lair to be given the grilling training of the Brothers.

Though in frame he was larger than the rest of the novices, he quickly absorbed all he was taught, proving more proficient in some of the necessary skills than others. At the same time the Master had seen that he was given lessons in the off-world trade tongue, passed to him information which seeped from the airport to the Lair, brought by traders and travelers. Though both Master and student knew well there were large and awkward gaps in what he absorbed with a will. His greater reach and strength as he approached manhood had awakened envy in his fellows, something he had long known that the Shagga Priest had fostered. However, he knew that he was competent enough for a mission and that the Master had had plans for him.

The Master and the force stone . . . Each Lair was endowed with such a stone and no one knew from where these came or what was the purpose—save that at long intervals their glow died. That was taken as a direct sign that the force of the Master had gone also and that he must

pay for whatever secret failing had brought about the death of his power. With the stone died also the Lair as this one had here and now. But it had been a long time since any Lair had come to an end, and it was a bitter thing which brought a faint touch of fear to every other Lair when it happened.

Jofre continued to meet the priest eye to eye. The man would see him dead if he could. But he could not, for Jofre had passed the first oathing four seasons ago and Brother could not shed the blood of Brother. However, the Shagga was settling his fate in another way. This was the season of mountain cold. To be cast out of shelter without weapons or full supplies was a delayed sentence of death—or so the priest believed.

"I am assha if not issha." Jofre spoke the words slowly as he might ready his knives for a final thrust. "Weapons you may take from me, for they are of the Lair. I claim therefore traveler's rights under the law." On this point custom would bear him out and he would hold to it.

The priest scowled and then flung away after the others, who were already moving off to make up their packs ready for the journeying to their newly appointed stations.

Jofre faced the force stone again. Slowly he moved forward. The light which had centered it was certainly gone—it was now as dull as the age-worn stone which held it. At least ten Masters had lived and died in its light—the eleventh had the misfortune to see that light fail.

The young man skirted the bodies of the lieutenants and climbed the steps. He expected some outcry from the Shagga though what he would do was no profanation. However, that did not come and he passed into the

darkness of the hall above, where the only faint light came from two lamps at the far end.

Between them lay that other body—the Master. For some reason Jofre needed to do this but he could not explain that reason even to himself. He came to stand beside the man who had saved his life, even though just perhaps because he saw in Jofre a tool to be well employed at a future date.

Jofre's hands moved Star-Of-Morning—Journey-into-Light. The fingers shaped that message in the air. Farewell-far-journey-triumph-to-the-warrior. As he did this there welled into him an inflow of strength, almost as if some of the will and purpose of the dead Master passed to him as a bequest.

Only a tenth night ago he had knelt at this very spot, had spread before him certain maps and papers, known the carefully hidden excitement of one being prepared for a mission.

"It is thus," the Master had spoken as one who shared thought, "these off-worlders change every world they enter. They cannot help but do so to us. We have lived by a certain pattern for ten centuries now. The valley lords have their feuds which have become as formally programmed as the IDD dances. They hire us as bodyguards, as Slipshadows to dispose of those whose power threatens them or whom they wish to clear from their paths. It has become in a manner a game—a blood game.

"But to all patterns there comes a time of breaking, for weaving grows thinner with years. So it comes for us— though many of the Masters would say no to that. But we

must change or perish." There had been force in those words as if the Master were oath giving.

"The Master of Ros-hing-qua has shown the way. He has oathed two Brother Shadows, one Sister Shadow off-world to men who seek easement to trouble on their own home globe. Word has come that they carried out their assignment in keeping with issha traditions. Now it is our turn to think of such a thing. There is news from the port that there has been talk of others coming from the far starways to seek the arts we have long cultivated. You are not of our blood, Jofre, by birth. But we claimed you and you have eaten of our bread, drunk brother-toasts, learned what was our own way. Off-world you can use all you know and yet not be betrayed by the fact you are born of us. Therefore, when the time comes, this mission shall be yours—either you will be sent to be the shoulder shield, body armor for some far lord, or you will be the hunter with steel."

Jofre had dared then to break the pause which followed:

"Master, you place in me great trust but there are those within these walls who would speak against that."

"The Shagga, yes. It is the manner of most priests to cling to tradition, to be jealous guardians of custom. He would not take departure from the old ways happily. But here I am Master—"

Yes, here he had been Master—until the issha and the door crystal had failed him. Jofre's lips tightened against his teeth under the half-mask scarf of his headdress. Could the Shagga have, in some way, brought this ruin here? There were tales upon tales of how they had strange powers but he had never seen such manifest and besides,

were such a thing possible, all the Masters of Lairs would rise and even the Shagga would face death.

Jofre knelt now and touched his turbaned head three times to the floor, the proper answer to one given a mission.

"Master, hearing, I obey."

He was not being sent forth officially, no. For no Lair would offer him shelter with the Shagga against him, nor did he want to remain where he was not a true brother. Off-worlder they called him. But as the Master had pointed out he had certain skills which could well be useful on any planet where men envied other men, or feared for their lives, or sought power. The spaceport would be his goal and from there he would await what fortune his issha would offer.

Now he left the hall and its dead and went directly to the storehouse, in which there was a bustle. A line of burden quir were waiting with pack racks already on their ridged backs. Hurrying back and forth were the Brothers, already in their thick journey clothing, loading on those ugly-tempered beasts all which must be transported now to their future homes.

The Shagga priest stood by the door but as Jofre approached he turned with a whirl of his robes to face him.

"Off with you—But first—There—" he pointed to the ground at his feet already befouled by the droppings of the quir, "your weapons, nameless one."

Under his half-mask Jofre snarled. Yet, this too, was a part of the tradition. Since they declared him not of any Lair, he could not bear the arms of one.

His long knife, his two throwing sleeve knives, his

chainball throw, his hollow blowtube. One by one he threw them at the priest's feet. At last he held but one knife.

"This," he said levelly, "I keep—by traveler's law."

The priest's mouth worked as if he would both spit and curse in one. But he did not deny that.

Nor did Jofre draw back now. Though the priest and the Brothers with their supplies tended to block the doorway.

"I claim traveler's right supplies," the young man stated firmly.

"You will get them!" The priest seized upon one of the boys just returning for another load. "Bring forth that prepared for this one. Then get you forth, cursed one."

The Brother ducked within and returned in a moment with a shoulder pack, a very small one, lacking much, Jofre thought, of what he would really need. Yet the Shagga had obeyed the letter of the law and if he protested, it would achieve nothing but to render him less in the eyes of these who had so recently been his oathed Brothers.

He took up the pack which had been tossed contemptuously in his direction and, without a word, turned and went toward the wide open gate in the wall. In that last meeting with the Master he had memorized from the map the route he must take. Of his destination he knew only what he had learned by study and by listening to the talk of the traders who now and then visited the Lair.

There was a road of sorts. However, that followed a winding way and he would lose time. By the heft of the pack he had little in the way of supplies. Though the Brothers were trained to live off the land, this was the beginning of the cold season and much which could be

converted to food would be hard to find. The herbs were frost burnt and dead; the small animals had mainly retreated to burrows. It was at least ten days travel on foot before he would reach farming land and then he must be wary of attempting to obtain supplies. The Brothers were feared by commoners. A Brother alone might well be fair game. No, it would be better to strike straight over the Pass of the Kymer, if that was not snow choked by an early storm. In a way he would thus be seeking out his own roots, as it was on the slope of the Ta-Kymer that the escapeboat in which he had been found had made a crash landing.

Jofre did not turn and look back at the only home he could remember. Instead he centered all his concentration on what lay before him, marshaling all strengths to face the mountain path.

The Shagga priest stood in the middle of that narrow room which had been his own quarters at the Lair. There were blanks of lighter strips on the wall where the rolls of the WORDS OF SKAG had been hung only moments earlier. All his belongings were enwrapped in weather-resistant orff skin bags to wait by the door.

He plucked at his lower lip as was his habit in thought, though there was so little skin to be gathered there.

Outside the narrow slit of window the pale sun was being cloud hidden. A storm, early in the season, that might most easily answer his problem. But no man could count on the whims of nature. It was best to cover all possible points in planning an attack.

There was one other object there in the room. A cage in which a black blot huddled. The priest went to haul out

that occupant. He held something which was neither bird nor mammal but a combination of both and faintly repulsive. The thing expanded leathery wings, releasing more of its disgusting, musty body odor.

Its head twisted and turned on a long neck as if it were trying to escape, not the priest's hold upon its body, but the glare of his eyes. Until at last the man's will overcame that of the Kag, the turning head was still, and it was held eye to eye with him as if being hypnotized, which it was after a manner.

There was a long pause and then the priest stepped quickly to the window and the Kag arose and was gone, spiraling out over the countryside, but still as much under his control as if he held it on a leash. It would follow, it would spy. When death struck down that upstart its master would speedily learn.

# ✳ CHAPTER 2 ✳

**JOFRE NOTED** those signs of the storm, yet he did not quicken pace. For the first hour after leaving the Lair he had country comparatively easy to travel. For he could keep for a while to the travelers' road. He swung along at the controlled gait for a long journey, with a divided mind which had come from his training.

One-half of his attention was for his surroundings and footing, the other probed into the future. He felt so oddly alone, though the Brothers, for the most part, operated singly, but always on a set task, and he was without that guidance. He set to gaining full control, first visualizing the map he was to follow, then examining in turn all the possible points of knowledge which could aid him in the future.

The history of the Brothers was thickly entangled with the intrigues and conspiracies of many small courts and kingdoms. All they knew of off-world came largely through hearsay. Many, such as the Shagga priest, wanted to keep it that way. Only because the Master had been far looking

and ambitious in a new fashion did Jofre have those scraps he clung to.

A city had been already established on the plain where the first spacer exploring starship had set down on Asborgan. Now there were, in fact, two cities, the old and a new one which had grown up nearer the port landing and in which there were strange off-world buildings housing beings of different races, different species even.

On the outer fringe of this newer city along the port side there was a third collection of buildings, seedy inns, trading marts in which there were few questions asked as to the source of goods offered. Here the outcasts of both Asborgan's native stock and the scum which followed the star lanes as a blot gathered and held a stronghold of their own.

Jofre had heard of the Thieves Guild, which spread talons to seize across half the star lanes. There was said to be a branch of that which had gained a foothold here, incorporating into its very diverse assembly native talent. In addition there were those who had met with such misfortune that they had fallen to a point of no return. He had been told of drugs which drove men wild, giving them great power for a short time, but condemning them to miserable deaths. All the evil which an intelligent mind could conceive gathered there in that dismal sink.

Yet that must be his own first goal. As a Brother he could not shelter in the old city—for he wore no lord's badge. Also there would be a need for coins to pay his way. The better portion of the space city would see him as a curiosity and so suspect. No, he must dive into the dark quarter until he could find his way about.

In his decision Jofre had no fear of either the law or the lawless. The conception that a Brother could be taken anywhere, used at any time against his own will, or the will of his Master, was inconceivable. He had skills of body and will, honed mastery of mind to shield him there. But when he tried to think to whom he might offer those skills now he found himself at a loss.

Finally, deciding that sure attempts at foreseeing were only useless, he shut down that portion of his mind and concentrated on the journey itself.

It was twilight when he came to where he must take the cutoff for the pass. Long trained to scout work, he could slip through the bare-branched brush and work his way up into the heights easily enough. He sheltered that night in a half cave where two great rocks tilted together.

Once he had his fire, hardly wider than his two hands held thumb to thumb, and had chewed the tough trail mix of meat pounded with dried fruit into a strip, he turned to the fitting of himself for what might well be the trials of tomorrow.

First he sought out The Center of All Things, concentrating on the mental symbols which marked the existence of that. Then he visualized the inner workings of his own body, the muscles, the nerves, the blood and bones, the knitting of the flesh. From his toes he began to use The Flow of Inner Life, drawing it up through him, into his mid body, his arms and shoulders, until his hands, where they rested on his knees as he sat cross-legged, grew warm and each finger tingled.

Into his throat, his head, the flood continued. There was a feeling of elation but that he was swift to dampen. He

was not summoning battle power. Only the strength needed for travel.

He breathed deeply three times, to lock in that warmth. Then he relaxed, aware that he had prepared himself as best he could. Now he set his sentinels of alarm that he might take a full night's rest. At least those were available to all travelers and so the Shagga priest could not refuse him them.

Jofre worked the three large pebbles out of their traveling bag and, with a knowing eye, in spite of the dark which had now closed in, he positioned them in the gravel about the rock. Such were quick to give alarm when approached by anything warm-blooded to which they had not been bound, as he had bound these with a drop of his own blood and the warmth of his bared hand.

Having taken his precautions, Jofre rolled in his double blanket and went to sleep, rest easily summoned by his long training.

There was no show of either moon tonight and clouds were heavy, though they had not yet loosed their burdens. Through their thickness sped the Kag. The creature lit on a spur of rock and hunched into a motionless blot of darkness, only to launch itself again and seize a warfin which had ventured out to hunt. Bearing the bird to its chosen perch, it ripped apart the body and fed ravenously, then settled to rest as had its quarry below.

Jofre awoke at dawn. He chewed another strip of journey rations, adding to that only a single finger scoop of yellowish paste from a small box. The Brothers did not depend often on stimulants but they had their own kinds of energy-inducing herbal concoctions. He gathered up his

sentries, returned them to their pouch, and swung his pack up on his shoulder. However, when only a few feet from his last night's camp, he paused to eye something protruding slantwise from the rubble which must have descended in a small slide from the heights he must now face.

It was certainly not the remains of any bush, or sapling. No, he had seen—and used—its like before. This was a pass staff which, in the right hands, could even confront a steel swinging opponent. The flash of recognition sent his hand out to close firmly about it.

The slide held it well in grip and he had to work it loose. When he had it wholly free he could see that the hook at its end had been bent out of shape, but it was still a weapon of which he could make excellent use. His issha was assuredly strong—

But whence had it come? He took several steps backward so he could view the upslant of the way before him more clearly. Then he saw it—a clean angle which was not of nature. There had been—still was—a wall!

Jofre closed his eyes for a moment and drew to the fore of his mind the map. No, he was certain that there had been no hint of any such along the route he had chosen. How could he have gotten so far off trace? He turned his attention to the staff he now held. It was old but it had been painstakingly carven of armor wood—that precious growth which could be worked by a great deal of effort, but once shaped would perhaps well outlast its maker.

He pulled off his thick glove and took the shaft into his bare hand, allowing it to slide along between his fingers as he held it closer to centered sight. Then that grip tightened. His breath came with the faintest hiss.

Qaw-en-itter!

Dead Lair, long dead Lair! And by all the teaching of assha a site to be avoided lest the ill fortune of that place still weave some pattern to entrap. Even as his own home Lair would now be regarded by any chancing close to its deserted compound. However—Jofre slid the staff back and forth between both hands as he sifted logic from superstition.

The Master he had served had been one to discount much in the way of rumor and legend. His outlooking for off-world contracts had brought him a wealth of contradictory information which he had sifted patiently, and for the past half year Jofre had oftentimes served as a kind of sounding board—since the Shagga priest and the Master's Right and Left Hands were all of a conservative turn of mind. The Shagga doubtlessly believed, and would tell it near and far, that the now dead Master's loss of assha had come because of that very turning from orthodox ways. But something in Jofre had responded eagerly to whatever speculation the Master had wished to voice.

Now he could remember that small warning mark on the map. However, there was a far better way to the Pass if one tried the ancient route from Qaw-en-itter. He would save perhaps a day's journey time, maybe more. A glance at the lowering clouds, at that threat of storm to come, made him think it would be worth the try.

Slinging the staff to be fastened to the lashings of his pack took only a short time. He was moving upward determinedly, watching for the best footholds, almost at once.

Over the years there had been a number of slides here. He came to a place where his path was closed by blocks of

masonry, perhaps a portion of the wall above, and he had to wriggle by. Then he came suddenly on a ledge which sloped upwards and showed the marks of very old tooling, undoubtedly one of the ways into the deserted Lair.

That was not what he wished. He must round what remained of the stronghold to locate the road on the other side. And the ledge was soon choked with debris. This was dangerous footing and Jofre walked with careful tread.

The half-destroyed wall arose on his right. There was the broken archway of a minor door but what he sought would lie beyond, and he shifted left, paralleling that offshoot of the wall. Something floated down, touched his sleeve—then another and another flake. The snow was beginning and, unless he would have himself walled from the pass, he must hurry.

Qaw-en-itter had been of moderate size, he concluded. Though so much of it was in ruin that he could not, without some waste of time, trace out its original ways. He tried to think of its history—there had been something—like a flicker, a scrap of memory came and went in his mind.

The master crystal here had failed, of course, or it would still be inhabited. But there was something else— the last Master—Jofre shook his head. For all his meticulous training he could not deepen that very faint feeling of having heard something.

The flakes of falling snow thickened, still were not enough to hide the way ahead. He had sight, if limited, and could keep from blundering off trail. Yet when he reached the point he had been seeking, where that other old path led upwards into the heights, Jofre hesitated. There was shelter here of a sort. Should the winds rise past the teasing

point which they now held and he be caught in the open on the bareness of the upper slopes, he would be in a perilous state.

This was a first storm. Those of the Lair had been trained to be weatherwise; they had to be. Part of him urged pushing on, another suggested a prudent delay. He could not hope to breast the pass if the snow became a true curtain.

On a quick decision he turned towards the end of the wall where the ruins beyond promised shelter. Edging around a tumble of stones, he came into what had been the main court of the Lair, There was a tangle of autumn-dried brush where the land had set its first grasp back on the forsaken territory. Brittle and sparse though that was, it promised better than anything he believed was available at a greater height.

Jofre nearly tripped on the first step which had led to the Master's hall, so enbowed was it with dried grass and drift from storms. He hesitated. To go on into that dark cavern which opened like a toothless mouth before him would take him out of the storm. But enough of the Brothers' belief remained in him to warn him off.

Instead he chose a niche to one side, where there had once been a storehouse, enough remaining of walls and roofing portion to afford shelter better than he could have hoped for elsewhere. There he set up camp.

The brush he broke off, or tore from its frail rooting in the pavement chinks, to afford him fuel for his small fire. As he worked to gather that the snow thickened, becoming more and more of a concealing curtain, and he knew that his impulse to night here had been right.

At last he settled in the small space he had made as stormtight as he could, but he felt no desire for sleep. Instead he knew the alertness of a scout in an enemy territory, his hearing, his sight, every sense he had reaching out to pick up the small hint of something which was not of wind, or snow, or natural to this ancient place.

For he could feel it more and more; it was like an itch he could not scratch because he did not know its source. There was that here which was not—Not what? Jofre chewed upon that question and found no answer.

He set out his sentries at the entrance to his burrow.

The portion of supplies he allowed himself was halved and he chewed carefully a long time before he swallowed each mouthful, as if that would stretch it to satisfy his hunger. What clung here? Were there indeed bases to old superstition and an abandoned Lair still held by the spirits of the last Master and his lieutenants? Without knowing that he did it, Jofre pulled the staff he had found across his knees as he sat cross-legged, was rubbing his right hand along the shaft, his fingers tracing the runes set there to identify the armory from which it had come. Suddenly he was aware there was a warmth in the shaft which did not spread from but rather to his moving hand. And then there was a sudden sharp shift in the staff, which had certainly not come by his will or from any movement he had made.

"Ssaahh—" Jofre was so startled from his carefully maintained calm that he hissed that aloud. What he was experiencing—yes, it was certainly that which he had heard tell of—had once seen demonstrated—and that by the Master on a scouting trip.

The half-broken weapon he had found on the rocks below was issha pointing! Issha? But the fact that this Lair was abandoned meant that there was no issha here—nor was he a Master to channel the power. Yet—this was happening!

In his now loosened grasp that shaft was pointing outward toward the snow. A long-set trap? He had also heard tales of such. Some of the Masters were rumored to have powers far beyond those of common men. He had dared to invade the accursed—was he now being drawn to the punishment for his impudence?

Because, Jofre also realized, he could not resist. He must carry through whatever action the weapon now urged. Loosing his knife for his other hand, he crawled out into the open, remaining there for an instant or two in the half crouch of Ward-the-attack-in-the-night.

Only the snow. Nothing moved through it or against the drifts it was building around the ruined walls. But the shaft was swinging in his grip with vigor, as if he were being pulled by a determined force on the other end. Now he was facing again the hall door.

> "By the blood oath, Brothers.
> By salt and bread, water and wine,
> By steel and rope, hand and foot—mind,
> By the ancients and the elders, Masters, and men,
> Thus do I swear."

He repeated the oathing of the assha, even as he would have done had he been sent with the rest to another Lair. And he followed, even as he would have had the long

gone Master of Qaw-en-itter stood on the rubble-strewn steps gesturing him in.

But it was not to the dark that the staff led him. As he reached the top step, the staff swung in his hand, slipping fast to thud butt hard on the worn stone. He looked down.

That butt was near to touching a patch of darkness, a patch of black which seemed to have a—Jofre went down on one knee and held out his hand, his fingers cupped over the blotch. There was a spark, as if he had used his flint against steel for fire lighting. Almost against his will those fingers closed.

Warmth—even as had been in the shaft when it had driven him into this action. He raised his hand, bringing what he had picked up to eye level. It was an oval perhaps the size of his palm, smoothed like a gem for setting. Black, so black that it might have been cut from the darkest of shadows. But as he cupped it in his flesh it gave forth—

Assha glow! But no—it could not be! When a Master's stone died did it leave a ghost of itself? No legend he had heard had told of that. However, had anyone ever lingered in a cursed lair to make sure? He wanted to hurl it from him, his clutch was only the tighter. What he had found was a thing of power, that he knew. Only he was not one who might wield it—

"No!" His voice sounded through the night and the snow. "No!" But there was a bonding; he could feel it; this was fast becoming a part of him. He strove to raise his own inner power to repudiate his find. There was no use—he could not hurl it away. Instead his hand, as if under the orders of a Master, went to his wide girdle and those busy fingers were working the stone into safe hiding there.

Jofre wavered as he stood. This—he could not summon any explanation for what had happened—but it would seem some power had fastened upon him. He turned to make his way back to his camping place. Through the snow from above came a flying thing. He breathed a whiff of musty stench and ducked as it seemed to strike directly at his head. An ill omen indeed.

Jofre struck out in turn at the wheeling half shadow. It screeched, arose and was gone into the night. Nor did it appear again. He settled into his shelter. Twice he tried to reach for the stone that he might examine it better in the faintish light of his pocket-sized fire. But his arm, his hand, would not obey his will. However, he felt it against his body, within the windings of the wide girdle its presence even through the folds of his thick clothing.

He began determinedly to Draw-to-one, Self-warrior-heart, Mind-of-seeker, so slipped into the innerways of the one who hunted in a strange and forbidden territory—even though that lay within himself. But for all his searching he found no trail, and he came out of that half trance stiff with chill, the pressure of the find still against him, knowing that he had done the best he could to arm himself against the unknown—now he could only face what would come.

The Kag beat wings to which snow clung and was flung forth again. It circled twice the ruins below but it no longer screeched nor attempted to descend. At length it broke the last circle and headed out through the night, winging its way north, away from Qaw-en-itter. Morning broke while it still flew, yet it did not perch to rest. It was nightfall again

when it circled another camp—though this a much larger one—and settled on the top of the empty cage.

A wrinkled hand and scrawny wrist was offered and the creature hopped onto that so that it was borne up to face eye level again the skull-sharp visage of the Shagga.

"Soooo—" the priest hissed at last. "He dares to meddle!" He considered the situation, weighing one thing against another. Tradition was strong; in spite of his hatred it bound him in some ways. None of the Brothers would move against one of issha training unless he had been denounced openly in a gathering of Lair Masters and the accused allowed speech in his or her own behalf. There was no knife or rope which could be dispatched openly against this four times damned off-worlder—not yet. But he must be watched—assuredly he must be watched.

As he thought he fed the Kag from a handful of wine-soaked herbs and put the now drowsy creature back in its cage. There was a second cage among the priest's baggage. As he approached that he looked up at the sky. Mountains would make no difference for his swift messenger and that one would reach the port city well ahead of that traveler he longed to break now with his bare hands.

He opened the cage and a farflyer pecked at his finger once and then came forth as the priest shrilled a summons. Again the priest and winged thing met in silent communication and then, with a practiced twist of the wrist, the man sent it up and out to complete its mission.

# ✳ CHAPTER 3 ✳

**THE MAN CROSSED THE ROOM** with a curiously effortless ease, a gait akin, as an imaginative viewer might think, to the progress of a fish through water. His tunic and breeches were of a lusterless, sober brown, though discreet front latches showed the glint of red gold, and the buckle of his purse belt was set with small gems which would betray their perfection only to a knowledgeable eye.

He was known in several sections of both the old city and that quick growth which fringed the spaceport as one Ras Zarn, a merchant from the far north, of middle rank, a good bargainer, one who paid all obligations promptly and fully. In two other places he had another identity and one of those places was this narrow windowless closet of a room, the only light in which came from utilitarian wrought iron lanterns supported on brackets on either sidewall.

The furnishings were meager, a single seat cushion and the knee-high table before it, which was bare, but the surface of which was thickly marked with scratches and small pits as if someone had driven a knife point into it many times over.

His arm was held out from his body as he came and on the fore of it was perched a farflyer, huddled a little together as it clung so, as if it were indeed close to the end of its wing strength. As Zarn seated himself on the cushion he held out his arm and the creature gave a hop which placed it on the desktop, as it did so adding a new series of claw scratches to those of innumerable times before.

It seemed disposed to make no other move until the man's hands went out, clasped firmly about the feathered body, turning it about so that it faced him. Then the fingers of one hand swept up, jerking high the head, elevating that so that he could stare into its unblinking eyes. Time passed.

Once, twice, Zarn nodded as if he were assenting to some speech totally inaudible in that cramped chamber. Then he relaxed a fraction and out of his purse pouch he brought a pellet of dull green. He gave it a sharp squeeze between thumb and forefinger and then discarded it before the messenger, whose released head made a quick peck at the delicacy.

Once that was done and the reward received, Zarn sat very still, looking at the opposite wall as if he were searching there for some map or message which was of importance. At length he nodded for the third time and there was a small quirk of the lips, a flash which was gone hardly before it could be sighted. Once more he offered his wrist and the bird hopped to that perch. Then he went to the far wall, pressed the fingers of his left hand in a complicated pattern and a door slid back to allow him into the very prosaic counting house which he had leased for use during his exile here.

Warning had been given; he would set into motion the

proper answer within the hour and he expected no ill results from his decided-upon plan. His weapon he had already selected and it would carry out his will as well as if it were his own hand wielding the silent steel or the choke of scarf-rope.

The storm which had imprisoned Jofre for two days in the ruins blew away during the second night and sun for the first time broke through those curtaining clouds. He was on the move at once. At this time of year such a respite must be made use of as quickly as possible. And some of the wind had moved drifts well enough for him to find the pass road.

He climbed steadily. It was not a road which would have suited a caravan of traders or any lowlander but to one from the Lairs it was as plain as that lower highway. Luck favored him in that there had been no slides here and the way was open, though he used the staff to sound the path ahead through any drift which did show.

The wind hit as he entered the pass and he clung to one wall of the cliff which formed it, moving crabwise at times lest some particularly forceful blast bowl him down. His inner strength was pushed near to the limit but the knowledge that once through this slit he would be on the downgrade again kept him moving.

Jofre was out of the cut and well down slope, to the first fringe of the evergreen trees which cloaked only the south side of the mountain range, before he paused long enough to eat. By sun height it was not too far from night and he must shelter out again in what protection he could find in the land. Also he was coming into occupied territory where

he must make every effort to pass unseen. There were outlaws in the mountains, though most of them denned up in more accessible country, but there were also foresters and trappers in the greenlands he was entering.

Though he did not now wear the full uniform of his kind, his late kind, still he was recognizable to any really suspicious eye. The traveler's clothing he had taken on sufferance at the Lair was a mixture which few would wear. He had the girdle knife, and the haft of the broken pole-hook, and he had all the powers of weaponless training which had been drilled into him since childhood, but such were no answer to a lance beam such as the lowlanders had been introduced to since the off-worlders had arrived.

The Master had had studies of such weapons, gathered from accounts and snatches of information brought back by Brothers who had served in the lowlands and returned once their service was done. But to obtain and master one of those weapons was something he had not yet achieved. The off-worlders were supposed to be forbidden to introduce such to a world where this craft mastery did not already exist. There grew up, therefore, a brisk smuggling trade. Only the lowland lords were as eager as the newcomers to keep such from the Brothers. Their long service as assassins and secret fighters had given them the label of being deadly with any weapon known to Asborgan. No one it would seem, save the Brothers themselves, wanted any new edge added to the murderous skill they already possessed. So though several of the Masters offered vast rewards for any strange weapon which could be delivered, so far none had come to them—instead only testimony concerning their deadliness and power.

Not only need he be on guard against foresters sweeping here for outlaw dens, but any lowlander would be his enemy on sight. Too many times had the Brothers on oathing been used by warring lords to put down rebellions or reduce some threat from the commoners. No, his safety lay in remaining invisible.

That night Jofre sheltered in a thicket of tree-tall brush at the lip of an ice-rimmed stream. He did not light a fire this side of the mountains and he allowed himself a very small fraction of his remaining supplies. Possessing no journey coins, eating and shelter in the lowlands would depend upon his wits and skill at thievery. Yet he was sure from what he had heard that there were those in the port city, could he reach there, who would be only too glad to add him to their following. The Brothers had no need to cry out their fame; history on Asborgan did it for them.

He had no coins, but he had something else. Not for the first time that day his hand touched his girdle and that lump within its folds. What he carried he did not know; but that it was valuable, he did not doubt at all. And he had heard Trader Dis, who had visited just before the end of the Lair, tell of the high prices one could get from off-worlders for any strange things from the old days. Jofre would not dare offer what he carried to any lord, it was too bound to the Brothers, but an off-worlder would not hold any such scruples. Yes, he would find a buyer; he would make sure of that. Having placed his sentinel stones, he set his mental controls to awake him at any change and at last slept. It was only a light sleep but enough to restore most of the energy he had spent this day.

It took Jofre ten of days to reach his goal. He used every trick of a scout in enemy territory to feed himself. Clothing had been changed at a farmhouse where the family appeared to have withdrawn for a day to the nearest village and he was able to select for his needs. So he left there cloaked and tunicked over his field suit, taking his other clothing with him in a bundle which resembled the jumble of belongings any tramping the roads might carry. It was difficult to shed the turban and half mask of his calling. He felt strangely unprotected with his whole face bared. And catching sight of himself in a wayside pool it seemed he looked upon a stranger.

He had the height of his off-world race, whatever that might be, which had always set him aside from those of the native born. But his hair was as dark as theirs. Only his eyes, the color of a well-burnished blade, were again different from the uniformity of brown known to men of Asborgan. In this rough clothing he might well pass for an off-worlder— except that his knowledge of the star lanes was extremely sketchy and he could well make a betraying error every time he opened his mouth. Regretfully, on the last day before he reached the port, he broke into bits the remains of the pole. That was too patently a Lair weapon and no lowlander would have ever picked it up. He must venture now onto the open road but before he did so he found a thicket and burrowed his way in. Once more he sought the Inner Life and drew upon it. His hands shaped the gestures—rising thought, keen eye, listening ear, ready hand, fleet foot. He drew deeper and deeper breaths as if he were pulling visible strength into his lungs now with each gasp of the chill air.

His eyes no longer saw the world about him as it was but rather as symbols etched in the air, each having its meaning and worth. That which grew was rooted, as strength must be rooted within him, the wind which blew, the declining sun, draw in their spirit, their force—

Now Jofre bared his dagger. This would be no oathing ceremony, for oathing had been closed to him—except the oathing to himself, his inner need. He had shed his glove and with the point of the weapon he touched the tip of each finger in turn with strength enough to raise a bead of blood.

A stiff shake of his wrist sent those flying. Then he put his hand to his mouth and licked each tiny wound, willing them closed. He had shed ritual blood and was now prepared for what would lie ahead, even though he had no mission except the search for such.

Ras Zarn excused himself with polished manners to the off-worlder. He knew exactly who this stranger was, that a linkage ran back and tangled through this man to others spaceflights away. Though he knew also that this Rober Granger had no idea that he knew.

"Your pardon, Gentlehomo." Zarn bowed again. "At this strike of the hour I have a meeting I cannot set aside, much as I would wish it, for indeed what you have to say is of the utmost interest. However, that which summons me will not be of long duration and I ask of your kindness that you wait for me—if you find that possible. I truly believe, Gentlehomo, that we can well strike a bargain."

He sensed the other's irritated anger at such an interruption. However, he was also aware of how much this

one needed what he, Zarn, controlled and he had no doubts he would find the man still there when he returned.

The house in which they had met had once been the town hall of a minor noble. Now it was cut into a warren of smaller rooms and narrow passages which might have bewildered any visitor who had not been furnished with a guide. Zarn turned right, left, and came to a room which had a second door on the outer world. The occupant there was already looking for him as he entered.

"Welcome, Lady." The merchant sketched a bow towards the cloaked figure. She could have been of any rank since that covering, though of good glas-wool, was of drab color and without ornamentation.

In answer to his greeting she inclined her hooded head but did not speak.

"You have had the message; you know what is to be done," he continued. "Remember, this one was high-rated. That renegade Master made of him a true Shadow. He must be taken so that which he now carries may be brought to us."

For the second time she nodded. Then spoke in turn.

"Honorable One, there is already laid on me a mission."

"Yes, but this can be accomplished before that is advanced. This is the oath-order."

"It shall be." Her voice was low but steady. Without any farewell she went out the other door into the open street beyond. Zarn rubbed one hand against another as if between them he was grinding something into dust. She would succeed of course; was she not the best he had ever seen in action? Another mission and perhaps they would have other plans for her—plans for the good of all.

He returned to his fuming visitor his mind fully at ease. With such weapons at one's command one was already the victor in any game. Now to business with this off-worlder and those behind him, and those behind them—Zarn speculated for a moment as to how far that line did actually reach.

There was no wall nor gates to hedge in the sprawl of the new city at the port. Though the merchants and administrators, the tourists (a few of them were coming now, mainly for the larox hunting in the west) and other law-abiding inhabitants were housed in five- and six-story buildings, some even with gardens, but all contained in barriers manned by private guards very much in evidence.

There was no place here for a penniless man, Jofre understood well; he pushed on at the steady gait of someone who knew exactly his goal toward the fringe where were the hurriedly built buildings put up after First Contact near a hundred years ago now. These had been "quickies" in the workman's tongue of that day, shoddily built, and never maintained past the bare necessity of keeping a roof on and not allowing too many holes in the doors.

Many of these housed traders too, those who sold a wealth of intoxicants from both continents of Asborgan, plus stray near-poisonous mixtures brought from off-world. To add to the wealth of drinkables there were the dealers in flesh, who made their wares visible in half-curtained windows during the busy hours of the night, and innumerable forbidden drugs. The police of Asborgan, the old city, had long ago washed their hands of any

responsibility for what went on there. Those inhabitants who were permanent might look after themselves, which most of them were viciously able to do, or disappeared for good, and those off-worlders of the better sort kept out of the "Stinkhole" and maintained their private protections. A few spacers now and then would wander in, but they came in pairs or trios and with stun guns in open holsters well displayed. Those natives from the lowlands beyond the city were seldom fool enough to even think of penetrating into that foul morass and anyway, having come to town, they automatically hunted shelter and amusement of the kind they had always known in the old city.

Jofre's hands moved twice. He had set "No see" pattern in his mind before he had started down the street which ran to the Stinkhole. Though he was well exercised in that maneuver, he had never employed it before except as an ordered drill. But all he had heard suggested that it should work. It was not that an invader could actually render himself invisible, rather that he projected some type of thought which shuttered him from casual sight of those he would move among.

The fetid odor gripped at one's throat. Coming from the austere cleanliness of the mountains, the order of the Lairs, this was like a foul fog. Almost one could see the vapors of decay and excrement rising from the broken pavement. The hour was one strike past sundown and the quarter was coming to life.

Several paces ahead Jofre saw his first spacers. They were clad in close fitting one-piece suits, a brownish-grey which almost matched the discolored walls about them, but was relieved on standing collars and shoulders with colored

patches, not all of the same design, symbols he supposed of either rank or duties. This trio were young and they walked with caution, glancing from side to side. He did not understand the remarks which floated back to him but somehow he sensed that they considered this visit to be something of a challenge.

Because he had nothing else in the way of a guide, Jofre kept in their wake. When they halted before a wide open door which was hung with a billowing curtain of grease-stained faxweed stuff colored a sun-brilliant orange, he paused, too, a step or so before him the opening to an alleyway.

There was a clangor of Whine drums from that doorway loud enough to drown out what the spacers were saying— they seemed to be in argument on some point. In fact those wailing notes were loud enough to drown most of the noises of this portion of the street.

Sound might be so blocked but not instinct. Jofre's head jerked to the left. Trouble—back in that black pocket of an alley. Not any cry of help to be heard with the ear, rather the reaction of someone fighting against odds. And in spite of the nature of the Stinkhole and the fact that its dangers should not be lightly taken Jofre moved—into the alley.

# ✳ CHAPTER 4 ✳

**JOFRE COULD SEE** those struggling shadows once he was within the mouth of that noxious way. There was slime underfoot and he adjusted to that danger. Backed against one of those oozing walls was a tall figure and moving in a concentrated attack three smaller ones. Jofre shifted the thong of his pack and went into action.

No steel here, unarmed tactics, he decided in a flash of thought—there was too good a chance of the victim being brought down in a mixed conflict. The side of his hand chopped between neck and shoulder of the nearest of the rat pack and even above the drums he could hear a cry of pain as the fellow reeled away. Something metal dropped from the attacker's hand to ring on the fouled pavement as he clutched at an arm now swinging uselessly.

"Yaaaaaah sannng—" The cry came from Jofre unbidden as he whirled to strike out again, this time with a lifted knee which sent the second assailant backwards. But their victim took a hand now. There stabbed out of the dark a spear of light no thicker than Jofre's thumb. It struck

the reeling man, then snapped to the left and showed for an instant a face rendered grotesque by a wide, near toothless mouth.

Both of those the ray had touched slumped. The man Jofre had first tackled was already careening down the alleyway, slipping twice and howling as he went.

"My thanks, Night wanderer." The words were oddly accented and Jofre stiffened. With all his need for caution he had betrayed himself with that battle cry. This other was addressing him by the name given by lowlanders to his kind.

Now the shadow which was the stranger stood away a little from the wall, stumbled, and would have gone down had not Jofre, without thinking, caught at a shoulder to steady him.

"You are hurt?" he demanded.

"I am—bruised—in my self-confidence as well as my flesh, Night wanderer. That there would come a day when such as that could move in on one of the Zoxan clan—alas, one is indeed led to face shame."

"If you need shelter—" Jofre began. He was not oathed to this stranger but neither could he walk away and leave him to be food for another pack of rats.

"Night wanderer, unless you have some mission of your own, I would welcome company—at least into the outer ways of this festering pit," the other replied frankly.

His forward move was a lurch and Jofre was again quick to steady him. There was something wrong about the arm the other had half raised to regain his balance; it was short, too short—was this stranger maimed?

Not only was he seeming short of part of an arm but he

was plainly limping as they made their way out into the crooked street. The spacers were gone and for the moment there seemed to be no one else nearby.

Jofre turned his head to survey the stranger he was aiding. Only long training kept him from betraying full astonishment. He had heard that other species not akin to his own were star rovers. However, this creature was so far from anything he had ever seen or heard tell of—except there was a faint relationship perhaps to one of the "demons" of old tales—that he was shaken.

The other more than matched Jofre in height, perhaps being a handsbreadth the taller. His uncovered head was domed and hairless, but about his neck, rising like a great frilled collar, was a fringe of skin which pulsated with color—now a dusky scarlet, though that was fading even as Jofre set eyes on it. The skin of the face and head were scaled, minutely prismatic. In the somewhat fore-pointed face, which was chinless, a well-marked and toothed lower jaw showed no fullness, the eyes were very large and by this garish light appeared to reflect small points of flame.

The stranger was wearing a spacer's suit monotone in color and with no badges to be seen. He was busy now settling one of those fabled off-world weapons into a holster at his belt. His other arm, that which Jofre still held onto in support, was but half the size of the right one and completely covered with the sleeve of the uniform which was turned back and fastened over it.

Having holstered his weapon, the stranger turned his attention to Jofre.

"Well met, Night wanderer—or do you agree?" Those

large eyes seemed to narrow a fraction. The voice had a hissing note which tended to distort the words a fraction.

"Who are you?" Jofre was startled enough to demand, bluntly.

The frill had lost its color, subsiding now to lie about the stranger's narrow shoulders like a small cape collar.

"You mean—what am I? There are no others of my kind on planet now, none that I have heard of. We, too, are wanderers of a sort but circumstances have led me to exceed the reach of my fellow clansmen for a while. I am a Zacathan—my call name Zurzal."

Zacathan! The Master had spoken once of that race. Old, far older than Jofre's own kind, their history stretched back into time mists so dim that no one now could penetrate them. Not a warrior-producing race, on the contrary they were scholars and students, the keepers of archives, not only of their own kind but of all those others they had contact with throughout their explorations into the pasts of many worlds. There were Zacathans to be found among the First-In scouts, for their particular senses and minds made them excellent observers and explorers. And there were fabled repositories of knowledge for which they were responsible, their long lives (when compared to other races) making them excellent record keepers.

Zacathans occupied a strange niche in the galactic world—serving at times as diplomats, peacemakers. Their neutral status was acknowledged and they were made free of any world they wished to visit.

But to find one in the Stinkhole? That Zurzal wore one of the stun weapons was only prudent for anyone venturing here; but why would he have come in the first place?

"I seek a man—"

Jofre tensed. Was mind reading also one of the arts this lizard man knew? If so, he wanted none of that art to be exercised upon him. He loosed his grip on Zurzal's shoulder.

"No, I did not read your mind, Night wanderer, I merely called upon logic. You, of course, wonder why I am here." He uttered a low sound which might have been laughter. "It is no place for a man of peace, that I agree. But sometimes one must overcome a number of obstacles to assure one success."

There was a silence between them. If the Zacathan waited for some reply, Jofre did not know what he should give him. Was the other hinting that he needed help in his search? If so, he had appealed to the wrong one.

"Master of Learning," Jofre gave him the honorific he would have given to one of the few scribes who jealously guarded the history of the Shadows. "I am new come to this place; I know no one herein. You must seek another guide."

"Are you oathed?" That demand came swiftly and with such force of authority that Jofre found himself replying at once with the truth:

"I am not oathed—the Brothers are no longer mine."

He was aware of the sharpness of those eyes which stared at him as if the Zacathan could indeed pry open his skull and sift out some answer.

"There is no outlawing of the Brothern that is recorded," the Zacathan said. "But also none will deny an oath. But— you are not of Asborgan and never have I heard of the Brothers taking into their midst a man of another race."

"I do not know my race, Master of Learning. I was found in the wreckage of a space lifeboat and I was so young that I had no memory of what chanced before the Master of the Lair brought me forth and back to be one of his followers. His issha failed, and the Shagga priest, who long wished none of me, denied me thereafter. But it remains I am issha-trained." And with that he ended confidently. It was no boast but a statement of fact.

"Do you wish an oath binding?"

Was that not what had drawn him here? Though in truth he had not dared to hope for any lord to offer him a House tie.

"Would not any in my position wish such? But I am not backed by any Lair now and the weight of the Brothers will not vouch for me."

The Zacathan nodded. "However, there may be an answer to two problems in this. Will you come and listen?"

It was a strange stroke of fate—there was almost something to be suspicious of in such a quick offer but at least he could hear the off-worlder out. Perhaps after his late experience Zurzal saw the need for a bodyguard. Well, Jofre was trained to that as well as the other uses of the Shadow ones.

"I will come."

He matched step with the Zacathan, walking on the side with the maimed arm. Already he had gone into bodyguard action, assessing each and every spot from which an attack might come. But though they met others, they were left alone and Jofre found himself beyond the Stinkhole and into that section of the port settlement where there were the hotels to shelter travelers.

They approached the largest of the buildings set aside for visitors from off-world, a tower which reached some ten stories above the ground to dwarf the highest of the old town's defense. Here was a clear circle of light about the wide door, showing in warning detail the guards, mainly, Jofre thought, of off-world stock and alert as their training demanded. However, at the sight of the Zacathan the one to the right raised his hand in salute. Whether he triggered some unseen mechanism or not, the door slid back without any needful touch to admit them into a place which, for all his training to be ready for the unexpected, almost brought Jofre to a halt.

Before them was a large hall chamber, one which might have swallowed up half the Lair. And it was divided by a series of tall walls into transparently sheltered circles, squares, alcoves. Some of these were vacant, others having company within.

The floor was not matted but in some places carpeted, in other sections grounded with what seemed stretches of sparking sand, in one place with what had all the appearance of thick mud, and in several what could have been well-cultivated grass starred with colored blossoms. However, the major roomlets were more conventional with a floor of thick carpet into which the boots sank. Here were no seating cushions and knee tables. Rather what looked to offer the same welcoming support of cushions were supported by frames raising them some distance from the floor. And in two of these so furnished there were parties of spacers, plainly of officer rank by the prominence and color of their badges.

Zurzal was threading a way which wound between

window-walled units and Jofre followed, though for all his efforts he could not keep his eyes from straying now and then to the occupants of other roomlets they passed.

In one which was floored with the grass (if it were grass) there were planted two of what looked to be misshapen trees, wide trunks extending horizontally. Perched on these were two beings of surely a very alien stock. One was fragile of body, the proudly held head was covered with what seemed to be curled silver white feathers. The eyes in an oval face were very large and set rather to the side, while the mouth and nose were united in what could almost be termed a beak. From a wide gemmed collar about the slender throat floated a series of panels of gauzy stuff, the color shading from pearl-white to rose, constantly rippling with every movement of the slender body they were apparently to adorn rather than cover. Jofre thought this must be a female, for her companion, plainly of the same strange species, had a feathered head with an upstanding crest, and feathers extended across his shoulders and down the outer side of his arms. The hands he used in quick gestures were more taloned than fingered. His clothing was more practical perhaps, what there was of it, as it consisted of breeches of a shiny material and boots quite like those of any spacer.

The birdlike couple were neighbored by a stretch of sand wherein several large rocks had been assembled. On these squatted things—Jofre could not at that moment accept them as sentient beings—not emotionally—they were too much like, or rather suggested, carvings the Shagga priests used to express the forces of evil. Yet their shelled, near-insectal bodies were at ease and two of them

held with foreclaws what were plainly large mugs into which from time to time they would dip a long tube tongue from between fanged jaws. Their attitude was so much like a trio of elders discoursing on a formal piece of business that Jofre was shaken.

He grasped the significance of this hall; its builders had made a conscious effort to suit not only humanoids but those of alien cultures. And for the first time it struck firmly home to him how very diverse life-forms along the star lanes must be—how utterly different, perhaps even repellent to his kind, some of those other worlds might seem, and how narrow his own life had been.

Zurzal reached the end of the corridor which ran between the "home world" sections of the lobby. Overhead this space reached to the top of the tower and was there roofed over with a yellow, partly transparent oval covering the whole of the circle through which any light outside would filter down changed into the likeness of sunshine. The Zacathan beckoned to Jofre and stepped upon a platform, which, when it held both their weights, arose, passing by two levels of balcony until it locked against the side of the third, and the railing there swung back. They were faced by the outlines of a door in the wall and Zurzal stepped forward to plant his hand flat against that. The panel moved and slid away and once more the Zacathan waved his companion forward into what was undoubtedly his own private quarters.

The glow of the lamp was very dim, but not enough to disguise the anger on the face of the man who stood facing a visitor. That he had not expected company was plain, for

he wore a loose chamber robe belted with a twist of cord about him. Behind him was the pile of sleeping cushions from which a private alarm had drawn him and in the air was the faint scent of the brewing herbs intended to settle nerves and drive away the day's cares—so much had the man called Ras Zarn taken to lowland customs.

A loose hanging curtain was pulled to one side and his unexpected and undesired visitor entered.

"There is no need—" Zarn near spat the words; at his side his hands twitched as if he wished nothing more than to make plain his resentment with a physical blow.

"There is every need," returned the other, low-voiced. Her cloak was all concealing, but with every movement its folds loosed a second scent into the air. "I have conveyed to my Master your instructions. He returns this: None that he oaths undertakes another commission until the first oath is blood erased. He is angry that you have questioned this and tried to lay a new duty on me. Though it does not greatly matter, as the path I follow now leads off-world and I will not be here to serve as your hound. I will be star borne at sunrise." She spoke without emotion though the other's growing rage was almost a tangible thing.

"By the Death of Shagga—"

She had been on the point of turning to leave, now her hooded head was on her shoulder.

"Master's oath—not Shagga—is my bond, and so it has always been. Apply to the Master for the weapon you wish, priest."

And she was gone. He twisted his hands together as if he had them about her neck. Fools, worse than fools!

Traitors if what he and others suspected was true! Now—
there was nothing he could do this night, save think. And
think he must.

# ✳ CHAPTER 5 ✳

**JOFRE SAT UNEASILY** and too comfortably on one of those platform-raised cushion chairs. He was facing the outer wall of the room, which was a curve as transparent as were the divisions in the lobby below. There was a faint sprinkling of watch lights from the old town, reflections of the more brilliant illumination here. At his side, on a waist-high table, stood a drinking vessel, seeming so fragile a too quick grasp might shatter it, the green of verjuice showing through its sides.

Zurzal, having equipped himself with a drink also—which as mysteriously appeared as had the verjuice in a wall space after the Zacathan had pressed some buttons—seated himself opposite his only partly willing guest.

"You say you are not oathed."

"I cannot be—there is no Master who will coswear with me."

Jofre had dropped his pack by the door. It would be ready to hand when he left.

"You are issha—is there any way that you can retreat from that?"

Jofre stiffened. What games did the alien want to play? Surely fortune had not been that good to him that he could find employment so easily, even for a short time.

"I am issha."

"I know something of the Shadow Brothers," the Zacathan continued. "It is part of the nature of my race to learn all we can about the ways and customs of others. It is true that your services are always contracted for through a Lair Master. How much power has this Shagga priest of yours?"

Jofre considered. "In oathing the Masters alone control us. The Shagga sometimes serve as special eyes and ears, they are advisors to the Masters—"

"The Masters can overrule them then?"

"Twice in our history it has been so. But to those who disputed with the Shagga misfortune came later—they were assha lost."

"As was your Master," Zurzal pointed out. "Could it be that he was a target then for Shagga ill will?"

Jofre swallowed. "He did not listen to advice he thought was too conservative, too lacking in a desire to learn new."

"So he therefore became one of the Elder Shadows."

"How do you know what—" Jofre flared.

"I told you, I would learn all that I can. There is talk in the old city of the Brothers, perhaps some of it rumor only; but even in rumor there is a core of truth. Think, Night wanderer, your Master was not a second voice for Shagga and he is now gone. Just as you have been hunted forth from the fellowship. You are freed by the very one who would condemn you, the Shagga. You have no Master save yourself. Therefore as a self-master you may be oathed."

Jofre swallowed. Dimly perhaps he had known a little of this but some back-looking part of him had not allowed him to put it so frankly.

"You want an oathed issha?" he asked now, trying to read the alien's face, which provided no features he could interpret after any pattern which he knew.

Zurzal took a long drink from his glass. "After tonight do you not think that I need a bodyguard? For a while I am not even a whole man." He set down the drink and his hand went to the sealing of his suit. With a quick jerk he had it open to the waist and back from his left shoulder and arm. For there was an arm there—or the beginning of one—a length of bone and flesh and a child-size hand.

"One of the attributes of my people," he informed Jofre. "We can regrow a lost limb but the process takes time and it is time I do not have right now. Therefore, I need aid."

"There are surely off-worlders who are guards—like those below—"

"They are not oathed men. You see, I know your customs, issha-trained. With an oathed man out of the Shadows I need have no fear of any treachery or carelessness. I lost this," he moved the small arm, "because I could not be ever on guard. I need you, Night wanderer. I offer you oathed status."

There was a pause and then the Zacathan continued. "What I wish to do here on Asborgan is only a beginning. Oath with me and it will mean the stars. You or any other in your place must have such a warning."

The stars—then what the Master had thought was true. On other worlds there were doubtless the same feuds, the same intrigues, the same covert wars for power that the

lords here played. And this Zacathan had already suffered maiming—which meant—

"You have a blood feud?" Jofre asked—such he could understand and be prepared to undertake.

"Not as those of Asborgan see it. But that is not discounting any danger, and such lies ahead. You are out set from your Brothern; in a manner of speaking I am also. But that I shall discuss only under oath. What is your word—?"

Jofre's right hand closed about his dagger and he drew that one long weapon left him. Holding it now between both of his palms, he went to one knee before the Zacathan.

The scaled fingers came to meet his instantly and the dagger was drawn from the sheath of flesh in which he held it.

"By the Great Oath"—so this off-worlder *DID* know enough of the Brothern to follow the form—"I call you out of the Shadows and into my service until my purpose is achieved or life is ended." Zurzal reversed the dagger awkwardly with his single hand and managed to press his forefinger down on its point. Dark blood welled in a thick bead and he smeared it on the dagger and held it out for Jofre to once more clasp double-handed so that that smear of blood was imprinted on his own flesh.

"I am bound—" he said shortly, making no move to wipe that mark from his hands as he returned his weapon to his girdle.

"So done. The hour grows late. Have you eaten, sworn man? Drink up, for I have much to talk of now and time itself is snapping at my heels."

"I have not eaten." Jofre's hold left a faint bloodstain on the drinking vessel. "But if time is limited, that is of no importance."

The Zacathan's long jaws opened in what must have been a smile. "I assure you I am not so blind to the needs of any employee. As it happens, I myself have not eaten." He crossed back to the opening in the wall from which he had taken the drinks. A button brought up light in a square and Jofre saw marks in a series cross that.

Then the Zacathan busied himself with the lower line of buttons before that light square was gone. "They do vespar well here," he said, "it is considered, of course, in this setting a novelty. And there are some other things I think you will find to your taste. We are not too unlike in our eating habits, we two peoples."

As quickly as he had gone to one wall so now he turned to another and set fingers in a ridge to open another door.

"This is the fresher," he said, "and here," he had found another doorhold and opened that also, light streaming up even as the portal went back, "are sleeping quarters. Settle in while we wait to be served."

Jofre merely glanced into the sleeping room. There were two bed places which looked to be as luxuriously soft as a district lord might aspire to. But the fresher drew him most.

Austere and barren to city eyes as the Lair might be, it was always meticulous clean and cleanliness was part of issha training. This tiled chamber did not resemble the bathing place he had always known but it promised a relief

The Zacathan had opened another door within that

place of ease to display a cubicle and now he indicated various small levers jutting from its inner wall.

"Hot steam or water as you wish, cold, soap power spray, and air-drying hose. Make yourself free—"

Then he was gone. Jofre rummaged in his bundle and brought out much creased but clean underdrawers, and shirt. But before he tried the amenities of that strange room he made a careful inspection. There was no entrance save that through which he had come and there was certainly no place where there could be a place of concealment. Not that he had any fears of this being a trap—he was oathed and, therefore, as tied to Zurzal now as if he were one of the Zacathan's scaled kin.

It took him a little time to master what the fresher had to offer and inwardly he marveled. No Lair Master could hope for such luxury as this and he savored the feeling of cleanliness afterwards; almost he wished he did not have to rewear his travel-stained outer clothing. But he made very sure that the stone he had found at Qaw-en-itter was again well secured in the wrapping of his sash girdle.

Zurzal was waiting in the outer room beside a larger table to which were drawn up two of the tall seats, these not so encushioned as the others. On the table itself were set out covered bowls and platters and two plates. By the side of each of those there was an array of knives and spoons and some odd-looking cutlery which ended in a set of points and which Jofre could not identify.

"It was good, lord," he glanced over his shoulder at the now closed door of the fresher, "my thanks for your offering—"

The Zacathan had already seated himself and whipped

the cover from the largest of the bowls so that steam and a smell, which made Jofre suddenly very aware how long it had been since he had last eaten, filled the air.

"I am no lord." Zurzal was now busy ladling some of the contents of the bowl onto the plate before Jofre as the younger man slipped rather awkwardly onto that elevated seat. "I am Zurzal, I do have a title—which means nothing on most worlds other than my own. I am called a Histechnic which only means that I have completed a series of studies to the satisfaction of my elders and betters. I am Zurzal. And you?"

"The Master named me Jofre."

"Jofre—" repeated the Zacathan, "sky given. Because of your finding, I suppose."

Jofre was again a little shaken at Zurzal's quick grasp of his name meaning, for that was a word of the high country and not the lowlands where a visitor might have traveled enough to learn something of the native tongues.

"Yes—" He eyed his plate now, drawing his knife to cut at the generous portion of smoking vespar which had been served him.

"Your Master made no attempt to report your finding to the port authorities?"

Jofre shook his head. "The Lairs have their own ways. He could have sent me to one of the valley lords but he did not. He was a man who kept his thoughts much to himself."

"I have heard that the Brothers are indeed secret in their ways; it is part of the faces they turn to the world. At any rate he gave you a trade, this Master of yours."

"He judged me issha," Jofre said and remembered his inner pride, which he had taken precautions to hide on the

day he had received the Three Weapons and the Cloak. Not that any of those had come with him on his being exiled.

He was having a hard time curbing his hunger now, making himself chew and swallow slowly. The food was diverse. As he had spoken, Zurzal had heaped on the plate before Jofre large portions from at least five of the dishes.

"You need my services—" Jofre was perhaps too abrupt in turning from his past to the immediate present but he had no wish to dwell now on what lay behind him.

"I do."

"What lord has declared blood price against you?"

"It is no feud, as I have said, like those of your nobles. There are those who are opposing me openly, and recently I have learned that there is an even greater problem in the nature of some who want what I am working upon for their own purposes. Those you took me from tonight might well not have been seeking my life, but rather my person and what I know."

Though earlier he had admitted hunger, Zurzal seemed more intent now on talking. He sipped from his drinking vessel, but, though he stabbed at a portion of vespar on his plate with one of the pointed pieces of cutlery, he did not yet raise it to his mouth.

"You must understand those of my stock," he said. "To us knowledge is everything. And one of the sources of knowledge which we hope to find are records—records of the Forerunners—"

"Forerunners?" That was one term Jofre had not heard before.

"We did not come first into space. There are worlds

upon worlds, some very old. It is a pattern with sentient people that they rise to a high point of civilization and then some inner lack or flaw within them saps the energy which sent them climbing and they decline, sometimes to actually disappear and be forgotten. So we are not the first rovers of the lanes; there were others before us and they left their traces here and there. There is a great reward posted for any major find which is made of such peoples—for they certainly were not all of the same stock or even the same time. Their civilizations may well have been as varied as our present ones. You saw in the lobby below life-forms which did not share a common beginning with yours. Yet all those are now citizens and equal under the galactic laws.

"Thus we have tantalizing hints on this world and that of other peoples, some we are sure were not native to the planets where they left these remains, but space rovers such as ourselves. One of my colleagues was able to find an entire planet city, stretching completely round the world which supported it, of a highly technical civilization. There are experts there now studying it under supervision.

"So many finds come by chance alone—but if there were some way that such could be traced—" There seemed to be tiny cores of light in the Zacathan's eyes; his neck frill was rising to frame his head and shading into a green-blue.

"And there is a reward for such discoveries?" Jofre thought he understood.

"Yes—but greater than any reward is the knowledge itself!" Now Zurzal's frill was a vivid fan.

"You are hunting such? But I have never heard of any old things on Asborgan and the Shagga priests have very

ancient records. If there was knowledge, they would have sought it out."

"No, I am not hunting Forerunners here—rather a man. I was in trace of him this evening. He may be the key to a great discovery—We have records and also we have access to special knowledge. I have a discovery I must try. At present I am not well accepted by my people; they believe that my research for the past few years has been for a very childish and no-purpose reason. I am young, as my people count years, and oftentimes the young are dismissed for thinking something can be done in a different way.

"There was a discovery made and ill-used on a world named Korwar. The results were so terrifying at the time that the man who backed that expedition saw that—or thought he saw that—the instrument used was destroyed and all the plans from which it had been manufactured were completely wiped from the records.

"But the idea of what had been done could not be denied and there was an undercover rumor of what had happened which spread. That there could be an artifact which would summon up an accurate picture of the past had now to be accepted. But the machine was gone and even mention of it was thoroughly suppressed.

"Not so well suppressed that it was totally forgotten, however. Two planet years ago those plans were rediscovered in a mass of material turned over to my home section of the archives by the Patrol after they had raided a Jack outfit. There was a mixture of reports, some log books of old ships taken by Jacks—and it needed sifting for anything of value. I was given the task of that

sorting—mainly because I was the youngest member of our group and considered the least responsible.

"But what I found was a complete plan for a probe, such a probe as would make any Histechnic give perhaps all his fangs for. I took this to my superior. He was not interested, pointing out this had been tried once with dire results and that my people would not tamper with anything of the sort. He confiscated what I had found and told me to keep quiet.

"I did. But I had those plans here." Zurzal laid aside his eating tool and tapped his forehead. "And keeping quiet I went to work until I had that scanner rebuilt. I ran one trial in a place I knew of and the result was astonishing, but it came and went in a flash and I knew that the remains on which I tried it were so well-known that I could be accused of falsifying evidence—which among my people, Jofre, is akin to oath breaking, if you can imagine that. Therefore, I must find someplace unknown where I could hope to tap into history totally newfound, and I also worked steadily on a true scanner, hoping to produce a way for it also to make a permanent record of what it draws from the past."

That the Zacathan believed in what he was saying was very apparent. That it could be done—well, Jofre would want to see for himself. Meanwhile it was more important to know who might be the enemy.

"It is your leader who would hunt you down now?" he asked.

Zurzal shrugged. "If he knew, he would oppose me legally, then I would have the Patrol on my heels. No, so far I do not believe they suspect what I would do. But the information on which I based my work was from a Jack

hold, and that means it could have been kept to be sold to the Guild—surely you can guess what possibilities their Veeps could see in such."

"Treasure hunting." Jofre could see. However, if the Thieves Guild was to supply his potential enemies, he had accepted a very direful oath indeed.

"Treasure hunting," Zurzal conceded but the Zacathan did not seem upset at the thought of taking on the most dangerous starwide organization—next to the Patrol—which existed.

# ✳ CHAPTER 6 ✳

**"HOWEVER,"** Zurzal had taken time to consume a good portion of what was on his plate, as if he must also do a little arranging of his thoughts, "it is not what the Guild might consider treasure, adaptable in their consciences as they are. No, what I want is knowledge—to find a place where there was a storehouse of records—"

"Does such exist?" Jofre had cleaned his own plate and was watching the Zacathan's neck frill a little bedazzled. It continued to glow as ripples of rich color spread along the creases.

"I spoke of the world found by one of my colleagues where a vast city covered the major continents. There were archives there and—maps—"

Zurzal swallowed another bite. "Star maps. Though the language of the archives is yet to be broken down for translation, there were certain symbols which we recognized. That was indeed a Forerunner world, a planet where a technical civilization had reached a peak before the end and yet they were in turn latecomers to the star lanes, for they had museums, they had visual records, of

much older civilizations which had preceded them. There were hints of finds to be made, which some freak of their own time prevented their making. My people impounded all such records with the blessing of Central Control. And it was my good fortune to be allowed some access to them.

"No, I do not hunt what the Guild would consider useful—the only market for my hoped-for finds would be my own people and, therefore, no market at all. I search for archives and perhaps the only way I can find them is by reaching into the past with the scanner for long enough to pinpoint the position of what I seek. Having made such a find, I will have redeemed myself in the eyes of my colleagues as well as added to the sum of our knowledge. None of my race could wish for a greater treasure hunt than that."

"Here on Asborgan—?"

Zurzal gave an impatient shake of the head. "No, as I said, here I seek a man, if he still lives. He did two band moons ago but he is in the last stages of graz addiction and I can only hope he still exists. He was the member of a First-In expedition to a world which, on Patrol charts, is named Lochan for the man who first made landfall there. What its inhabitants—they are listed as extremely primitive and at least nine points away from human—name it we do not know.

"As a primitive D class world it is off-limits to all but the smallest of Free Traders, those who nose around the lanes for the crumbs and are regulated by the Patrol as to what they may carry. There IS trade, however. A kind of clay which, when ground into sand texture, is highly

desired by the potters on Reese, and there is some exchange for unusual furs and other oddments.

"But there is also a ruin which was reported by the First-In scout and then partially explored by the first expedition. They made certain records of the finds, one of which—" The Zacathan left his seat and went to a set of shelves on the other side of the room. He came back holding a box hardly bigger than his hand, which he put down before Jofre with the instruction, "Look!"

There was a round of glassy substance not unlike a mirror in one end of the box and into that Jofre obediently looked. The surface of that disc was changing color and now he could see what might have been a picture of a portion of a strange landscape. The ground was dull, black-sprinkled grey and would seem to be bare earth with no form of vegetation. From that sea of coarse, dull colored sand projected a straggle of rocks, so eroded that one could not tell whether they were a showing of the planet bones or the work of men.

The picture was moving, drawing closer as if he were approaching closely one of those rock humps. Here there had been a clearing, the sand had been dug or pushed away, and then it was as if Jofre stood at the edge of that pit looking down. The uncovered base of the rock reached deep, until it joined another at right angles. And on that second there was a flashing marking.

"The F ray brought that out." The Zacathan was beside him. "It must have been set with great care to have lasted so long a time."

"What is it?" Jofre was completely mystified.

"It is a symbol which has been found twice before and

each time it indicated a storehouse," Zurzal informed him. "Only there was to be no follow-up; the expedition was attacked by desert dwellers. Two men escaped, one dying before they reached the landing port, the other very badly injured. He managed only to bring this recording with him but he was unconscious and could not explain its value nor even where they had been excavating to discover it. His brush with the natives appeared to plunge him into a deep trauma—for a year or more he was plagued by nightmares and had to be kept sedated. He resigned his position, dropped out of sight, and turned to graz. It was as if he had faced something so terrible that he dared not live conscious of the past at all—"

"The natives?" Jofre looked away from the small mirrored picture.

"Perhaps—very few of them come to the port and those that do any trading with off-worlders keep much to themselves. They seem to travel in fear themselves. There must be some menace which they do not discuss with outsiders.

"However, this," Zurzal took up the box again, "and the memories of that man are all the clues we have to what may be the greatest discovery of this generation. That same symbol elsewhere led Zammerly to the cache of star maps on Homeward, and the same sign brought Zage to the lost library of the Woland Priest Kings. It is as if some of the Forerunners deliberately marked such sites either for preservation or for a future exploration which never came to be. Thus Lochan is the goal, and the site of this," he tapped the box with one finger, "depends on the memory of one Garsteon z'Vole, who is now living out what is left of his life in the Stinkhole."

"They say graz rots out a man's mind. His memory may be already gone," Jofre pointed out. To him this seemed a business in which there were too many loopholes through which failure could thread. But he was oathed and it was now his business as well as he could carry it out.

"That can only be determined by meeting the man. Which perhaps we can tomorrow."

To that Jofre was ready to agree. He refused the comfort of the second bed in the Zacathan's inner chamber, taking his proper place, as a bodyguard should, in front of the doorway. The carpeting in the room was far softer than any sleeping pallet he was used to and he knew that no one could enter without his knowing.

That the Guild, having heard of Zurzal's boasted scanner, would be interested he could well believe. Even in the mountain Lairs they had heard tales of how the vast criminal network took into its clutches inventions and discoveries which it kept for all time. Jofre could understand that if what Zurzal claimed for his find was true, it could well be put to other than archaeological searches. As for himself he would believe you could see into the past when such a scene was directly before his eyes.

In a Lair tower to the north at that same hour, which was near midnight, a Shagga priest bent his shaven head over a brazier which gave forth a trickle of reddish smoke, drawing that deeply into his lungs. His eyes were shut and he rocked his body back and forth in a rhythm which matched the words he mouthed in a hissing whisper. He was going deeper perhaps than was prudent. Hate had set him on this road in the beginning; now there was a touch

of fear. The contempt he had earlier felt had diminished; this adversary was stronger than he had ever conceived he would be.

He collapsed at last, huddled in upon himself as if he would hide from what was about him. The arts of the priesthood were very old; those which they transmitted to assha and issha were only the surface of what powers they could summon. He had been a teacher all of his ordained life but at times he had also been a seeker, probing into some ways which, if not completely forbidden, were warned against. It was only his fear which drove him to try this.

Jofre awoke from his doze immediately alert and ready as his training had prepared him to be. For a moment he did not stir; he looked through only slits, keeping his eyelids near closed to deceive any watcher; at the same time he readied himself. That he was not alone, of that he was so sure that his hand moved serpent still and quick under the edge of his sleep cover until his fingers could close about the handle of his dagger.

Still he waited. His ears quested for the sound of breathing. There was a faint light from the upper part of the walls where they joined with the ceiling, enough to give him full sight. He heard nothing, saw nothing.

Then there was a stab of heat, great enough to bring him up to his knees, his hand at the stretch of his girdle on the right side of his body. There was a lump there, the stone he had brought out of Qwa-en-itter! And through the cloth which hid it he could feel warmth, for the worst of that touching flame had eased.

At the same time that sense of another presence was gone, as if he had snuffed out a Lair lamp. And the warmth went with it. Shagga—Shagga tricks! He was as sure of that as if some priest still stood there leering at him. The priest who had expelled him from the Lair company had certainly held no kind thoughts towards him, but why would he want to carry on any feud now that Jofre was no longer contaminating the Brotherhood? That pain—he worked the stone out of the girdle folds. There was no light in its depths now—it was opaquely dead. But there was still warmth in it as he handled it, turning it around in his hand. Whatever it was it answered to Shagga power. Perhaps it would be far better for him were he to discard it now. Yet he could not. It was as if the artifact had a will of its own and had oathed itself to him.

Jofre shoved it once more into hiding. He took the position of far-seeing—the door was made fast and he must dare thus for caution's sake. Nonetheless he planted his shoulders against the portal it was his duty to guard, firmly enough so that he trusted any movement there would alert him, before he began the Descent-to-the-heart—forcing his breath into the slow, regular pattern, using his will to wall away all thought.

He had always excelled in this since he was issha made—in fact to the point that the Master had used him several times without advertising the fact, in his own affairs. Perhaps some quirk of his off-world-born brain adjusted easily to this skill.

Now having reached the Center, where was the path? He might be standing in a circle of light from which led radiating rays to form roads. He sent out thought and was

again in live memory, in Qwa-en-itter, his hand reaching for that ovoid he still carried. There was a flicker of light, a spark, as he touched it. Yes, a thing of power—very old power. And the Shagga—Jofre tried to find the path which would lead back to that one who had come spying. But nothing remained on which he could fix to draw himself.

A lash of will took him out of the Center. His hands began to move in the ritual patterns which summoned strength—to both mind and body. He could feel the rise of that strength, the way it filled him. The rest of the issha preparation he could not continue. He had only his dagger—the small knives, the sword, the flask of blinding powder, the hooked rope which could be either a ladder or a weapon, those he had been forced to leave behind. He felt their loss now; not being able to complete the Readiness worried him. If the Zacathan truly wanted him as a bodyguard, then with the day's coming he must see about acquiring the familiar weapons he had been deprived of before he would be fully at ease, a formidable trained issha. Where in this lowland country such weapons could be found, Jofre had no idea, but he must make plain to Zurzal their lack might cripple him in the future.

However, with the morning he had no time to speak of his need to the Zacathan; the other had anticipated him.

"You must have supplies," Zurzal said briskly, having summoned another of those very satisfying meals out of the wall. "I have heard that you or the Brotherhood can accomplish much with bare hands—but there is no reason to try and prove that. We shall see about more conventional ways of defense."

✳✳✳

Seeing about that brought them to a warehouse-shop where Jofre, trailing Zurzal into a smaller room, nearly gaped as wide as any field laborer as he viewed racks of weapons, cases of them, an armory so superior to that of the Lair that the latter would seem a play place for children. However, a second and more measuring survey showed him that there were few of the conventional issha arms here. Those small throwing knives easy to be hidden—he could see none in the case which held mainly daggers and some blades long enough to be short swords. There were no whirl chains, no hook ropes.

"Over here." Zurzal was beckoning to him. The seller of these wares was a lowlander, though he wore the formfitting clothing of the spacers. A Tarken, Jofre placed him, one of the hereditary clan of merchant guardsmen. He had opened another case and was taking out those storied off-world weapons, such as Zurzal himself wore, the sidearms which could either stun for capture or burn to a crisp an enemy.

"Take your pick," the Zacathan bade him as Jofre joined the other two by the case.

Jofre looked uneasily to the salesman. He had his own needs, but to reveal them now would instantly label him for what he was in front of this lowlander. On the other hand were he to be summarily equipped with weapons with which he was unfamiliar, he could well be defeated in an attack before he started.

He stared down at the stunners. Then put out a hand hesitantly and picked up the nearest. It did not have the familiar balance of a dagger or sword, did not fit easily into a trained hand. Though as he examined it more closely it

appeared to be a simple enough mechanism—one closed the fist thus, then within easy reach of the forefinger were two buttons. Jofre raised it and squinted along the short barrel at the wall—yes, just so must one aim it. He laid it back with its fellows and picked up the next. A man must feel at home with his weapons, not just take the first offered, thus he hefted them all before nodding and making his choice.

"This—" It was the one lying in third place, and somehow in his hand it felt the best. "However—there must be other things—" Again he looked across Zurzal's shoulder to the salesman. How much dared he reveal by his choices? It was as if the Zacathan read his thoughts, for Zurzal turned to the Tarken and at the same time reached out and laid his hand on Jofre's shoulder.

"Ras Quan, this issha is blood oathed to me," he spoke deliberately. "As his New-master-one I must equip him properly. Let him then choose what he believes will serve him best."

Tensely Jofre waited for the Tarken's reaction. But there was not so much as a flutter of the eyelid to suggest that such a request was in any way out of the ordinary.

"Seek, Night wanderer." At least he was giving Jofre the name lowlanders bestowed upon his kind. "We have very little call for the Shadow weapons here; you may find that most are lacking."

Jofre nodded curtly and swung on his heel, going back to the display of knives and swords, eyeing as he went the various arms hanging on the walls. There were two small knives which might do for sleeve weapons, though whether they could be easily concealed in any clothing save the

wide-sleeved coats his kind favored he was not sure. However, they looked enough like those he had practiced with for many hours to be familiar and he indicated them. A sword—if they were bound off-world into places where the weapons would be those lasers—swords would be useless. He eyed them wistfully for a moment and then shrugged.

A climbing rope he could devise himself but he found with some excitement a large bowlike container full of polished hooks, well barbed, and of those he selected a dozen, running his fingers across the metal in search of any flaws. Such he could conceal in a turban wrapping if he must.

There was no use, he was sure, to search here for a sleeve box of poison dust, nor other subtle weapons of the Lairs. And he had to be content with what he picked out, the hooks being fastened for transporting within his sleeves, the knives and the stunner joining his dagger in his girdle.

But it seemed they were not yet done with shopping for the Tarken led the way into another room and within a short time Jofre found himself with a totally new wardrobe, the suit of a spacer, a cloak which the Zacathan said was meant to shed water, underclothing, new boots which felt curiously heavy as they were soled with the plating for ship-bound travelers. In addition there was a bedroll and some of the aids to make easier camp life. Though Jofre privately could see no reason for such pampering of one who was out of the austere life of the Lairs.

He wondered now how Zurzal was to pay for this. As a sworn liegeman Jofre was entitled truly to weapons, the

livery clothing of his employer's house, just as he would be entitled for, as long as the oath held, transportation, food and lodging. In the natural course of things a wage sum would have been transferred to the coffers of the Lair from which he came—but that would not be necessary in this transaction.

But no bar pieces passed between Zurzal and the Tarken—rather the Zacathan merely showed the other a band on his wrist on which glowed a number of markings. Then in turn Zurzal pressed this to a pad the Tarken produced. As they went out of the place Zurzal explained and turned his wrist well out into the daylight to show Jofre.

"Each world has its own form of exchange for goods and services. But there are ways of transferring such credit without having to pass it into the form of another planet. Thus—" He flexed his hand and the wristlet was a gleam in the thin sunlight. "I have funds on several worlds to draw on, and pay from those funds may be demanded by merchants on other planets. It is a simple system—"

Jofre thought he could see the flaw in it. "If that is stolen and used—"

Zurzal shook his head. "It is blood joined to me alone; it will not work for any other. Now, let us go ahunting for this spacer."

He turned quickly into a side street, threading a way he seemed to know well, heading again for the Stinkhole. Jofre slipped a hand across the new weight of those recently added knives. Last night his unarmed skill had been put to the test; he wondered if this time his ability with steel would be called upon.

# ✳ CHAPTER 7 ✳

**THERE WERE NO BURSTS** of eye-tormenting light from any of the smoldering doorways, no whine of drums. Today they might be walking through a sink of long-deserted squalor. One or two muffled figures kept close to the verges of the pavement, since the center of that was a riverlet of corruption. Only the thick stench was the same, puffing out at them from the opening of every alley as if the Stinkhole itself had life and nauseous breath.

Zurzal seemed to know where he was going. Jofre was a step behind, every issha instinct alert. He did not like what he could not see but was sure was lurking in the stained walled buildings, in every one of those alley mouths; he did not like what he heard—which was nothing at all. Certainly there should be some sound.

As Zurzal took a sharp turn to the right, a moment's glance around placed Jofre. This was the same place where he had come to the rescue of the Zacathan the night before. To venture into such a trap was more than foolhardy.

At least a small measure of light had come with the day and Jofre could see the path ahead, choked as it was with rubbish. The alley was dead-ended by a portion of the building on their right which extended at a sharp angle. There was a door at floor level and up the narrow slit of this wing a series of windows, all covered with boarding.

They passed the site of last night's skirmish. The noisome debris underfoot had been churned and there were signs of some heavy object having been drawn along through the muck—doubtless one of their opponents taken away. A sound brought Jofre into action. He was before his patron, a punch of his shoulder sending the Zacathan back against the moisture-running wall while he half crouched in defense. Out of the disturbed muck and nameless mounds ahead poked the nasty white snout of a ku-rat—the largest Jofre had ever sighted.

His hand went from the hilt of his dagger to the far less familiar grip of the sidearm. He brought the weapon up, sighted and fired. There was a screech, then the twisting body arose from the rubbish in which it had sheltered to curl into both silence and a motionless ball. Jofre stared at the creature. A lucky shot certainly, he had had very little time to practice—save in dumb show—before they made this expedition and he must not believe that his accuracy with the off-world weapon was more now than rank fortune.

"The power of the first part," Zurzal observed from behind him as Jofre still sheltered the Zacathan with his own body, "is enough if we meet more than rats—to stun is allowable. I think that a burn-off even in this place might bring some retribution down on us."

Jofre made the adjustment before he returned the weapon to his unfamiliar overbelt. He had changed into the new clothing before they had started and he regretted deeply the loss of his wide-sleeved overshirt, though he retained the girdle which had always supported hand weapons. To be reduced to a dagger and this stunner-blaster meant double caution on his part.

In two more strides the Zacathan reached the door in that wall which blocked their path. It looked as set-in as the boarded-up windows above, as if it were sealed firmly. Yet the off-worlder did not appear to be baffled by this. He drew the taloned fingers of his useable right hand down the splintery surface, scratching into wood spongy with rot.

At waist level those fingers stopped to circle about as if outlining some lock which did not appear. Then Zurzal drew his own weapon, examined the setting critically before he made a small adjustment, and put the barrel to the door. There was a flash and a crackle of sparks ran from that point of contact. A moment later the Zacathan resheathed the weapon, put palm flat against the door to push. Reluctantly the barrier gave, showing a thick gloom within.

"This is a back way," Zurzal's voice dropped near to a hissing whisper. "What we seek lies there." He jerked his head toward the wall of the building from which this portion angled.

Jofre's hand was quick. His fingers closed about the Zacathan's sinewy arm.

"I first," he made that an order. "Which way?"

"Right. There should be a stair near. The man we seek has lodging, such as it is, near the top floor. He is, I think,

very near the end. The report made to me is that he has not been seen for three days now."

Within the house there was a thick effluvium of old filth, the result of beings of more than one species being crowded in long-uncleansed quarters. The two invaders found the stairs easily enough, for there was an orb light, near exhausted by the feebleness of its glow, suspended over the well of the steps.

Now there were sounds, grunts, the rumble of speech, and once the throb of a hand drum, a smashing of what might be glass, and again a scream which held both rage and pain. Zurzal continued to climb; Jofre, eyes darting from wall to wall of the stairway, ears and nose alert, edged after him. They reached the third level of the stair and Zurzal stopped, fronting another door.

This time there was a waiting latch and he caught at it, throwing the door open. The room on the other side had once been of fair size, but a partition which did not reach clear to the ceiling had turned it into a pair of alcoves. The stench was now overpowering. In the nearer of those alcoves was a sleep mat and on that lay a body wrapped in a discolored length of bed covering.

Zurzal felt in the pouch which was clipped to his belt. He brought out a package which, without opening it, he squeezed vigorously in his one hand. Now another scent joined the rest, a cloying one which seemed thick enough to be visible in the room.

The bundle on the mat stirred, shifted, sat up. A bloated-faced head wobbled on a neck seemingly too thin to hold it, then a bony hand came out of hiding and made a wide circle through the air. The eyes in that puffed face,

which at first had looked unfocused, now centered on the Zacathan. A slobbering tongue crept out from between swollen lips and then a voice which was thick and hardly to be understood spoke a single word:

"Give!"

Zurzal ripped open one end of the drug bag and that wavering hand strove to flatten and hold steady as the Zacathan shook onto the palm a wad of seeds and leaves. Dropping some of the stuff in his haste, the man on the pallet crammed it into his mouth and those jaws so hidden by fatty tissue now moved as he chewed.

The effect came within a few moments. The sagging body on the sleep mat sat straighter. There was a certain dim intelligence back in the eyes to be sighted in the constrained light through a half-masked window.

"You—" The word was mumbled around that cud which the spacer still chewed.

"As I promised," Zurzal returned calmly. "Enough of this to take you to the end—" He gave the bag a little shake and once more the smell of the drug was wafted about.

The bulbous head nodded. "Fair—fair bargain." Then the mouth moved as the speaker spat the pulp of his chewing onto the rotting floor. "I have—" Now two hands emerged from his wrappings and he was tugging at that covering, pulling away from his body.

He was bare of any clothing Jofre could see. In spite of the bloated face and head, his body was a rack of bones covered with greyish, grimed skin. But he wore around his neck a chain which sparked in the light—iridium! How could such a derelict possess that? Supported from that chain was a round medallion of the same precious metal.

Long broken nails scrabbled at that until it opened and a tiny dark roll fell out. The ex-spacer weighed it in one hand, and for a moment, in spite of the ruin of that face, Jofre thought he saw a flash of another man who had once been.

"Fair—fair bargain," the spacer stuttered a little. "But—you may find it not so good. Not so good." He shook his big head from side to side. "Give!" he demanded.

Zurzal dropped the packet of graz in the seated man's lap and took the roll, slipping it into his belt pocket.

The spacer's one hand clamped on that opened bag as if he feared it might be taken from him. But with the fingers of the other he swung the pendant from which he had freed the roll back and forth.

"Beyond—call—duty—" He looked up at the Zacathan and then he laughed horribly, his huge face a mask such as one of the Shagga imagined demons might wear. "Get out! You have what you want, lizard man." The more he spoke, the firmer his voice, the clearer his words became. "You have everything but luck, remember that." Greedily he pawed at the bag, brought forth another wad of the drug and crammed it into his mouth, dropping his head back on the bed place. It was plain that he had nothing more to say.

"What do you have?" Jofre asked as they edged out of that horrible box of a room.

"The coordinates of the place on Lochan which I must visit. He was a hero once—did you see that medal? Through everything he held onto that."

Zurzal's voice was somber as they retraced their way down the staircase. "He is very near the end," the Zacathan continued. "The supply I took him will surely see him out and he will die in what poor comfort that has left him. He

was a hero—once—" The repetition of that phrase rang in Jofre's head as they stepped once more into the alley and headed back into what was a cleaner and brighter kind of life.

Ras Zarn stood again in that small private chamber of his, and again he held a farflyer. There was a weariness about him these days. Sometimes fortune turns against a man—then to fight his way through obstacles becomes twice the battle. He was no longer as young as his appearance made him seem to these townsmen lowlanders. And he had been long away from the north and close touch with that which demanded his inborn allegiance. Just as those who gave secret orders were far removed and uncaring about his problems.

They were set in the old ways as tightly as a sunken worm in its shell and perhaps all which would ever get them out was how one dealt with that worm—smash the shell itself.

Zarn shivered with a quick glance from one of the walls to another. The bird in his hands raised its head and quickly he put his other hand over that, cupping it gently, blinding the creature. No one knew, would ever know, just how farseeing the Elders were, nor what strange powers they could call upon. It needed only one small misstep, one planting of a seed of suspicion, and he himself could be a target no matter how well he had served in the past.

Sighing inwardly, he seated himself at the floor table and set the farflyer on its well-scratched surface. Lifting the shielding hand, he looked into the eyes of the north-bred creature.

He gained no comfort from that voiceless communication. His lips drew into a bitter grimace. They made their own rules, disregarding the fact that this was a spaceport, that a section of it was not under planet law, but rather that of the outlanders who policed travelers as long as they stayed within the confines outlined for their supposed safety.

An emissary could be sent in but he would be as visible, in spite of all the preparations of the Elders, as if he marched behind a challenge drum. Oh, the watchers were out; Zarn had learned much these past few days. However, the fighter was now oathed—to an off-worlder. And only this very morning had the news come that that off-worlder was ready to leave planet, taking the subject with him. If they meant him to be followed off-world—but why? Such an expenditure was beyond anything Zarn had ever been authorized to put out.

To arrange now for an assassination was to ask for not only failure of that mission but perhaps the uncovering of at least part of the net he had been cautious years in weaving. He could only report facts—those apart seemed to expect miracles.

Zarn stared at the wall. The feathered messenger uttered a plaintive sound and the man's head jerked. His hand went quickly to his belt pouch and he brought it out again with the globule the creature gobbled before settling down on the tabletop, scaled eyelids closing over those large eyes.

The merchant arose stiffly. They gave him very little choice and part of his present burden was the fact that they refused to make plain to him why and wherefore. What had

this renegade Shadow done which made him the focal point of such a stir? What was it he carried? That spark of cupidity which had made Ras Zarn an excellent merchant flared briefly. If he could learn that and turn it to his advantage! But how—how?

Zurzal checked once more the carry bags. The labels were firmly attached.

"We shall transship at Wayright," he said. "Luckily that is a refit planet and sooner or later a trader bound for Lochan will planet there. Then we shall have cramped quarters for the rest of the trip." He looked at Jofre. "You are not space wise—some cannot adapt to such confinement. On the passenger transport it is another matter. But a trader is built first for cargo and only takes passengers on reluctant sufferance."

Jofre shrugged. "What has to be, is," he commented. However, inwardly he had begun to wonder. He had never, before these past few days, even been near one who traveled the star ways. Yesterday they had gone to the port station and he had seen the waiting ships standing nose skyward—there had been such a difference in them—from a swift courier of the Patrol, to a wide-bellied Company freighter. The passenger ships ranked somewhere in between and, looking at them, Jofre had felt an odd small chill, to venture into the unknown in one of these—But men had been doing it now for hundreds of seasons. There were disappearances and wrecks, dark stories of ships devastated with strange plagues, which wandered with a crew of the dead until they were blasted by a Patrol cruiser or were caught by a sun. Space was not kind nor cruel; it

was the fortune of travelers which made it one or the other.

As for him, there was no choice. He was oathed and if that took him into space, so be it. He would move into this new world as he would move into an unknown strip of territory, with every sense alert, even though what he might have to face would not yield to any weapon he knew.

He again wondered at the Zacathan's seemingly inexhaustible funds. Jofre's passage had been promptly paid. In fact Zurzal had opened for him an interplanetary account and showed him how one could draw upon it. Into that his wages would be fed automatically every quarter. For himself, however, he was dubious about such a pay method. And surely the Zacathan must be wealthy beyond the means of even a valley lord to so arrange matters.

He had booked passage for them on a passenger ship due to depart before sunset tonight and they were on their way now to board. There were small scooter carts belonging to the hotel which loaded both passengers and their luggage. Having heard so much of Zurzal's scanner, Jofre was silently surprised that no box or container which could contain such was loaded aboard the scooter they chose. But it was not his place to ask questions.

However, there was a feeling of uneasiness which settled on him as they approached the landing stage, where groups of passengers before them were filing onto the lift, to be hoisted aloft into the ship. Did that come from the shrinking of the planet-born who had never been in space, or was it a cautionary impulse triggered by something else?

Whichever it might be Jofre was on guard. There were a number of attendants around but none of them showed the characteristic features of the Asborgan-born. These

were mainly off-worlders and some were truly alien. However, it was one planet-born who centered Jofre's regard. In this very mixed group he might not have attracted the general eye, for he was wearing the livery of a high lowland house and accompanying a young Highblood.

His livery was not in any way suggestive of what might really be his duties but to Jofre there was no mistaking a Shadow—even though he had never seen the man before.

The position he was careful to keep, about two steps behind that of the young Highblood, was that of a guard, even though only the hilt of a ceremonial sword showed at his girdle. So another of the Brothers was bound off-world on an oathed mission. Jofre might have given a surreptitious gesture of recognition, but his own status was too equivocal. The chances were that they would never meet.

These two were well ahead of him now, almost as if the young lord was very eager to get aboard. And the Asborgans were already swinging upward on one of the lifts by the time he and Zurzal reached the takeoff mat.

They stepped onto their own transport, one of the attendants sweeping their baggage up beside them, and began to swing upward. Jofre fought his sudden, and to him shameful, reaction to that rise. Instead he made himself stare determinedly down at the port, and beyond it the old city, and beyond that—the only world he could remember.

# ✳ CHAPTER 8 ✳

**WAYRIGHT WAS A CROSSROADS** for the star lanes. The many differences between races, species, sentient beings, which Jofre had been introduced to at the spaceport hotel on Asborgan, were here set forth even more plainly. He had to keep tight rein on himself not to turn and gape after the passing of what might be a vast lump of dough riding on a small antigravity plate and putting forth now and then eyestalks to survey something which caught the fancy of that particular traveler. Even an imagination honed and trained by issha teaching could not supply an idea of the world from which *THAT* had come.

Though the humanoid form was the more prevalent, there were also insectoids, some scuttling along on six legs, others, taller even than the Zacathan, progressing on powerful hind legs alone, using their upper and middle limbs in quick gestures to augment their click-clack talk. He caught a glimpse of one of the crested males of the bird people and, next to him, a warty-skinned, broad-bellied creature which resembled one of the pond dwelling

amphibians of Asborgan. What passed here began to be like a nightmare in which eye refused to accept what was to be seen. Jofre fell back on an issha's refusal to be tricked even by his own senses.

The street was divided down the middle by a board rail of what gleamed like metal. Down that glided seated platforms which picked up or dropped passengers along the way. But Zurzal had chosen to walk. The Zacathan was apparently absorbed in his own thoughts. He had not spoken since they left their quarters.

This thoroughfare was lined on either side by many-storied buildings of an architecture new to Jofre. The first floors were square, as were those above; however, each was smaller as the structure rose floor by floor. And that larger section so left as a balcony surrounding each floor was occupied by potted and tubbed vegetation interspersed by seats and tables of different sizes and shapes to accommodate very dissimilar bodies.

This was a way planet, a meeting place for several of the major star lanes. Its principal industry and the livelihood of its natives was based almost entirely on serving the needs and desires of travelers en route to hundreds of different worlds. Beyond the inner city there were parks, carefully landscaped to catch the eye and tastes of a very mixed lot of visitors and there were amusements in plenty to fill any idle waiting hours.

The building towards which Zurzal headed was one of the more imposing ones. There was a deeply set insignia over the wide door and the automan that stepped aside when the Zacathan showed his identity disc was, Jofre was certain, armed.

The door opened automatically and they were in a wide hallway with many doors along each side. Zurzal did not halt his confident advance until he had reached the third of those on the left side. Again a door slid at their approach to admit them into a room thickly carpeted, containing several easirests and a wide table behind which, half-crouched, half-resting its thorax on a high cushion, was one of the insectoids.

As Zurzal approached, the alien, with one of its middle limbs, pushed into place between them a square box crowned by an upstanding, fan shaped attachment. The insectoid's claw tip touched a button at the same time it chittered its unintelligible speech.

"Welcome, Histechneer Zurzal Our resources are at your command." The words clicked mechanically from the direction of that fan, and Jofre realized it was a translator.

"Rest and refresh yourselves, far travelers," the insectoid continued.

Jofre, however, did not follow Zurzal's example as the Zacathan seated himself in one of the easirests, rather he stationed himself in a proper guard position by the door, a point from which he could keep the whole room and its occupants in constant sight.

"Greetings to you, Fifthborn," Zurzal spoke directly to the fan and was echoed by a series of sharp clicks. "It is well with hive and hatchlings?"

"Well. And with you, Learned One?"

"Well." Zurzal's return was as terse as the others. "I would take now that which is mine."

The insectoid's middle limb clawed at another of a range of buttons running down one side of the desk. "There has been an asking—" The fan squawked.

Zurzal shifted in the seat which instantly accommodated itself to his body. "Sssssssooooo?" The hissing which underlay all his speech suddenly was more apparent. "What kind of an asking, Fifthborn?"

"From one of power, Learned One. This one also has dealings with the Hivehold and to no small profit. He is one to be listened to."

"Sssss—" again that hiss. "And the name of this powerful one, Fifthborn?"

"He is—" the insectoid appeared to hesitate, "well-known enough—the Holder of Tssek."

The metallically sharp words brought silence. Jofre moved a half step forward. His issha sense caught that silent tensity in Zurzal's body, a sudden rigidity of spine. The Zacathan was not pleased by that answer, rather he found it disturbing.

"The Holder of Tssek," he answered now, slowly, spacing his words as if he would keep all emotion which might underlie them carefully hidden, "is known, I am not. What does he want with one who has been discredited even by his off-world peers? There is no reason to be interested in me."

"The hive repeats only messages given for the relay, Learned One. There is one named Sopt s'Qu, who is a highly placed follower of the Holder. This one is now at the Inn of the Three Fountains and wishes speech with you. He left the message some five daybreaks ago. There was no other message save that that one would see you as soon as possible."

"Well enough." Zurzal had relaxed a fraction but still it was apparent to Jofre that he was disturbed. "My thanks to the hive for the courtesy of message passing."

The insectoid made a gesture of assent and then pushed another button. "That which you left to hive care we return to you, Histechneer Zurzal." The words bore some of the formality of a ritual.

"I have been out of touch with many things for a space," Zurzal remarked. "There have been changes which a prudent being should know?"

The insectoid placed the sharp elbows of its higher pair of arms on the desk and latched that set of claws together. The feathery antennae on its head inclined towards the Zacathan.

"Changes? Not many and minor ones only, such as occur with the passing of time and can never be countered against nor truly foreseen. There are rumors of Jacks operating in the Alaban system, and there is the usual unrest on Vors—but there they are never happy unless they are unhappy—a most strange people. Of course Tssek is about to celebrate its Holder's Fiftieth."

"An auspicious occasion." There was a dry note in Zurzal's answer to that, as if he personally disagreed.

Before the insectoid could answer, if he were inclined to do so, a section of the wall at the left opened. Jofre was at half crouch at once, hand to belt butt, and then straightened, but did not release his hold on that weapon hilt as the small antigrav plate raised to the height of the tabletop and made for a landing on that. The insectoid lifted off its cargo, a black case with a handhold set in the top but no sign of any hinge or fastening on its smooth sides.

"Your hive desposit, Histechneer."

Zurzal was on his feet and approached the table, his hand out to close about that handle.

"I accept. My thanks, Fifthborn, for the courtesy and the aid of the hive."

"May you prosper in your going, Histechneer Zurzal."

"May the hive prosper with many hatchings, Fifthborn," Zurzal returned. He half bowed and the insectoid echoed him a little awkwardly, its body not made for such action.

As they issued forth from the building Jofre would have taken the handled box from the Zacathan but the other shook his head. "This I take—then if any harm comes to its contents I am alone responsible. But I do not like what I have heard."

"About the Holder of Tssek?" deduced Jofre.

"Just sssssooo—" again that hiss. "The Holder is bad news in any instance. Why he should be interested in me I have not the least idea but I am going to keep glancing over my shoulder from now on—"

Jofre shook his head. "The looking is mine, I am your oathed. But a man should know what he can of his enemies—who is this Holder and why is he considered a man of power?"

"It's a story, all right," Zurzal returned. "Let me get this back to our inn and into their safe room there. Then I'll tell you what I know. Which is common knowledge to most of stellar space in this quarter. My people have had no dealings with Tssek." He seemed to be speaking his thoughts aloud now. "What was there, suitable for inclusion in the archives, was routed out long ago. It is an old world and mainly inlooking, being occupied with a number of bloody events in the past."

Jofre was alert as they returned to their lodging but there was no sign that he could detect that any of that

mixed multitude thronging the streets had the least interest
in them. After Zurzal had turned his burden over to the
security captain the Zacathan led the way onto one of those
terraces ringing the building and took a seat at a table
which was screened on three sides by the potted growths
and well away from its nearest neighbor. Having dialed
drinks from the button menu on the table, he settled back
in his seat, looking thoughtfully at Jofre.

"The hive tenders do not mention things they consider
of little interest. Therefore, this business of the Holder is
important enough to lead them to pass it on. They are the
conservers and transferrers of credit; their vaults are
entirely safe and have never been raided; they are keepers
of a great many secrets. Doubtless even a number of the
Holder's!

"Now—we come to the matter of Tssek. Over the
centuries since First-In contact that world has not been too
healthy a place, not only for off-worlders but for its own
people. There appears to be some quirk in character there
which leads to constant intrigue and war. For a long time
there was no stable government, merely a string of very
quarrelsome and warring small nations.

"A little more than a century ago there was born one of
those individuals who appear in all our histories from time
to time—a person of charisma and with inborn qualities of
leadership to make him supreme. On Tssek this was Fer
s'Rang. He set about vigorously and within twenty years he
had united one continent under a government which for
the first time appeared stable and likely to last. From there
he went on to bring the eastern continent also under his
control.

"Not only was he a born leader but he had the happy gift of being able to pick just the right followers for each job. And Tssek settled down into peace for the first time in the memory of that world. Things went very well indeed. Fer s'Rang, after he was proclaimed Holder, opened the spaceports for trade; he sponsored manufacturing and raised the standard of living and was generally what is seldom found, a genuinely benevolent dictator, and Tssek prospered.

"There was some dissatisfaction, of course; there could not help being, given the past history. But it was growing less and less. Then there came the Great Ingathering.

"All the clans which had been warring were invited to this. War was already a thing of the past and it was to be a peaceful celebration. In the midst of the festivities Fer s'Rang died. It was also a peaceful death, expected since he had been ailing for some time, though it was accepted that the exertion he had been put to in the last weeks of his life had told on him. He fell dead while receiving the homage of the last of the families who had caused him trouble.

"His second-in-command at once took over and it seemed for a space that there would be no change in what Fer s'Rang had started. However, the government began to tighten here and there, to dominate quietly, to take over. Now Tssek is a tight dictatorship and from all rumors a very unhappy world.

"The present Holder keeps aloof, as far as I have heard, from any off-world contact. And, as you know, only when a world is one of the Great Council can there be any examination of its internal problems. Tssek has never

applied for such an inclusion. The rumor is that Fer s'Rang was on the verge of it when he died.

"There is a good amount of trade with Tssek. They provide a number of very much needed minerals as well as manufactured goods. But off-worlder contact is limited to the spaceport, as it is on any non-Council world, even as it was on Asborgan. There is good reason to believe that the Holder is anything but beloved by his present subjects. However, that is not for off-worlders to meddle with."

"But this Holder wants contact with you—" said Jofre slowly.

"Just sssoooo—and why? Not for anything I think I would have an interest in," Zurzal returned.

Jofre's movement was so sudden that it might have been intended to deceive the eye. The nose of his sidearm appeared on the surface of the table, pointing past the Zacathan at the screens provided by two of the potted plants which were large and thick enough to be considered bushes and far too good a cover. The Shadow was on his feet in one supple movement. Though the eyes of his companion glittered and his frill stirred Zurzal made no move himself. Instead he raised his voice a fraction.

"Company expecting welcome moves in the open," he stated, then swung around in turn, though he produced no weapon of his own.

Their answer came from another direction: a man advanced into the open with the casualness of one moving about his proper business. He was fully humanoid—perhaps even Terran stock—but small. And he lacked the heavy browning of skin developed by a spacer. Against the high collar of his tunic his chin was jowly, and his eyes were

small, set in darkened pouches of unhealthy grayish-
appearing skin.

They were half-shadowed by the bill of a uniform cap
generously embroidered with glittering thread, a matching
device worked also on that high collar, and modifications of
it up the sleeves of his tunic. The color of that tunic was a
dead black, as were his tight breeches and the boots
beneath. He also sported a wide belt from which hung,
close to hand, a blaster sheath.

Jofre's second move had taken him crabwise, so that he
was now in a position to defend the Zacathan from both
this newcomer and that bush screen behind which his alert
senses told him there was at least one more lurker.

Slowly the uniformed man smiled. "You are to be
commended, Learned One, on the alertness of your guard.
Harse"—the bush in the pots shook a fraction—"come out,
man. We have no quarrel with the Learned One. On the
contrary we come with open hands." And he held up both
of his, palm out, demonstrably empty indeed.

From behind the screen of vegetation moved now a
second man, much taller than his officer but wearing the
same black clothing, though this was plain except for a
shoulder patch in the jagged form of a red lightning bolt.
He walked a little stiffly, holding his hands carefully away
from a belt on which there were a number of loops all well
occupied by rods of various sizes and lengths.

The officer clicked his fingers and Härse, if that was the
subordinate's name, wheeled so that his back was to the
three of them, forming a barrier between the table and the
trio now by it and the outer world.

The Tssekians might be playing the part of being

harmless in the most straightforward forms their culture recognized; however, Jofre did not relax. His trained senses could not pick up hints of anyone else in concealment. However, he had little idea of what weapons that festoon of belt equipment might represent and he was not to be caught off guard. Nor did he retreat from his position of guardianship for his employer as the alien officer moved closer to the table.

"I am addressing Sopt s'Qu?" Zurzal had leaned back in his seat with the appearance of one fully at ease. Yet Jofre sensed that the Zacathan in his own way was as wary as he was.

"News travels fast—" Was there or was there not a note of irritation in the other's comment? "Yes, I am Horde Commander Sopt s'Qu at your service, Learned One." And he sketched, so neglectedly that it bordered on an insult, a salute. "You are doubtless one who does not wish to waste time in formalities, thus I will say plainly that I have business to discuss, Learned One, a proposition to benefit us both."

Zurzal, with a flick of his good hand, indicated the chair from which Jofre had arisen. His oathed took two steps back, still in a position to view both the Tssekian officer and the firmly planted back of his subordinate, now playing screen for this meeting.

Sopt s'Qu's thin lips still sketched a half smile but he plainly was not pleased with Zurzal's greeting. He was undoubtedly used to a more receptive audience when he spoke of business. But he seated himself and was at a slight disadvantage with the greater bulk of the Zacathan looming at the other side of the small table.

"Since we have set aside formality," he continued, "I shall come directly to the matter. My Great Leader," his hand flapped up again as if he were saluting, "was informed that you were to be found here. He also knows that you have suffered from the refusal of your peers to believe in your splendid achievement of past retrieval. You seek now for an occasion—and a site—to demonstrate the value of your discovery. You are offered such with every facility which you may desire—you need only ask—"

"Most interesting." Zurzal's faint hiss was still to be detected. "And what moves the Great One to such a generous offer?"

"Belief in you, Learned One," came the prompt reply, "and in your discovery. You wish to prove that you can show the past; this is the fiftieth year of Our Leader's rule, of the sad death of Fer s'Rang. We can offer you an opportunity which will bring you fame, not only planetwide, but which will reach the stars, convince all doubters you can do what you claim to do. The Holder invites you to Tssek, to install your time scanner at Marlik and bring back the death day of Fer s'Rang. At the moment of your retrieval of this great event there shall be ready a planetwide broadcast to carry the scene to all of our people. Can you ask for more in the way of making known the value of what you have discovered?"

"Your Illustrious Holder must have heard also," Zurzal said, "that this discovery of mine is far from being perfected. That the former trials had no more than a very fleeting success. I can promise no better results and because of that I cannot, of course, accept this offer. Were

the Holder to arrange such an impressive audience and occasion and then there was a failure—it would be more than a disappointment—"

"You are too modest, Learned One. Our Leader has made a close study of your achievements in the past. He believes that you are far nearer to complete success than your words now warrant. And he will see that you are well rewarded—"

"No." Zurzal was unusually curt. "I do not promise what I may not be able to produce. My thanks to the Illustrious Holder, but until I am sure of the worth of what I have to offer, I will not risk the disappointment of any who would seek to back my experiment. He will understand the logic of that, certainly."

Sopt s'Qu's features had taken on a rigidity. "My Illustrious Leader is not a man to be easily disappointed."

Zurzal stood up. "No man accepts disappointment easily. But neither does any life flow with continued smoothness. I am sorry, Horde Commander, but my answer remains no—I am Zacathan and we are sworn to the gathering and preservation of knowledge. Yes, I wish to use my discovery in that cause. But until I am sure of success I must keep my actions to myself. If I can find the proper rhythm for the scanner by experiments, then I shall be only too glad to allow it to be used on any world to recreate such scenes of planetary history as the inhabitants wish to experience for themselves. That will be a proud day, but it is still far off. Thank you, Horde Commander, but make this point clear to your Illustrious Holder: I do not offer that which is not well perfected."

The Tssekian arose also. "I am sorry, Learned One. You

have just thrown away that which would have brought you great glory."

"If so the loss is mine." But the Zacathan did not sound in any way disappointed. He nodded his head in a small salute as the Tssekian with no other word left them, his man falling in behind him as he passed the sentinel post.

"Now," Zurzal said slowly, "I wonder what lies behind that. I think perhaps I should speak a word or two in some places. There may be an interest in Tssek I have not heard of formally. Oh, well, we shall not be upshipping off to the Holder's hold, that is certain."

Only, of course, it was not.

# ✳ CHAPTER 9 ✳

**THE STRIKE CAME IN** their own quarters and just at the first sign of dawn. Jofre had been uneasy ever since their meeting with the Tssekians, as he was sure that Sopt s'Qu was not one to consider the argument finished. He thought once of the possible theft of the scanner but at his questioning, Zurzal had informed him that no one but himself understood its use. The various modifications he had been adding to the discovery originally made were not ones which existed now anywhere except in his own scaled head.

Though the Zacathan went to sleep early, Jofre continued to prowl their suite, slipping from wall to door to wall as if he expected each time he entered one of the three rooms to find a foe waiting and ready. He had asked the Zacathan about the various weapons Harse had apparently carried in plain sight (and if he had those in sight *WHAT* might he have in concealment?) and Zurzal had admitted that it was certainly true that the very warlike breed on Tssek might have perfected something new—or

rediscovered something old, not yet generally known in the space lanes.

The outer door was locked on their palm signatures. As long as they occupied these rooms and made sure to set palm to the plate if they wished to be undisturbed, there could be no forcing that—short of equipment which would alert the whole inn. The windows were also sealed and locked where they opened onto the terrace outside. Jofre himself had taken the precaution of moving tubbed foliage out of their carefully symmetrical pattern in order to clear the space to the banistered edge of the balcony offset. He had in addition dropped two of his warn buttons at strategic places on that terrace.

Yet with every precaution taken he could not relax. The issha sense was awake; that which he had been so long trained to do was taking over. It was well within reason that the Tssekians might attempt to capture Zurzal. With the Zacathan and his machine both in their hands they could believe they would have no trouble in forcing the action they wanted. But why were they so determined? Zurzal had questioned that himself several times during the evening. He seemed sure that if they had full knowledge of what he wished to do, they also knew how chancy would be the success. To link the experiment to planetwide broadcast and then fail would discredit the Holder as much as the Zacathan himself.

"They play some game," Zurzal had said at last. "But it is not ours. I wish we had better luck in our passage. Lochan is a fourth place world, the only visitors are Free Traders. I do not have unlimited funds—for I cannot draw upon the resources of my House since they have disowned

what I would do. Thus we have to wait for a Trader already bound for Lochan to take passage—I cannot just charter the ship on my own. However, this is the port from which such take off, and sooner or later one will appear."

To the wary Jofre such waiting, especially now, was like a silent war. This city was a maze of strange buildings of which he knew very little, though he made every attempt to study maps and mark out the principal reference points. The throngs of visitors (many kinds of whom he found it very difficult to name as "people" at all) added to the general dissatisfaction the whole port raised in him. The sooner they could be free of this place the better—it was far too removed from all he knew and he had almost begun to wonder if all those skills which had been assha honed would hold in such diverse surroundings.

For the third time he made the round of the rooms, moving noiselessly, his night sight enough to take him in the circuit. He would pause every few steps to listen, sniff, call on his warn sense to pick up anything out of the ordinary. This was the second night he had spent so and he could not stand guard thus forever.

It was the faint flicker of one of his warn stones which brought him along the wall, flattened against that, to peer out on the terrace. His stunner was in hand, but in the other he had one of the throwing knives on which he would first depend, since it was an old and familiar arm and he knew his skill with that.

There was something moving in a slow sweep in towards the edge of the terrace. A gravraft such as he had seen in use for transport through the city. Jofre raised the stunner—

It fell from fingers suddenly rendered limp, a grasp which would not obey his will, any more than his knees would continue to hold his body upright. He crumpled forward, facedown, and found that he could hardly breathe, as if the muscles of his chest, the power of his lungs was being crushed out of him.

If assault had been meant to cause his death, the attackers did not know the quality of their victim. Jofre's inner defenses rallied instantly. He went into withdrawal, his only answer to the unknown until he could learn the nature of the weapon being used.

Though sight, hearing, other senses were dulled to near unconsciousness, he was still aware enough to know that there was movement now in the room, confident, assured, as if those invaders had nothing to fear. Would they take the commonsense action and kill him as he lay? So far they had moved around him, heading towards the inner room where Zurzal slept.

The pressure holding him immobile remained steady. Only issha defense kept him breathing shallowly! Then— he had been seeking the Inner Heart, the core of strength to hold to. There was a sudden flash, a shock as if he had heedlessly thrust a hand into a fire. He was aware of that hand now instantly. It was crumpled under him at an awkward angle, the fingers still curled as if about the stock of his missing sidearm. But he could move those fingers— a fraction. And the strength for that came from—The find he had made in the mountains—that he had brought out of Qaw-en-itter—the stone!

His thoughts seemed to slide in and out of a cloaking darkness as if he were bog-trapped. He fought to hold to

them. Then there was a sudden explosion of pain in his side as he was struck a sharp blow there. And very faintly followed an explosion of sound, hardly more than a whispering, which seemed to be an argument of sorts. The answer came when he was roughly hoisted and dragged out of the room, over the terrace, to be dumped on a surface which vibrated under him—the lift platform.

A moment later a weight rolled against him and he smelled the musky scent of the Zacathan, who was plainly also helpless in the hands of these captors.

The platform gave a quick bound upward and it seemed to Jofre that it was whirling around. His precarious hold on consciousness grew even less, though he had somehow been able to move his hand so that the palm lay across the very slight bulge which concealed the mountain talisman.

There was clearly no move he might make now; he must wait until he could work around or break whatever the compulsion was which held him so pinned. But he could hold to the Inner core and so far had been able to survive. While a man lived there was always chance— which favored one who was ready to seize upon it.

How long they were airborne Jofre could not tell. It was much lighter and though he could not turn his head and dared not even lift those eyelids more than a slit high, he surveyed what he could of his surroundings.

The craft on which he was unwilling cargo was just that, a transport for cargo. And it had at least three passengers besides him and the limp and silent Zurzal. Two of them crossed his very restricted line of vision. One was Harse, and the other could be his twin. The third member of the party remained at an angle behind where Jofre lay and he

could not see who it might be. But Harse's presence made plain that this dawn raid was a ploy of the Tssekians.

The lift gave a sudden drop, bringing Harse, who was in line of sight at that particular moment, to mutter a guttural sound or two and clutch at the rail, waist high, behind him. Another downward fall and they landed on some surface, with force enough to raise Jofre's body a fraction from the lift flooring and let him slam back again.

That slight change in the angle of his carefully masked sight showed him a tall reach of space-scoured metal. They had made landing close to a ship. Having done so, they were now in a hurry to get this particular cargo on board. Harse and his fellow ducked under the rail and then showed again with boxes which they dumped on the lift. One on the top tottered and fell forward, its weight bringing a red wave of pain through Jofre's leg. Once more the lift arose and was maneuvered closer to the side of the sky-towering ship. And into the cargo hatch of that he was slung along with the Zacathan, though the latter was immediately carried out of Jofre's very limited sight.

Harse appeared again, turned Jofre's body over with a kick and proceeded to search him for weapons. His belt knife and sleeve knives were jerked out, and hands felt over him but the Tssekian seemed to be quickly satisfied that his prey was now totally unarmed—too satisfied.

Though much of what Jofre could depend upon for offense and defense was gone, no issha was unarmed as long as he had control of his body. To regain that was the immediate task in hand. Jofre had not dared to experiment with even the smallest move while he had been under the eyes of his captors. But his hearing was slowly sharpening

once more and he could detect now the sound of metal-shod space boots going away. Nor had they apparently left any guard.

He had been able to straighten the fingers of that hand which lay against the hidden talisman. Which was a suggestion he could not overlook. In his mind Jofre built a picture of that oval stone as he had studied it many times over. The dead, opaque darkness of it did not repel, rather it drew attention, as if there was a need within it—

The stone—dare he cut concentration from his surroundings to focus fully on that? Yet he felt that such a reckless move was the only one left for him to make.

Thus it was—his inner sight shut out the world, concentrated on the mental picture of the stone—he sought thus with all the intensity of assha strength of mind.

His hand raised a fraction from where it had fallen across his body when they dumped him here. The fingers moved in one of the Six Signs, those which led to the Great Call. Still he held the stone in mind grasp—thus it looked, thus it was!

The second hand tingled as life returned. He was dimly aware of that and raised it to join the other, so that the fingers could interlock in the pattern of "Seeking Strength of Mountain Winds."

He drew each breath a little deeper, moving sore ribs where that kick had struck. Slowly, with infinite care, he shifted one leg and then the other. There was a dim light in this cubby, enough for him to see boxes and containers which might be cargo or supplies. There was air enough to breathe, there was—

Jofre's body tensed and then he forced it to relax. That

sound through the walls. This ship was taking off and, unprotected by any cushioned seat in a passengered cabin, he must face the brutal pressure of lift-off.

It came as a blow delivered by a giant fist and brought with it darkness. All he had so painfully won was negated in an instant.

In one of the upper cabins a woman lay breathing shallowly, her face drawn into a grimace. Then they were planet free, but she did not immediately loose herself from those restraining straps which had assured her safety. Her strained grimace was now a frown and she had the appearance of one listening.

At length she shook her head, as if denying some disturbing thought, and did arise from her resting place. Only to reseat herself cross-legged, her hands lying one on each knee. The movements of her body were now infinitesimal yet they were following a pattern as formal as might have part of a ritual dance. Her face had smoothed into a mask, ivory pale, in which blacklashed eyes were closed. The brilliant scarlet lines of her lips moved, shaping words which carried no sound. She began to sway back and forth at a more noticeable rate now. Her hands lifted— were held out before her. However, she did not open her closed eyes to watch the intricate patterns she threaded fingerwise through the air.

This was good—good! She could feel the power rising in her, arming her as these off-world louts could never dream one might be—

There came a shock, sudden, hard. Her eyes opened wide, her mouth shaped a cry which was not uttered. NO!

This was impossible—beyond all knowledge—this could not exist—here!

Zarn—almost as swiftly as her thoughts had been interrupted and her weave strength shattered, her mind tugged at memory. Was—this what Zarn hinted at when he tried to seduce her from her mission and send her on a quest he merely hinted at?

She was frowning again, calling on every scrap of that memory. Truly Zarn had been excited to a point she had never seen. And the Shagga priests—they prided themselves highly on their imperturbability. But here—on this ship? The last time she had touched that kind of power had been back in Rama-di-frong when she had fronted the Lair Master and been given this assignment, proud that she would be a pioneer in off-world dealing. This was something which was so incredible that it must not be allowed to go unnoted, direct as her mission was.

Reaching for a box of prismatically glittering metal clamped for safety on a shelf behind her, she loosened its thumb lock and brought out a round hand mirror, raising it to the level of her face, inspecting her reflection critically. She had no vanity; that was never a part of issha training and was quickly dealt with whenever it arose. What she did now was view one of her weapons carefully. She had value and she could raise that value; she had been trained since childhood in the various ways she might use that particular weapon.

Now, she allowed the mirror to fall to her knee and gazed sightlessly at the near wall of the cabin. This new mystery—it was intriguing and demanding, yet it must not get in the way of her assignment—nothing must defeat

that! However, these Tssekians were not particularly clever. Devious, yes; truly clever, no. There were ways people gave away their secrets though they did not speak them aloud nor inscribe them in reports. Supposing—just supposing this Sopt s'Qu had learned something of issha lore, had managed to obtain for his master that which she had sensed was now on board. That would be a danger. In the right hands it would mean a full control—of her. Her hand tightened into a fist.

They had taken off very suddenly. She had kept to her cabin as the role she would play demanded. But those others had been working on some plan—she was only a side issue, she had been sure of that—had meant to make it certain that her worth advanced highly before they reached this Holder. Thus it might not be to control her— though she must leave no suspicion unexplored—but for some other purpose.

She must now make very sure of her territory even as a hover spy soared over the land of some mountain lord. Rising, she began to make certain preparations which required access to several pieces of baggage, the contents of which had been most carefully selected.

There was the taste of blood in his mouth, a runnel of it from lip corner. The practice must have been a fierce one today. Jofre opened his eyes, but not on mountain sky. He was looking up at a ceiling not too far above him. His body ached with an ever-growing reach of pain and it was very hard to draw a breath.

This was certainly not the Lair arms court. Nor were these smooth walls around, as he painfully turned his head

to discover, the rough stone of a Lair chamber. Where—where was he?

He allowed his aching head to drop back the few inches he had been able to raise it, stared at the roofing overhead and tried to remember the immediate past. Then he was aware of the vibration which thrummed through his body, spreading upward from the floor on which he lay. A—a ship—! Slowly it came, though it was adding to his pain to probe and hunt for that memory.

# ✳ CHAPTER 10 ✳

**JOFRE WAS NOT GIVEN LONG** to mine for memories. There was a thrust of brighter light into his prison and he made himself go limp. Better to discover the nature and number of any opposition before he put his own drained powers to the test. His almost closed eyes once more limited his field of vision but he knew that at least two had come to stand beside him and there was a guttural exchange over his body.

Hands pawed for a hold in his armpits and his feet were gathered up by another. The two of them edged out of the store cabin with his body and made their way down a much better lighted corridor. He was able to peer surreptitiously at the one transporting his legs—a man nearly as bulky as Harse and wearing the same uniform. They came to the foot of a ladder and he was dropped unceremoniously to the floor. A rope fell over his head, the loop of it crammed under his arms, tightened about him. He heard the click of boot plates on the flooring, saw that one of the men was ascending the ladder while the other dragged and

378

pulled at him, getting his body into place at the foot of that climb.

He was to be hoisted up like some inanimate object but better still to let them believe that he was still unconscious. Were he indeed aboard a ship, as he was almost certain now was the case, there would be little chance of escape anyway. Best to let them believe that they had a really helpless prey within their hold.

The sharp jerking of the rope taking his weight from above aggravated the aches which had now grown beyond his power to count. That captor coming behind steadied his body now and then but certainly not for Jofre's comfort, rather for the aid of the one hauling him up.

They passed two levels, coming to a halt on the third. Once more he was dropped flat and this time they worked the rope off him. Then he was carried again, down a short corridor, until they entered a cabin of some size opening off that. Jofre plunked to the floor, only under him now there was a padding of some type of carpet and the air was not so stale, rather carried an almost fresh scent.

"As you see, Learned One, your fears are quite unnecessary—we did not leave a dead bodyguard behind us." The voice was familiar; Jofre fought to match it to a face.

"It would hardly have served your purpose to do so—" the hissing note in that voice he did recognize was exaggerated. "You will release him at once!"

"Learned One, we are ordered to give you all possible assistance—as long as you, in return, agree to consider yourself our guest—As a guest you certainly will not need a bodyguard—the Holder's hand would fall sharply on anyone daring to do you harm."

"You will release him," the Zacathan repeated. "You have given me no proof that your Holder has any peaceful thoughts toward me either. You have stripped my oathed of his weapons, he is harmless. Look at these bullies of yours, each overtops him by a head—could make two of him. Do you fear a man who has been held in stass until you have leached the strength out of him?"

"You are a man of peace, Learned One. It is well-known that your kind do not offer any threat to sentient beings. Why do you care what happens to this?" The toe of a well-polished boot swung into Jofre's very limited view, prodded him.

"He is the opposite of all you believe in, one who lives to kill, is that not so?"

There was a moment of silence. Then Zurzal answered, "This man is sworn to me, after the way of his own people; his trust lies in me, mine in him. You would have something of me. Very well: bargain, Horde Commander—or have you never heard of that?"

"Hmmm—" It was not a word, merely murmur of sound. Then there came a cackle of laughter, harsh, having nothing of humor in it. "So, at last we have touched you, Learned One. Good. You can have this one—as long as you conduct yourself as our . . . guest."

Jofre's body jerked. No one had touched him but that near rib-crushing weight which he had battled all these hours until it seemed as much a part of him as his body suddenly lifted.

"We leave you to yourselves then, Learned One—" There was the clang of boots, then the sound of a metal door slamming into place.

Jofre rolled on his side. He was dragging deep breaths. Getting one arm under him, he managed to raise himself to a half-sitting position. Zurzal stood by the bulkhead where the door showed its outline. By the Zacathan's position he was listening intently. Jofre rolled a little on his knee until his shoulder struck against a well-padded seat secured firmly to the floor. Gritting his teeth and calling on his reserves, he somehow got to his feet and stood, supported by that.

Now, when his own struggle was somewhat eased, the full force of what had happened struck home at him, almost hard enough to set him reeling again. He had failed in his task of preventing the very thing which had happened to them, betrayed the issha. There was only one answer to that, but one which he dared not make, not yet while the Zacathan lived and he was oathed.

Zurzal turned back from the door. His neck frill was extended and he raised a hand to smooth it down. In two strides he reached Jofre, swung the younger man around and pushed him down into the chair which had been his support.

"No warrior is the less if he comes up against the surprise of superior weapons." The Zacathan struck directly to the heart of the shamed confusion in which his cabinmate writhed. "They used a paralyzing stass ray; by the look you took it full force. Nothing save titanium armor can withstand that and neither of us were so equipped."

"I am your oathed—" Jofre muttered, unable to accept any such excuse. "I should have kept closer watch—"

"You are my oathed," Zurzal struck back sharply, "and as such you are on duty. And so shall it be until I release

you. It is a marvel that you are still alive." He eyed Jofre up and down as if expecting to sight something unusual. "They could not leave your dead body—they brought you along—to space the evidence. But on my demand they had to produce you."

The Zacathan had come to stand directly before Jofre and now the long taloned fingers of the lizard man moved slightly. Jofre tensed and then, with all his will, relaxed. He did not know where Zurzal had learned the finger speech of the Brothers and indeed his messages had been somewhat clumsily delivered, but they were forceful enough. The two of them were under surveillance, perhaps, Jofre thought, by both eye and ear.

"We have something of a voyage before us," Zurzal continued speaking, though his fingers twitched in a different pattern. "They are transporting us directly to Tssek. It is the Holder's desire to use the scanner to produce a viewing on the fiftieth anniversary of that event, the passing of the leadership long held by the Illustrious Fer s'Rang to himself. I am to employ my time en route to making sure that the results will be just as he wishes."

Watch, wait, listen, look, those fingers spelled out, the orders given to any spy about to be planted in an enemy lord's holding.

"I am at command, Learned One," Jofre found his voice which sounded unusually harsh in his own ears. "What aid I can offer is yours."

"Well enough. Now," Zurzal went to the wall and pushed some buttons, "we shall see you fed. The stass leaves a man weak. Then—well, I have notes to be studied

and perhaps a few experiments to run. Some will not require training and your aid will be of assistance."

A tray had come in answer to the Zacathan's order and he carried it, burdened with sealed containers, over to place on Jofre's lap.

"Eat—ship's rations, of course, but they are palatable and nourishing."

There was a drift of mist-thin weaving lying across the backed seat in the woman's cabin. She plucked up a fold of it between thumb and forefinger to eye critically. This was of fabulous worth, twice-woven spider silk—the cost more than even a Lair Master could raise. The color was strange—or perhaps one might say unfixed, for, though the basic shade might be a very pale green, as the folds rippled there were rainbow flashes along each edge, patches which glowed and faded with every move of the length.

Her own personal taste was for richer, deeper colors, but training, severe and critical, had taught her to suit her robing to the demands of her mission. Such stuff as this was truly the gift of a world ruler and when the time came she must show it off to the very best advantage, both of the gift and of she who had the wearing of it.

No jewels—except the moryen fire stones for a simple girdle to refrain the fluttering stuff so that it might outline her body, bracelets of the same to make certain the eye was led to the delicacy of her wrists, the slender beauty of her hands. She would not use the cheek lacquer overlay; rather a moryen fastened between the near-meeting arch of her brows—she considered her choices and made up her mind. Then, deftly, she refolded the robe, which seemed to cling

to her hands as if it did not want to be laid aside, before seating herself and lifting her eyes to the expanse of the wall.

The metal casing of the ship's cabin was not starkly plain here, rather there was a heavy scroll of pattern which was gem-brilliant in places. Her lip curled a little. Much as she inwardly rejoiced in color she found this display too ornate, lacking in taste. But it was not the patterning which she was viewing, rather she searched for a point which days earlier she had discovered, a water stone, into the blue-green depths of which she could channel her thoughts to outreach—

There was no true reading of the minds about her. To her knowledge barriers had never been pierced to that extent. Body language she was well versed in and she could pick up emotions, especially when they reached a certain intensity. However, that ability had served her well and she applied herself to it whenever she could be sure of privacy and quiet.

They were very satisfied with themselves, these Tssekians. So long had they held power that they had forgotten the useful curb of a little self-doubt. Certainly they were very apt to underestimate what they did not fully understand—a fault which might be safely used if the necessity arose. This one who named himself Horde Commander—her dealings had been with him and he was as clear to her as a cup of springwater from the Neeserdene heights.

There was the ghost of a smile about her lips as she considered the matter of Sopt s'Qu. Any issha-trained woman could have controlled him in three meetings,

maybe less. She knew him for what he was, but she was after much bigger game.

There—that was this Sopt s'Qu; she caught a touch of his vast conceit, which was like a whiff of smoke in the air. Yes, he was very pleased with himself, swollen with success—too swollen. She considered that quickly. He was pleased with more than just her presence—the thought that he had in her a new toy for his master—he had achieved something else.

Her fingers moved. What else had he on board, or knew, or would receive in the future, to move him to such a fatuous belief in his own rise in the world?

She could not leave this cabin. It had been made plain to her that her presence on board this ship was not to be generally known. And she had accepted that, knowing that privacy would give her time to build her inner strengths for what would come. But now she wanted some touch with the ship world, to learn what was happening outside the walls of her own luxuriously furnished cabin. To perform, any issha must have all the information possible.

The only contact through which she might learn was Sopt s'Qu. So be it. She concentrated her gaze on that spot of sea-bright green on the wall and unwound her will to spin it as an intangible noose to summon the Horde Commander.

And the faint chime of the cabin bell came soon enough. She spoke only one word to loosen the inner locking:

"Enter."

Then as the Horde Commander strutted within, his bright eyes sweeping her up and down, she made a graceful

obeisance, her own eyes lowered submissively, her attitude one of gentle waiting on his will.

"You have all you wish, Gentlefem?" Almost he spoke a little uncertainly as if he were not sure why he had come.

"You have given me of the best, Horde Commander." She made a small gesture to encompass the cabin and all that was in it. "I have specially to thank you for the tapes." One slender finger pointed to a small pile of discs. "It was most thoughtful to provide me with such information concerning your world—and your Illustrious Leader."

"What do you think of Tssek then, Gentlefem?"

"That it has very much to offer in every way," she returned promptly. "I think fortune smiled on the day we met, Horde Commander. You have shown me a very bright future."

Without being asked he settled himself in the second chair near that part of the wall which held the stone she held in focus. In her there was a prick of anger. He was making very plain what he thought of her. And she must make no move to destroy his summation of her character— the varl toad!

"So you like what you have seen on these." He indicated the discs. "Ah, Gentlefem, how much more will you like it in reality! And the Holder will indeed make you free of a very pleasant world. He can be very generous—when he is pleased."

She allowed herself a slight lift of eyebrows. "And you think that he will be pleased?"

"By you? He would have to be man without a man's body not to admire you, Gentlefem. Also we bring him not

only your peerless self, but also the lock he can place on his future."

"You speak in riddles." She must be very wary, but also she must learn what she could.

"Riddles of time, Gentlefem. We have on board one who has mastered time—in his own way. And he shall master it for the Holder. You have doubtless heard of the Zacathan race?"

She triggered memory. Her briefing on Asborgan had not been too wide; there had not been time for as much as she would have wished.

"They are a race who study the past." Out of some corner she brought that.

"The past dealing with the Forerunners and on many worlds," the Horde Commander amplified. "Now and then through their delving comes some great discovery, for they are ingenious at following clues to ancient mysteries. We have one of their trained Histechneers on board, who is to do just that for the Holder."

Sopt s'Qu looked very pleased with himself. "He will be greatly beholden to our Leader, who is giving him something his own people have refused to allow him: a chance to penetrate the mystery of time itself. This will be a discovery which shall make Tssek famous."

"And how does this Zacathan master time?" She was genuinely interested. All space goers knew of the Forerunners. And now and then rumors of finds from that ancient past filtered along the star lanes.

The Horde Commander grinned thinly, his lips seeming to find it difficult to shape such a move. "He claims he has a way. Our Leader is inclined to believe

him—and the chance to put it all to the test lies now on Tssek. Our Holder approaches the fiftieth year of his taking power. He wishes to show to all the planet the event which transferred the rule from Fer s'Rang to him."

She allowed her eyes to widen in a calculated expression of wonder. "What a happening! How pleased this Zacathan must be to be a part of such action."

Sopt s'Qu lost his smile. "He is very modest, this Learned One. He objects that his preparations have not been successfully tried. But of course those who have knowledge which leads to power have no desire to share their secret. Once he has talked with the Holder and understands the advantages of the chance offered him, he will be quite ready."

But, she fastened on the thought, the Zacathan was not a contented party to this experiment, whatever it might be. She knew so little of his people. How effective could opposition from him be and what might such opposition do to impinge on her own mission? She wished she had at her command learn tapes—not like those which the Horde Commander had showered upon her, showing all the best of his Tssek, but those same which would give her an insight into what might prove to be a complication.

Then, there was that other—that touch she had made earlier. Surely somewhere on board was an issha-trained mind. And, since she alone had been assigned to this mission, she feared interference from that mysterious other. Who was the prey of the stranger? Why sent and by whom, that other lurker in Shadows? She dare not ask; though, as she eyed Sopt s'Qu, she longed to be able to

enter his round skull and tunnel it, seek that information which meant so much to her.

The Zacathan was a player she had not been prepared for. Was the lurker she had sensed connected with him, sent to spy on this strange time reader? Or a stranger from another Lair hired to perhaps a similar mission as her own? She felt anger again. She was issha, fully able to account for victory by herself alone.

But who and where was that other?

# ✳ CHAPTER 11 ✳

**JOFRE HAD KEPT SILENT** after he had cleaned up to the last crumb all the food in the container Zurzal had shown him how to unseal. The Zacathan had produced a small black box which he tapped on one side and then stared intently at some curling lines of different colors which writhed, tangled and wove across the slick upper surface of that artifact.

In spite of what the Zacathan had said Jofre bitterly chewed upon his own failure. It was plain that much of what he had learned in the Lair would not apply to weapons which could be used from some distance with devastating force. Therefore, he must set himself to assess what he had that he could use. Would these off-worlders also be impervious to such dealings as the Shadow use of practiced invisibility? Might they be made, as any lowlander, to look at him and not see—see in the sense which would alert their thoughts? Would they even have a readable body language? He could not be sure until he tried. At the same time any experimentation on his part must be very carefully done.

Zurzal clicked off his small screen of patterns and Jofre, out of his desperate need to learn the worst, broke the silence.

"Learned One, you have traveled the star lanes very far, have you not?"

"Not as much as many of my kind. By our standards I am quite the beginner—a novice with the blade as your arms instructor would put it."

"I know only the ways of one world—truly. It might be well that I know more if I am to be of service to you, Learned One."

Zurzal nodded and smoothed his neck frill, which continued to show a fluttering at the edges, betraying his uneasiness though he appeared to be lounging relaxed in his seat.

"You deal in weapons," the Zacathan began abruptly. "Very well, we shall begin with those." He launched in the even tone of an instructor who expected full attention from his audience and he had it. As he continued Jofre could almost have been startled into a denial that such things were possible. For Zurzal went from hand-to-hand combat to the fiery destruction of worlds, and back again, outlining the innumerable ways of dealing death among the stars.

Jofre's first shame became a misery eating at him. He had been so believing that there was nothing the issha could not in the end defeat and now he heard of weapons so outré that they sounded like the demon myths of the Shagga priests. Most killed at a distance—killed, or—as the ray which had brought him down—rendered the victim entirely impotent. The stunner he had been so wary and yet proud of owning now measured by these brutal tales,

for the Zacathan spoke plainly of the different deaths which could be met, had no more value than a rock some land grubber of the plains might pick up in the futile desire to defend himself against an osscark on the prowl.

Issha training—even the hints of his Assha-trained Master—was enough to assure him that this must all be true. Therefore, oathed though he was, he was worth nothing to Zurzal off-world. Why then had the Zacathan taken him on?

"There are the like of the Brothers along the lanes, are there not?" Jofre was trying to frame that question so that if they were overheard it would not reveal too much.

"You have seen the guardians of Tssek—felt their power. Each world has their elite guards and fighters."

"Learned One, what use is such as I on these worlds you have spoken of?" Jofre forced the point; he had to.

Zurzal did not answer in words. The forefinger of his useable hand twirled, tip pointing down—Spear-seeking—grave-ground—then it flicked in a sudden sidewise movement to suggest the covering of that hole.

Jofre caught his lower lip between his teeth. Where had the Zacathan learned that? It was a death order such as was given among the Shadows to a designated killer. From the hand which had stopped moving he raised his eyes to meet Zurzal's.

By all the rules of the issha trained, he had not only been confirmed in his oathholding but informed that he would remain so in full trust even under death threat. And Zurzal met him full eyed, so that he realized that the Zacathan meant just what he signed.

"A man who is weapon trained," Zurzal spoke again in

his lecture voice, "can be taught those weapons which are new to him if he is open to the learning and not so tightly confirmed in his beginnings that he cannot see the value of change when the conditions are right. There is something else—most of these ably armed and trained men of other worlds do not possess issha. Nor any equivalent to that—therefore, they are in a way maimed when they meet one who possesses it. Consider that well, my young Shadow."

He leaned farther back in his chair and closed his eyes as if he had indeed finished with instruction, leaving Jofre to take to pieces and consider, near to word, all he had been told.

There were the outside weapons and even among his own kind those were diverse and many. But there was the inner strength—issha and assha cherished. Jofre set himself on that inward journey to assess what he did have—to build upon any shred he could find, not spend time regretting what he did not. The Quietness of the Center—that enfolded him and he opened himself fully to it. He "saw"—saw the muscles which lay under skin and knew what each could be called upon to do—saw the steady beat of heart blood through his veins and knew what must be done in time of injury to seal off the vital parts. His body was a weapon and that belief had been pressed upon him with brutal force from the beginning of his training—the body first—and then other arms—even makeshift objects which could be called upon to expand the reach, toughen an assault, raise a tight defense.

Deliberately his memory turned to the arms field of the Lair, refought rough battles there, where broken bones and

sometimes even life itself was the payment for a moment's inattention or folly. These off-worlders cherished weapons afar—which meant that one must somehow nullify their range, reduce a struggle to the body to body—since he lacked throwing knives, poleax, sword.

What he had was himself and, of his bones, blood and flesh, he must make the best possible use. If any of these strange weapons came within his reach and he could gain mastery of them, so much the better, but desire was not a fact and it was facts he must cling to.

There would be, he thought as he came step by step, breath by breath, from the Center and fastened again on the outer world, little chance to try any ploy while they were aboard ship. Even if by some totally unheard of smile of the Assha Gods he might be able to somehow seize control of the ship, he would still be helpless within a metal shell, surrounded by enemies, and unable to command the forces which would take them planetward.

Therefore—wait—the patience of the issha was well-known, another of their unseen weapons. Wait and learn. He must know more now of this Tssek, of what they might face upon disembarking there.

He shifted his weight a little and Zurzal looked at him.

"What is the nature of Tssek, Learned One?"

The Zacathan nodded as if he were answered a question he had not asked.

"It is what is termed a heavy metal world. There are many great cities wherein factories turn out machinery for mining—not only the mines of the north mountains which appear to be bottomless in their promise of rich ore—but

also for shipping off-world. Machines work and the people labor with them. It is very different from Asborgan."

Well, he had half suspected that he would not be favored by fortune even in that much. Jofre nodded. He was being shunted into an entirely different life. But he had one rock to cling to—issha training. That was not of machines, but of men. If men came to depend upon machines so greatly, would they strive to keep also in balance with the Quiet of Center?

"It is a contentious world," the Zacathan was continuing, "or once was. Parts of the land are rich in minerals, or in soil able to produce bounteous crops. The people are—or perhaps we should say were—inclined to greed. Generations ago there were a number of nations which warred, each striving to take over some advantages they believed their neighbor controlled—a good port, a fertile valley, mines newly discovered in the upper ranges.

"It was then that they forged ahead in the making of weapons. Rumor suggests that some of the dissatisfied dealt with the Guild, buying up off-world weapons which they might copy in their own way. Which may not be too far from the truth, for the Guild is noted for fishing in disturbed waters.

"Then, as has been many times over in the history of numberless worlds, there arose to power their leader of genius. In a single generation Fer s'Rang, as I have said, united the Tribes, united them as a whole world. He proved, however, to be unusual in the fact that after he made himself Holder of Tssek that act indeed meant the saving of his world. Peace brought trade and the factories turned out products which could be sold off-world. The

people prospered—except for a handful of the old noble families who resented their loss of power and made of themselves an irritation to the Authorities.

"Fifty years ago—these of Tssek are long-lived and their medical science was much advanced by their wars—there was a final meeting arranged between Fer s'Rang and the two most important rebels. Fer s'Rang died—"

"Assassinated!" Jofre could follow this kind of politics very well.

But Zurzal was shaking his head. "No. He seemed to have died quite naturally, though he was still, by the standards of Tssek, only in middle age. They believed some inner hidden weakness hit. At his death he had made plain that he was to be succeeded by the man who is the present Holder and was then his trusted second-in-command. It is that ceremony which the Holder wishes to reenact by the time scanner for all of Tssek."

Jofre used finger speech. "Then there is something he must prove." To follow this idea was easy.

"He wishes," to Jofre's surprise the Zacathan answered him aloud—did he not care that there might be those same ears he warned of earlier? "He wishes to recover the past for the glory of Tssek, for the edification of those born since that historic hour."

Words which held a very clear meaning. It was necessary somehow that this Holder make plain the fact that the rulership had indeed passed peacefully to him and by the will of his own lord. Therefore, there must be those who did not believe this; there were questions being asked somewhere—and with force enough so that the Holder must make his answer very plain. Even though Zurzal had

warned this messenger that perhaps the time recaller would not work—the Zacathan had never claimed that it could, he only hoped that it might. Which meant—Jofre's lips turned up in the thinnest of smiles—the Holder had some plan he thought would make the experiment foolproof. That was something to consider. The Brothers had taken part in subterfuges of one kind or another— played major roles in some. This was not a strange and alien form of warfare.

"Learned One," he said in the quiet tone of one stating a fact, "if anyone can show the Holder what he wishes from the past, then that one must certainly be you."

They were not visited again by the Horde Commander. Twice Harse appeared with messages from his officer, asking if all was to the Zacathan's liking and if there were anything he wished. The pretense of honored guest was now being played to the limit.

On the appearance of the Tssekian guard Jofre made himself as inconspicuous as possible while he studied every movement of the man's body. At first Harse had kept his back to the door, outside which Jofre could hear some movement—which suggested he had come with backups. But on the second visit he was forced to cross the cabin to give Zurzal a tape case and explain that this was a mock-up of the ceremony of which the Zacathan was to be an important part, sent to him to study.

Jofre could have taken the Tssekian during that short meeting, he was sure of it, but it would avail him nothing. Not on board ship. In the meantime he might seem for periods to be dozing himself, but instead he was actively exercising issha fashion.

When the tape was run and Jofre invited to look at the small screen of the reader there appeared a building of formal and austere architecture with a wide audience hall. Centered in this was a two-step dais on which were several chairs alined. Though the tape was in color the apartment was bare, grey-white wall and showed no attempt at decoration. There was nothing to view except the static dais and the chairs.

Then flashed on a second scene in bright color but so static that those in it might have been caught in the same paralyzing stass which had held Jofre prisoner. They wore brightly colored clothes with the look of uniforms and there were a sprinkle of jeweled insignia everywhere. A voice, using trade tongue, came out of nowhere in explanation:

"The historic meeting between the Holder Fer s'Rang and the Lords of Nin and Vart as shown in the painting of Re s'Dion."

Five men were seated in those chairs on the dais; the sixth stood among them, one hand upheld as if to underline some point of speech. Two of his listeners were leaning forward as if very intent on what he was saying. The other three did not appear so moved. Now Jofre sighted a seventh man on the lower step of the dais towards the back where the shadow overhung and nearly erased him from sight: the present Holder in attendance.

Jofre could see very little of the man, his head was turned away so that his face was only a slice of cheek. Yet there was something—Jofre wished there was some way of sharpening the screen or bringing the scene closer that he might catch more details of that near-hidden man. He could only guess, but it seemed to him that the position of

one hand was odd. It seemed to be raised breast high and flattened horizontally as if it supported a weight and yet there was plainly nothing resting there.

From the time the Zacathan had told him the history of this scene Jofre had fastened on the relationship between Fer s'Rang and the man who had succeeded him. If this shadow figure was the Holder-to-be, why was he not in a more important position at this meeting? Certainly he was not on the dais, where one expected the second-in-command to stand.

"Learned One," Jofre asked, "after the death of Fer s'Rang was there any trouble? Any claim that he was the victim of some attack?"

"Far from it. His personal physician revealed that he had been suffering from a fatal illness for several months, that he had really made a supreme effort to rise from his deathbed to cement the alliance pictured here. It was cemented over his body by those shocked into fellowship by such a loss."

Still—Jofre was too well versed in the devious tricks played by the valley lords to completely accept that story. It was far too convenient for the present Holder—an alliance at the death of his predecessor, sworn to by men who had doubtless been completely stunned by that death—too much a whim of fortune. He had heard tell of other deaths, carefully executed to order by issha trained to complete anonymously action requiring months of tortuous intrigue. Not that it mattered now what had happened fifty years ago—unless Zurzal's time scanner could produce a copy of just what they were viewing now.

"Can it be done—that scene brought into being again?" He wriggled one finger at the screened picture.

"You can answer that perhaps as well as I can." Zurzal's good hand arose to rub across the growing stump of his maimed one, as if the renewing flesh and bone itched as might a wound in the progress of healing. "I have had some fleeting successes, it is true."

He did not continue but Jofre thought he could pick up what the other was leaving unsaid, that Zurzal was honestly wary of any success in this venture. Which meant that they could have only a fleeting value to their captors.

Frustration bit at Jofre but he could do nothing, save prepare as best he could for the first chance he would have which would promise even the remotest chance of escape.

In the days which followed he had to fight against the constant urge for action. He refused to let himself walk the floor as sometimes his body demanded, wanting to be free. All he could do was draw upon the Center—

There was one small thing to which his mind continually turned—the fact that when he had been, he was sure, very near death from the stass weapon, contact with the stone from Qaw-en-itter had somehow given him the strength to hold on. He took to studying the stone and made small discoveries, though he was cautious about it— it came from a cursed place and some of the darkness which gathered there could well cling.

He found that if he held it cupped between his palms when he did his Center seeking, he was brought much more quickly to the state of body awareness he wished. Once, when trying a memory exercise he pressed it to his forehead and nearly dropped it when he was answered with a painful burst of jangled images which even left him partially blinded for some very frightening moments.

Something kept him from showing his find to the Zacathan. He only brought it out when Zurzal was resting or deeply occupied with the studies which had to do with the scanner. By now Jofre was convinced that what he held could only have broken off of the Lair stone whose death had signified also the abandonment of Qaw-en-itter. No one—except the Masters and the senior priests—knew the relationship between men and the Lair stones. Those were assha—of the innermost of the Shadows. Nor had Jofre ever heard of anyone possessing an artifact such as he had found.

Perhaps a prudent man would have left it where he had discovered it—any Brother would—but—it remained that he was not by birth or blood a Brother—he was an off-worlder. And when he thought of that he knew a trickle of cold within. From what world had he sprung in the beginning? How did that other breeding limit—or aid—the issha now ingrained in him?

There would be more than one trial ahead to test both his limits and his successes, and all he was must be pushed to making certain he faced all squarely and alert.

# ✳ CHAPTER 12 ✳

**THEY DID NOT TOUCH FOOT** to Tssekian soil once they had earthed. Rather Jofre found himself squeezed in between Harse and one of his look-alikes on the second seat of a flitter which had made a precise connection with a landing platform. While Zurzal was wedged in with the Horde Commander and the pilot on the fore seat. Just as his first glimpse of Tssekian architecture via the vision screen had impressed him with stark utility and no concessions to any softening of line, so did the loom of the buildings between which their present vehicle streaked its way offer a vague threat, as if each was a sentinel on duty and those of the population about were prisoners.

They did not linger in that somber pile of a city but rather sped on into open land beyond. Jofre could not move enough in his seat to see what lay below them. But the walls were gone and, except for sight of a distant skeletonlike erection or two, they were now in the clear.

Their craft apparently had reached maximum speed and was being held so. However, they were not alone in

the sky. During their flight through the city they had passed a number of similar craft and, once they had reached the outer ways beyond that stand of buildings, a second flitter hung close, a little behind, but apparently bound for the same goal.

Jofre had made no resistance to the somewhat rough handling which had steered him to his present seat. Neither of the guards broke silence, and their craggy features were set in stolid, almost stupid, patterns. However, Jofre was well aware that in no way must he underestimate these followers of the Holder. He was lucky in that he had not been placed in bonds and would continue to be most biddable while he noted all he could pick up from his surroundings. Both of these guards were trained, though not, he believed, in the more outré systems of the issha. Armed or not, and given the smallest of chances, he could take them both. But that must wait upon a time when such a move could be made profitable. At least they had not stassed him again and he was given that small freedom.

The flitter fell into a circling pattern and began to descend near a building some four stories high. It was not the stolid block of the city structure but rather a different design altogether. There had been some ornamentation about the windows and one could catch flashes of color through those as if they were curtained. Then their craft set down on a perch extending from the side of the building just under the rise of the top story. Facing them one of those windows had been expanded into a doorway by which a man in a brilliant yellow tunic stood waiting.

At the sight of the Zacathan he bowed—apparently the subterfuge that Zurzal was a welcome guest was to be

carried on. Jofre was given a sharp dig in the ribs to send him after his employer as the flitter took off, just in time to clear a landing spot for that second craft which had followed them from the city.

The yellow-tunicked man was waving Zurzal in before him and a meaty hand on Jofre's shoulder hurried him in the same direction. He gathered, by the placing of that goad and a certain tenseness of his two guards, that they did not want any passenger which the second craft might have brought to be seen.

She did not have to be seen. The strict training of years kept Jofre from any halt in his step. He did not turn his head as every atom of him wished. Here—! Who was she? *What* she was he knew from that faint whiff of scent which had reached him. Only in the Lairs was that distilled, to be one of the minor weapons of the Others—the Sisters, of whom he had seen exactly two in his full lifetime, and then only from a distance. Daughters were few in the Lair and those were born there, not recruited from the land at large as the Brothers mainly were in childhood. Their fabled prowess in their own field was the bed from which legend and rumor both grew mighty tales.

One of the issha—and a woman! He allowed his arm to swing loosely by his side, twice brushing the thigh of the guard who had herded him to the doorway. His forefinger and thumb moved. She might never sight that signal, nor sighting it, have any desire to reveal herself. Certainly she was here on a mission and he could not believe that that had anything to do with him or Zurzal. But the fact that she would be under the same roof—or so it would seem— was a new factor to be considered.

She certainly was not following them. He caught no trace of sound and that faint touch of scent on the air was gone as he passed into the room beyond that door. Nor did they linger there, for the Zacathan's guide had already reached a matching portal on the other wall of the small chamber and was bowing Zurzal through. While Harse and his companion, paying no heed to any such formality, propelled Jofre along in their wake.

A twist down two corridors and they entered a room where the walls were an eye-searing riot of color, great sweeps of brushwork in vivid shades seeming applied with no reason in sometimes crisscrossing directions. The floor was thickly carpeted in a material possessing the texture of some kind of fur—and there was furniture gilded, carved, and inlaid, within tawdry splendor which fought valiantly with the walls. It was a room in which to keep the eyes shut if possible.

"Ask whatever you wish, Illustrious Learned One." The man in the yellow tunic was speaking trade language in an oily voice which matched his moon-round face and thick-lipped mouth. "All is at your command."

Jofre's guards had not crossed the threshold; that hand on his shoulder had merely propelled him within. He stood where he was and Yellow Tunic had to take a side step to pass him in order to reach the door. As soon as that closed Jofre went into action. A single stride brought his ear flat against the panels and then he nodded. They had been locked in.

Zurzal's snout grin was plain to read. He put the box he had refused to let anyone touch on a table which stood in the middle of the room.

"We are indeed honored guests," the hiss underlay that observation.

Jofre had been forcing himself to eye those riotous walls. The Zacathan had been sure on board ship that they were under observation—how much more certain that must be here in the enemies' own home territory. He had to blink and blink again; staring too intently at any of the swathes of color hurt his eyes. Perhaps that was exactly what was intended—to keep any inmate from a prolonged examination of the walls.

"For how long?" He thought he dared ask that aloud.

"For as long as is necessary to satisfy the Holder's need of us."

That was an answer which could be translated two ways and one of them deadly.

Jofre set himself to inspect their quarters. They had been favored with a suite, all lavishly furnished—including a room with a pool of water which bubbled a little at one end from which there arose a cloying scent. Zurzal stooped and dabbled a finger in that.

"Sooooo—Yes, we are indeed honored guests—and well prepared for. This might well be my Zoxan home quarters—even the vantan pool for relaxing."

Jofre had gone on to another discovery. Although the walls of this building had been pierced by those windows he had sighted during the descending circle of the flitter, here there were no openings on the outer world at all. Nor was there any sign of another door such as the one through which they had entered the apartment. They were sealed in as much as if they had been escorted into some valley lord's deepest dungeon.

There was a sound—Jofre's head twisted so he looked to the wall from which that had come—a thin wailing, shrilling which made him wish to raise hands to cover ears. It slid up and down a scale worse than any Whine drum.

"Yessssss—all the comforts of home," Zurzal continued. "Now that is the second movement of Zamcal's Storm Symphony. It is a pity I am not a lover of Zamcal's work—something a little lighter would be more to my taste."

As abruptly as it had begun that wailing ended. Jofre shot a side glance at the Zacathan and saw a taloned finger move in assent. They were under observation. But he also commented aloud.

"It would seem, Learned One, that your voice is enough to summon or dismiss."

"Yessss—how very enterprising of those who designed these quarters. We shall doubtless find much here for our benefit. Now, I see that our luggage, such as it is, has preceded us. Shall we deal with that?"

Jofre was surprised to discover that his own shoulder pack had indeed appeared along with Zurzal's personal baggage. It had been ruthlessly ransacked and anything which could be classed by the inspector as a weapon had been taken. However, as he crouched on the floor, Jofre slipped his hand along the edge of the overflap and felt that reassuring resistance to his fingers. So—the Makwire remained to him and, even though it might be nothing against a stass gun, he felt a surge of satisfaction. Every inch of that hidden chain was known to him by weight, by feel, and he knew just what it could do in close quarters.

Zurzal was prosaically stacking his clothing and other belongings away in a chest but Jofre merely dragged his

pack to one side, allowing his shoulders to sag as he did so. If he were in luck, any watcher would believe that he learned of his weaponless state and was cast down by it.

It had been midafternoon when they had earthed on Tssek—it must now be close to evening. Where was that other he was now sure was under this same roof—and what did she prepare—and for whom?

She was making herself felt indeed. One glance at walls, nearly as violently disfigured as those in the Zacathan's suite, had brought an instant and vigorous protest. Screens had been hurriedly found and set here and there and even lengths of cloth hung to cover those eye-torturing lines. Her own baggage was extensive and she refused to allow the maidservant they had produced to touch most of the contents, inspecting the girl's hands disdainfully and dismissing them as being too rough to be entrusted with her fine belongings.

All the time she was bending these Tssekians to her will in this enjoyable fashion, another part of her mind had fastened on one thing. Those other two, plainly prisoners who had preceded her from the ship to this place. One was a Zacathan, so of course, the one Sopt s'Qu had been so vocal about. The other one—Without thinking her right forefinger touched the thumb beside it. Issha—! She had been right. And—surely it would be too much of a coincidence to believe that this was other than that outlaw Zarn had been so intent on eliminating. He was certainly taller than any of the Brothers she had seen—but she must be wary. To make any move before one knew one's path was the way of a fool.

Besides her own mission must and would come first. She would take the first step to insure that this very night.

The messenger they had expected arrived at last. As the man who had ushered them into these quarters, he wore a yellow tunic, this also garnished by gold lace as if he strove in part to outglitter the walls about.

"Illustrious Learned Ones," he introduced himself, "I am Dat s'Lern at your service. Is all to your liking?" He addressed the Zacathan only, but his eyes had lingered for a second on Jofre who sat cross-legged against the wall, his shoulders a little hunched, his demeanor very much of one helpless and sulking because of it.

"Your hospitality, Dat s'Lern, leaves nothing to be desired," returned Zurzal blandly, "except of course the small matter of our freedom."

"Freedom? But, Illustrious Learned One, that is, of course, entirely yours—"

"In return for?" Zurzal was lounging in one of the easirests, showing no form of polite return to any effusiveness the other might offer.

"In return for your word, Learned One, your word that you will be willing to await a peaceful meeting with our Leader." The man's right arm swung up in a stiff salute. "He wishes nothing but your comfort, truly, Learned One. This is his country place for rest and relaxation; it has many amenities; please make yourself free of any you wish to sample. Your—guard, however—" That stare was turned once more in Jofre's direction.

"Yesssss—" Zurzal hissed as the man paused, "What of my guard? You have left him empty handed, disarmed.

Do the noted warriors of Tssek fear attack by his bare hands?"

"Learned One, it is only by special favor that he shares your quarters. The regulations state that personal guards are permitted only by the favor of the Holder and he does not give that often. Perhaps—since your service is about to mean so much to him, he may make an exception. However, even if your guard is made free of this place, he will bear no arms; that is forbidden!

"Now, Learned One," he had stepped back towards the door, "I am to summon you to a meeting with the Holder; he has most graciously invited you to share his evening meal The Holder lives simply here—he does not dine formally, rather wishes to be able to converse easily with those he has a particular desire to meet."

Zurzal arose from the easirest. "Since I have also a particular desire to meet him at the present moment, this is very fortunate. Lead on, House Master."

As the Zacathan passed Jofre his hand shaped the message: "Watch out!"

As if he needed such, Jofre thought, with a small bitterness—though his NOT watching out, being prepared for all eventualities, had landed them right here. The door closed behind the Zacathan and the Tssekian, and he was left to brood.

Except brooding was a waste of time. Either his eyes had become somewhat accustomed to those flashing walls or else some of the strident color had been dimmed. Perhaps the whole effect was meant to distract newcomers into these apartments, throw them somewhat off guard. Now he made no move to rise from his position near floor

level but he began a squinting survey of the nearest spread
of flashed, crooked lines, and splashes of raw color.

Within a short time he believed he had located at least
two spy holes in that length. Jofre gave his eyes a rest by
centering outward sight on his two motionless hands and
concentrating the inner strength. He was alert enough not
to be startled when the door slid open—foresense had
given the proper alarm.

Harse entered with a tray which he dumped
unceremoniously down on the top of the table. He stood,
hands on his hips, fingers brushing in passing significantly
against his festoon of belt weapons, his thickish lips snarling
as he stared at Jofre. Then he grunted something in the
guttural local tongue and went out.

The issha-trained needed no ear to door to assure
himself that he was locked in—perhaps even with a guard
at ready. But—his tongue swept across his lips as if he
savored the seldom known taste of lar honey—he could
have taken Harse. He knew that as certainly as if the action
had been carried out in full.

One studied each tiny movement of the enemy, each
flicker of eye, which foreran action. These Tssekians made
so plain their contempt for their opponents, their
overwhelming confidence in their abilities, that they held
and handled themselves as awkwardly and transparently as
the youngster new come to the Lair arms court. Yes, he
could take Harse—and when the time came he would. But
he must know more of what lay beyond that door.

With the quiet pad tread of a hunting ossack Jofre went
to the table and uncovered the dishes. Drugs? Poisons? He
did not think the latter—but the former might just be in

the Holder's program for keeping his unwilling guests under control.

There was a rich and mouth-watering savor rising from the larger plate. Jofre touched fingertip into the thick gravy about the chunks of unidentified meat there, and transferred that taste with a lick of his tongue. Though each world might have its narcotic drugs—with all those of Asborgan he was familiar, he could sense nothing of that like here. But—

Jofre thrust fingers into his girdle and freed the talisman from Qaw-en-itter. It was the only touchstone he had and assha matters were quick to warn of danger. Hiding what he did by cupping the stone within his palm, he passed it closely over the dish and then squinted between his fingers at the stone's surface. There was no hint of life within that ovoid though it felt warm to his hand as it always did. So— well, life was full of chances—he had long ago been rendered immune to the poisons of Asborgan—he could hope that held here. They had supplied him with no eating knife and his own was gone. He was forced to use his fingers as might any land grubber who shared a common pot, but he ate, slowly and chewing each bit to the limit, alert to any change of taste in any mouthful, though that did not come.

They had supplied him with a square of cloth on which he could wipe his greasy hands, and as he did so with slow strokes he went back to his study of the walls, through narrowed eyes as if that lethargy which comes from a full stomach was already creeping over him.

# ✳ CHAPTER 13 ✳

**"ILLUSTRIOUS LADY,"** that girl actually stuttered and she had a harsh voice into the bargain. If she who now named herself Taynad Jewelbright was to be properly served, she would have something to say about the selecting of her servants. These off-world lar beetles were going to step smartly to her gripharp sooner or later.

Taynad was surprised, however, though of course she would not show it, at the summons that pompous fool of a house master had just delivered. She had expected a first interview in private, not to be told to report to a food table and eat in public—even a valley lord had better manners than to approach the highest rank of Jewelbright so. But what could be expected from those who had no proper issha shaping?

The robe she had long ago selected for this first meeting must be the one, though it was not entirely proper for such an occasion. However, one would not expect this Holder to be aware of the nice graduations of formal robing as practiced in a Jewel House.

She stood to allow this inept maid to settle it over her shoulders, but for the rest she pushed the girl away and clasped her own girdle, plucked the hold collar into just the proper angle, and then leaned forward towards the wide mirror—at least they had not stinted her there—to place the moryen gem on her forehead. Moving back a little she examined her whole reflection with a very critical eye.

Her specially bleached skin was faintly rose under its firm ivory surface. The hair so carefully cared for and induced to grow over the years to a proper length for a true Jewelbright beauty was very dark in contrast to the ever-changing colors of her near transparent garment, but it was not black, rather when she moved there were glints in it of deep rich red. Her features were well shaped and had been schooled into the masklike expression to be worn in open company.

Well enough, she had prepared her weapons—now it was to the arms court to see how well those could be used. She saw the maid's face reflected over her shoulder in the mirror as she arose fluidly. The stupid child was in the proper state of awe—let her hope that a like effect would fall on the company waiting to be met.

The maid hurried to open the door and Taynad swept through, the veiling which was her gown swirling in ever-changing color about her. At least she was being given a proper entourage. There were four of the hefty guards statue still at attention, their eyes not daring to follow her, as they came to life and fell in about her. While the house master trotted like an ushound back to his master at the fore of their small procession.

They passed down the hall, passing several open or half-

open doorways and Taynad was well aware that she was on view. She also fed upon the emotions which the sight of her awoke. Easy—easy these Tssekians—it certainly must be that they were totally unacquainted with the Jewelbright. Were all their women as clumsy and heavy bodied as the servant they had inflicted on her? She probably had no rival, though she must not be overconfident. Sometimes the tastes of off-worlders ran in strange patterns.

The house master ushered her into a high-ceilinged room with the same color-scrawled walls which made her suppress a shudder. In the exact center of what seemed an overlong room for the purpose was a dais crowned by a table and several chairs, each one upholstered in a vivid color which inclined to war with the hue of its neighbors.

One of the occupants of that dais had arisen and now stepped down, his arm swinging across the breast of his overly ornate jacket in what was doubtless meant to be a gesture of greeting. The Horde Commander—

Taynad inclined her head at just the proper gracious angle, indicating that she acknowledged his right to so meet her. However, it was the man who had not stood, who instead sat, slightly hunched, in the mid chair at that table, who was the important one. She placed two fingers on the back of the hand Sopt s'Qu extended and matched step with him as he turned back to the dais.

Below the first step she dropped the touch and curled gracefully forward in the First-Time-House-Greeting obeisance, bringing her two hands together, fingers pointed upward, under her chin and lowering her head, but not so far that she did not have full view of the two at the table.

One of them had arisen in proper courtesy and she knew him instantly for the Zacathan. The other continued to sit, staring at her, though she had not missed that sudden widening of his eyes. He might put on the seeming of one encased in boredom, one who must be coaxed and teased into whatever these Tssekians deemed was the proper height of pleasure, but certainly he had not seen *HER* like before.

"This Jewel one," she used the trade tongue, though she might have spoken in his own guttural sounds—only it was far better that these believed her lacking in knowledge of their speech—at least for a while, "arrives, Illustrious Lord of Many Lands and High Towers."

He made no move except for one hand and he snapped the fingers of that. From somewhere below the level of her sight, hidden by the folds of the golden cloth which enveloped the table, arose a furred creature.

It was about the size of a two-year-old child and humanoid enough that, as it jumped to the arm of its master's chair, it squatted on its haunches and held its upper limbs and paws as one would use arms and hands. Its body was covered sleekly with a tightly curled fur growth of dull grey-blue. The head was round with the snout seemingly pushed back towards the skull, so that the flesh there was wrinkled. Eyes which were apparently pupilless, like opaque copper gems, were overlarge and were now regarding Taynad oddly. She gave it a quick glance, unable to judge what it might be.

Ears long, shaped like pointed leaves, the tips of them bearing tufts of fur, flanked the skull on either side, set well back on the head. Those tufted tips now tilted in her direction.

Issha knowledge gave a certain rapport with all living things. Those of the Lair had contact with and made use, on occasion, of flyers, creepers, runners which were native to the mountain heights. But Taynad sensed here something which was not quite animal. Was it a potential danger? The Shagga priests, she knew, had such control over some creatures as to even make of them weapons. Had this Holder such a protection in this thing?

She could not continue to hold her position of formal greeting without losing face—that command of the situation which she must retain at all costs. Was this thrice-cursed world ruler never going to make her any welcome?

He was leaning a fraction forward again and this time she felt a little more at ease; there was no mistaking that she had begun to awaken his interest. Shoving aside the creature he had summoned a moment earlier, he got to his feet.

As Sopt s'Qu, he was a short man, seeming almost of a different race than the tall guards—which, of course, might be true. His skin was very fair and bore no trace of beard, nor did he show any great signs of age—the life span on Tssek must be a greatly advanced one. His hair came to a sharp peak over brows which slanted a little upward and was nearly as dark as her own. On one cheek there was a distinct pattern of red lines as if he had been tattooed.

"Our house is honored." The timbre of his voice was oddly rich, almost he spoke as would a legender of a lord's hall, trained to make the most of every possible inflection. It held warmth which drew but which was in contrast to the man himself. "Will the most Gracious Jeweled One guest with us?"

Shoving back his chair a fraction, he moved around the table and took two steps down from the dais. Beside her Taynad heard the indrawn breath of the Horde Commander—apparently she was indeed in the process of being given some extraordinary honor.

Then the Holder held out his own hand as his subordinate had earlier, and with confidence and the air of one only claiming what was rightfully her own, Taynad advanced to touch fingers. Only it was not polite and formal finger touch which greeted her, rather he actually grasped her hand in his and she recognized the gesture of one taking possession. The first encounter—he must believe that it would be wholly all his desire. She meekly allowed him to steer her up to the dais and install her in the chair next to his.

The furred creature had made no sound but had continued to eye her, and Taynad felt a twinge of uneasiness.

"This is our good friend," the Holder had gestured toward the Zacathan, who bowed where he stood. "The Histechneer Zurzal, who will lend the fruit of his great learning to our project. And"—he let his hand fall so that his fingers slid from the nape of the furred creature's neck down its back—"this is Yan." He gave no other explanation of what purpose the creature served. Instead he reached out and selected a round blue fruit from a dish before him and dropped it into eagerly reaching paw hands.

Servants appeared with food and it would seem that the Holder did not encourage speech while eating, for his eyes were mainly on his plate, several times sending a portion of some proffered dish to either the Zacathan or Taynad by a finger flicking gesture alone.

She ate daintily and lightly, sipping very carefully the full-bodied drink poured into the crystal goblet by her right hand. It was an epicure's meal rightly enough and she would have had a hard time putting names to the contents of the dishes.

The Zacathan was as much a teasing point of interest as the Tssekian ruler. It would seem that he was now an honored guest. Did that mean that he had agreed to whatever project the Holder had in mind? Listen—not only to words, her thoughts urged, but to the inflection of voices if and when these about her began to converse. Very much could be learned from that.

With the passing of time the violent patterns on the wall had dimmed. Jofre moved from room to room of the suite, each time apparently on some small errand which he dutifully carried out, searching for other spy vents, to learn that they would certainly be under observation, for all the chambers that made up their quarters were so supplied.

During their last days on the ship he had managed to make plain to Zurzal that he must learn something of the Tssekian language. The Zacathan had the ability of his species to pick up an alien tongue quickly but Jofre did not trust himself to do likewise. Asborgan speech and dialects he knew in plenty, even as he knew finger speech. And the trade tongue had been required study for several years in the Lair, but other-world tongues were difficult.

He was well aware that space travelers often encountered peoples whose physical makeup alone kept them from sharing a common speech with strangers—then the translators such as he had seen in use at the hive bank

were in common use. But he must be able to learn enough on Tssek to operate. Jofre refused to believe that he would not get the chance to strike for their freedom sooner or later.

Now he deliberately made use of one of the appointments of the suite that Zurzal had pointed out earlier in passing. There were buttons to be pushed on the rim of a box set into the wall. Then on the screen above that flashed into life scenes of people, bursts of talking, even of music which was sometimes harsh and sometimes stirring. He seated himself before this now and brought the screen to life. Not only his ears but his eyes were trained on what he watched with issha concentration. There were movements of the mouths which sputtered and spoke, very faint changes of position, all which could be studied. Zurzal had given him a short briefing in the local dialect—limited even more to trade tongue which everyone knew could not contain the real nuances of constant speech.

He began to catch words whose meaning he did recognize and repeated them under his breath. What he was watching he took to be a sharing of general news. Then that faded and what followed appeared to be reenactments of some kind, for the Tssekians employed in the action wore clothing unlike any he had seen so far and they moved with a certain formality which almost aped ritual ceremony.

To make any sense of this was difficult but Jofre persevered. It was an exercise, just like any other of training, and only constant usage made any exercise profitable. He was frowning intently at a scene wherein a bound Tssekian had just been deprived of his head, apparently to the dismay of a number of females who had

been forcibly lined up to watch this disaster, when the screen went black for a second, only to come to life again showing a face so enlarged that it nearly covered the whole area.

"—enemies—die—in honor—unite against—the Great Destroyer—"

A click and the face was gone, but the scenes it had superseded did not return, and, though Jofre fingered the control buttons in every possible pattern, he could not gain any change in the dark screen. But he was very certain that that face had had nothing to do with the program he had been watching and the few words he had understood were intended to be an arousal for those who heard them.

There had been anger and fear—the anger for the moment overriding fear—in that shouting voice and issha instinct picked it up easily.

Jofre was still trying to gain back some life from the machine when the click of the door behind him brought him to his feet. Had his use of this installation triggered some trouble with the Tssekians on guard? His hand went to his girdle where earlier he had carefully wound in the Makwire.

However, it was Zurzal who entered, though the door was shut so quickly behind him that it was close to a slam, as if his escort was glad to have him safely back under lock and key again.

"You have had a profitable evening, Learned One?" Jofre asked.

It was plain to see by the yellowish tinge of the Zacathan's neck frill that he was not completely at ease. What a mercy that the issha kind did not have such

betraying body part. To learn control of something such as that might tax even a Lair Master.

"After a fashion. We are not the only guests the Illustrious Holder has seen fit to gather to him. She must have shared our ship—even though we knew nothing of it. It seems that Sopt s'Qu has truly thought to please his master; he has imported a Jewelbright!"

So—Jofre had his answer. Not all jewels of any establishment were issha—Sisters of Shadows—but it was a very useful cover for any assignment those were given.

"A Jewelbright," he echoed the Zacathan but, at the same time, holding his right hand where only Zurzal might see it in spite of all those spy holes. Jofre sketched the thumb to forefinger, the recognition signal of his own kind.

The reptilian eyes of the other narrowed only a fraction. Jofre knew that Zurzal had picked up that identification and that now they must both wonder what this new player, whose part in the game they could not guess, was about to do.

"It costs more than four lords' ransom," he said as one commenting on a wonder, "to select a Jewelbright for personal service. This Horde Commander must indeed wish to curry favor—"

Gain favor, Jofre wondered, or had Sopt s'Qu imported a weapon, the danger of which he himself was sure no Tssekian could gauge?

# ✳ CHAPTER 14 ✳

**JOFRE KNELT ON THE TILES** which encircled the large bathing place of their quarters. Zurzal's body was stretched out in apparent ease, a turgid greenish liquid hiding much of his length. But he had one shoulder hunched over the edge of that miniature pool, the one which ended in the very slowly growing arm replacement, and the small fingers of that undersized hand were moving along the tiles, trailing through a violet soap smear.

Though the oathsman was apparently just waiting with a roll of towel across his shoulder, he did not miss the least movement of those small fingers. Zurzal was mapping out for him the ways outside these rooms as far as the Zacathan himself had followed them.

But what the Zurzal spoke of audibly was something entirely different.

"The Illustrious Holder," he commented, "is well served. He also possesses a Jat."

"Learned One, a Jat is—?"

"Something one would not expect to find this far from Varingholm. There is a ban on their export therefrom—"

"A Jat is?" Jofre persisted. That the Holder had another possession which was or seemed to be as rare as a Jewelbright of Asborgan meant resources—or power.

"No man really knows," Zurzal continued. He had brought the palm of the baby hand down on the soapy tile, splashing away any marking. "They are not animals; though they are apparently unable to communicate except through vague mental images, they do not live in communities or apparently share any of their lives with another of their kind. Nor are they, by most of our standards, yet judged to be sentient beings. There was a nasty traffic in them some years ago—their home planet raided by slaving Jacks. And those who could be located and liberated were returned to Varingholm."

"Of what value are they—their hides?" Jofre persisted.

"By the Teeth of Naman, no!" Zurzal appeared to be honestly shocked as he clambered out of the bath and reached for the towel Jofre held ready. "Even a Jack would be fire-blasted by his own kind if he suggested such a thing. They are—it is difficult to put it into words—the brains of Central Control are not sure how they do what they do— but they are calmers, possessing an odd ability to project to those they company soothing thoughts, and, in some indefinable way, actually appear to heighten the mental processes of their owners as well as warn against perils to come."

"How could they be enslaved if they possessed such capabilities?"

"Easily enough—through stass. They were carefully kept incommunicado until they were purchased and then and then only were they released. They bond at once with

the person who provides them with food and water when they are again alert. But they are a very valuable warning signal against anything which or who threatens their bond master and they never willingly leave that owner."

Another shield for the Holder then—this Jat. But it was not the Holder against whom he must now act. And he was going to make his first move this very night. Brother to Shadows they called the issha—very well, he would now appeal to Shadows for cover.

He had signed to Zurzal what he would do, and, though the Zacathan, it was plain, did not altogether approve, he did not forbid. Perhaps he thought Jofre did not have a chance to go exploring.

Jofre had selected his first shield with care—a large cushion. So big it was more a body rest than a promised patch of comfort. Zurzal was going to bed, leaving the liquid to gurgle out of the pool. Jofre followed him as far as the doorway of that chamber and then flopped down across the portal on his chosen bed, as any bodyguard must do, were he weaponed or not.

He made a fussy business of settling himself, seemingly finding his choice of bedding difficult to arrange to his satisfaction. While doing so he slipped the Makwire from his girdle. Then he dropped near the edge of the cushion, his left shoulder against the door itself. The lighted walls had dimmed yet again—perhaps the Tssekians' own cleverness in trying to provide guest comfort was going to work for him.

Slowly, Jofre edged the floppy cushion rollaway from him, subsiding behind it. He had made much of arranging his pack for a pillow and that remained in place. Then, an

inch at a time, he began to move along the wall. It all depended upon the angle of those spy holes. They had been set, as far as he had been able to determine, so that those who used them could survey the most of the room—but that meant they were aimed mainly at those walking or sitting. He shifted over to his stomach and was digging his fingers into the carpeting, keeping to a worm-flat advance along the wall.

He thrust the thought of time from him, rather drew upon that shadow-sight-hide trick for a spy. The corner of the wall faced him. With infinite slowness he came into position to head down the next with which it had right angled. Another corner and he had reached that wall which held the outer door. For a very long pause he lay facedown, sending out every possible extension of his senses to reconnoiter for him.

They could well have fastened on him by now, even watched him, waiting for him to make his big attempt and then fasten upon him, to deliver a double blow. That idea he forced away. His study of Harse and the other guards had suggested that they were not subtle thinkers, perhaps not skilled in any unusual form of fighting either, depending only on their chosen weapons and brute strength.

Once at the door he came to real danger as he must get to his knees to deal with the lock. They did not use the sophisticated body heat locks he had seen in the hotel on Wayright, rather he had been aware every time they had been visited of a faint click.

Now his fingers crawled up the surface of the door, the end of the Makwire caught between two. The forefinger

located the small depression and he felt a surge of satisfaction which he instantly suppressed. With the most delicate touch he turned the fine end of the wire, to pass back and forth across that depression until it caught!

Using it as he might the finest of tools, Jofre pressed. To his joy it sank a fraction and then hit a barrier. Now—the hair-thin wire he had worked out of the length of Makwire twisted under his bidding. There followed a click, the hair slid cleanly in, and, as quickly, he jerked it out and resealed it into the thicker part of the coil.

He was on his feet in one movement so swift it might even deceive any watching eye, his palm flat against the door, the wire a-swing and ready in his other hand.

The door gave no betraying sound under his urging. There was a whiff of odor which he recognized as that which clung to the clothing of several of the guards due to their smoking of crumpled native leaves.

That scent alone was a guide. Outside the door the hall was lighter than the room within, giving Jofre a good sight of the man who was leaning against the wall, his shoulder only inches from that doorslit. Suddenly the Tssekian yawned widely and straightened a little. Jofre froze but the man did not turn toward the door he was guarding.

Did not turn, no, but with that small movement rather delivered himself squarely into Jofre's hands. The issha sent the door open and his right hand through in a blur of movement. His fingers thudded home on the neck of the Tssekian before the befuddled guard knew what happened and the man folded forward. That nerve pressure had not been enough to kill, Jofre wanted no bodies to betray him, but it would keep the fellow unconscious for a space of

time, perhaps even leave him unable to account for what
had happened—it sometimes worked that way.

Jofre squeezed through into the hallway, pulled the
bulk of the guard to a cramped seating position with his
back to the door which he had drawn closed. He stood
assaying the situation. There did not come the sound of any
alarm. Which, of course, did not assure him that such
might not have been given.

But he had gained freedom, at least for a space, and he
must use that to the best advantage he could. Also, and
that healed a fraction the wound to his self-esteem which
their kidnapping had dealt, he was in the act of proving
that issha training had some answers to even off-world
technology.

He did not rise to his full height, rather scooted along
at a crouch, but he was swift and he reached the end of the
corridor where it linked to the next in seconds. This was
the way to the dining room which Zurzal had outlined in
the soapy rings.

It was deserted, there were no signs of guards along
it, and all the doors were closed. There could be
someone in wait behind any of those but Jofre had to take
that chance.

This was not to be an escape but rather a reconnaissance,
thus he must take no chances. He slid into the dining hall.
The light here was very dim, and only night sight alone was
able to assure him there were no watchers. There were two
other doors, wide ones which could be thrown open to
accommodate a whole squad of visitors at a time. He
opened each in turn cautiously. One showed another hall
of closed doors, the light very dull. But not enough to hide

that other guard. Jofre pulled back instantly and waited, Makwire ready. He dare hardly believe he had not been sighted.

However, there was no alarm and he slipped around the wall to that other doorway. This gave abruptly onto a terrace and the open night. He could smell the scent of growing things and hear the splash of water as if from a fountain. Several steps below the terrace lay a garden and into this, with the ease of one coming home to the familiar, Jofre quickly faded.

Many of the scents were strange, growing things particular to Tssek, issuing from various forms of vegetation. He flitted from one welcoming shadow to the next, surveying as well as he could his surroundings. This garden did not give on the open countryside, but rather was set in a well with the four walls of the building standing to form its limits. There were doors at intervals in those walls, but for the moment Jofre did not test those.

He had early sighted the lighted windows a full story above the garden level. The light was dim, cut by drawn curtains, and the three windows from which it issued on a line. Someone was awake there, of that he was sure.

Moving in immediately below that beacon he surveyed the wall. With the proper equipment—now denied him—he would have found it an easy climb. At the same time any such action would spotlight him against the pale wall at once to any other intruder in the garden. Regretfully he decided against that.

It was while he was still fingering the wall's roughish surface, reluctant to leave such a chance to spy, that he was interrupted by a sound. Instantly he went to cover and

from his brush-screened position he saw a figure flit from the door in the wall below those intriguing windows.

The invader did not come boldly, rather showed something of the same stealth Jofre was employing. And, his curiosity fully aroused—for why should any rightful inhabitant of this pile act like a rooftop thief?—Jofre moved closer and then took a limited step or two along the path the other followed. The newcomer emerged from the thickest shadows when reaching the pavement surrounding the central fountain.

A woman! The enveloping cape the other wore, even the hood to veil the head, could not disguise the swing of body and telltale signs of sex for an issha. For an instant he thought of the Jewelbright—if this were indeed she, he might have his chance to learn more of this unknown Sister.

But the small breeze stirring branch and leaves about brought no whiff of the betraying perfume. Then she whom he spied upon pushed back her hood a fraction so that he could see features which certainly could never be assigned to any peerless beauty.

She crouched down beside one of the two benches set to face the fountain and, though the long cloak masked her movements, Jofre thought she was in some way hiding or withdrawing from hiding some object.

He could catch, even through the continued tinkling of the fountain a faint scraping sound, even a click. Then she was on her feet again, hurrying back the way she had come. He watched her disappear before, like any trail hound, he went to sniff at the place she had been busy.

His fingers touched moist earth, crumbs of it. She had

not taken time to sweep entirely away the traces of her work here. His nails caught under the edge of a flat stone like those which paved the section of earth between bench and fountain and the rock yielded to his pull. Carefully he used his fingertips since it was too dark in this corner to depend upon his eyes to explore the find. What he examined by touch was a roll covered with some slick material, the whole perhaps as big as his hand. Jofre was greatly tempted to take it. To his exploratory pinch the contents within that narrow bag yielded a little—nothing stiff or hard. He could, in spite of all his prodding, discover nothing solid. This might not be a conventional weapon nor even the fruits of some theft—unless what had been taken was some type of record.

At length he decided to leave it where it was. If he had time to stand spy here, to discover if what he had uncovered was merely a way place for message exchange and not a secure depository, he could doubtless learn—but that time was not his—not this night.

He had already been away from their apartment too long. To be sighted by the reviving sentry was the last thing which must happen. Regretfully he replaced the stone and this time he made sure there were no crumbs of soil about to betray that it had been moved at all.

Back he prowled through the dining hall, down the corridor. To his relief the guard was still wall supported and yet as unconscious as he left him and he was able to squeeze within the narrowly open door and begin the same worm's journey back to his sleeping cushion.

Once stretched out there he allowed himself to relax, loosed the strains he had put upon every sense during that

night's journeying. And that relaxation allowed him to slip into the slumber which he had banished so ruthlessly earlier. He did not try to relive his exploit, to wonder about what he had seen—there would be plenty of time for that later.

Though there was no sun beaming through a window to waken him, the daytime glow of the walls appeared to arouse one with the same efficiency. He stretched and became aware that the Zacathan was standing near, watching him.

"Only one with a quiet mind can sleep so well," Zurzal observed. "No dreams, Shadow, to plague you? That is well. We need clear minds and ready spirits—"

Jofre sat up. "We need these minds and spirits to a greater degree than ordinarily, Learned One? I await orders."

"The Illustrious Holder has thought that he would like a demonstration—"

"I thought—" Jofre was startled enough to begin when Zurzal interrupted.

"It seems that there are those the Holder would like to have see a small exhibit of what can be expected. The crew who are to arrange for the broadcast of the Fiftieth time scene believe they can work better if they are shown what to expect."

"The time scanner in the hall—"

"Ah, no. The Holder wishes something a little less impressive. There are some ruins from the old days within a short distance. It has been arranged that we visit those with the scanner—and a selected number of guests—this morning."

And if it does not work, Jofre wanted to ask, but thought better of it. He believed that Zurzal had been given little or no choice, that the Zacathan was caught earlier than he had expected in a tight web of what must be deception. Oddly enough, however, Jofre detected no sign of disturbance in either the Zurzal's voice or actions, his frill had not risen.

It was midmorning before they were escorted out of their quarters by Harse and his usual squad of guards, Jofre being ordered at Zurzal's demand to carry a bag which the Zacathan insisted held auxiliary equipment. Once more they entered a flitter waiting on a terrace approach above ground level and took off, heading out towards a range of hills which appeared to lead upward, like the beginning of a giant flight of stairs, into fog-dimmed shapes of mountains.

Jofre saw that other flitter already landed as they set down and standing by it the Holder and—This woman was as well robe-wrapped as the one he had spied upon the night before, and yet he was sure of her identity. The Jewelbright had also been brought to watch this phenomenon of time past.

He was able to pick out the weathered ruins which were their goal, so time eroded that there was little to be seen above the drifted earth. This was a country of rocks and what vegetation existed was a meeting of small drab plants clinging to crevices and the rough parts of the stones.

Jofre had favored the Jewelbright with a single glance. Though there certainly was not much of her to be seen, even her hands were concealed within the wide, enveloping folds of the cloak, and the hood was drawn well forward to shade her face. That cover-up might have been

in protection against the furies of grit which breezes, funneling down the cut in which they stood, whirled about them.

Sopt s'Qu was very much to the fore but he was not a happy man, rather one who displayed every sign of nervousness. Perhaps even more than Zurzal he feared failure. But he spoke up loudly as they joined the other party.

"This is a place of which there is no mention, even in the First Archives. The Holder wishes to see what the time scanner will make of this. Perhaps there can be little hope of such far reach—"

Was the Horde Commander trying to provide them with an excuse? If so, Zurzal did not fasten on it. In fact there seemed to be very little uncertainty about the Zacathan—he was all business, beckoning to Jofre who went down on one knee and unrolled the bundle he had carried, setting together the rods within as Zurzal had earlier demonstrated, to make a holder for the scanner. In order to steady that on this rough ground it was necessary for Jofre to hold it in place while the Zacathan worked.

At last Zurzal looked over his shoulder. "I have set it to the farthest extent possible, Illustrious One, since this site is said to be so old. We can only hope that it comes within range. Now!"

Jofre nearly jumped, for that last word had the force of an order as Zurzal reached out with his good hand and pressed firmly down on a lever.

# ✳ CHAPTER 15 ✳

**THERE WAS A SUDDEN UPRISING** of the grit-filled wind between them and the well-eroded stones. Or was it that? Jofre blinked and blinked again. That mist appeared to be thickening in places, thinning patches showing between spots. Color—a warmth of that. But it was like trying to see through a bog mist which swirled and eddied, enveloped and revealed.

Figures—yes! At least dim shadows which were not fixed, but appeared to move backward or forward. He saw with sudden clarity a single face which held so for no longer than it took him to expel the breath from his lungs, but he would take full oath to the fact he saw it.

It did not hold long, that mingling of denser shadows in a mist. Then it was gone as Zurzal clapped the edge of his hand down across the lever.

"No—!" That protest had come from the Holder; he alone of their company had found a voice.

"Yesssss—" Zurzal hissed. "Would you put such a strain on this," his hand caressed the scanner, "that it cannot be

435

used without lengthy recharging? You have a time limit set for that which you wish to see the most."

"Yes," the Holder nodded, "yes, that is so. But—why do you say this scanner will not work, Learned One? Have we not just seen it in action?"

"Have you seen. clearly, anything more than unidentifiable shadows?" the Zacathan countered. "It is a clear picture, a full one which I seek. Now I must rework the setting on this, make very sure that it will serve as well as it can the next time it is called upon."

What brought Jofre's glance upward to the heights which backed those anonymous ruins he never knew. But a glimpse of that flash there sent him instantly sidewise, to sweep the Zacathan from his feet, rocking the scanner perilously askew.

There was no sound, but a smell of scorching fabric. He felt the smart of a burn graze along his shoulder as he continued to grind Zurzal down against the rock, shielding the other with his own body.

The others were shouting; he heard a crackling and, even though he did not see them clearly, he knew that blaster beams were cutting back and forth overhead, aiming at a point well above, perhaps that from which the first beam had come.

Zurzal was struggling in his hold and for a moment Jofre resisted the Zacathan's fight to free himself. Then he realized that the other was attempting to move away from that exposure into the lee of one of the crumbling stands of weathered block. Jofre aided that with a stout push. Now they were crouched tightly together in the small measure of protection that hollow offered them.

The Holder's flitter took off, seemingly by a straight upward leap, whirled and turned back towards the outer plain. Their own craft was also quickly aloft, heading not after the first ship, but along the range of the heights with now and then the crackle and flash of a blaster beam aimed from it to spatter and slice rocks. There was no sign of any return fire.

Not that that would mean they themselves were in the clear. Jofre, surveying as much as he could see of those rock walls without offering himself as a good target, fully expected an attack from above. And he was not the only one to so judge trouble. Though the flitter which had transported them was hunting aloft, the guards who had been so ready to keep him under control were both still at ground level. Against the light grey of these rocks the dark shade of their uniforms made them visible, though they had taken cover as quickly as he and Zurzal.

He watched Harse twist a little in a crevice between two piles of the ancient masonry and wriggle a tube loose from that fringe of arms he wore at his belt. Sliding back a little so that he could gain all the protection possible from his cover, the Tssekian fitted that rod to the weapon he had already openly in hand, making the barrel near twice as long. Again he plundered his belt arsenal and produced something he cradled in the palm of his hand until he could fit it into the mouth end of that barrel.

Having so prepared, Harse inched forward once more to the very end of his cover and the weapon in his hand moved slowly, pointed well up towards the heights. At length he apparently had it centered to his satisfaction. There was a click sharp enough to be heard even over

the crackle of those blasters being fired indiscriminately above.

What he released arose almost lazily, angled inward toward the cliff face. Then it struck and Jofre flung up his arm a little too late to save his eyes entirely from a torturing burst of vivid white light. A second later sound beat at his ears. When he could again see through his watering eyes there was a glowing scar down the rock face; a good portion of wall had simply vanished. Harse sat back, his hand slipping along his weapon almost as if rewarding its action by fondling it as he might a living thing.

The flitter had ceased firing and was now coasting along, quite close to that scarred wall as if those aboard were inspecting the results of the attack. Then it spiraled down towards the level space from which it had earlier arisen.

Could they believe it was all over, Jofre wondered. He absently brushed down his side and then snatched away his fingers. That beam had come close! The fabric of his tunic was blackened, he ripped it a little to look at that line of smarting flesh his earlier touch had awakened into protest. However, save for the burn graze he could see no great harm.

Then his hand was jerked away and Zurzal bent over him, pulling the brittle cloth apart.

"It is nothing," Jofre said quickly. "No more than one would get being careless at a campfire."

"Yessssss—" Not only was the hiss very loud in the Zacathan's speech but his frill was extended to its furthest extent, throbbing an ever-deepening shade of crimson. "You have served, oath bound." There was a certain

formality in those words and Jofre forced himself not to allow himself any credit. What he had done was only such actions as he had been pledged to. He drew together his slitted tunic.

"Someone wants you dead," he said slowly. Zurzal had been directly in the line of that first fire.

"Me dead—or that out of commission—" The Zacathan had sense enough not to stand up as a target to any who might still linger above, but he was wriggling toward the scanner.

That was tilted on its tripod; Jofre himself might have pushed it out of place when he had made that jump for Zurzal. On the ground there was a blackened line inches away from the machine. No, Jofre was sure, it was the Zacathan and not his scanner which had been the prime target.

Harse and the other guard were on their feet and walking freely toward them from the flitter. Of the Horde Commander there was no sign and it might well be that he had joined with the Holder's group in that swift flight.

"Move it—" Harse approached the two by the scanner. "We go—now!" He jerked a thumb at the scanner and then at Zurzal and Jofre. The latter glanced upward. There was only that new blackened scar on the cliff side and it would seem that these believed the battle—if battle it had been—was now over.

The man with Harse advanced purposefully on the scanner and Zurzal swung out his good arm to ward him off.

"No hands on that—" His now blood-red frill was still up. "We shall do it." He beckoned to Jofre.

Together they dismounted the scanner, nor would Zurzal pay any attention to the attempts to make him hurry as he examined it carefully and supervised Jofre's two-handed disassembling of the stand. Only when that was packed away to his satisfaction would he pick up the carrying case of the scanner and start for the flitter by which most of the squad were obviously impatiently waiting.

Jofre was occupied with speculations. The attack, he was sure, was truly meant to take out Zurzal and perhaps the scanner—but first the Zacathan. He was sure that the Tssekians were well aware that only Zurzal could properly set up the machine—or was he wrong there? Did they believe that, after this rehearsal, one of them could do as well? Still he was very sure that that attack from the heights had *NOT* been part of any plan made by the Holder. Leaders of nations did not use themselves as bait.

Therefore—who—?

He was chewing on that as they packed into the flitter once more. But this time he had shoved past Harse and taken his place beside the Zacathan. When the Tssekian tried to shoulder him back the Zacathan faced around.

"That is my bodyguard. I am alive right now because of him. No thanks to you and your men here. He rides with me, he stays with me—from now on or I shall not be coming out of my quarters. This I shall make very sure of with your Holder himself!"

Harse scowled but did not seem sure enough to protest and Jofre found himself in the fore of the flitter with Zurzal as they winged back across the plain.

From this more open seat he could better see the

countryside. Up to the foothills it was level, apparently much of it covered with a thick vegetation which on Asborgan would have made it pastureland. But he could sight no beasts at graze there and he wondered if this world had any species that lived so. They were about halfway back when they were passed by a flight of six larger flitters flying in formation and boring steadily towards the place of the ruins. If the Tssekians had decided that they were not yet sure of the fate of the one who had launched the attack, they were going to make very certain now.

As they came down to the landing stage on the Holder's headquarters Jofre gained some idea of the size of that building. It was certainly larger than any on Asborgan and any inn on Wayright. Surrounding the outer wall were a series of small domes, slits in them open toward the sky. Through those slits pointed what could only be the barrel tips of weapons too large for any one man to wield. It was plain that this was an armed camp, which meant enemies—who—how many—where?

The teachings of the Assha Masters swept to the fore of his memory. Weaken your enemy from within, lead him to believe that his own trusted underlings will turn against him, the strongest fortress can fall to inner rot. But he needed to know more—much more.

Was this a hint of a power struggle between two leaders—the Holder and would-be ruler—Sopt s'Qu for example? The importation of a Jewelbright as a gift—how much did the Horde Commander know of the true nature of the woman he had brought? Trained issha she was—even the hair on her head could become a weapon at her will. The skills of the Sisters were legendary. They never

came for any purpose but that of secret war—she would not have been oathed except for that and she would not be here were she not oathed, no matter what amount of treasure an off-worlder offered for her.

Was the Zacathan in some manner an unknowing weapon in a hidden struggle? It would seem that he was feared or his death would not have been intended. But one small point of good had come out of that—he had, as Zurzal had certainly been quick to recognize, now the right to demand the constant attendance of Jofre—might even gain back for the bodyguard some of the weapons of which he had been shorn at their capture.

They were speedily escorted back to the suite of rooms which had been their prison. Zurzal had spoken only once, as the door had been opened and they were motioned within:

"My life has been threatened. If I am the guest the Holder proclaims, then I must be told by whom and why I should be fried by blaster!"

Having delivered that, he turned his back on the guards and stalked within, the case of the scanner still held carefully in his arms as if that were something he would do all he might to protect.

Once the door was closed Jofre instantly laid ear against it. Yes, they had stationed a guard outside. At least the one who had been on duty there last night had never reported any difficulty. When the Tssekian aroused he probably had been afraid for his own skin; he might well have believed that he nodded off on duty.

Zurzal placed the scanner carefully on the table as Jofre dropped the bundle which contained its supports on the

floor. Some of the red had faded from the Zacathan's neck frill and now he swept up his hand in the impatient gesture Jofre had seen him use before, striving to settle the fluttering skin to his shoulders.

"The scanner," Jofre broke the silence, "it worked. I saw a face—"

"The timing," Zurzal shook his head, "it was too inexact. How could it be tuned when one did not know the general setting one would need? Yes, it worked. But it has worked even better before when there was a more definite dating to be calculated. What is important now is who doesn't want it to work at all?"

"Could they believe that with you dead they would have control over it?" Jofre advanced what he believed could be a very logical argument.

"There is always a good measure of stupidity in this or any other world," hissed the Zacathan. "However, they have not pressed me to discuss this," he rested hand on the scanner, "with any of their men of learning who might be considered able to grasp the principles of its controls. No, I do not think that that is the answer. The Holder wants me—he wants me to use this—he does not want a dead man and a useless piece of hardware to spoil his plans."

He turned away, to face Jofre squarely. "Meanwhile, let us see to you, oathed. Off with that tunic—"

Jofre protested, but to ears not prepared to listen. He found himself speedily divested of tunic and shirt, seated on the edge of an easirest while the Zacathan squeezed a jelly from a tube he produced from among his luggage.

"You were very lucky, oathed." Zurzal's hand had the lightest of touches as he spread the ointment over the

reddened skin and slapped a flesh seal over it. "That was on full or you would not have taken so wide a scorch as you did. There will be no scarring and there is no reason why it will not heal well. However, we shall not let them forget that you seem to be the only one who was marked in that action, and because, weaponless, you fulfilled your oathing. On Asborgan I believe I could demand a wound price from them."

Jofre flushed. "It is no real wounding," he muttered. "I failed you once—when they took us—did you expect me to fault every time?"

"I cannot see there was any failure. You fronted a weapon you knew nothing about, were caught by something which could well have caused your death. You are a very tough fighting man, oathed, to have survived stass holding as well as you did. The issha are certainly highly regarded, I know, but I was not aware they had ribs like tillenium to keep them breathing—"

Jofre had pulled on shirt and tunic and was being careful with his girdle, holding as it did both the Makwire and the talisman. But not careful enough, for the ovoid slipped out of hiding, struck on the floor and landed near the Zacathan's feet.

# ✳ CHAPTER 16 ✳

**JOFRE SWOOPED FORWARD** but he was a fraction late; Zurzal had already half stooped to eye the artifact more closely. Against the light shade of the carpet it presented the appearance of a giant drop of some unknown liquid frozen in shape.

The Zacathan put out his hand. However, when it hovered over the ovoid, he jerked it aside just as Jofre made a determined grab for it. From his stooped position Zurzal was staring up at his bodyguard with a keen measurement.

It was almost as if he were questioning the younger man's possession of such an object and Jofre responded to that sensed demand.

"Mine!" His hand closed about the stone and he felt the familiar flare of warmth in the cup of his palm.

Zurzal straightened. "Yours," his word came in agreement. Too quick an agreement? Was the Zacathan trying to placate him?

Slowly Jofre opened his hand; he had no true explanation for what he held. But if an oathed could not

trust his lord, then he was indeed a man without hope or being.

"I do not know what it is—" he said slowly.

"A thing of power." There was no doubt in Zurzal's quick return. "And without a doubt very old." He was shaking his head as if to deny one of his own thoughts. "But there is no record of any Forerunner remains on Asborgan—perhaps that is from off-world—"

It was Jofre's turn to gesture denial. "It is of the assha." At the moment he was sure that all his speculation concerning his find was correct. "I found it in Qaw-en-itter—a Lair which died four generations ago. I—I am sure it was part of the great stone—the Masters assha heart— though I have never heard before of any such retaining any life after the fail of assha—"

"This retains life?" Zurzal's voice came quietly, hardly above a murmur.

At that moment Jofre remembered where they were— that those eyes in the walls might well be turned upon them. Rather than answer in revealing words, he hunched a little, bringing the stone up between their bodies and loosed the tight grip of his fingers. He could see that point of light at its heart—could the Zacathan? Or was it all some ancient spell set by one of the Shagga?

"Interesting—" was Zurzal's comment. "It is a luck talisman then?"

Jofre's lips tightened. Let this off-worlder dismiss his find as one of those luck pieces such as the lowlanders gave credit to—sometimes wearing them on chains about their necks. Very well, let this be thought a talisman—a superstition. He did not raise his eyes but—he sensed—

this was what the Zacathan wanted—that he be lessened in the sight of any spy, a ruse. He dared to give the ovoid a toss, catch it lightly.

"Well, Learned One, I have a good measure of luck since I found it"—or, his thought added, it found me—"so I shall not deny that." He tucked it away again in the folds of his girdle. "One of my calling needs any help fortune may send."

"And we need luck that this has not been injured by our recent skirmish." The Zacathan turned back to the table where he had parked the scanner. Taking the machine from its case, he set it on the tabletop and then crouched down so that he could view it at eye level from a number of angles.

Jofre watched with interest, though he understood little of what was going on as the Zacathan's one good hand touched here and there, his large eyes squinting along the surface as if he were bringing to bear on some target one of the large weapons of the Tssekians. At length he settled back on his heels.

"As far as I can say without actual testing, it has not suffered. As for testing—" Now he stood up and laid the scanner on its side, hooked a clawed finger at the side of a small plate there and jerked it up. Within that cavity were two coils of fine wire of a particularly vivid blue-green wound in even patterns around what would appear to be a core of another substance—that a sullen grey-black.

"Sssoooooo—" the hiss as well as the lifting and coloring neck frill of the Zacathan suggested agitation of some sort. "Power—perhaps one more viewing and then it must be recharged. We have no chance to experiment."

"When is this viewing these Tssekians want? Can they provide the power you need?" Jofre wanted to know.

"The viewing is within two days. As to the other—I shall find out." He shut that pocket in the side of the scanner. "That was folly, errant folly," he hissed again, "to waste what I had on that peep show this morning!"

"I do not think you could have said 'no' " Jofre observed. "This Holder is not one to have his wishes denied. And— it worked! You proved that, did you not?"

"Worked? Raised some shadows and near got itself— and us—fried. I can do without such examples of its proficiency," snapped the Zacathan. "What is done is past—there is what lies ahead. At least they can give us a proper dating this time and not too far in the past."

Jofre noted that "us" the Zacathan used so easily. It was as if he had suddenly advanced from a mere oathed to an accepted kin sworn. And that brought a quick touch of warmth within even as the assha stone had given him in the past.

Taynad turned the thread-slender stem of her wineglass between two fingers. Her lips smiled provocatively as her thoughts raced. The Holder's performance this morning— the man was afraid for his precious skin! This—this weldworm was what she must court with all her skill, soothe into contentment, encase in feeling that all was right with his world and there was no need for fear. She could have spat the wine she had just taken into her mouth into his face! No, control, control that contempt, make of it a weapon.

At least she had had a chance to learn much these past

hours. Now as soon as she could get this booby occupied with all the various acts to make sure of his continued safety she must start piecing together her scraps of true knowledge.

The first was, of course, that the Holder of Tssek believed himself anything but secure in his exalted position. In the past sweeps of the timekeeper since they had returned to this fortress of his she had heard orders given, raids planned, lists of suspects made—names marked for death, for imprisonment, for questionings.

There had been returning reports also. Of suspected nests of rebels which had been found deserted when the raiders moved in, of the disappearance of a number of those whose names appeared on those lists. It was as if the failure of the attack upon the Zacathan and his machine had been a signal, somehow broadcast farther than any mirror flicker or flyer message, to take cover.

And with each reported failure that man by the table had tensed the more, spoken fewer words, become more—dangerous! Yes, perhaps she had indeed misread him—even a vomink caught in the trap could flay the hand of the hunter who did not brain it in time. The orders for death were now outweighing those for imprisonment. And such summary deaths began to be listed a few at a time.

Would this put an end to whatever game the Holder wished to parlay with that machine of the Zacathan? She did not yet believe so. He had spoken twice of the ceremony and of those who must be brought one way or another to attend it.

It was true that the Zacathan did possess something which could not be explained save as what it was, a

recreator of the past. She had gone to view the action at the ruins very much a skeptic, and had been practically convinced that he could do what they said he could. However, were his scanner to turn up nothing more than ghost-mist forms such as they had seen that morning, she did not understand the Holder's dogged demand that the ceremony of the great Ingathering be so reenacted.

She was suddenly aware that there was a lull in the constant flurry of officers reporting and being dispatched again. The Holder had arisen from his seat and was approaching her. Taynad set the wineglass down and went immediately into the welcoming obeisance.

"Your pardon, Jewelbright," he put out his hand and she straightway set hers in it, allowing him to so draw her to her feet, "these matters are harsh; I am sorry that you have been witness to them. But all is now arranged, so that we have time for more pleasant things. I have not yet shown you the inner garden. The langian are in bloom and you who are such a connoisseur of perfumes will find these to your taste—"

As he spoke he was drawing her on. There was a scuttling at his other side. The Jat that had not been present at the morning's fiasco was there now accompanying the Holder closely. If all they said of that creature was true, and she had heard much from the maid last night, then it was certainly a good weapon against any close attempt at assassination. She allowed herself to speculate on whether the creature could be won away from its allegiance, though as yet she would not make any move in that direction. Instead she used the speech of the Jewel House, meant to soothe, to compliment, to enhance the

ego of the patrons—not with bold and open flattery but rather with the most delicate innuendo.

The garden proved to be in the heart of the fortress-palace, the four walls rising to encompass it. She could hear the play of a fountain, and even the sounds made by insects. A flying thing with huge wings outspanning a body no larger than her little finger hovered before her. Without thought her hand went out and it settled, so lightly she could hardly feel its touch, fanning wings of brilliant green which appeared spangled with inset gems of blue and gold. Its beauty was enough to startle her out of her thoughts for the moment.

"A lashlu." The Holder was regarding her with something close to benevolence. "Have you any such on your world, Jewelbright?"

"Not such as this." She held her finger very still, hardly daring to breathe. In those few seconds it chose to remain with her it was as if she had stepped out of time, away from all she was and what had brought her here, all that she must never forget.

It was the Jat which broke that moment of otherness. For the first time since she had first seen it the creature uttered a cry, scuttling ahead and out onto the pavement of flat stones which ringed the place of the fountain. There it went down on all fours, its wrinkled-in nose close to those stones, clearly on the trail of something.

The Holder had halted and his hand brought Taynad to a stop also. He was watching the actions of the off-world creature as it fastened its attention on one of those grey squares. Its forepaws, which were so like hands, suddenly sprouted claws as if it could extend normal nails to far

greater distance on demand. These it curled about the edge of the stone and heaved, the rock turning easily in its grasp as if very lightly set in place.

A fast scoop of paw into the hollow beneath the stone tossed out a lump of grey-brown which might be a bag. With the very tip of its claws the Jat urged that find towards the edge of the pavement well away from the two standing watching.

"So—" The Holder dropped his touch on Taynad and took a step or so closer to view that small round of what might be plumped-up hide. All expression had been wiped from his never too expressive face. He reached for his weapon belt, not as heavily laden as that of his followers but showing the jewel-inlaid butt of what could only be a blaster.

Then that was in his hand with one quick movement.

"Away—" he made that sound almost a whistle and the Jat obeyed instantly, leaping backward to them.

The spat of fire caught the bundle cleanly and from that core of flame burst smoke and a strange scent—Taynad found herself coughing, her head shaking from side to side as if she could banish that odor or escape it so.

Smoke and flame were gone, there was nothing left but a charred black mark on the stone where the Jat had rolled it. The Holder, blaster still in hand, stood over that now, looking down at the charring.

"Sooo—" he said again. "Here—?" He made a question of that last word but Taynad had a feeling that it was not addressed to her. Then he came back to her.

"Fair One, it seems that this servant of mine," he snapped his fingers and the Jat moved closer so that he

could draw his hand caressingly across its rounded skull between those two stiffly up-pointed ears, "has nosed out some contrivance which was ill meant. This place," he lifted his head and stared beyond her at the rich wealth of growing, blossoming life, "was meant as a sanctuary—but even here there is no safety. I must crave your pardon, for this is a thing which must be carefully examined and I must ask you now to excuse me."

He escorted her with punctilious ceremony back within the building and then left her with the guards and that maid she could not yet rid herself from, dismissing her so in a way she found irritating. He was not going to explain just what menace he had blasted out of their path, that she had to accept. But it did not please her—there was too much in his attitude now of one who considered her only something to be thought of in an idle hour, not a real part of his life. That lack of true interest in her she must deal with, and by every way she knew. She must become more important to the Holder than the Jat or the blaster—far more.

Though they had not left their quarters (they probably would not have been permitted to do so, Jofre had thought from the first) the two prisoners were aware that much must be going on in the fortress-palace. Jofre strove to free senses for outer-questing—always an uncertain thing but needed now. He must assess what he could pick up—at least a little of what was in progress. Issha touch caught—as if a fog invisible to the eye but very apparent to one's inner consciousness seeped through the walls. Something which brought with it the same feeling of ever-abiding

dangers and evil as hung over the dark alley of the Stinkhole. Save that there he had been free to defend, and here he could not even be sure of what weapon the enemy might produce—or whether there was but one major enemy or more to be reckoned with.

He firmly dismissed all conjectures and concentrated on his inner exercises. The Makwire was always there in his girdle for seeking fingers, and those very fingers themselves were ready to be weapons. The Zacathan for the first time showed signs of worry, prowling back and forth across the room, going now and then to inspect every inch of the scanner as if he expected it to be somehow invisibly attacked unless he kept a careful watch.

They were fed from trays brought by guards, though Harse was not in charge, rather the fetching and carrying was done under the supervision of an officer who did not address them and whom the Zacathan made no attempt to question. The food was good and Jofre was almost sure that it could not have been tampered with. This close to the time when Zurzal's skill with the scanner would be demanded, the Tssekians certainly would not in any way attempt to drug them.

Three times Zurzal called again for the tape Sopt s'Qu had supplied of the scene of the Great Ingathering and sat for a long space of time before it in study, as if by his will alone he could somehow transfer that picture to the scanner and have it appear when desired. Yet it was always the same and the Zacathan would shut it off with a hiss of exasperation.

His neck frill was in constant agitation and the colors, while not bright, ran through a variety of hues. Zurzal was

not taking this waiting with the same philosophical adaption to circumstances as he had earlier shown. Jofre debated concerning a second assay at exploration by night and decided against it. The Zacathan was plainly not ready to settle in and he had no desire to leave the other alone.

In spite of his attempts to forget her, his own thoughts played with the puzzle of the Jewelbright. That she was assuredly issha he had not the least doubt, yet she had not responded to his Slip-shadow recognition signal—if she had seen it and somehow he believed that she had. That she was on an oathed mission must be the truth— otherwise she would not be here—no issha would willingly leave Asborgan on some whim. No, she had been introduced into the Holder's household for a very definite purpose, even as others of her Sisters had from time to time found themselves in the halls of lords they were oathed either to protect or bring down. And somehow Jofre did not believe that this one was here to protect—no.

He felt a certain frustration that he could not share his speculations and doubts. Not only did there remain the fact that they might be constantly under observation through the loopholes those violently patterned walls contained but he had no right to interfere or betray another oathed.

They spent a restless night and in the morning Zurzal attempted to view the world through that screening device Jofre had earlier watched.

"That is their monument to the past." The Zacathan identified a building which flashed onto the screen while a voice blared out in the native tongue a stream of words so fast Jofre could identify perhaps only one in ten.

The screen viewed the structure from slightly above, as

if they were seated in a flitter swinging in there for a landing. Jofre caught sight of something to the far right.

"Spaceport!" He was sure that he had seen, through an opening between that forest of grim buildings, the rise of a ship on pad.

"Yessssss—" the hiss of the Zacathan was low. "To the south, I think."

They would surely be transported again by flitter Jofre believed. If they made their move, once aboard that, could they hope to reach the port? But what good would that do—

Zurzal might have picked that question out of his mind. "There is a Prime Control base there—otherwise off-world ships could not land. Reaching that—"

"The Patrol would protect us?" Jofre allowed his doubt of that to be plainly read in his tone. "The port at Wayright must have been patrolled—yet here we are."

Zurzal nodded. "Yessssss—that is sssssooo—but we were but helpless baggage then and they treated us as such."

"And as we come in with blasters ablaze and demand aid here—" Jofre could not believe that the other could be so naive as to believe that.

"I am Zacathan," Zurzal said. "My race has immunity on most worlds. Also, when we raise our voices, planet lords listen. I think we would have a very good chance to claim sanctuary."

"But first we have to get out of there—" Jofre jerked his thumb to the scene on the screen. That had changed somewhat. They were now looking at the loom of the building from ground level facing an impressive flight of stairs. And those were occupied, with rows of statue-

straight, well-armed guards, and behind them a massing of people moving restlessly back and forth as might waves kept out by the barriers of a portside landing.

"Just sssssoooo—" replied Zurzal, but he was looking now, not towards the screen, but at Jofre. If the latter had also been befrilled that appendage might have gone into a rising flap. He was being challenged in a way and he found that there was that within him which was rising with a fierce eagerness to meet that challenge.

# ✳ CHAPTER 17 ✳

**THE TSSEKIANS,** it would appear, had also foreseen that the task of ferrying Zurzal, Jofre, and the scanner to the place where they wanted them was going to be a problem. Perhaps they could not reduce the two to the point of becoming baggage to be towed around with impunity, but they mustered such a guard that each of the off-worlders was wedged in between two towering Tssekians and under constant eyes of those matching step with them.

There was no way in this compact and ever vigilant company, Jofre had to admit to himself, that he could make a move towards freedom. When the flitter landed them in a cleared space which guards held open with cracks of riot staffs before the steps of the Ingathering hall, he needed only to see that seething sea of a crowd to realize that massed bodies alone could wall them from escape.

Through the subdued roar of the voices about them even the commands of their guards did not carry and they were shoved in the direction of the steps leading upward.

So they came into the long hall which had been shown them on the viewer. There was the dais, the chairs which had been midpoint of that older scene, but there was no one on that perch now. Gathered below and to one side was a clot of brightly uniformed men with here and there a woman in rich robes and bejeweled. To the fore of that small assembly was the Holder with the Jewelbright a step or two behind him, the Jat reaching up one paw to grasp the edge of his brilliant golden tunic.

Between the newcomers and the chair was a spiderweb of wires, interlocking a number of installations all set at different angles and heights but meant to focus on the dais. These were under the control of men also in uniform but intolerant of the guards, giving harsh orders now and then.

"They prepare the broadcast." Zurzal had somehow managed to come near to Jofre.

They certainly must be very sure of the results they wished, the Slip-shadow thought. But how could they be? There was some trick in this—there must be. Only he could not ferret out what it was nor how it would work.

The guards pushed the two of them on, Zurzal insisting on carrying the scanner as usual. They had to be careful of those crossing lines on the pavement as they advanced. Zurzal opened the case; Jofre, as before, unrolled and made ready the supports. The Zacathan lingered on sighting the scanner so that it was aimed at just the angle he wished. Behind them rang out orders from one of the broadcast experts.

Jofre shot a glance to the left. The Holder looked at perfect ease, exuding such an air of confidence that Jofre's own wariness became like a taut string within him. He

continued to steady the scanner with his right hand but his left rested on his knee not too far from the end of the Makwire in his girdle.

Having made a last finicky adjustment, the Zacathan turned his head toward the Holder and nodded.

Jofre had turned his attention in another direction—in time to see one of those attendants at the nearest of the broadcaster machines hurriedly slip a cone over the forepoint of his machine. Had there been a mistake in the setup that must be remedied at once? The off-worlder had no idea how those machines worked but there was something in that hasty action which, to his watchful eyes, presented a suggestion of trouble.

Their guards were impatiently motioned away by those running the other machines, though there were protests until one of the officers from that brilliant group marched over and snapped an order which made them move. Zurzal and Jofre were alone well beyond arm's length of any of the Tssekians for the first time since they had left their quarters.

The Holder raised his hand at the same time Jofre's fingers closed about the end of the Makwire. With a supple twist of the wrist the issha freed it, to lie three quarters of its length among the mass of wiring. The possibilities he had before him now had doubled. And he was sure that, aided by the last few days of practice, his wrist had lost none of its cunning.

Zurzal reached over and pushed the control of the scanner. Three breaths later there was a shimmer on the dais, which had more life and gathered more quickly into definable shapes than that mist had evoked at the ruins.

From the massed group of notables to the side arose a
hum of astonishment. It was plain to Jofre at least that they
had really not expected this response. What had they then
expected? Something to issue from the unknown machines
about them?

The shimmer was gone; they might have been looking
at an enlargement of the same scene Jofre and Zurzal had
studied on the record given them. But this was no frozen
picture. These people on the dais moved, shifted in their
seats. The representation of Fer s'Rang moved, raised his
hands, spoke—words which rang out and even seemed to
echo hollowly down from the ceiling above.

And the picture held, grew bolder!

Jofre shifted weight. Those about him seemed bemused
by what they were watching. His chain weapon was a
serpent ready to strike.

Taynad stared at the dais and then quickly looked to the
Holder. He had taken a half step backward as if he had
been confronted by some sheer surprise which he had not
thought to face. Beside him the Jat jerked at his tunic,
waved its other paw in the air, plainly distraught by the
emotions broadcast now from the man it was bonded to.

The Jewelbright sent one swift glance at the other man,
the Horde Commander. There had been a smirk on his
face, but now there was forming another expression
altogether, one rooted in fear. Her fingers moved as she
flexed them. Emotion was so thick that it lay about them
like a mountain fog exiling each from the other, and it was
true fear!

However, almost all eyes were fixed on the dais, on

those actors out of time. Jofre looked now for the one who had puzzled him in the painting they had been shown, the man who had lingered on the lower step. His hands—

On impulse Jofre gave a small shove to the scanner and it seemed, in answer to that, that figure became not only brighter to the sight but somehow more dominant in the scene. Its hands went to mouth level in a swift movement as the representation of Fer s'Rang turned to address one of the other seated lords.

The Great Leader made a sudden movement, raised a hand to the side of his throat. He took a step forward, his other hand sawing at the air and then he crashed down. While the man on the step below was already in motion upward to raise him, his hand sweeping across the dying man's neck as he did so.

There was a rising howl of sound and Jofre saw that those at the machines about were frenziedly busy. He put his weapon into use. It twisted among the cords on the floor. He gave a jerk with full shoulder strength, aware that Zurzal's scaled hand had joined his in that hold.

The nearest of the broadcasting machines crashed down. There were screams and cries and that scene on the dais abruptly disappeared. Zurzal was again back at the scanner.

A blaster bolt of fire skimmed from the mass of officers. There was struggling there and the screaming of the woman. Guards moved in—two of them towards Jofre and the Zacathan. But Jofre was ready. He took a leap, not away, but at the men and the wire flicked to imprison a wrist holding a blaster. The Shadow jerked the one who had held it forward into the line of his own comrades' fire.

Again Jofre struck and the other guard dropped his gun, caught at his face, hands over his eyes, as he screamed thinly.

Other blaster beams were sweeping back and forth. Jofre grabbed up the weapon one of his victims had dropped and tossed it to Zurzal. Pacifist the Zacathans might be, but they were ready to protect their own lives and Zurzal fired twice. Jofre was jerking at that mass of wiring across the floor, sweeping it back and forth until its tangles brought down two more of the guards.

Then he had their weapons, the precise blows he gave both of the entangled men putting them speedily out of the fight.

He looked back over his shoulder to the Zacathan and gestured with one of those hands in which he tightly gripped the weapon, expecting every breathless moment to be either cut down by a stass ray or fried by a blaster.

Hostages? Jofre looked to that milling mass of spectators. There were uniformed guards plowing into that for there were apparently a number of small fights in progress. He saw bodies in bright uniforms lying underfoot. And some of the guards had apparently turned against their own officers.

The Holder? The man was gone from his position.

Jofre tensed. It was as if a voice had shouted in his ear, someone at his side had screamed aloud in fear. Yet it was not sound but raw emotion and he swung towards that. He had reached the edge of the dais, that man whose fear was being so broadcast. Dragging at him as if to urge faster flight was the Jat and behind those two by several steps the Jewelbright.

Jofre gave a leap which carried him over the wreckage of the wires and landed behind the Holder. In a moment his arm was over the other's shoulder, bringing pressure to bear on the Tssekian's throat.

"Be quiet," Jofre hissed in the other's ear, "and move— or you die!"

The Jat was kicking at him, but not with enough strength to shake that hold. Now another moved beside him.

"These witless waglogs have turned on each other to the death. It is as if the Old Ones have sent them mad!"

He knew her scent. At least she was not oathed as bodyguard or he would have now been dead.

"Move!" He shoved the Holder around the end of the dais to where the Zacathan, blaster in hand, stood over the scanner. Jofre could see over his prisoner's shoulder now. There was such wildness in the struggle in the audience hall that the Jewelbright might indeed have been right. These Tssekians could have all been struck mad, for they were fighting each other. Now there dropped on ropes from above other armed fighters, both men and women, wearing no uniforms except a band of green about the upper arm, and these moved in upon the fighters.

To reach the outside they would have to win through that mess on the floor and Jofre was not sure they could. He was trying to evaluate all possible advantages, if there were any, for this action or that, when a party of those who had come down from above began to draw in upon the four of them in a grim-faced half circle.

"Pass us—or this one dies!" Jofre shouted in the trade tongue, hoping that he would be understood.

The leader of those confronting him, a man as tall and

wide-shouldered as Harse, and certainly with all that guard's grim presence, made no move to lower his own weapon. Jofre staggered; a sudden and more vicious attack from the Jat had nearly rocked him from his feet. But a moment later the Jewelbright took a hand in the matter and captured the creature in a grasp strong enough to pull it back.

Zurzal had shouldered the scanner, paying no heed to its tripod stand, using a side strap above the maimed arm to support it, as he covered the distance between them in two strides.

"Pass or this one dies!" Jofre tightened his hold on the Holder's throat. The man was already gasping for breath, his hands flailing out to no purpose as he had no weapon now and Jofre was positioned out of reach behind him.

"There is a problem here." The leader of the opposition had again edged closer so that his voice carried even through the clamor. His weapon hand was steady but Jofre, reading the subtle change in the other's eyes, did not think that he was about to be crisped at once by blaster fire. At least the fellow was speaking trade tongue. "You have what we are very anxious to get—yield your prisoner—"

In Jofre's grip the Holder struggled wildly. It was plain to the issha that this was not a friendly party seeking to rescue their leader.

"Why?" It was not he who asked that question but Zurzal. The Jewelbright said nothing, merely held to her place beside Jofre, both hands gripping the upper front limbs of the Jat in spite of the creature's frenzied fight for freedom. That she possessed issha-trained strength was very plain to see.

"He is more our meat than yours, Learned One," the green-banded leader returned promptly. "We have certain plans for him."

One of his squad moved closer and growled a sentence. The melee in the chamber seemed to be dying down. Here and there a knot of uniforms still fought, but it was apparent that those who had swung down from aloft were fast gaining control of the conflict.

"Plans for us also—" Jofre stated. "What are those?"

"Not perhaps what you might fear," returned the other. "Learned One," now he spoke directly to Zurzal, "you have served our cause even inadvertently." With his free hand he pointed to the scanner which now dangled down the Zacathan's back. "We are a little in your debt—even more when you turn that one over to us. I think you will find us grateful."

Two of the squad, one of these a woman, Jofre noted, split off now and came inward, one from either side as if to box in him and his captive.

"These are rebels." For the first time the Jewelbright spoke and flatly.

"Partisans of freedom, lady." The leader was smiling now, almost gallant in his attitude, but there was no lessening of alert menace in those still edging towards Jofre.

"And our coming—was it part of a plan which you also shared?" asked Zurzal. "Well," he did not wait for any answer, "perhaps we can deal after all. Though I think that your party had another end for me in view two days ago."

The leader shrugged. "We have hotheads, such are the

bane of any party, Learned One. Those who made that decision have been disciplined for it. Now—give us that man—"

Jofre interrupted. "One does not throw away a weapon untried, Commander," he gave the man the only rank he could guess. "You admit that your followers tried to burn us down at the ruins. How can it be that we are now to forget that? You did not take this prisoner; we hold him—"

"So you can decide what is to be done with him?" queried the other. "How long can you stand there, guard, and hold him? You need both hands to the purpose, are you then able to sprout another pair to beat us off?"

"He will kill—" It was the woman approaching from the left who spoke then. "We need that one for—" She stopped abruptly, near in mid word as if she realized that she might be giving away something of importance and the commander favored her with a quick frown before his eyes clicked back to center on Jofre.

"What do you want?" he demanded sharply then, plainly impatient to settle the matter—if he could—as quickly as possible.

"What you spoke of earlier, Commander," Zurzal had adopted the same title, "freedom. We are here against our will—we were kidnapped to order. We want nothing more than to ship out from Tssek and go our own way."

The commander studied the Zacathan, then his attention turned to Jofre, and last of all to the Jewelbright.

"This off-world female was not brought here by force but to play another game of her own. She cannot claim otherwise."

"Any game she was to play," Jofre said, "is now ended.

She is off-world—she has not meddled with your ways—can any speak against her?"

"She is what she is," the scorn in the woman's voice was near as hot as blaster breath. "We want none of her—let her return to her own kind and swim in their dregs."

"Let us reach the port," Zurzal said swiftly. "I do not know what ship may be there ready to lift. If there is none then let us enter Patrol custody—do you not agree that that will keep us away from any meddling here?"

"We need give you nothing," the man who had earlier spoken in Tssek to the commander, burst in. "Stass rays—"

Jofre stiffened. It was true, they could be taken again as easily as he and Zurzal had been back on Wayright. As long as he must keep his hold on his prisoner he could do nothing to prevent such an attack.

"You forget, At s'San, we do have something to thank them for. Did they not show us the true death of Fer s'Rang—though that service was quite unintended." The commander smiled thinly. "No, we shall give them what they wish—the female also since we have no use for her kind—and even that squalling thing," he pointed to the Jat who was crying out in a thin wailing. "Such are not for our world; let them go. Escort them to the port and turn them over to the off-worlders who keep the peace for their own kind. But first—give us—him!"

Could these orders stand? Could he accept the word of this rebel commander? But Zurzal was nodding in agreement and Jofre must accept the bargain as became an oathed.

He loosened his grip on the Holder and at the same

time gave the prisoner a push forward. Those two who had closed in from the sides were on him in an instant, and one pointed with a rod straight at the Holder's head. He stiffened with a jerk which nearly raised him from his feet and then toppled forward, caught in stass and so completely helpless.

Three of the squad bore him away but six more fell in around the off-worlders, forming a hollow square, moving forward at a trot which they were forced to equal. The Jewelbright had swept her shimmering robes up with one hand. She had tweaked out of her cloak of hair one of those hidden cords the same color and texture of the tresses in which it had been fastened and thrown that in a noose around the neck of the Jat, so pulling the creature along as one might a hunt-hound.

There was still fighting in progress and twice they had to battle their way past opposition from one of the stubborn pockets of beleaguered guardsmen. There was no flitter waiting for them, rather a ground transport into which they were crowded while their guard took position around them, weapons ready.

They turned abruptly from the main streets where struggles were still in progress, winding a road through lesser ways, some nearly alleys. There were bodies to be seen here and there. Once there came a blaze of blaster fire crisping the side of their vehicle inches away from where the Jewelbright crouched. She winced but made no sound and Jofre was so tightly jammed against her other side that he could not see whether she had been burned by that fire's touch.

The transport skidded around a corner and they could

now clearly see the space port. The great gates had been firmly closed and within their perimeter were to be seen the black and silver uniforms of the Patrol as well as the grey worn by the space employees. Also there were weapons very much to the fore.

But there was no warning to stop as they approached. Though neither did anyone move to open the gate. The nose of their vehicle was nearly touching that when they came to a halt.

The Tssekian guards stepped aside and allowed the three off-worlders and the Jat to face the barrier. A man wearing Patrol dress and one in space grey, who had the insignia of Port officer on his right shoulder, moved a little forward.

Zurzal hunched the strap of the scanner higher on his shoulder and raised his good hand in the peace salute.

"We claim refuge under the Code of Harktapha." His frill was high and a deep crimson and his hissing near serpent-strong.

The Patrol officer took a stride which brought him to that section of the larger gate which might be opened separately as a small door.

"Who are the hunters?" the officer asked.

Zurzal's frill fluttered and the hue darkened. "We are not hunted, First Officer. These have brought us out with orders that we reach here. We are from off-world and there is war on Tssek which does not concern us."

"You will drop all weapons and enter singly," came the command. "You will abide by the code, surrendering to judgment concerning that which brought you here."

Zurzal nodded. "Agreed, First Officer." He tossed to

one side the blaster he had belted when he had given the peace sign. Jofre wound the Makwire about his hand into a coil and sent it earthward. The Jewelbright produced from somewhere about her person, so swiftly he could not sight where it had been hidden, a slender but, as he knew, most deadly knife and added that to the collection on the ground.

Moving one by one, Zurzal in the lead, then the Jewelbright with the Jat on leash, and finally Jofre, edged through the gate door which was opened only far enough to give them tight passage. Jofre's empty hands stirred in a sign he did not know he was shaping:

"Out of dark, into light."

# ✳ CHAPTER 18 ✳

**THOUGH IT WAS WELL PAST** the mid-hour of the night, there was still a lamp alight in an upper room of the old town house. A shadow swept across the wall in an even pattern as Ras Zarn paced the room. This night he was ridden by the need for physical effort, to somehow expend the tension which crippled him during the day, which made it more and more difficult to make decisions swiftly and correctly.

Might the Night Gnawers of Garn feast upon their lives! He fought to keep control, to not throw back his head and voice the howl of frustration which seemed near to suffocate him. Could any one of them in his position have done better? All well for them to issue orders, but the ability to obey was not in their power to enforce—unless they would decide to make an example of him and set up some other fool who, given the same situation, could certainly do no better.

*THEY* could hunt across the hills as they had in the past to bring down prey. There was no way any one man could

hunt the star lanes. It would require centuries to even sift through a small portion of the star ports. Such a search was madness even to think of!

He had given them one solution but they would not accept it. Secrets—they were not prepared to share their secrets! But there was no other way. If the Guild accepted that they were to hunt for a man, if the matter could be presented to them solely as an act of vengeance—a chance. Though for the most part a Veep of the Guild would not concern himself with such a minor matter, under certain circumstances he or she could be led to give such orders. That was a kernel of understanding on which he, Zarn, could build—though there would be a price.

However, there was the problem of the prey—had he yet learned the value of what he had stolen from the cursed Lair? Supposing during a hunt the Guild would discover what their quarry had in his possession?

Zarn's fist was at his lips and he gnawed on his knuckles. This night he had sent his strongest message. It must be acted upon at once, for the Guild contact was not going to wait on the favor of a priesthood they did not recognize nor consider of any import in their own deliberations.

Time was fast running out. They must either depend upon these others who had the wide-flung organization which could locate a man off-world, or they must admit defeat. And to do that was to perhaps open a future which would—

Zarn shook his head. He went back to the low table, dropped down to the mat seat behind it, his fingers scrabbling among a number of small sticks littered there. Each was notched in a different pattern, one which could

be read by touch, even in the dark. But he had no need to try to sort out again those orders, threats, demands.

There was a muted sound, hardly louder than his own labored breathing. Zarn's head came up, he was on his feet at once, to pass through a concealed doorway into that narrow room where there was a panel high in the wall open to the night sky. Through this his awaited messenger had come to perch on the desk table. It uttered two plaintive squawks as the merchant reached it.

His hands went out to stroke and gentle the flyer. Then met those avian eyes with his own compelling gaze. This was one of the best trained of the shrine flyers. At least they had accepted that the task demanded the very best weapons they could bring to the field.

Zarn plucked the message from brain to brain. His tongue tip swept dry lips. His life—well, he had known in the end it would come to this—his life in the balance against victory. But they were giving in, if reluctantly; they were agreeing that his suggestion could now be the only way.

So—in hope he had already made certain moves; now it was time to follow those up. He gave the flyer its reward and left it squatting on the desk top, the opening in the roof unclosed. There would be no message he could send now—that he wanted to send. What he would do needed no interference from those at a distance who had never encountered the players he must draw into the game.

Dawn was smoky pale in the sky as he began to set into action the plan he had labored on. He sent another messenger, this one two-legged and from his household,

with a very ambiguous report that he had lately obtained certain wares from the north which might interest that particular buyer.

Down in the larger chamber devoted to business he oversaw the unpacking of two bags, the setting out of his bait—star stones worked by Hemcreft himself. The High Shagga had parted with those as easily as if they had been implanted toothwise in his jaws—but they were unique enough to hold this Xantan.

He had time to compose himself fully, to practice the Six Exercises of Quiet and Preparation. So it was with his usual composure that he faced the woman who answered his summons.

She was clearly an off-worlder, a thin-bodied figure with elongated arms and overlarge hands. Her dark skin had a metallic sheen and looked very smooth, almost as if she were indeed encased in some hard coating. A great deal of it was exposed by her scanty clothing which consisted mainly of strips of shaggy material which might be the fur of some strange beast and was of a violently vivid flame color, showing even brighter against the grey-black of the body it wreathed around. Her head was swathed in a large turban that flashed a border of jewels, the seeing of which gave Zarn a hidden satisfaction. It was plain that this envoy of the Guild had a liking for gems, so that what he had to offer should prove tempting.

"Gentlefem"—he bowed and escorted her to a pile of seat mats well raised above the floor to accommodate her longer limbs—"you honor this house of trade."

She raised her first set of eyelids and opened the inner ones halfway. Her narrow, almost snoutlike, mouth was not

meant to shape a humanoid smile but it twisted somewhat in what might just be the equivalent of such.

"The wares of Ras Zarn," her trade tongue had a rasp as suggestive of metal as her body, "are well known to produce treasures. It was spoken to me of a special shipment—"

She had not glanced once at the display on the table. However, Zarn believed that she had not only surveyed it but at the same instant had been able to value it.

"As you see, Gentlefem." He waved a hand toward the gems set out skillfully on a darkened strip of leather which enhanced their incandescent silver and gold natural coloring.

Now she did turn a little on the mat seat, that exercise twisting her long neck (looking far too slender to support a large head made even more bulky by the turban). Both her outer and inner eyelids were fully open. She made no move to lean forward a little farther to touch the gems, merely regarded them. Zarn did not doubt in the least that she knew to a quarter star crédit their value.

"A showing, Merchant Zarn, a showing. But—"

"A buying—no?" he said quietly. "Ah, well, it was the Gentlefem I considered first when these came to me, knowing how great is her ability to pick the best and make the finest use of such. But if they do not suit your taste, then I am most sorry to have troubled you."

Her mouth worked again and those second inner eyelids half closed, surveying him now, rather than the display of stones.

"We buy and sell, both of us, merchant. If I buy, what then is the price?"

Inwardly Zarn relaxed a fraction. She was willing—at least enough to discuss matters. But any deal with the Guild was tricky, very tricky.

"There is a story to be told, Gentlefem."

She made a sound which might either have been a sigh of boredom or one of impatience. "There always is when one of you wishes to deal with us." She was frank enough anyway.

"We seek a man, a traitor, one who has betrayed us blood and bond."

The woman raised a hand as if to straighten the mound of her turban.

"Your world is wide, but I do not doubt that you have the means for tracking him—Shagga!" She mouthed that last word almost as if it were an accusation, but Zarn was not taken unawares. No one could deny that the Guild had their own seekers of knowledge, that they kept account and learned all they could of any they might have future dealings with.

"Unfortunately he is off-world. Before we could put hand on him he blasphemously used the code which had been stripped from him and oathed with an off-worlder— a Zacathan."

"Ah, yes." Now the woman did reach out, and, with one of her long equal-length six fingers, tapped the table below the first jewel in line.

"That lizard skin is one I have heard that your own people have an interest in." Zarn ventured the first push. He must assume more authority or else be defeated before he began.

"We have an interest—slight. Not one that moves us particularly at present," she said.

"We are ready to award interest with payment—" His very slight gesture indicated the array of jewels.

"That could be taken under consideration." She arose from the pile of mat cushions. "Word will be sent before nightfall."

He was forced to be content with that, but he was hopeful. The rumor which had reached his own well-enlisted spies was that the Zacathan was of particular interest to the Guild. They could already be laying a web for that one. However, any company their prey might have at the time might then be summarily disposed of unless a neat profit would change that part of their program.

Had he been able to use his own eyes and ears as well as he wanted to, his relief would have been the greater. The woman made her way directly to the spaceport and there in the lounge where those who waited for a ship to take off she had taken a seat and sat as if only idly interested in what was about her. She did not wait long before a man in spacer suiting but obviously of her own species came to stand before her. She greeted him with the slightest of nods and he sat down at the empty seat facing her.

"That mud-based toadling," the language she spoke was not trade and it was a murmur of words run together until they seemed to be a single sound, "offers a respectable amount—the Shagga must have combed out their private treasure boxes."

"For what?"

"The Zacathan oathed a renegade of their tamed killing order. They want him back—they are highly primitive in their thought processes. This traitor of theirs went off-world with the Zacathan."

"They want him dead?"

"No, I believe that the death dealing is something they desire to be strictly their business—they want him."

"As an oathed guard he will defend the Zacathan."

"Yes. However, there are ways and means—The main point remains that the Zacathan be allowed to proceed as he himself wishes until the proper time. I understand that there has already been some difficulty on that point—"

"The Tssekians were not in the picture as we knew it then. We have to sort that out."

Her mouth moved in that twist of a smile. "Doubtless there has already been set in motion a plan to deal with that. But—do we accept this other offer—the renegade to be taken and returned here? The price they offer is tempting."

"And this Shagga can be depended upon to come through when the deal is properly completed?"

"He is no fool. Guild bargains are kept, as he and all the stars well know. This can be done I am sure—and the extra bit of sweetening he is ready to offer will please the Council. They just must be sure our merchandise is not harmed in any future action."

"Very well, make what arrangements may be demanded." He stood up. "We lift at the fourth moon hour. Shall I see you aboard?"

"Of a certainty, yes, and with some interesting baggage. These star stones, Talor, are worth even perhaps a fourth grade organizer's ransom—should some sum as that ever be asked."

Zarn had made his first move; he did not linger before following through on the second. Once more he sorted out

the rune-inscribed sticks, setting them first in one pattern and then another as if striving to find one which suited him best. There was no possible other choice. Yes, one of the Shadows had gone off-world as bodyguard to that young lordling. He was not of top grade, nor experienced, and the reports on the renegade had been clear.

Outlaw that he was, he was well trained, though he had never been sent on a mission. But that mind-twisted Master of his had given him special instructions—some the Shagga on station in that Lair did not even know; he could only suspect. He was certainly a fool also—the renegade should have been assigned another Lair and quietly disposed of there. But instead he had been loosed—

Luckily that brain-empty skull of a priest had had him monitored when he crossed the mountains or they would never have known what happened in the dead Lair. But that Shagga was now busily repenting his first stupidity and would be for some time to come; no one need worry about *HIM*.

However, they must accept that their prey had training well past novice grade, perhaps approaching that of a Hand, young as he was. And with what he carried—No, they could not, even if the oath law permitted it, detach the young lord's guard.

Nor must they depend solely upon the Guild, even if the latter were willing to seal a bargain. The Guild wanted the Zacathan—or rather what they hoped to wring out of him. While the renegade was oathed and would defend his charge to the death. Not even the Shagga who loathed him would deny that he was truly issha-trained and firmly set in their pattern.

Also—Zarn tapped his fingers on the tabletop inches away from the sticks. What if the renegade began to understand what he had taken out of Qaw-en-itter? What if he would become—a Master? Assha strength might defeat even the Guild entrapment.

Who—? It must not be left to the Guild. What if they (and he had the greatest respect for their Veeps and experts) also did a little delving and discovered that taken from the dead? They might even strike a bargain with the renegade—his life for his find—taking as an excuse for such dealing that the Brothers had deceived them in not mentioning the prime reason for their hiring.

Zarn shivered. Were that to happen—He would envy for the days of life still left to him the fate of the Shagga who had first loosed this blot upon the Shadows. To dispatch another issha—one of greater training and experience—off-world? He had no time to wrangle with the Shagga Over Heads for that. The longer the renegade remained loose off-world—and only the Foul Three of Trusk knew what he was doing besides guarding the Zacathan's back—the more chance of his becoming greater than they could hope to handle. He might even be able to give the Guild a surprise or two.

Which left only one choice and he had already been denied that. However, under the circumstances this time she would have to agree. Her oath could be dissolved with the permission of the Sister of the Inner Silences. Such action had been taken several times in the past—need must overreach custom when there was demand.

But how then was he to reach her—off-world? There would be only one organization—outside of, of course, the

ever-present Patrol—which could bear such a command along the star lanes after having first located her to whom it was to be given. The Guild again—

Zarn sighed. He poked at a roll of leather. Wealth beyond the raising of any one Lair—at least four of the richest had been stripped to gather that. And the Guild were no unpaid benefactors—they would demand more for such a task. Still—deep in him he was certain of only one thing: he could not trust the Guild to the point of blood oath—the Sister who had already gone starward would carry out any true order to the death.

Get her free from her present bond—and he had only until the Guild Veep returned to do so. He swept the sticks together and rolled them into a bag he thrust into a concealed holder under the low table. This he must do himself.

The roll containing the jewels he took to the wall behind the seat mats and touched several places there to open a small cavity. But before he stowed his packet inside he surveyed the present contents of that hiding place. With a sigh he flicked another box into place beside the packet, and then closed the cavity.

For him to approach the House of Jewels openly in daylight and be sighted, would cause talk—and not the kind of talk his position in the old city welcomed. But there was no help for it. He could only depend on a hooded cloak, such as one of the mountain priests wore, or a disguise—a very flimsy one.

The Mistress of Jewels received him in her own chamber and listened to his terse outline of what had to be done and why. She frowned.

"This you ask casts a stain on honor. We are also issha, and we live by the Five Oaths! Once a mission has been honorably taken and the Shadow oathed, only a successful completion—or death—releases the Sister. You ask much—too much!"

"This is a threat to us all." Zarn dared not tell her the truth; only a handful knew it and if he spoke without permission he would be word-broke—disgraced until he could not even redeem himself with his own life taking.

"In what way, Shagga?" She was not going to give in easily. He could feel the sweat beads gather at his hairline in spite of all his inner effort to appear above emotion.

"I cannot be word-broke," he decided that he could be this frank with her, "but it is such a danger that we have not known since the Refusal of Gortor." The mention of that portentous action which had nearly wiped out all the Shadow breed was never uttered idly. Surely that would impress her!

Her eyes had widened slightly and now her fingers sketched Ward-off-Perils-of-the-Far-Night.

"You swear this?" she asked.

Zarn's knife was in plain sight. Deliberately he extended his heart-finger and pressed the tip of that sharp narrow blade into the flesh, until a bead of red showed. Withdrawing the knife he held out his hand where the drop of blood welled larger. The woman looked straight into his eyes and then down at that finger. With her own heart-finger she touched his and Zarn knew inwardly a great relief. She had accepted, she would do it!

"The oathed one has gone off-world, there is no way a Shadow message can reach her—" the woman continued.

Zarn shook his head. "There is a way, that I also oath swear."

For a moment she looked dubious. But the promise he had just given her was so binding she had to accept that he believed he could carry it out.

"Very well. The word is Flow Cloud."

The word which would trigger oath release—Zarn almost shivered. That was something sacred, by custom used only by a Lair Master to release one from a mission accomplished. To pass such to another was a perilous thing, but in this he had no choice.

Once again in his own chamber, the packet and box from the cavity prominently ranged before him on the table, he busied himself with another small twiglet of stick, this of a dull black in color and no longer than his heart-finger. With a very small tool, such as one who set gems would use, he made his scratches on the stick. First the release word and then the second oathing—one which would bind the Sister to her second and most important mission. He was barely finished in time, for one of his household came to announce the return of the Veep. If she agreed—but she must! He called on that inner way which, it was said, one truly in difficulty could use as an inducement—holding to it like body armor as the off-world woman came in.

# ✳ CHAPTER 19 ✳

"**YOU UNDERSTAND** that under the 1732X you must be held." Patrol Captain Ilan Sandor eyed his listeners coldly. "If the Tssekian government demands that you be turned over to answer charges of fomenting riot, of plotting, you cannot claim sanctuary here."

"We are escaped prisoners." Zurzal's return was as evenly voiced. "We were brought to Tssek against our will and in defiance of interstellar law. I have not yet heard that kidnapping is a legal form of obtaining immigrants."

"You have one story—"

"Backed by a truth reader," Zurzal interrupted. His neck frill was stirring. "We had no voice in our coming here; we were kept prisoner by the then recognized government—forced to accede to certain demands made upon us."

"And you precipitated a revolution!" the captain snapped.

For the first time the port officer spoke. "As you have seen, Captain"—he motioned to a number of reader discs

lying on the desk between the two parties—"there was preparation for such a rising long in the making before the arrival of this Learned One."

"With"—the captain showed no softening—"this infernal machine of his! That at least we can take care of—"

Zurzal's frill flamed a violent yellow-red. "It is under the seal of the Zacathan explorative service, Captain. I do not think that even your all-powerful organization is going to dispute ownership."

"You, Learned One," retorted the captain, "are no longer a member in good standing of your service—and because you meddled with this very scanner of yours! Any protest will have to be entered through your Clan Elder and, since we are half the galaxy away from your home, that will take quite a time to resolve."

"I am on detached service, Captain. Consult the authorities if you wish. You will discover my credentials in order. My search. Before my journey was so brazenly interrupted, I was on my way to Lochan. I have already shown my authorization for such a study. That this has occurred on Tssek, is, I assert, no fault of mine."

"It remains that there is a civil war in progress on the other side of that fence," the captain waved at the nearest window opening onto the port, "and that you have had a hand in stirring it up, willing or not willing. You have transgressed against the creed of your own people as well as the central law of noninterference."

"Captain," again the port commander spoke, "is it not better to wait and see? There is abundant proof which you yourself have viewed," again he waved toward the discs,

"that a strong underground movement was underway even before this Learned One and his bodyguard were brought here. That the attack came at the time it did was also certain. They had knowledge—my listening service is not a questionable one—that the Holder planned to broadcast his carefully edited version of the Great Ingathering. The overturn of his plan was caused because two of the technicians selected to set up the already prepared broadcast of his own editing were members of the underground party. They were prepared to sabotage his efforts. When the Zacathan was brought in it added a new factor they had not planned on. But in fact, Learned One," now he addressed Zurzal, "you did show what might have been the truth fifty years in the past. This was a support they had not counted on, but one they speedily turned to their advantage. For what your scanner showed was broadcast over more than half of the machines, picked up by underground installations and passed on. The broadcast had already been arranged as the signal for the uprising, and they moved in."

"Their control is not yet complete," the captain stated. "It is difficult to believe that they will prevail over such fortresses as Smagan or Wer."

"Thanks to our friends here," the port officer nodded to the three on the other side of the table, "they have the Holder. As do all who rise to power he has for years systematically weeded out all below him who could question his authority, depending on those linked to him so tightly that his fall would mean theirs also. They may hold out in pockets because it means their lives, and even rasrats will turn and fight if they are cornered, but there is no

longer any leader to rally them and there has long been
jealousy and infighting among them."

"You have been watching the building of this situation
for long, Commander?" Zurzal's frill was lightening in
shade.

"As the one responsible for this port I have had to make
observations," the other agreed. "Every form of
government sooner or later reaches a plateau from which
there is no longer an upward advance. Since the lives of
sentient beings do not remain static, there follow changes.
As your people know so well, Learned One. So it happened
here. But when the rebels win they will have something to
thank your guard for—that they have the Holder."

"As I have said!" the captain scowled, "interference with
the native government—"

"You would rather, Captain, that we be dead?"

Startled, it was not only the Patrol officer but all the rest
of them who turned now to look at the fifth member of the
party. Gone were the floating, seductive garments of the
assured Jewelbright. Taynad had asked for and changed
speedily into a spacer's drab garb. The long waves of her
hair had been tightly braided, and were now bound around
her head, though the wealth of that hair made it seem she
must be wearing a turban.

"Yes," the captain had almost instantly adjusted to her
entrance into this meeting, to the implied criticism of her
question. "There also remains you, Gentlefem. I believe
that you arrived here by the invitation of the Holder, is that
not so?"

"Having done so," Taynad returned calmly, "there is no
reason for my remaining once he is no longer my host. My

very presence in his company would probably have damned me with these rebels. I owe my continued existence to the Learned One and his guard. And I am duly grateful. I hardly think, Captain, that you are going to hand me over to Tssekians—"

Jofre was sensitive to what she was doing, using trained will-power. Even though she had not turned it on him, he could feel the gathering force of it. And he did not believe that this Patrol officer, disciplined as he might be, could stand against the issha assurance of the Jewelbright.

"Why did you come?" It was not the officer but the port commander who asked that bluntly, and she answered as fully:

"The Holder had (I saw *him* cut down in the hall and so he is no longer my employer) a Horde Commander who was ambitious. He had gone off-world hunting the Learned One here as an offering to his master, and on Asborgan he chanced to learn of the Jewels. As was custom he bargained for my services. I was to be another gift. He had plans—" She shrugged. "I was a weapon; he did not have time to use me."

"Now that we have discussed a number of explanations and scraps of news," Zurzal cut in, "may we return to the main point of this meeting? I have suffered a crude and unnecessary interruption to plans I have been making for years. It is my intention that I carry those out and I do not think that anyone, Captain, is going to produce a good reason why I cannot."

"You will wait until there is a settlement here!" returned the Patrol officer flatly.

Zurzal spoke then, not to him, but to the port

commander. "Commander, you have shown that you have ample reason to believe that my coming here had in reality nothing to do with the present embroilment. You also know that my appearance on Tssek was entirely against my will. By Stellar Law can we be held in this fashion?"

The commander looked neither to the Patrol captain nor to the Zacathan, instead he was studying with great interest the nails on his right hand.

"He's right, you know," he observed. "We have proof of the kidnapping, of the fact that he was being used against his will. He has claimed refuge under the Code of Harktapha—that has held since the first spacers met with his kind. We have no quarrel with Zacathans—their knowledge is ever at our service—their persons are diplomatically sacred—"

"This one presumes too much!" the Patrol officer interrupted.

"In your opinion—" The three words brought a sour silence from the captain. His hands clenched on the edge of the desk as if he would upend that innocent piece of furniture and send it in the general direction of those three across from him.

"So, Learned One," as if he need expect no more interruption the commander turned again to Zurzal, "what is your will?"

"I would return to Wayright and carry out those plans of mine," returned the Zacathan. "My guard goes with me and this gentlefem also, if it is her will."

"It is," Taynad agreed. She added nothing to that and Jofre wondered what thoughts clustered now in her head. Since he who had oathed her was dead by what the

issha-sworn would consider chance, she was free from
employment. Would she, once more on Wayright, seek to
return to Asborgan?

"Also," she was speaking again, "there is the matter of
the Jat."

"That can be easily attended to." The Patrol officer
must have been glad he had a clear and definite answer to
that. "It will be returned to its home planet."

"In the condition in which it now exists?" she queried.

The officer looked to the port commander for an
answer.

"Unfortunately, the creature has gone catatonic and
cannot be roused," he reported. "The bond between it and
the Holder was so harshly broken as to send it into a coma.
The medic reports that nothing he has been able to do will
restore it."

"It might be well to let me try." To Jofre's surprise the
Jewelbright spoke. "A broken bond might indeed break a
mind, but a transferred bond—"

"Can this be done?" the commander questioned.

She hesitated for only a second. "My kind have certain
powers, Gentlehomos. I have developed a liking for the
creature and I saw more of it when it was with its bond
master than any of you. Let me try to transfer the bond."

"But it still must be returned—"

"Let that be decided after we see how this will work,"
said the commander. "Yes, Gentlefem, I shall give orders
that you are to try this—and may you be successful."

To Jofre's complete astonishment she turned her
head and surveyed him. "This is one of my world," she
indicated him. "The training he has been given grants

him a certain rapport with other species. I will need him to give me aid."

Jofre had no chance to talk to her alone. She had admitted obliquely that she knew him for what he was. But that that would constitute any tie between them was chancy. The commander escorted them over to the medic quarters and there they looked down upon the small body which had balled itself almost into a knot on one of the bunks.

"It still lives," the medic reported, "but it has had no food nor drink, and the heartbeat is very slow. It is close to death."

"Yan searches for he who is gone, that one who became his other half." Taynad seated herself on the edge of the bunk and leaned over, to gather the Jat into her arms as if it were a hurt child.

"Medic, on our world we have certain training which can unite us with other living creatures beside those of our own species. It may be that we can reach Yan and bring him back. We can only try."

The medic shook his head. "Gentlefem, I fear it is hopeless. But if there is anything you can do—"

He went to seat himself on a stool at the other side of the room, watching them intently.

Taynad, the Jat still held against her, moved carefully around on the bunk, so that as much of her back was now presented to Jofre as possible. He could guess the next step. Though he had never been a part of such linkage, yet he was well aware there were cases in which it would and had worked.

Now he seated himself behind Taynad's back and

dropped his hands on her shoulders. The inner commands he knew and gave one by one, each taking him further to the Center. As yet he was aware of nothing but his own search for full control.

With one hand Taynad stroked the small body which she cradled so close to her. She began a soft crooning in which there were no words to be distinguished, only soothing sounds.

Jofre within himself found and fastened upon that strength he sought. Now he drew—launched—as he might a dart—what he shaped. He could feel the feed of it from his center, along his arms, into her body—Then—!

Touch, immediate linkage, being borne along by another's demanding will. A wall against which that will struck, and then began to beat in a heavy pattern, seeking a weakness, a way of entrance—

Swifter grew those blows, steady and unrelenting the draw upon Jofre. He summoned up more and more to feed, to strengthen—

The resistance lessened reluctantly, as if a bit crumbled, and then another. Before him now was a whirling chaos of terror, alien and therefore threatening. Jofre braced himself and held. What they shaped together now was not the battering ram which had found them a way into this place of rolling terror and loss, but rather a thread to be caught up by the churning of what abode there, twisted, tangled. And they were content to have it so for now— though the payment was heavy as there was feedback of that terror, those waves of negative force. They must not only hold their small contact, but protect themselves into the bargain.

Now! She had not spoken, but the order reached Jofre as if it had been shouted like a battle cry. He sent forth a surge of power, the thread tightened as she spun. It was well enmeshed now in the chaos, it held. Yet it formed a path for them. Dark, cold, nothingness slipped along towards those two who dared to touch.

The room was gone, Jofre was aware only of a battle which he could not see, only sense. This—this—Frantically he hunted a shield, a weapon, something to stop that dark counterflow.

As if it lay heavy in his hand he knew now what he must have. The stone out of Qaw-en-itter. Asshi—if it were assha—force—if it could bring him that force. Though he continued to hold to the thread the Jewelbright had spun, yet he groped within him until he in turn touched! Yet this was no chaos—rather ordered energy. His inner self buckled as he strove to harness it. Too much—he was like one filled with fire which ate outward until all which he was might be consumed.

Ruthlessly Jofre fought to turn that wave, that fire, to harness it to the thread. And so it did—whether by his efforts, or perhaps because it was attracted in turn to what they were spinning out from issha strength.

The thread had wound and now was in a whirl which had begun to thicken, to encompass the darkness as if that had substance. And the darkness drew in farther and farther upon its own core until it was like a single nugget of pain and fear. This the thread netted and drew towards its own source.

Jofre was aware again of the woman beside him, of her body trembling in a hold he had tightened to keep her

erect and steady. Then the last remaining fragments of the break-bond spread into him and his clasp on her shoulders would have fallen away save that there rang from her to him the issha touch—enough to steady him.

He accepted the break-bond as he would swallow some bitter potion if such an act was necessary. Then made one more call, issha—assha—he could not tell which answered but, as the blowing out of a lamp, the flash of a blaster, the darkness was gone.

Into its place there flowed something else—a warmth which was not of his own, not issha at all—alien—yet with no harm—rather lightness of spirit, peace of mind and heart. Jofre realized that their linkage still held but what it had done was more than they had thought—the Jat was free of that despair which would have killed it—but it was—rebonded—with them!

He could see over Taynad's shoulder that the creature was no longer a hard ball in her arms. One of its small forepaws was raised, drawing the blunt finger growths down the Jewelbright's cheek. It chirped inquiringly and she gave a small cry and hugged it closer, rocking a little back and forth as might one who had feared for a child and now found that fear had gone.

"Friend—" Jofre's head jerked. The Jat had moved in Taynad's hold and was now looking over her shoulder to him. Again its forepaw advanced, to stroke caressingly his hand which still caught at the Jewelbright. From that touch came the warmth and peace which he had earlier felt, but increased, as if fueled with the same power as one of the starships.

"You have done it!" The medic was standing over both

of them, staring down at the Jat, which kept its hold on Jofre as well as remaining within the circle of Taynad's arm.

For the first time Jofre heard the tinkle of the Jewelbright's laugh.

"Perhaps not as the Patrol captain might wish," she returned. "I am afraid that he will be unable to follow orders even now—Yan has rebonded with—" She glanced at Jofre. Her face had a slight softness which had gentled the masklike beauty she had always turned upon them. "Yan has bonded with—us!"

"And," Jofre swiftly spoke for himself, "I do not think that you can try a second time." He was surprised at the warmth of his own feelings. Issha were not bond-worthy except by oath, and certainly no oathing had passed here. Or had one which was deeper and wiser than that of Lair knowledge?

The woman also, he was sure that some of his feeling at least had been shared by her, known to her now. Which was a muddle—they had indeed wrought thoughtlessly, for it would seem that the two of them were now linked in a way unknown to their breed before—by one small, warm, and peace-spreading creature. He wondered what complications they had both drawn to them by what they had done.

He loosed his hold on Taynad, feeling a little awkward, but he reached forward to draw his hand in a half caress across the hobbling head of the Jat, between those up-pointed ears.

"You are sure?" The medic was demanding. "This is going to present a problem—"

"We are sure," the Jewelbright answered calmly.

"Though we could have done no other to save the little one's life. Bond-breaking," she shivered and her arm tightened a fraction about the small furry body, "is deadly."

The medic looked at them both indecisively. "I shall have to report—" And with that he was gone.

Taynad waited until the door closed behind the spacer. Then she squared her body around on the bunk so she was facing Jofre as well as she could.

"Brother." She had freed her one hand from the Jat and gave him finger greeting.

But dare he answer her as Shadow to Shadow? That was deceitful and not issha way.

"I am no longer of the Brothers," he said, watching her face carefully, waiting for that small softening of the expression to vanish. "The story is a long one, Jewelbright. But thus it stands—" And quickly he sketched all which had happened to him since the morning when the Master had paid the Dead-Stone-price and he himself had been denied. Though he did not mention his night in Qaw-en-itter nor his find there, for that was something he felt he could not share—there was too great a secret about it and he must have the unlocking of that first himself.

"You are issha—for all the blathering of the Shagga," she returned unexpectedly. "Have you not followed the proper pattern and oathed yourself—and to a lord who is well worth the serving? Do you think we could have linked to free this one," she glanced down at the Jat and then to him again, "if you were not a true Shadow? The Shagga sometimes take too much on themselves."

He was startled by her questioning of authority. Perhaps in some fashion she, too, had had something to be

angry over after some priestly encounter. But that she accepted him—with a lift of heart he solemnly made the gesture of welcome and dared to change it so that it was not just to a Shadow met in passing but to one who shared a common goal.

# ✳ CHAPTER 20 ✳

**ONCE MORE** they were gathered in the office of the Patrol captain but this time two more had been added to their number. These were Tssekians but not in the uniforms the unwilling visitors had seen everywhere during their travels in the city and at the keep of the Holder. It seemed to Jofre that they were trying to make a special effort to break with the restraints of their former clothing. For one wore a one-piece suit of green girded by a brilliant scarlet belt and the other a loose shirt of crimson over dull purplish breeches. But both were armed, carrying a fringe of various weapons about their waists and slung across their shoulders, and the speaker for the duo was a woman.

"We have no quarrel with the Learned One," she spoke the trade tongue with an accent as if it was one she was not used to using. "He and his guard were brought here against their wills and what he would have used for the purpose of increasing knowledge was not misused—it showed us the first great treachery of that one—" Her lips moved now as if she would spit, though she did not. "That which is his

and that which belongs to his man, we have brought with us."

Zurzal inclined his head in a small formal nod. "My thanks for your courtesy. I bear no ill will to those of you who now rule here."

"This other," the woman had only nodded curtly in answer to the Zacathan, as if she had already dismissed him from her mind and all dealings with him were completed. Now she was looking at Taynad. "This other was also brought here for a purpose—but one differing from your case, Learned One. Therefore, she is not to be judged as you—"

Jofre stirred. He had had little time to do more than acquaint Zurzal with the news that the Jewelbright was issha and that her mission was aborted with the fall of the Holder. Now he saw her head come up and she met the Tssekian woman eye to eye, almost in direct challenge.

"Why did you come—plaything?" There was scathing contempt in that last word. But Taynad showed no sign that any sting of that reached her.

"It seemed that the Horde Commander Sopt s'Qu had some thought of pleasing his overlord," she returned calmly. "Thus I was included in this plan."

The Tssekian scowled. "Sopt s'Qu is dead," she said flatly. "The one he served will be held to face the wrath of the people. What should be done with you?"

Jofre tensed but Taynad spoke before he could make any protest.

"The man with whom I made my bargain is dead; the man for whom that bargain was made will be otherwise occupied. My reason for visiting Tssek has ceased to exist."

The Tssekian woman continued to measure the Jewelbright and there was nothing soft in that harsh stare.

"Your kind are without value," she almost spat the words. "We want no taint of you in our lives. Since you had no time to work any true mischief here, we shall send you off-world with these others."

"That is your right," conceded Taynad, "nor have I any wish to remain here."

"You brought with you gauds—"

"To which you are now entitled," Taynad interrupted. "Since such were of the Horde Commander's gift and so belong to Tssek. I do not ask for any accounting of them."

"Well for you!" The woman was determined not to be bettered in their subtle struggle. "So, off-worlder," she now looked to the Patrol captain, "these are now your responsibility. Let them return to their own places, we need nothing of them. The Council meets tomorrow; we shall be speaking with you again concerning regulations for off-worlders—some of those will be changed."

She stood up, adjusted a fraction the swing of her weapon slung across her shoulder, and moved towards the door without another word or look.

"Well, it seems it is all decided," the port commander said briskly as the two Tssekians disappeared. "There is no reason, Captain, why these three must be retained to answer questions now—or at least I cannot imagine any. According to the wishes of this planet's people the sooner they are gone the better. There is the courier attached to the port service which is due to lift for Wayright. Quarters may be a little cramped," he spoke now to Zurzal, "but the courier service is fast and there is no other ship due for

some time. In fact the local disturbances here may be a warn-off for freighters in company service. They will want to be sure the new regime is well rooted before they start negotiations again."

The Patrol captain was frowning.

"Learned One, I intend to send a full report of this whole matter to headquarters. This is very close to interference with planetary affairs, and, if proven, that can keep you safely out of space wandering. You, Gentlefem," he said more slowly, "were also undoubtedly intended to interfere with matters as they stood. That you did not have a chance to do so was merely fortune. I shall recommend that you be returned to your Asborgan and not permitted off that world again."

She did not answer him but the Zacathan did. "Send your report, Captain. You will be following the proper procedure. But know this, I shall also offer an explanation of what was done against my will; also I intend to speak for this gentlefem who was legally hired by the laws of her own world, brought to Tssek and then, not only dismissed from service but deprived of the payment promised her. She dealt in good faith and therefore cannot be held responsible for what another deems she might have done— a very unsure assumption.

"For the present I consider her as one of my party and ask that she accompany us to Wayright without prejudice. You cannot condemn anyone for a crime which was not committed and perhaps never would have been except as you speculate."

The port commander was nodding in time to the last words. "He has the right of it. Submit your report, Captain,

and I shall also submit mine. The Tssekians find no fault with these people; instead they freely admit that the Learned One was kidnapped. That his machine worked in part, even aided what they had planned to do, for it betrayed the fact that the Holder had been a traitor to his predecessor. I can believe that such glimpses into the pasts of all of us might turn up some unpleasant and dangerous decisions and events. However, it is the Learned One's desire to use his scanner only in the field of archeology—to present a past so far removed that its summoning will have no effect on the modern day."

"It is wrong—" the captain exploded.

"As you see it. But let us leave such judgments to the higher authorities. What happened on Tssek was a forced use of what might be a very important thing. Now," he spoke once more to the Zacathan, "you will leave with the courier and I promise you as quick a trip as possible. I cannot assure you there will be no questions raised when you reach Wayright—but that will be your concern."

"We shall be most pleased—" Zurzal said. His neck frill, which had shown some traces of color and a tendency to flutter at the edges, now lay peacefully at rest.

When they had time to themselves the Zacathan spoke to Taynad. "Since they have deprived you of your wardrobe and other necessities of travel, allow me to make up that loss at least in part."

"You are very generous, Learned One." Her answer came in a colorless voice. The Jat had hunted her out and now cuddled against her. "I cannot promise any repayment. In the eyes of those I return to I may be considered one who has failed."

"Death cancels an oath!" Jofre broke in. "Sopt s'Qu is dead. And the Holder will soon be, judging by the attitude of these Tssekians we have just seen. Also—were you oathed directly to him or to his subordinate?"

"To the Horde Commander."

"Who is, I repeat, dead. You cannot serve a dead man."

She could, of course. That, too, was part of issha training, but there was no reason for her to use her knife on herself in this situation—the oath was not a full service one he was sure.

"At any rate," she returned, "we have to wait on the fate shadowing us. Much is changed by time."

Their voyage back to Wayright was both swift and smooth. For Jofre it was a far more comfortable one, even though their quarters were crowded. He had hoped to establish some closer communication with the Jewelbright. But she spoke only of service things, mainly of the Jat. And it was that creature which drew the two of them together.

Jofre was startled to learn that he could exchange vague thought-speech with Taynad if the Jat was with them both. This was something new in his experience and in the Sister's also he believed, though she did not admit to it. Zurzal was greatly interested and set up some tests, but when he himself strove to try the same form of transference of ideas it was a failure. Apparently only the shared bonding allowed this.

At ship's night measure before they planeted the Zacathan made a serious suggestion to Taynad.

"Gentlefem, I know of your way of life, and also that you are issha-trained. Perhaps what I have to offer is too far removed from that which you know and desire. But I

would like to ask you to join with us—not oathed but as a partner in what is to be done on Lochan. That is a planet about which we know little—and where we would venture is wilderness. It is, I have been informed, a harsh world and not one to tempt a visit. There is danger to be found there. However, danger is not new to the issha-trained and your success with this small one who is alien to all of us, might be a factor for success or failure of what I would accomplish.

"For if you can bond with a Jat, then binding with other alien wildlife can certainly be hoped for. And where I would go the wildlife is said to be one of the greatest perils."

She was smoothing her long fingers down the Jat's furry back, sending the creature squirming and uttering small mews of pleasure. Away from her fantastic robes, dressed in the severeness of the spacer garb she had obtained at the port, she looked like another person.

Taynad studied the Zacathan. What she had seen of the man suggested trust. She was not sure that Jofre had been right, that death had broken her oath-binding. After all, by his own admission, the guard was no longer a true Shadow Brother. If she returned to Asborgan—if she would be able to return there—she had no funds and those possessions which she might have been able to pawn to secure such had been taken by the Tssekians—she might find herself in a difficult position. Doubtless on other worlds there existed the equivalent of Jewelbrights with their own manner of life—but to her that was a mask, a disguise only, and to think of it as *ALL* of one's life was distasteful. The Zacathan's suggestion promised hardship, but she had

come from perilous and sometimes near-vicious schooling; she had no fears that she could not do as well as Jofre if it became a matter of survival. There was much in this offer which did interest her.

The binding with the Jat was something which still made her feel warm and good inside. Suppose she could indeed develop such a talent with other forms of life? It was truly something to consider seriously.

"Learned One, I cannot make answer until I know what awaits me in Asborgan. It may be that I shall be tied by another's will. But—let it be as you wish for now!"

"Fair enough," Zurzal returned. "We may have a period of waiting at Wayright port, for ships to Lochan are few."

Taynad continued to gentle the Jat. Good, time she could use, not only to settle her own possible future but to discover what there was about this disowned Brother—she shot a glance at him as he stood checking some list the Zacathan had handed him—which gave her always the sense of hidden power.

His off-worlder blood showed in his greater height, even though beside Zurzal he was made to look small, slim, boyish—He had ice-grey eyes also, instead of the brown ones she was used to seeing, able to warm with fire, when the issha displayed skills in the arms court. Yet he moved with the unmistakable ease of any Shadow she had seen.

What had Zarn said concerning him when the disguised Shagga had attempted to get her to forego her mission and go after him? That he was a renegade, one who was the first in generations to break the Code of Vart, that he had stolen something of power—Still Zarn had been very wary

in that part of his explanation of why Sister should turn against Brother.

She knew well that what Jofre had told her about his outlawing from Ho-Le-Far was the truth. Deep-trained could not so deceive deep-trained. He believed that it was Shagga hatred which had denied him his proper life and certainly it was Shagga hatred which had set Zarn scheming to bring him down.

They had linked to free the Jat and linkage would have speedily revealed to her any darkness in him. But—there was something—that power—a strength which she was well aware he possessed. Oddly enough she was also sure that he did not realize what he had—it was as if a man carried a bit of stone, perhaps as a luck piece, not realizing that what he grasped in truth was a gem of great price.

What made one Asshi? Oh, there were ceremonies and trials, all manner of testing. She had never been at such a raising herself but she had heard talk of such. Could it be that this off-worlder who was not of the true blood possessed that necessary extra core of power? Then—yes, it would explain the Shagga hatred—all the rest. They would never allow among them a Master who was not born of their own breed.

Nor would they—her thoughts carried logically forward—would they wish one with issha training and perhaps such dormant power, to really escape them. Better the death the Shagga had planned in the mountains, they would think. And perhaps most of the Brothers and Sisters would agree. Assha were jealous of their standing; it was the base of their inner powers, something which must not be questioned.

Taynad summoned now her own inner reactions to this outlaw. There was no hatred—why should there be? Hatred could be seeded, grown, used judiciously when it was needed to enhance inner power, but one did not nourish it without cause. He had been ready to stand for her before the port authorities; she had sensed that as completely as if he had spoken aloud.

He had linked, securely and well. And he had bonded—with the Jat—and perhaps also—at this new thought her head jerked a fraction—bonded with her? But that was impossible! There had been no oathing. Nor had this Zurzal offered that either when he had spoken of Lochan. He would take her free of any loyalty tie and this Brother would accept her so—she was sure of that.

The Jat had fallen asleep and she laid the small body on one of the cushions of the bunk. She gave a sudden shake to her head and loosed the curtain of her hair as it must be before she sought the Center. The other two in the cabin were very intent upon the tapes the Zacathan had borrowed from the captain of this ship, data of distant worlds. If they noticed her, Jofre would realize what she did and would not disturb her.

Deep, slow breaths, control of mind, closing out of all which was about her. In—in to the Center. Her hands moved in the long familiar patterns although she was no longer aware of them. In and in and in—She knew the calm, the waiting force, and encushioned herself in it. As she would do before any trial of strength, Taynad fitted herself with that armor, those weapons, no living being had ever seen.

It was like being free to swim in some pool of pure and

fragrant water, turn lazily and circle, feeling the flow of that force about her. Yet there was the prick of warning which came now. Not too long—one dared not linger here too long. Reluctantly she roused once more her will, out, away—it was sluggish that response, then it grew stronger, swept her out into the world once again. She was once more Taynad, save that for a while she would be a little more than she had been. No Shagga, no Master, no Mother-sister, had ever learned how to hold to that force for long, how could a lesser issha hope to do so?

It remained that she must wait for a period—learn if those who controlled her would reach for her again. When she entered into this bargain there had been no time limit set on her off-world stay. She had not been dispatched to deal death but rather to subtly bend a man to another's will, and that she and those who had selected her were sure she could do. But there had been no promise that this would have been a short mission or that when it was finished she would not return to her Lair.

They planeted on Wayright in the late afternoon, using that part of the giant port which was reserved for couriers and Patrol ships. There was none of the heavy traffic here which engulfed one at the passenger port some distance away.

Jofre had expected that they would be met by a guard, marched off to another debriefing by the Patrol. He had his suspicions that the officer on Tssek had no intention to forget them and the danger he believed them to be. However, they were picked up by an antigrav ground transport and, with their scanty luggage, transferred to the

city, back to the pyramided inn from which they had been snatched—was it weeks—or even months ago? Space-time and planet time differed in a way Jofre found amazing.

As the outer door closed behind them they were received with the suave diffidence shown them before under this same roof, speedily escorted to a suite of rooms on the second rise of the building. Jofre made for the windows at once and examined the latching, even though he hardly believed that the same trick would be played on them twice. Surely there was not a second dictator ready to have his past scanned.

# ✳ CHAPTER 21 ✳

**"WELCOME,** Veep Tetempra, welcome indeed!"

She noted the exact depth of his bow as well as the carefully cultivated joy he was so quick to express at her appearance in the conference chamber where he had had his temporary rule. This Salanten was harboring some thoughts he believed unguessed. She would have to take steps sooner or later. Just now there were more important decisions to be made.

"Glad hour to you also, Salanten. There arose no difficulties during my absence then?"

She fitted her gleaming body, bending her stick-thin limbs easily, into the waiting seat at the head of the conference board. Her turban flashed two new jewels, her personal selection from that hoard the Shagga Voice had reluctantly bestowed.

"Nothing of great import, Veep. Routine merely." He was of the old Terran stock, and the pride of such sometimes got out of hand. Though he had come up through the ranks and knew exactly how he stood and how

firm that standing might be considered at present. Now he began to rattle off his report and Tetempra listened, twice condescending to tap out a note on her own recorder.

There was a new market for Kamp opening up in the northwest sector. And the illegal trade in Varg furs was showing a generous profit. So good a one it might even be well to see that the Jack outfit in charge of that poaching be replaced by one of the Guild's own fleet. Have Fengal evaluate that. The rest was petty, planet-bound stuff. He was deliberately smothering her in such details, hoping to bore her so that she would be adverse to more than very random checkings on such activities as he had managed to corner under his own control. There were a number of those—yes, this servant must be bound to the orders of those over him and not free to meddle on his own.

But she allowed him to come to the end of his dull reporting and did not interrupt. Although twice she made mental note of matters her own special eyes and ears were going to check on.

"And you bring us new business, Veep—?"

She narrowed the slight slit of her inner eyelids. He certainly must be watched. Business for "us" indeed! Did he rank himself as one who could speak at any time for the Guild?

"There will be a conference at the hour of the second moon rise," she made no direct answer to such effrontery and was even more irritated that he did not seem to be aware of the snub. "Summon all department heads—"

"Lan Te is on the eastern continent."

"Send out the summons." She made no other comment

but raised her long hand in a gesture he could not overlook as meaning dismissal.

For several minutes she sat playing with her personal recorder, slipping it back and forth in her fingers as she thought, trying to fit one bit of information to another in order to form the whole upon which a decision must be based.

Then she spoke to the voice box at her right hand.

"Send in the one who waits—"

The woman who appeared in answer to that abrupt summons wore a shabby spacer uniform, its badges proclaiming her a communication expert, but those were tarnished. In all she gave the appearance of one perhaps bumped from a berth and unable to make a new connection.

Her face was bloated, the cheeks distended and shivers ran over her body. The Veep studied her.

"Very, very good, Ho-Sing. An excellent disguise. And what do you have for me?"

"The Zacathan and his guard were kidnapped and have left planet on a Tssekian Force fighter. It seems that one of the Horde Commanders, Sopt s'Qu, took him from his quarters at the Auroa Inn. They did it by flitter and loaded the prisoners on board at once—they had been stassed— the guard looked near death. The ship lifted them as soon as possible."

When the woman stopped speaking Tetempra clicked her long nails on the tabletop.

"We knew that the Tssekians might try this," she said, "they moved fast."

"They had another passenger also, Veep."

The nails were now motionless.

"Who?"

"A woman of Asborgan—one of those trained to give pleasure—and of the highest rank—those called Jewelbright."

"Ah—" What Zarn had parted with in the way of knowledge, besides the jewels, was now to be added to the picture. That was the one he had spoken of at their second meeting, the one to whom the Guild, in the manner of speaking, owed the increase on their fee.

"What do they say was the purpose of this Jewelbright's visit to Tssek?"

The woman shrugged. "What could her purpose be? She was a gift to the Holder. Doubtless she was to whisper into his ear at the proper moments any word her sponsor would wish passed on."

"Tssek—" Tetempra's nails began to tap again. "Four shipments of arms to the far west there—and a different touchdown, not a true port for any of them. The rebels made an excellent deal and they must be very close to the fruition of their plans. It may go hard with the Zacathan— and his guard, if he survives the trip—should Arn's'Dunn win this squabble. What is the latest news?"

"None as yet, Veep. We have the eyes out, the ears ready. Wayright is covered."

"When there is news, bring it at once."

With no parting salute the woman turned and was gone. That one was to be depended upon, Tetempra considered with satisfaction. She had handpicked her herself and the reward which had been dangled was very great. Nor would it be skimped—this one was well worth her hire.

There was nothing to do now but wait. But she could find plenty otherwise to deal with. There was the matter of the ship they would need, if and when they could get the Zacathan away from Tssek and once more on the move along the path *THEY* chose—though the fool thought it was all his doing. It showed that even such as a Zacathan could be subtly managed into obeying the desires of another. All had been going so well until these mire-eaters of Tssek interfered. Though if Guild calculations were right about Arn's'Dunn, the Illustrious Holder and any henchman of his would speedily have very little to say about anything.

She would present at the conference the bargain with Zarn and she had no expectation of anything but success.

It was a ten-ten of days later that Tetempra's chamber safe alarm brought her awake. This Farcar Inn was Guild owned, through a proxy, of course, and had a number of additions for the comfort and convenience of its occupants. The Veep pressed a button set in the frame of her bed, pulled around her a length of thick blue-green cloth and stalked over to the wall farthest from the window.

At her touch the concealed door opened, and, slipping into the very dim light of the room, was the woman she had interviewed before.

"What has happened?"

"Opher has reported in—not from the port, Veep. No, there was the landing of a service courier and on board were all three of those you wish knowledge of—the Zacathan, his guard, and the play woman."

"A service courier! They were under some form of arrest?"

"The signs were not of that. An antigrav was summoned and they all went to the same inn where the Zacathan was staying when the Tssekians took them. Also—Opher reports that they have a Jat."

"Sigsman gave that to the Holder four seasons ago when we wished certain privileges. But—a Jat does not leave its bond master. That needs some thinking about also.

"Tssek must have come to a boil. But why this woman with them? She is a new complication."

"What we can learn, Veep, we shall."

"You continue to do very well, Ho-Sing. I am well pleased."

"One asks no more than that, Veep. I have already ordered that a strict watch be kept."

It was the third day after their return to Wayright and Zurzal had been summoned twice to service headquarters. He returned each time with a flaring frill and a refusal to talk for a while after pacing the room like a caged orzal. The scanner had been carefully returned to the guardianship of the hive as if the Zacathan feared that it might disappear were he to leave it out of safekeeping.

Jofre had known something of impatience also. He needed weapons. Even the Makwire was lost to him now and he felt almost as if he had been stripped of his clothing as well. On the third morning he ventured to break into Zurzal's preoccupation with a mention of this point.

"Of course!" Zurzal was immediately attentive. "A man must always be supplied with the tools of his trade if he is to be set to work. But this is not a place where I have the proper contacts—"

"There is one Istarn of Vega." The cool voice of Taynad somewhat startled them both. "It is said that he offers weapons from half a hundred worlds to those who take pleasure in collecting such things."

Though Zurzal had urged her to gather a new wardrobe, she had made no effort to return to the rich garments of her supposed trade. She had selected a second spacer suit, lacking any insignia, and seemed, when wearing it, to be able to take on a kind of enwarping drabness. Jofre knew that she was summoning her own form of the Shadows invisibility.

Only her hair remained to mark her as different from any woman crew member on leave, for, though she kept it braided tightly, it still formed a heavy crown for her head. That, Jofre also knew, she would not part with willingly, for it was a weapon she might call upon in need.

"Istarn," Zurzal repeated first a little blankly as if he had not heard the name before, and then added with more force, "Istarn—but of course—it was he who turned up the Balakan mirror dispatcher that Zanquat has in his collection. I have never met the man but I thought he dealt mainly in antiques—not the weapons of this day."

"Learned One," Jofre said, "we of the issha have been trained with weapons those of these strange worlds believe to be primitive, for the use of barbarians only. However, it might be that this Istarn would put a collector's price on what he has to offer and that would be too great to pay."

"Istarn himself does not deal here on Wayright," Taynad continued to impart information the other two began to wonder how she gathered. "His shop is on the Second Way—where those bored while they wait for their

ships spend time and money on things which seem strange
and new to them, but have little real value. We have the
knowledge to pick from among rubbish that which will
serve."

Zurzal gave his hissing laugh. "I do not know how you
got this information—"

For the first time Jofre saw Taynad's lips curve in a true
smile. "Learned One, I listened—after asking a question
or two. Yan," she patted the head of the Jat that, as usual,
was clutching at the edge of her tunic, "is very much an
interest to the maidservants. They have come and asked to
see our little one. And they talk freely when doing so. I
have learned of the best shops, those which have quality
merchandise and do not put up the prices when a
passenger ship planets, the eating places and the specialty
of each, again where one may expect to get the best service
for the credit outlay. So eventually I learned of Istarn."

"To our benefit," Zurzal returned. "Very well, let us off
to this establishment and I shall leave it to the two of you
to equip yourselves with what you believe will be most
useful."

In the arms courts of the Lairs a weapon was judged for
efficiency. The truth of a blade was in its forging and
edging, of all other implements for battle in their usability
and strength. Valley lords of Asborgan might prance about
with gem-hilted sidearms. A hilt wrapped with well-
seasoned lacing to keep it from slipping in the hand was
what the issha-trained judged by—and no one could fault
the value of any Lair wrought blade, lance, hand hook or
the like, that value rested in the weapon itself and not in
any ornamentation.

What confronted Jofre in the shop of this so-called weapon merchant were not the tools of his trade but rather trumped-up bits of glitter misnamed for the blades he knew. He stared at the display of what the shopkeeper spoke of as "swords of value from Vega" and thought privately that one good blow from any one of those would speedily separate blade from hilt, perhaps even shattering the blade. These caught the eye most certainly but not the eye of a warrior. What did he care if a hilt was of tri-gold in the form of a washawk with emerald eyes—or something of the same stupid description when he could see very well that the blade attached was not nine times forged, or even six times worked!

"These are toys," he said in Lair tongue to Taynad. "What does any want with such—unless to pick out the jewels, melt down those hilts and use the blades for hide scraping?"

"Those off-worlders who are the buyers here do not intend to *USE* them," she replied as softly. "They are for show only. But there is a second display beyond. Perhaps—"

He was impatient enough to move away and lost any other word she might have said.

Yes, there was a second display—or rather it was not an arranged display to show off the offered weapons, rather a pile, in a darkish corner, of dull metal, long uncared for, with nothing in that mass to catch the untaught eye. Only when he stopped there and looked for himself—could he mark possibilities. This clutter might be what was tossed aside in some smith's forge, things to be melted down and reworked—at least that is what it looked to be at first sight.

However—no arms master would have been so quick to devalue—that! His gaze fixed upon the peeling leather sheaths, twins, and the matched blades they sheltered. He plucked one forth. Dulled, needing a honing, yes. But the steel—ah—that he knew for what it was. Heartened, Jofre drew the second knife and found it as sound as its twin.

Taynad was busied separating a choice of her own from the rusty jumble. Luckily the proprietor had been detached from them by the entrance of several off-worlders whose rich robing proclaimed hearty credit ratings and who were fascinated by the gemmed display.

At the end of some careful choosing, even a bit of surreptitious testing of the elasticity of blade, Jofre had at his hand for bargaining the twin knives, a short sword, and a collection of wicked-looking hooks which, when wedded to a length of chain he had loosed from the pile, would make a Makwire far more suitable even than that which had served him on Tssek. Unfortunately other familiar aids to a guardsman were not to be found. Perhaps he was lucky that he had discovered as much as were useful among these apparent discards as he had.

Taynad had a blade which was near the length of a short sword encased in a sheath once covered with a grimy brocade which was now peeling from it in strips. At the top of the scabbard showed also the hilts of two small knives and she had worked one out of the damaged sheath to show, unrusted, an almost needle-thin weapon perhaps as long as her hand. Such were perhaps meant for eating purposes but they were close to those weapons the Sisters were well-known to hide in hair coils or hanging sleeves, and Jofre had no doubt that she would be able to put them

to the best service. She also had a Makwire chain, which she was twisting about now inch by inch to test it, for there were stains of rust on her fingers where she handled it. However, beneath that surface flaking it appeared to be strong enough to satisfy her.

"Gentlehomo and—Gentlefem—" The salesman looked at Taynad as if she were indeed an oddity in such a place, or else her air of knowing exactly what she wanted from this dingy heap was a surprise to the seller. "Have you made some discovery—? But this—this is of second rating. You would be better with the swords from Lanker, or the ruby-headed daggers of Grath. Now those are proud weapons."

"They are," Jofre returned, "but not to our purpose—"

"No," Taynad struck in, "we do not seek weapons of fine show, but rather ones we can use to demonstrate various forms of fighting. We think to display combat for show."

"So? Are you then from the Arms Court of Assherbal? It is known that his battle displays are very lifelike—close to the real—blood spilled, even."

"Something like is what we aim to do." Jofre picked up her hint quickly. "No, Gentlehomo, what price is put on these?" He indicated what they had set aside. The salesman eyed their selections with a disdain he did not attempt to conceal. Certainly his attitude had become brusque—that of one dealing with persons below the social rating of those he commonly served.

He quoted a price well within the credits Zurzal had transferred to Jofre's new account and for the first time Jofre made use of that ever-present aid to off-world living.

Their selections were bundled into a sack in a hurry as if the salesman did not want it seen that such dingy wares

were going out of his shop, and they returned to the open street.

They were passing by one open-fronted shop where there was a sprouting of tables edging out into the thoroughfare and for each some stools. The aroma of food was strong enough to combat and defeat the scents wafting from a place of perfumes across the way.

Jofre nodded towards one of the tables. "It smells good," he said simply. For it did, better somehow than the exotic dishes which were constantly offered them at the inn. Taynad gave a heavy sniff and then showed him again that very fleeting smile.

"So it does, and no Shadow food either. Yes, let us try it to see if it tastes as good as it smells."

They seated themselves at one of the tables, Jofre allowing the package of weapons to lie on the floor between his feet, and consulted the menu printed in trade and displayed as part of the tabletop between them.

Not too far away a woman in a spacer's uniform chose a table and settled into a seat there. The occupant who was already there greeted her with a nod. He was humanoid to about the fifth degree, but his heavily furred body, erect pointed ears, and wide well-toothed mouth, showed he did not share his companion's Terran breed.

"Those then." He did not look at Jofre and Taynad, and his voice was very soft, nearly a growl.

"Those. I pass them on to you, Lenoil. She wants them well watched. And do not take them lightly, they are of a trained-for-fighting breed—the most feared on their home world."

"One world among many," her companion replied. "We all have our champions. Sometimes such do not survive—"

"No! No interference with them, only watching," the woman said swiftly. "Watch and report—you are staying at the Auroa as are they; therefore, you have better chance to keep an eye on them. Be sure that eye is ever there."

# ✳ CHAPTER 22 ✳

**THE ZACATHAN** walked in upon a scene of concentrated industry. His three companions were seated on the floor and each was busy. The Jat was drawing back and forth through a length of oil-stained cloth a supple chain. Beside him Taynad honed the narrow blade of a very small knife and opposite them both Jofre was fitting another chain, thicker, well able to support such a burden, with a series of wicked-looking hooks, pausing now and then to test his work with a swing or two of the metal line.

"Luck, Learned One?" They had all three looked up at his coming but it was Jofre who asked that.

"As yet none. Almost one could believe that there was some pattern we are not able to understand—" He paused as if not knowing just how to put his thoughts into words.

"A warn off by the Patrol!" Jofre suggested.

"I hardly think so. We seek Free Traders, and they do not take kindly to official warning unless those are delivered with force. Two such ships have planeted within the last ten days. One is already chartered by a party of

engineer-techs to transport them and their equipment to Helga. The other carries no passengers and is mainly an asteroid mining ferry."

"It may be a long wait, Learned One." Taynad had not halted work on her knife while she listened. "It seems you deal with the whims of fortune now and that is always sheer chance."

"Yet there is no better place to await any transportation than here," Zurzal returned. "I have spread the word as to what I wish. And this is on route to Lochan—which is why I chose it as a base in the beginning. Have you consulted those?" He indicated the three tapes lying on the tabletop beside the reader.

"It seems a place about which very little is known," Taynad commented, "if that is all which we have to consult, Learned One."

"A barren land," Jofre struck in, not that that was any deterrent as far as he was concerned. The northern stretches of Asborgan were certainly sere and stripped enough. "It seems to be mainly desert—"

"As far as we know. Yes, that is all the information on file," Zurzal assented. "It does not have too promising a reputation—there is no great trade to be found there— small stuff—some strange furs, odd minerals—"

Taynad fitted the newly sharpened knife into a small sheath of her own devising, one actually woven from strands of her hair. "Then why should anyone go there—or is it that this Lochan might have other uses for outworlders—a hidden base, perhaps?"

"Guild dealings?" Zurzal shook his head. "It was well combed for any off-world activity after the failure of

Desmond's expedition. There is no defense against Patrol sensors, unless the establishment would be a major one and Lochan certainly could not support such."

"Treasure?" Taynad submitted another surmise.

"Not the kind which would draw the average trader. Though it was the matter of some artifacts turning up in the cargo of such a one which first directed us to Lochan. What we seek there is another kind of treasure than would draw Guild interest—knowledge. There is good reason to think there may be one of the Forerunner repositories there."

"The Guild seeks knowledge, too—" Taynad commented. "Is it not rumored that they discover what they can which may be put to their own uses?"

"The scanner!" Jofre had fastened his last hook and was coiling the chain to accommodate those additions.

"Which will not serve them," Zurzal answered. "We learned long ago to protect our tools from wrongful use. Were any other to attempt to use the scanner, it would destruct. That is built into every tool of the sort which we lift from our own world."

"How long a wait then, Learned One, until such a ship as you wish sets down here?"

"Not too long. There is one which made the run to Lochan five planet months ago. It has made two runs and each time to a near planet. The ship is old, the captain not one, I have been told, who is ready to push into any other territory. We can expect the *Haren Hound* to be in port soon if all goes to the past pattern."

Jofre had moved to the wide window-door which gave upon the balcony servicing this portion of the floor.

"We are being watched," he said flatly. "I do not think we are off the Patrol's hook yet."

"The watcher?" Zurzal demanded quickly.

"Differs. We could slip them if we wish. We would rather learn who they are and why eyes and ears are set on us. To learn that perhaps it is well to let them go about this Shadow business for a space longer."

Tetempra was already seated at the head of the table in the wide room which could be entered only through her personal office. There were five of her staff flanking her and at the other end of the table, awaiting any orders, Ho-Sing.

"They have rearmed themselves, this guard and the woman, with barbarian weapons—such as can only be used in hand-to-hand combat. Doubtless they prepare so for the wastes of Lochan. Our people cannot penetrate into their suites because of the Jat—it is very quick to sense anyone who is not friendly to its bondmates."

"It can be removed—" came the suggestion from an obese and warty-skinned member to her right.

"And give them warning? Nusa, have your brains begun to addle already? I thought your skin-shed season was yet well off. No, we do not move against them. But there is this other matter—the message—the order to be given to the Asborgan woman. So far we have not been able to separate her from her companions. But a bargain is a bargain and this one must be carried out. Ho-Sing, have you any new thoughts on reaching the woman long enough to pass a message without the others knowing what has happened?"

"This morning the room maid spoke to her of the

Fragrance baths—she showed interest. The maid receives a percentage of what any guest spends at the Tri-lily—she will endeavor to send this woman there. The maid's in debt to Dabblu; she may be reached through that—though the hotel staff are supposed to be incorruptible."

"Excellent. This you will move on, Ho-Sing. When this one goes to the Tri-lily one will meet with her—seemingly by accident—to the beholders—but for our purposes. Let it so be arranged."

"The ship, Veep Tetempra?" Salanten being officious once again, her eyes slitted to mere threads though she did not turn those on him, rather focused her attention on a small com before her.

"The Learned One is waiting for the *Haren Hound*. We have prepared the way very well in that direction. Gosal is due in very shortly—the new drive we installed in his bucket of rusted bolts has delighted him; he is very willing to be able to pay for it in service. Which is well since any cargo he has lifted in the past could not pay for a wind wheel!"

"Do the Patrol have a watch on them?" One of silent others spoke. "The Tssek business could not have made the authorities happy."

"Ho-Sing?" Tetempra looked to the head of her Shadow service.

"None we have picked up and Everad has scanned for them. But—"

"But what?" Tetempra demanded when the other continued to hesitate.

"I think that they—at least the guard—the woman—guess that they are under observation. We have been using

the utmost care and they have done nothing to throw us off—"

"Still you sense it yourself, Ho-Sing?" the Veep concluded for her. "Very well, have one of your force make some error which will suggest he is Patrol or planet force inspired. They may well be expecting that and will go about their business freely. I can leave that well to you."

"Why does that priesthood on Asborgan want the guard so much they offered us such a price?" Again it was Salanten pushing himself forward.

"He has been outlawed by them. All these priesthoods and religious overlords turn vicious if any of their followers begin to think for themselves. I gather they wish to make an example of him. He seems to be on passable terms with the woman at present but once we pass on Zarn's message we may cause complications for them all."


"It is a thing that travelers indulge themselves in," Taynad said as they shared their meal on the terrace. "I think," she continued, "that the maid is probably paid a small fee for suggesting that one goes—if one *DOES* go thereafter."

"We are not just travelers," Jofre said sharply. Their few excursions into the whirl of the city round them had been all for very practical reasons, the obtaining of weapons, clothing, finding out from information sources what they could about possible transportation and the planet Zurzal wanted to explore.

"This might be a chance," the Zacathan said slowly, "to discover more about those shadows you believe are hovering around your trail. Yes, I know it would mean that

Taynad would take off on her own, but I believe that there is that in issha training which favors the individual over even a duo. By all means, Jewelbright, try this new sensation, you may have something to import to Asborgan on your return."

He did not like it. Jofre was opposed to her going out alone even at midday and in a city so well policed that no casual crime had existed for years. Nothing must disturb the well-being and peace of the travelers on whom all Wayright's industry was centered. Why did he have this inner warning? Did he fear some improbable attack on Taynad? Certainly all his training would turn him against such a thought—issha did not doubt the skill and ability of issha—she was very well able to take care of herself.

Then—what was it? The fact which had been nibbling at him now for days, that she seemed to accept the Zacathan's offer of employment with no thought that her home Lair might see matters very differently? She had not been oathed to this as was he, and without the oath—Then there was a freedom which could turn to enmity on the demand of a Lair Master. That she could not return to Asborgan without assistance was true. But it would take time for the happenings on Tssek to filter back to that world and meanwhile she had to live. There was the Jat and the linkage; Jofre kept coming back to that for assurance. Surely the creature linked so to them both would display uneasiness, perhaps even more, if Taynad did not mean exactly what she had said to Zurzal. Still—

There was no use in following her to this Tri-lily for it was a luxury establishment for females only. He was also somehow sure that she would know what he was doing if he

tried to follow her, at least to the door. For the moment there was nothing Jofre could do and he resented it.

To escape his own thoughts he started a practice session, concentrating on learning just what could be done with his new weapons, the Jat squatting on a cushion to watch him with very round eyes.

The establishment of the Tri-lily was imposing but in an oddly discreet way, as might a Jewelbright slide into a mixed company and subtly let her presence there dawn slowly on those about her. There was a living doorguard, not a robot voice box, to bow Taynad into a room which somehow wrapped one around with a feeling of relaxation and peace. How this effect was accomplished she had no idea, and indeed her issha suspicion tightened. There would be no wearing away of her own core of control, no matter what outward signs of enjoyment she might need to summon.

"Gracious and Illustrious One—" A slender female shape moved from between two misty blue-green wall hangings.

They were prepared to pile it on; Taynad's professional interest sifted it all. Greeting suitable to some highborn, but delivered with apparently complete sincerity. She gave several points to the manager here—perhaps even a Jewel House Mistress might be impressed.

"Bright day," she responded pleasantly, but allowed to creep into her voice a faint tone of uneasiness as if indeed she were a little daunted by such ceremony. "I have heard— there is a maid at the Auroa who spoke highly of the restful value of your services. Such are new to me—but—"

"You were interested enough, Illustrious, to come and see what there is to be offered? We have many services—but since you have not visited us before, perhaps it is well that you begin by making your season choice—"

"Season choice?"

"Yes, it is known that beings differ greatly in their reaction to environmental changes. Perhaps on your world spring is the season which holds the strongest meaning for you—during which you feel at the best. Or you may look forward to the ripeness of summer—the soothing warmth—the cloudless skies under which living things rise to their fruitfulness. There are those also who find autumn stimulating—the first crispness of freshening winds, the savor of the land which has been touched faintly by frost. And there are those, though they are fewer in number, who like the bracing of storms, the clear cold of mornings when ice begems twigs and branches. We have these, Illustrious, ready for your service."

Taynad was intrigued. For a moment she held a flash of memory—of being young—running barefooted across a dew-wet strip of tiny mountain meadow to sniff the first star flowerets of the year.

"I think I choose spring," she found herself saying.

"If you will come this way, Illustrious, you shall meet spring—"

One of the curtain panels on the wall was looped aside and she stepped ahead of the attendant into a narrow corridor not more than three strides long, and so came into a second room. Or was it a room? She could not actually see any walls except a fraction of the one embracing the door behind her. There was a mass of greenery to the sides,

and, centering, a pool into which flowed liquid. She might have come out into the open of one of those mountain valleys she knew so well, except this had no skin roughening winds tunneling down it, and the softness of the air was a caress on her flesh. There were fragrances carried by those lightest of breezes, clean, fresh scents of newly awakened growth reaching for new life and renewal.

The attendant beckoned her on to the side of the pool. There were places there for sitting, cleverly hollowed into the seeming stone. Some were so placed they would allow entrance into the pool. The attendant indicated one larger rock.

"You place the fingers so, Illustrious. Within is the spring robe for your use, also there are certain balms and essences. The spring maid will be with you when you are ready—only touch this," she touched another spot on the rock chest, "and she will come at once. What is your pleasure, Illustrious, as to other refreshment? We can offer the spring drinks of near a hundred worlds—"

Certainly not the one of the Lairs, Taynad thought, at least not that which was left in the spring—the sour dregs which survived a winter's supply.

"Something light—kind to the inner parts—" Taynad was sure she could detect any danger from a drink meant for some other species.

"Lily dew, then. This is collected from flower petals at dawn, Illustrious. It lightens the spirit, calms and soothes—" She produced a flask carved from green stone and poured a portion into a crystal flower shaped glass which she half-filled before passing it to Taynad, who cradled the fanciful container between her hands and took a deep sniff of its

contents. She could detect nothing save a faint sweetness akin to the perfume of a slowly opening flower.

"Your thanks." Taynad raised the cup toward the attendant in a small salute and sipped. It was good—holding the chill of a mountain stream, with a faintest shadowing of flower honey.

"May you enjoy your spring, Illustrious. The maid will come at your call." The other bowed her head and then disappeared behind those curiously veiling bushes.

Taynad, glass in hand, went to survey the contents of the coffer in the rock. There was a shelf set in its raised lid which supported a number of locked-in bottles and boxes. And in the coffer itself were the folds of a green robe. She must follow the custom, she supposed, though she shed her clothing a little reluctantly. The robe was as fragile as one of her Jewelbright gowns and as transparent. She made no effort to unbraid her hair. What she carried within that concealment she intended to keep with her.

Having folded her clothing into the coffer, she hesitated about pressing the summons for the promised maid. Instead she sipped slowly at the drink which had been poured for her and took two steps down to one of the curved seats where she could slip her feet into the pool. The water was flesh warm.

Jewelbrights were accustomed to the highest forms of luxury Asborgan knew—many of the noted ones could command more service and pampering than lords' ladies. Yet this place somehow offered too much—it was a Jewel House carried to the highest degree but she had no duty to hold her here.

She still had not summoned the promised maid,

wanting to settle herself into the sensations this place summoned, but there was movement behind her and she looked around swiftly.

From here, the rise of greenery hid even the door through which she had come. Now out of the hiding of that stepped a tall, nearly bone-thin figure, certainly by her strange clothing no employee of the Tri-lily, or at least Taynad did not believe so. That clothing appeared to consist only of long strips of thick furry material of a brilliant scarlet, which stood out in eye-aching intensity against the smooth green, wound about her, to Taynad's reckoning, abnormally thin frame. Her long neck seemed too fragile to keep aloft the huge mass of her head where a large turban covered three-quarters of any skull she might have, its folds hung with a dripping of dazzling gems. Two of which, Taynad noted quickly, were ayzem stones— from Asborgan—and of the first water—the kind which the Shagga kept jealously in their hidden treasure places.

This newcomer moved stiffly, as if her knobby joints did not have the easy play known to most humanoids, and she came directly to stand before Taynad who had risen to meet her.

The long fingers of the one hand lifted lazily from the other's side to sketch a sign. So—Taynad waited, calling on all her training to show no sign of surprise. That signal she had never expected to see off her own world. It was an identification she could not deny.

# ✳ CHAPTER 23 ✳

**THOSE STRANGE EYES** with their double eyelids made her secretly uncomfortable. It was as if this alien stranger possessed some unnamed sense which could sift into her mind. Yet Taynad was not otherwise aware of any such invasion. She had never met any save the Jat and a very few of the highest trained Asshi Masters who could do more than pick up emotions their owners wanted hidden. Thought reading might be common somewhere along the star ways, but she had never heard of any who had encountered it. Which did not mean that it could not exist. Taynad suppressed thought quickly, closing off the way to the Inner Center.

"Gentlefem"—though it might give the other the advantage at their meeting, Taynad chose to break the silence first—"you have come to me. What is your wish?"

"You are direct—that is an attitude I like," the other returned. "What I come for is a matter of business—your business, Jewelbright. I gather that your work on Tssek came to an unfortunately abrupt end—though, of course,

through no fault of yours. Sopt s'Qu was not noted for complex mental labor at any time, and he reached well above his abilities in that matter. Since you are now free, I bring you a message." One of those long hands burrowed beneath a looping of the body scarves to seek a hidden pocket and produce two small sticks, shorter than the fingers that offered them.

Taynad accepted them with a reluctance she would not allow to be seen. She slipped first one and then the other between the balls of her thumb and forefinger, the small markings making an impression on her flesh that she could read.

Zarn again! But this time he had called in formidable backing. She was quick to read the mark of the First Sister of her own Lair. This was official, then. They had selected her for a new mission.

"You are to inform me—" she said slowly.

"By Zarn's word you already know what is wished for. This guard who has attached himself to the Zacathan—it seems he has proven traitor to your people, or so Zarn puts it. They wish him returned."

Taynad twiddled the twigs between her fingers.

"And to return him from off-world?"

The alien slitted her inner eyes. "That will be arranged for. However, not at present. Zarn will have his wishes fulfilled but at *OUR* timing. And that is not yet. I have heard of this oathing of your people, that you cannot break such a bond once it is taken. Have you oathed with the Zacathan as this renegade has done?"

"No, I have merely pledged my help in another matter—"

"Which is suitable. Render him that best of services; he must be made grateful to you. Perhaps then the loss of his guard shall not be too regretted. But you know best your own business, Sister to Shadows."

"And your part in this?" Taynad refused to be cowed by the other's air of complete control of the situation.

"Nothing to interfere with yours, Shadow. We have in part a common goal and your people have seen fit to recognize that. Good hunting—when the time comes."

The stranger turned and vanished behind one of the bush curtains. Taynad was left with the feeling that she had just met a wielder of power—akin to a Lair Master. And who would have such power and yet be interested in them? There was only one answer she could assume—the Guild. So they were taking a hand in some game still not plain to the players?

However, did that one who had just gone have the right to pass along a Shadow order? There were these message sticks she herself held now—Zarn and those behind him would never have entrusted such to this alien unless they considered there had been an oathing—though not directly between Taynad and any employer. And such a situation she found doubtful.

She had to think this out, and carefully. Tucking the two small rune sticks carefully into the hiding places her braid offered, Taynad sat for a very long moment staring into the pool before her. Then she turned and pressed the button for the attendant she had been assured was waiting. As long as she was here she might well make use of the amenities spring had to offer before she went back into the world where decisions waited.

*＊*

Jofre sat at the small walk side table. The Jat perched on the second chair beside him. Those passing back and forth on errands of their own were an ever-changing show of strangers, enough to hold the interest of any idle spectator. But he was wondering where, in that shifting series of strollers and tourists, lurked the stalker he was very sure was interested only in *HIM*.

"Watch—"

A thread of thought—but Jofre had carefully schooled himself during the past few days to receive such without showing that he knew. Taynad was better at communication with the Jat than he, but the creature could reach him at times. He fished into the depths of the glass before him, speared one of the tart-sweet wedges of fruit which had been floating on the liquid and brought it out, holding the tidbit to the Jat, whose paw flashed forth to seize it.

"Where?" Jofre tightened and strengthened his thought question to his best ability.

"Red—" It was almost no use. The Jat was obviously communicating more, but all Jofre could pick up was that one exasperating word.

Red—what was red—so much so that the Jat could use mention of the color as a guide—around them?

Red—it was a common enough color—he had caught sight of at least two feminine robes, a short jacket—even a head covering of that shade during the past few minutes. But those had been passing. Since he had settled here, surely his tracker would be more or less anchored nearby.

Red—and he could not look for it obviously. The Jat

pawed at his arm—wanting another fruit? Perhaps, but Jofre's senses were alert, perhaps something more. He turned his head a fraction that he might look more closely at his small companion and saw one of those ears twitch as if an insect had dared to alight there. Red—

At that far table. And it was a red, unusual enough to rivet the attention all right, yet he dared not risk a direct glance.

Instead he turned the glass which held the dregs of the drink and went to fishing for another fruit bit. The shiny material of that container was opaque—reflective—he had a smeary sort of mirror which he could watch with impunity.

The man at the other table was humanoid in proportions and stance as far as Jofre could judge. But the general whole of his appearance was alien indeed. Instead of the usual clothing, which here planetside followed a pattern mostly akin to travel suits, this diner (for the stranger was consuming with very apparent gusto small, frantically wriggling creatures it plucked up from a platter before it) had limited wearing apparel to a kiltlike garment reaching to the knee and below that boots which were so tightly modeled to the legs and feet one could see the play of muscles through the substance of their making. The area of displayed skin was a dull black but the head, shoulders and a wedge descending the back in the form of a manelike growth were covered by long thickish bristles of a deep crimson.

That such an easily noted being could have been selected as a "shadow" amazed Jofre now that his attention had been directed to him. The features were decidedly

human in character and there were ruffles of the bristle growth over each eye. As far as Jofre could judge the other was paying no attention to either him or the Jat. Yet Jofre trusted Yan that this was someone to be watched.

If he had even Taynad here to back him, he would have departed with the attitude of one about some business and so make sure that the maned one did leave his meal to follow. But Taynad was not here and he wondered how long it would be before she did arrive. The Fragrance place was six shops farther along the avenue and it seemed to him that she had been there a very long time.

The maned man finished his plate of wrigglers, patted his middle and gave a belch. No matter what race or species he might be his public manners left much to be desired.

Jofre fished the last fruit out of his glass and presented it to Yan, leaving that drinking vessel placed so he still had a distorted glimpse of the other diner. But Yan suddenly gave a cry of pleasure, both of his ears swung forward and he wriggled off the chair to run to meet Taynad.

Fragrance indeed! Jofre picked up a mingling of scents as she came along, moving with that languorous glide that he had not seen her use since they had left the great hall on Tssek. She had slipped well back into her Jewelbright armor again.

"It was a pleasure?" he asked, rising to greet her as she arrived, the Jat holding to one of her hands.

"It was spring—" she said, and sighed. "Truly there is much to be learned when one travels. So you missed me, little one?" She smiled down at Yan. "Did not this tall warrior treat you well?"

"We should be getting back." Jofre had taken a step or two closer to her, presenting his back to the maned one and making a quick signal to alert her.

"Time flees when one is at ease," she answered. "Yes, perhaps it is well to return. Zurzal may at last have news for us."

She had made no sign that she had understood his signal but Jofre was sure she had. Now, for quicker passage through the crowd that was thickening on the street as the afternoon advanced, he swung the Jat up to his shoulders and felt the paw hands take a good grip on his turban. Though he had not gone back to the full head covering of the Lairs he had once more assumed a style which made him feel more comfortable.

Taynad let him get a stride or so ahead, stopped as if to adjust a boot buckle, then she light-footedly joined them.

Her forefinger moved. The maned one was following. But for now they had no reason to try and evade him since they were only returning to their temporary quarters.

"This place is stifling," she broke out suddenly. "I find myself thinking with a strong desire of the slopes of Three Claws, or even the Grey Wastes. How can one live ever in such a turmoil?"

Jofre was surprised. He himself had been suffering from the feeling of one entrapped in some lord's vor stockyard with the herd turned in to share it with him. There was always something new to be seen, that he would agree, but one tires of constant change and variety. Also of this enforced idleness. Though issha discipline taught patience and he had thought that he had learned all the Lair lessons well. But perhaps what she had said gave him

a chance to discover answers for a question or two which had been plaguing him.

"If there comes word from Asborgan—you are not oathed—"

"No." Her answer was almost harshly abrupt. "But my mission was meant to be one of some length when I left Su-ven-ugen. They will not think of me as being free now and the message which the Patrol promised to deliver will take some time to reach the First Sister. Perhaps because I am without funds, since those of Tssek saw fit to confiscate what I had, I am in debt to the Learned One and it may well be that in the end the Elders will decide that I must work out what is owed. Anyway, oathed or not, I have promised the Zacathan that I will return service for service as long as he needs me."

"It will be a different kind of service than that you trained for—" Jofre was partly convinced that she meant exactly what she had just said.

"It is well to have more than one kind of experience," she remarked. "Do you think that the Learned One will succeed in what he wishes? I know that his scanner showed the past on Tssek, but what of Lochan? It seems to me to be as much of a gamble as when one tosses kust stones for wager."

The Zacathan was not in the suite when they entered and Jofre made his meticulous search through the rooms and across their section of the balcony terrace as he always did, the Jat trotting behind him as if it too could sniff out any hidden danger. Was the red-maned one lounging in the lobby below? And what did whoever set him on their trail want? Was it a ploy of the Guild? That was a point to

be very well considered. From all he had ever heard Jofre rated the Guild very, very high as a potential enemy.

When the Zacathan returned his frill was standing high, not flushed scarlet as from anger or frustration but the green-blue of satisfaction with the world.

"Fortune favors us at last," he began even before the door had closed behind him. "The trader who has made the Lochan run twice has planeted. Not only planeted, but the captain is ready for a return. It seems that he took one of those chances which the Free Traders often do and managed to barter directly with one of the desert tribes. What he picked up are a new type of gem—good enough value to have one of the auction houses take on sale.

"One cannot keep such a find a secret; he well knows that there will be others heading in there now—since the trade rights for Lochan have never been auctioned. The Patrol may take a hand—but they cannot by law deny the captain a return trip to realize on his own discovery. He will want to harvest all he can before the rush begins. Which means he is already loading supplies—"

"But will he take passengers also?" Jofre wanted to know. If the Free Trader had an outstanding discovery to exploit, its crew might well be jealously on guard against everyone.

"I had already had contact with him before his last voyage. He knows well that what I would accomplish there will have nothing to do with his business. I have sent him a message and I expect a quick answer. If he wishes to lift soon, we must be able to move—perhaps at a moment's notice. It would be best we think of packing now."

Zurzal's enthusiasm was such he was sweeping them

along with him. Though Jofre took time out to make a very careful inspection of the arms he had acquired, together with the stunner which Zurzal had managed to secure for him with a permit near twisted out of the Patrol, the same for himself, and Taynad.

The Jat squatted on a wide pillow watching the girl do her packing in her own quarters. A fast move—her hand went to the braid wreathing her head to touch the ends of the twigs there. Perhaps this was best—if she could stall a little until this ship swept them away—She shook her head at her own thoughts. Why did she resent and shrink from this order which had been delivered?

Because it was not an oathing such as she had always been taught was right? Because it had been so delivered to her by one she knew was Guild? That the Shagga would turn to the Guild for aid went against her deepest beliefs. She was a trained killer, a weapon in the hands of those whom she was sworn to serve. But the Guild was not the Lairs with their old tradition of a certain rigid honor. Also—Zarn said that this Jofre was an outlaw, a traitor—the story he had told her was one she had come fully to believe, having had time to observe this man over days and through sharp demands made on him and his skills.

There was nothing about him to make her think that he was in any way enemy to the Lairs. Rather, it seemed to her, it was the spite of some priest which lay behind it. Then—why had they not killed him out of hand? Taynad stood very still, a half-folded undergarment in her hands. The basic oath of them all—Brother—Sister—do not delight in the blood of their kind. Perhaps that priest had been afraid to kill Jofre openly lest he be called to account

for that—perhaps he had hoped that the harsh season in the mountains would do it for him. As for the reason for such a strong hatred—it lay encoiled in what she had sensed—that in this issha there were surely the seeds of Assha. Yes, the Shagga would never allow a leader of off-world blood among them; they were too fixed in the ancient ways. So they wanted him—but they wanted him returned so that he could die now under their hands and only so would they feel safe.

Now she could understand those orders. She dropped the garment and freed the twigs from their hiding place in her hair, running them once more to be touch read. Betray him to the Guild, see him safely taken.

An order—but not an oath! Her head went up as if she faced the First Sister in her own Lair. She was not oathed by the mere words of Zarn's sending—there must be the ritual and blood must flow—she would be one who betrayed.

They would say she was not oathed to the Zacathan, but she was indebted to him. And those of the Shadows paid debts, blood signed or not. No, she was not going to make any attempt to contact that woman from the Guild—perhaps time would favor them all and see them aboard this trader before she could be met again with any more demands.

For a moment Taynad stretched the twigs between her fingers. Almost she applied enough pressure to snap them. But she did not follow through—there was enough of custom to hold her from doing that. She tucked them back into hiding and determined to let the future arrange itself into its own patterns.

# ✳ CHAPTER 24 ✳

**"PASSAGE,** yes, that you may buy. Once on planet you shall be on your own, and Lochan is not friendly." The voice was a deep-chested growl, sounding oddly from this undersized man who eyed them upward from beneath heavy bushy brows as if he was highly suspicious. In contrast to those unduly thick brows his skull was bare of even a fringe of hair, the space-browned flesh of it sprinkled over with darker patches of skin here and there. Captain Gosal was far from being attractive personally any more than his rusted and worn, space-battered ship.

Jofre, his shoulders planted against the wall of the small cabin, was not only unimpressed but wary. If it were his choice, he would be off the *Haren Hound* and as far from its battered length as he could get. But it would seem that Zurzal had discovered they had no choice. It was either this ship or perhaps no chance at all, and since the debacle on Tssek the Zacathan was apparently ridden more and more by the need to get to the goal he had tried so long to reach.

"You have a flitter—" His frill was fluttering. Jofre could

actually feel the effort Zurzal was making to keep his emotions under strict control.

"That will be in use. You have heard my terms." This captain was favoring the Zacathan with none of the honorifics which bare courtesy would have suggested he use. Instead he was deliberately trying, Jofre was certain, to make any contract with him as unpleasant as possible.

"It will be necessary for us to strike inland—near the Shattered Land—" Zurzal's hissing was more apparent but he still spoke on a level note as if he did not really understand the captain's hostility.

"Go where you will after we planet. I am not an arranger for travelers—I do not offer tours—There are plenty here who are eager for such as you to come to them."

"For approved planets only." Zurzal still held tightly to his emotions but the flush of color was rising in his frill. "This is a matter of exploration, or discovery. I understand you yourself have recently made a lucky discovery on this same world. Well, such as you are about to exploit I have no interest in. I seek old places—those of the Forerunners."

"You are confederation backed—why then do you come to me? Where is your First-In ship? I am a trader, not a searcher—"

"Perhaps not a searcher for the same things," Zurzal returned. "But, yes, I have cleared this voyage with the authorities—on the *Haren Hound*—"

The captain's head snapped up. Under that brush of brows his eyes showed a reddish glint.

"You cannot make any Free Trader rise to your will

unless it is under charter, and I am not—for all your official clearance!"

"There is the matter of time," Zurzal pointed out. "When is your rumored auction—tonight! You have forced that into a rush, which means you need to get planet free very soon. There will be those ready to sniff along your trail and see what they can pick up for themselves."

The captain did not answer at once. His full-lipped mouth was closed as a trap might spring upon a victim and there was a dusky flush spreading up from the unlatched collar of his tunic to color even that bare dome of skull.

"So—by the thrice-damned rules you force yourselves on board—knowing that I must be accountable for your arrival on Lochan. Very well, you have set up the stars in this game, but perhaps the comets lie in other hands. You will pay—"

"I fully intend to," the Zacathan returned. "Full voyage accounts for four."

"Four?" The captain glanced from Zurzal to Jofre and back again as if trying to separate each of those fronting him into a second.

"A party of four. You will find it listed with the port authorities. It has been so listed for a ten days—"

"You were very sure, lizard lord."

"I have had news of your voyaging for some two planet years, Captain Gosal. Lochan has long been my destination as it has also attracted you."

The captain spread his hands palm flat on the small table already untidy with a drift of tapes and a speaker.

"Very well. But you will take us as you find us, without complaint. We are no wallowing passenger liner. Your

quarters will be tight and you will give vouchers for your own supplies to our steward. Also—the license runs only while you are on board. On Lochan you make your own way, for there the law favors me. I need not detach from this ship any personnel nor equipment which I need for my own use. And all of what we have is so needed. So think about that, lizard lord, before you move in."

"What if it is as he says?" Jofre asked as they boarded the port flitter to return to the inner city. "He could dump us in some wilderness and not have any questions asked? Does it work that way?"

"It can. However," Zurzal did not seem in the least upset by such a dubious glimpse into the future, "there are other factors. I have made a study of Lochan as far as is possible. Unfortunately, as you know, the discoveries of the single expedition whose path we would follow were lost in the fate which overtook them. But the First-In Scout's report was on record in our own archives and with it similar data gathered by traders such as Gosal, but not having this luck that he has apparently had with the new find of his.

"He may not be willing to provide us with transportation once on planet, but the landing he heads for is known—and there is a port there. It is not manned by off-worlders but there seems to have grown up something of a trading settlement about it. And where there are traders there are those to visit and supply the trade. We have the Jat—"

"Yan? But what has it to do with—?"

"Communication, Jofre. All we must do must be begun by communication. And there have been some hints that certain of the rulers of the rovers in the lands we would

visit have been intrigued by the sparse off-world contact which has been. Oh, I believe it truly"—he turned his head to face Jofre squarely and his frill was up, flaring blue-green—"I was meant to do this—and I shall!" There was an aura about him which Jofre recognized. Just so had it been with an issha-trained when he was oathed for a mission. He could only trust blindly for now that the Zacathan could carry this through and follow his lead—but in reality he had no other choice—he was oathed.

Oddly enough when they had picked up Taynad, Yan, and their baggage and returned to the ship they found a different reception waiting them. Gosal, who was apparently hurried, paused to actually welcome them aboard with a thin veneer of courtesy. They were shown to the two cramped cabins far down in the ship, Taynad and the Jat bunking down in one, Jofre and the Zacathan in the other. The stowing of their baggage took some time and some of it had to be given room in the cargo hold. Jofre expected trouble over that but the crewman who aided him in stowing it away so was ready enough, if not talkative.

Jofre was surprised when the captain, with special invitation, made them free of the other small cabin which served as a gathering place for off-duty members of the crew. He felt it necessary to accompany the Zacathan whenever Zurzal took advantage of that hospitality but he found it almost as claustrophobic as their own quarters.

Gosal seemed to have, now he was in space and as it might be master, changed his opinion of the Zacathan.

He not only willingly answered the other's questions concerning Lochan to the best of his ability, but twice summoned his cargo master and his steward to supply

various items which they were the more conversant with, having dealt with the natives for supplies and met with the local traders.

Once free of Wayright the captain was in a good humor, even talking freely about his own good fortune in discovering the new gems which would make his fortune and that of the *Haren Hound.* He had kept back from the port auction a couple which he displayed. Even in the rough, without any cutting or polishing, Jofre, as unused to such wealth as he was, could detect their unusual flash of color.

"Koris stones now," Gosal had said at that display. "They bring a high price—'course that is mainly because they give off scent when one wears them against the skin. The *Solar Queen*—they made such a killing with them as brought one of the Companies after them—a nasty scrape that was. So far we're in luck. We're registered and the auction credit—most of that—goes to the planet bid. We've got us nearly two planet years and we're going to make the most of 'em!"

"Where were these found?" Zurzal asked.

Gosal laughed. "Now that would be tellin', wouldn't it? Not that I think the likes of you, lizard lord, would be any threat to this deal. But a trader keeps his secrets—they're as good as credit units on the register."

He and the steward both had stories of the trading parties who came in from the outlands to the port. Though they both said frankly that they found the aliens difficult to deal with—that there were rigid customs and certain patterns to be followed in any attempt at communication.

While Jofre and the Zacathan listened to traveler's

advice in the leisure cabin, Taynad kept closely to her own appointed cubby. She felt some of the same claustrophobia as plagued Jofre. The mountain-born of the Lair were not at home in situations which seemed too much either prisons or traps.

She had been so sure that she would have been approached again by some emissary of the Guild acting for Zarn before she had left. But that had not happened. Did such neglect mean that they had taken as a matter of course she had accepted their mission? But if she were to entice Jofre into some type of trap, should that not happen on Wayright, where there were many ships lifting daily and he could be returned to Asborgan with the least difficulty?

Gosal had made very plain that the only exit from Lochan would be this ship she now traveled by. It was a puzzle, and puzzles were never to her liking.

She spent much time with the Jat, trying to tighten the mind ties between them. Once or twice the creature actually sent her a mind picture which held, if mistily, for a fraction of time. Taynad worked carefully, fighting down her own determination and eagerness to perfect what she could do with Yan.

When the Zacathan was busied with his own calculations for the scanner, which seemed to occupy him by fits and starts, Jofre would come visiting and though she distrusted the wisdom of doing so the Jat himself drew the guard into their experiments. They discovered that reception was far clearer when Jofre and Taynad were linked by touch and both concentrating on Yan at once. So this they tried to perfect and hone as they would their selected weapons.

Jofre wondered at these crewmen, most of whom spent the longer parts of their lives encased in these metal wombs. He felt that a man would go out of his mind facing day after artificial day and night of this imprisonment. He had his mental exercises, his work with Taynad and the Jat, even the necessity of making mental notes for anything picked up in the conversation concerning Lochan which could be put to future use. Also there was the knowledge that sooner or later this was going to come to an end.

It did at last: the orders came to strap down for entrance. And the settling of the ship on its fins was as steady as if it had planeted on a recognized landing port.

Jofre longed to see what lay beyond the shell of the ship, to be able to breathe again more than the stale air which seemed to give one always a dull headache. He went through the ritual of checking his weapons, so much a part of his drill that he no longer was truly conscious of it.

They had their cabin luggage to secure. Jofre hoped that they would spend no more time aboard than was necessary though he had not the least idea where they would shelter on Lochan.

As they came out on the runway which stretched beyond the slice of heated ground where they had ridden the tail flames down, he was astounded by what lay about. The port on Asborgan was two planet generations old. There were a number of off-world buildings which had come into existence there for the convenience of travelers.

Wayright was a whole planet of ports, it existed only because it was a travel center, and all its resources were gathered to support and provide for those using the star ways.

What he looked out on, over the Zacathan's shoulder, was dull rock, fairly smooth in the vicinity of the ship and seared with the burnoffs of other landings. Beyond the edge of that was an undulating stretch of plain which appeared to reach to the horizon without any break except a huddle of what might be very rude shelters a good distance from them. The sun was blazing hot, even though it could not have been more than mid-morning. And heat, which was more than that just born from the rocket-scorched earth, reflected back to them. There seemed to be no vegetation which he could identify as such—unless the uniform dull yellow of the ground was some low-growing herbage. The sky overhead was a palish blue with a hint of green. It was a forbidding place, doubly so to one mountain bred.

"There you have it, lizard lord." Gosal swept a thick-fingered hand in the direction of that smudge on the desolate prairie land. "That is the one and only city on Lochan that I have ever heard tell of. I think you will find accommodations limited there. There is a welcoming party coming—"

There was indeed movement away from those blots on the yellow land, heading in the direction of the ship. Jofre had expected the captain to have out the flitter and ready that to reach the distant settlement but he seemed perfectly willing to await the arrival of the native party. Though he did unhook a com from his belt and hold it ready for speaking, thumbing the on button in a moment or two.

What he jabbered into the mike was either code or native tongue, totally incomprehensible to his listeners.

Jofre had little liking for that action. He did not know what he feared, but he had that alert within that this unknown was not to be trusted.

They had seen all the tapes on Lochan that Zurzal had had to offer, but the material the Zacathan had been able to locate had not dealt with this scrub of a port but rather with the planet at large. Jofre knew that the greater part of the continent on which they had landed was this stretch of plains land, arid for most of the year. It supported some nomadic tribes who traveled to find herbage for flocks of weird creatures upon whose meat and fleece they built their existence.

It was to the northward that Zurzal's interest was centered. There, somewhere beyond present sighting, were the remains of a very ancient earth turmoil, ragged beds of age-worn lava once vomited forth by a narrow chain of now eroded mountains. It was a land even more sere than that they could see now. And, knowing that, Jofre was even more uneasy. Had the obsession of the Zacathan brought them, badly prepared, into such country wherein no off-worlder could hope to survive? Had they the use of the flitter they might have had a chance, but he could see none if they attempted to strike into the unknown with any other form of transportation.

The cackle of conversation between Gosal and his unknown contact continued at intervals. Zurzal had transversed the rock of the landing field to the edge of the yellow line, Jofre with him. He was right, the guard saw, as they came to the ragged edge. The ground ahead was thickly grown with a carpet of vegetation which was more like long and ragged moss than grass. Also it was busy with

life as there were small puffs of insects which arose at their coming, circled and settled again.

Jofre jerked as one of those winged dots which had alighted on his hand delivered what was either a sting or a bite. He hoped that the immune shots they had all gone through on Wayright would help and that nothing more than that single sharp pain was going to plague him in consequence.

The caravan from the "port" reached them at last. They had withdrawn into that small shelter the shadow of the ship offered, for the beat of the sun was strong. Jofre had seen many aliens on Wayright but the motley party which straggled now from the plain across the rock to the ship seemed to him to unite all the possible whims nature might have indulged in during a fantastic dream.

They were not carried on antigrav plates, nor were the mounts they rode akin to anything Jofre had imagined might exist. In the first place these bearers did not run four-footed, but walked erect using two trunk-thick back legs for propulsion. Their skin was bare of any hair or fur he could distinguish and seemed to be merely warty and puffy flesh, dark in color, nearly approaching the shade of the rock over which they now padded. Their heads were out of proportion to the rest of them, too small, and yet in a way disgustingly close to human though there was no sign of intelligence in their tiny eyes. Across their shoulders rested wide and heavy yokes which ended in loops of dangling chain that supported flat plates somewhat like the boards of swings. These they constantly steadied as they went with their great balls of hands. And in those bobbing swings rode the rest of the party.

On the first mount one of the beings transported a passenger who was clearly humanoid, perhaps even of distant Terran descent, dressed in what was almost a parody of a port commander's uniform. His companion who had the other swing of this first bearer startled Jofre. That dull black skin, the bristle of fire red hair—this might have been the twin of that alien—the man himself who had been watching him back on Wayright—except there was no possible way that the other could have reached Lochan before them, nor was there any place in the cramped quarters of the trader where he could have been concealed.

The human stared at Zurzal.

"I am Wok Bi, Commandant of Lochan Port," he announced in a voice which had a metallic quality. "This is a closed port—there can be no visitors."

"I have this." Zurzal held out a small coil of message tape already snapped into a reader hardly larger than a ring.

Wok Bi's glare did not diminish but he took the tape, gingerly, as if he feared that it might be an explosive device of some kind. Zurzal appeared to have no doubts of the efficacy of what he had brought in the way of introduction.

# ✳ CHAPTER 25 ✳

**THE SELF-ANNOUNCED** port commander activated the tiny reader, though he seemed uneasy about taking his eyes from the Zacathan and Jofre long enough to absorb the message there, giving a couple of quick glances in their direction and losing nothing of the scowl with which he had welcomed them. Meanwhile Jofre made a study of the commander's force.

There were four of the huge transport creatures. And each had two passengers. Besides the red-maned one, there were three others of the same general appearance, save that their manes, instead of being flaming red, were of the same yellow shade as the land over which they had traveled. Jofre thought that if they lay facedown in that moss stuff, they might even be invisible. Another of the group from the "city" was closer to the conventional humanoid and unlike his companions wore an enveloping robe of grey, like the rock underfoot, over which there sprawled a pattern of meaningless and formless lines. His round skull was as hairless as that of Captain Gosal and the skin was yellow as Haperian honey, with a sleek overcasting

as if he had been carefully rubbed down with a doubtful grease. His features were blunter than those of the maned men, his mouth so wide and lipless in appearance that it might have been merely a slit cut in the puffed skin.

His eyeballs protruded until Jofre wondered if he were able to close the wrinkled lids entirely over them. And the eyes seemed to be like surface mirrors, giving nothing away as they met Jofre's and swept on. His alienness was even more apparent than that of his maned companions, but it would seem that he occupied some position of authority among them, for two had hurried to aid him from his traveling sling and fell in a pace or so behind as he waddled towards the commander.

The last two of the party slid off their swings but made no move to advance. Like the greasy one they wore robes of grey but these lacked any touch of pattern. One swung back an arm as if impatient of that covering and Jofre saw muscular yellow flesh—but more, a weapons belt from which hung a curved blade as brightly kept as any of his own steel.

Though they wore robes, they remained aloof from their fellow in the like garb. However, their faces had something of the same general traits—the wide mouths, the protruding eyes. Only these boasted head decorations of a kind, a ragged kind of crest running from between the eyes on the forehead back to the nape of the neck. Jofre could not distinguish whether that was artificial or, as Zurzal's frill, a natural flap of skin.

"You presume much—" The voice of the commander jerked his attention back to the Zacathan and the man who fronted him.

"I do not presume, Commander. I ask no more than what the Central Control has for centuries of your time granted my people. We are the Keepers—"

It was plain that the commander was impressed against his will, either by the unperturbed attitude of the Zacathan or by whatever credentials had been a part of the message on the reader.

"This is a closed planet, Learned One. We have no facilities for expeditions, nor would such be allowed if we did. There is life out there"—he swept a hand towards the horizon—"which considers any stranger rich prey. You are truly a fool if you believe that you can reach even the edge of the Shattered Land."

For the first time the oily one took part in the conversation. He gabbled a stream of squeaks, high and thin, and very strange when proceeding from his massive body. Zurzal made a quick grasp at the array of tools hanging from his belt he had equipped with care just before their landing. His taloned hand swept out of its loop a disc which he swung up before the speaker. The man gave a squeal and backed off a step, while those two who had established themselves as his attendants snarled, showing fangs as sharp as the knives which had appeared, apparently out of nowhere, in their hands.

"A translator—my speech to you, yours to me," Zurzal stated calmly, though Jofre was at his shoulder, ready to move if those two yellow-maned toughs did dare an attack.

There was a squeaking from the disc and the oily one started as if a fassnake had arisen from the ground at his very feet and was weaving its war dance in the air. Then those huge eyes blinked. One of the puffy hands sketched

a gesture in the air between them. Jofre thought he needed no translation for that—this native of Lochan was warding off evil.

"Off-world evil!" The squeakings suddenly made sense. "Who are you—serpent skin—to travel our land? What do you seek? It can be nothing good."

"I seek knowledge, and that is better than ignorance, Worshipful One. What I may be able to find will be freely shared with your learned ones. Are you not one such yourself?"

Again those huge eyes blinked. The hand trembled as if again he would form the ward sign, but he did not carry that through. Instead the tip of a green tongue appeared between those narrow lips and ran from side to side as if to prepare the way for some important message.

"To share knowledge—" the squeaking became words. "That is always to be desired. But what knowledge can you give us, off-worlder, which will be of use to us? Your own laws will not allow you to bring things which are of your high knowledge—have we not been told this many times over?" There had come about a change in the priest, if priest the man was, and Jofre thought he could recognize the type by now. He did not need any translator to understand that the other, once past his first repudiation of another and doubtless to him inferior sorcery, was now busy calculating what could be accomplished by a show of, if not friendship, then neutral acceptance.

"There is knowledge and knowledge, Worshipful One. Some it is lawful to share, and that I would open to any who wished to learn."

"To every bargain there are two sides," the disc

translated. The squeals had an almost impatient sound as if the priest felt Zurzal was refusing to come to the point. "For what you give, what must you receive?"

"That we can discuss together—at a better time and place," the Zacathan said firmly, before turning to the commander. "We are prepared to follow the regulations, Commander, even as you. You have seen our credentials. Do you question them?"

The man who had given his name as Wok Bi glanced from the Zacathan to the priest. He eyed the latter with some surprise, Jofre believed, as if he had not expected such a response from the native.

"No question," he said brusquely. "We have little in the way of accommodation—but there is part of a warehouse in which you may camp. Follow the Deves, they will see you back to the port."

He turned his shoulder a little, shutting them out as he approached Gosal.

The two robed men were back in the swings, their huge carriers already turning to depart. Jofre shrugged on his shoulder pack and helped the Zacathan adjust his and a sling which held the scanner. Taynad came down the last few feet of the ramp, Yan running beside her, her own pack in place. They would have to depend upon Gosal to see to the arrival of the rest of their supplies.

As they tramped from the rock to the thick moss their heavy space boots crushed well into it and the insects arose. The Jat whistled and slapped at its arms and legs and Jofre swept the small creature up to hold onto his pack, settling his own shoulders under that increased burden and trying not to feel the sharp sting of the bites as he went.

The bearers made better time than those who trailed behind, but since they knew their goal, the four off-worlders did not try to stretch their pace any. The constant attacks of the moss insects was irritating, but Zurzal's scaled skin apparently protected him against the worst of the bites. Only Jofre and Taynad had to call upon their stoicism to tramp that path. The Jat was apparently now free of such attacks, since the disturbed life, so busily defending its territory, did not rise high above the moss.

Closer to hand the "port" did not make any more of an impressive sight than it had from the ship. The buildings were all low, not more than one story, and apparently constructed of slabs of the same turf over which they had traveled, molded together, the now disturbed moss mottled in color to brown, and a dark red.

There was no pretense at any order, no sign of marked-off streets. Apparently the buildings had been thrown up where needed and to the builder's fancy at the time. At the opposite end of the way they followed there was a wider space in which crouched more of the swing carriers sans their yokes. Several were chewing as a ruminant might on a cud and others were very apparently napping. The breeze from that section brought a thick odor which the off-worlders found unpleasant and which hinted that these were not altogether cleanly citizens—if citizens they were and not animals.

Their guide into town brought them to a slightly larger sod building and, without dismounting, one of the swing riders motioned to the dark open doorway of that before the carrier shuffled on.

"Shelter," Zurzal commented and led the way within.

A long room had been divided by partitions which neither reached completely to the low roof nor clear across the width so that there was a passage running along beside the cubicles which perhaps were meant to serve as separate rooms.

Most of these were filled to corridor openings with bales, large earthenware jars, baskets which appeared to be woven from some manner of reed. And the mingling of smells was nearly overpowering. The Jat set up a wailing cry and pulled at Jofre's head as if to try to turn it around and so move his mount away from this place.

Luckily there was a vacant cubicle only a short distance from the outer door and Zurzal pointed to that.

"Certainly not the most luxurious quarters," he commented. "However, I think the best we can count on for now."

Jofre unlatched the Jat from his hold and handed the small struggling body to Taynad before he made his safety survey of this darkish hole. There was light, certainly far from the brilliancy of any room on Wayright or even the lamplit quarters of the Lair. These wan beams filtered out of bunches of what looked like the herbage of the plains but of a much darker shade, stuck haphazardly along the upper edges of the partitions and the wall behind.

The floor appeared to be an uneven surface of rock as if surface soil and growth had been rolled back to clear the space. It was certainly solid enough to ring under the tread of his space boots and he thought it could conceal no unpleasant surprises. While the walls appeared so thin, he was sure that a determined assault could bring any one of the three down, but it would seem they had no choice.

"That priest," Taynad had soothed the panting Jat and shrugged off her pack, "he is one to be watched." She knew she stated the obvious and she was sure in her own mind that the Zacathan was well aware of it.

"That priest," Zurzal countered, "may be our key to what we wish." He divested himself of his own burdens but he placed the scanner carefully between his feet as he stood, one hand on hip, looking about him. "That one wants power—knowledge is power—it is sometimes simple."

"It sounds simple," Jofre returned, "but the working out is perhaps far more difficult."

At least Gosal saw to the delivery of the rest of their equipment, sending it in on an antigrav which belonged to the ship and which he certainly had not offered to them. Jofre, remembering well-bitten legs, added another mark to his score against the Free Trader.

They saw the inhabitants of the port only in passing. No one came to the warehouse to which they had been so summarily dismissed nor was there any sign of either the commander or the priest. It would appear that their arrival was now a matter for total denial. Though Jofre had sighted at least one of the armed robed ones passing along the stretch of ground outside the warehouse door at rather regular intervals, as if he walked a beat.

Zurzal seemed content to wait. Patience was inborn in his long-lived race, but it was a virtue which the two from Asborgan had learned the hard way to cultivate. Since there was no sign of an eating place, they reluctantly broke open some of their own supplies and ate a very frugal portion as the day swept on toward evening.

More and more of those giants who supplied

transportation were returning to the place where off-worlders had seen their fellows relaxing earlier. Some of them were burden carriers and others had their smaller swings occupied with the maned aliens or, once in a while, a robed one.

With the coming of evening and the setting of the sun there was a change in the temperature. The heat which had grown almost to a stifling degree began to dissipate and there arose a wind sweeping in from the north which had a decidedly cold edge. Jofre had taken position on guard at the door of the warehouse itself. There had been no intruders during the afternoon to get at any of what was stored there and they seemed to have it for themselves.

"One—come—" He did not really need the warning of the Jat. It would seem his own battle-honed sense was keen enough here to pick up that feeling that there was a stranger headed for their quarters. Certainly there was no lighting of the "streets" in the dusk but there did seem to be a haze of dim radiance bobbing along towards the doorway at a pace a person might walk.

Jofre did not step into direct sight himself and now he was aware that Taynad was moving in at an angle behind him as might any Brother when the alert was given. One of his hands was on the hilt of a throwing knife. They had set out from Wayright with stunners, only to have theirs put under seal by the captain as contraband on Lochan. Only Zurzal, because of his maiming, had not been deprived of his weapon. Here one was back to the bladed weapons Jofre knew best.

The pinch of light brought a glisten from a round face. If not the priest from the landing site, then another of his

kind. And there came through the dark not only an odor which suggested a long-unbathed body but, in addition, a thin whistle.

"Let him in." Zurzal moved out, ready to bid their visitor welcome. Jofre obeyed but fell in on the heels of the Lochanian. He knew without being told that Taynad and the Jat shared sentry duty now and that his place as guard was with the Zacathan.

The light of their cubicle was strong enough to show that this was indeed the one Zurzal had spoken to. In one pudgy hand the fellow held a loose ball of stuff from which spun the thread of feeble light. His bulbous eyes glistened in that glow, as subdued as it was.

Zurzal was ready with the translator. "Greeting, Worshipful One, you have been awaited—the hour grows late." There was a kind of snap in the Zacathan's voice; whether such a nuance was translated into the squealing by the disc Jofre could not guess. But he was very sure that Zurzal was prepared to take a firm stand with this visitor.

Those wide lips puffed forth a breath which was foul. And then squeaked in answer:

"The Axe of Rou comes or goes not at the will of off-worlders. There is little patience—what would you do here, stranger?"

"I seek, as I have said, knowledge. Your world is old—it has seen many changes—is that not so?"

"Rou works as it is willed. The earth and all which forms it is for *HIM* as the mud of the under leaf is to the maker of pots, as the knuckle of iron to him who fashions a blade. But what do you know of these changes you speak of? You are not one with Rou."

"Rou exists in many forms also," Zurzal answered. "Can it not be that it is by *His* will we stand here this night? Axe of Rou, would it not be to such a close-held follower as you that revelations would be made? Or is it that the Axe merely speaks for another who is closer to the ear of Rou?"

"I have the ear of Rou." The squealing arose to a high pitch. "Say it to me, off-worlder, and I shall judge whether this be business of Rou's Own or not."

"Very well." The Zacathan stooped and laid a hand lightly on the scanner case. "This I carry, Axe of Rou, is born of long study and the use of very ancient records. It has the power to bring to light matters lost in the long seasons forgotten by men whose memories cannot hold so much. There is a place in the Shattered Land which bears a certain mark. That was discovered by some knowledge seekers before me. But they did not possess such an aid as this one and they were driven away before they could obtain much which they were sure could be learned. Therefore I have come to carry on this work and see into the ages behind—"

"Only Rou can look behind more than one lifetime!"

"So can I not, without this. But it is the learning which Rou allows men that has brought this into being and the glory will be *HIS* when the great find is made."

The priest wiped the palm of his light-free hand across his triple chin. He was like all of his kind, Jofre believed, seeking what could lie in such a matter which would further his own gain.

"What would you need to do Rou's Will in this matter?" The demand was abrupt. Their needs would also present a bargaining point.

"We need a guide to the Shattered Land, and transportation for ourselves and our gear." Zurzal was as quick to deliver his needs.

"The Shattered Land—it is a place of the Long Dead, of the damned Ones who followed Vunt. You will find no true follower of Rou to enter there. But—" The squeaking voice paused for a moment. Jofre tensed, sensing that what was coming now was of the first importance as far as the priest was concerned.

"There once was land where Rou had *His* place. And—yes, there are very old stories that there was powerful knowledge to be found there—left behind when the Will of Rou twisted that part of the world with fire and the shaking of the earth. But why should we allow such knowledge to fall into the hands of off-worlders? By what right do you claim the knowledge which was once that of Rou's children?"

"None," the Zacathan returned promptly. "I freely surrender all claims to what may be found if those of Rou will it so."

"Then," came back the priest with a rush, "what do you gain, off-worlder, if you surrender any knowledge treasure which may be found? Why do you, and these with you, willingly go into the Dead Land if you gain no benefit from your labors?"

"I will make with this," again the Zacathan indicated the scanner, "a record, one which you will be free to see. It is my wish to prove that I can set aside the mists of the past. With such proof I can visit other worlds and on each I can add to the store of ancient knowledge. To my people, Axe, such is the primary work of our lives. We find in any

discoveries value, whether it is something which can be seen and handled, or whether it abides only in the minds thereafter."

"There must be a considering of this," the Axe replied. "You will be told what the answer will be." So abruptly he turned and waddled away.

"He has a reason," Jofre ventured. The issha might not be able to read minds but they were aware when alerted to certain emanations of emotion. He was certain that the Axe was indeed taking time out to think and that, behind his assent, if assent it would be, there would also be a scheme set in motion.

"There is one on guard," Taynad said in a low tone from the door to which they had followed, more slowly, their late visitor.

"We could not expect less," Zurzal asserted. "But I think we need fear no more attention until our friend is ready to move."

# ✳ CHAPTER 26 ✳

**IT WAS ONLY PARTLY** impatience which rode Jofre. He held Zurzal's knowledge to be far above even that of the Shagga priests—and put to better use. However, he also knew that the Zacathan was so fiercely determined to prove the efficiency of the scanner that he might be led to overlook any hidden threats. Its use on Tssek had confirmed for Zurzal that he could do this, but to be able to deliver a find from Lochan would reestablish his credit among his own peers. And that was a situation which Jofre could understand very well, even though he himself could have no hope of a triumphant return to Asborgan and an addition of issha status made by the Shagga.

The sheer mechanics of a crossing of the long tundralike plain to the northern country was always to the fore of his mind. That they could tramp it carrying all their supplies was out of the question. From the scanty tape information they had studied so carefully they knew that the Shattered Land would be a far greater obstacle even than the insect-infested tundra.

"We can make no deal with Gosal?" he asked, though he was sure of the answer. "Even if he would give us use of the one gravity sled—"

"Those carriers," Taynad added as if she had been following some line of reasoning of her own, "are they natives or beasts, servants, slaves—? The Jat has tried to reach them by mind touch—there is nothing there."

"They serve both the maned people and those they call Deves," Jofre commented. "But even with such aid could we reach our goal while our supplies still hold out?"

Zurzal's toothed jaws showed in a grin. "We shall have another visitor," he stated. "One who will come by dark."

And Jofre, who had quickly retaken his place as sentry, was startled as there was a warning from the other end of the warehouse, that where there seemed to be only solid wall. He saw movement and knew that Taynad was on alert, slipping from their cubicle to the door of the next, the Jat close beside her.

"It is all right," Zurzal said, his hissing voice carrying easily. "Bright evening to you, Commander!"

That port official who had been so obstructive at their landing passed close enough to one of the moss torches to show his face, pausing in the light a second or two as if to make sure they recognized him, before he slipped into their quarters and settled himself cross-legged facing the Zacathan.

"You are a fool, Learned One," his voice had the rasp of exasperation in it. "There is no way under the Heavens of Lochan that you can succeed in this."

"Men have succeeded on thinner chances than the one I have been offered, Wok Bi. And you have your orders."

"Orders!" The man flung up his hands in a gesture which suggested that this was indeed folly. "You head willfully into country where one expedition came to a very bloody end. There are what—four of you—one a woman—another a Jat—you would need a squad of Patrol to even venture over the border there. It is madness and you are forcing me to be a part of it."

"Your orders are plain," Zurzal returned placidly. "Yes, we are a small party, but that means we have less to transport. It is the transport that we must now consider."

"No Pungal owner will lease out to you and I cannot make them." There was a small note of satisfaction in that. "And on your own feet there is no possible way to reach your goal before Change-season."

"There are the Gar," Zurzal said.

"Gar!" The way Wok Bi said that name made it sound as if the Zacathan had hissed it.

Gar—Jofre remembered. There had been a brief note concerning them on one of the tapes. They were the nomads of the inner lands and the off-worlders would have to transverse those in order to reach their own goal.

"Yes. Captain Gosal has a mixed cargo. There were Gar dealers to meet us at set down. And those have caravan trails inland. With fresh goods some one of them will be moving out."

"The priests will not hear of it!" Wok Bi fell back on a second objection.

"I think that there will be a change of thought there, too. Now—the Gar caravans must have been transport other than these Pungal—"

Wok Bi shook his head. "No, not this side of the Var,

but they do have carriers which are steady movers. It is said that sometimes they keep the trail for a full day and a night at a time since their drivers have learned to sleep a-swing. On the other side of the Var—there you would have to take your chance with what the Wild Ones use—they have mounts of a sort—I have seen a couple of specimens of them—running four-legged, with a sweep of horn—and nasty tempered I am told. Also that you might be able to make any deals for a guide or beasts of burden beyond the Var—that is very problematical."

"Commander, you have done your duty in stating frankly all the perils we must face. I shall, of course, give you a tape absolving you of blame which might come from some catastrophe. But go on, we shall."

Again the man threw up his hands. "On your head be it. There is also this—within the Shattered Land none of our coms work. If you are caught in some trouble, you cannot call for any aid—not that we would have any to send you."

"That is also understood," agreed the Zacathan.

"Be it on your own heads then." The commander got up. "I do not expect to see you again. If there is any hope of fortune, may it be yours. But I doubt such exists."

They settled then for the night, Jofre taking the first watch once again, well advised that the warehouse door was under surveillance from the outside. He thought of Zurzal's stubbornness. To an oathed the wishes of his patron were law. He might advise if called upon, but the central core of any operation remained the choice of the one to whom he had pledged himself. After all, men of the Lair had served very threatened causes before, and the triumph of some of them over great odds was the material

for the Legend singers. No man could see the future and it was best to live but one day, one night at a time. His fingers sought within his girdle for that small pocket he had fashioned and drew out the stone. There was no heart fire in it, but it was warm and that warmth reached within him, far—banishing the ghosts of foreseeing. He held it so until Taynad moved up to take his place as sentry, closing his hand quickly when he heard those faint stirs in the dark which marked her coming. This was his secret only and he would hold it so.

However, Taynad had thoughts of her own. She had taken the measure of this Zacathan and she believed that if anyone could succeed in what sounded like a fever-born dream quest, it was he. There was something else. She found the twigs of her braids and once more fingering read their message. If not capture—kill! But to take the life of a Brother was to break-oath. And not to follow orders was an even greater break-oath. The Shagga wanted Jofre—they would find the means of contacting her even here—since they had joined forces with the Guild. The latter was as legendary as the issha-trained in achieving what its members were set to do.

Why did they want him? And why, if they could not take him bodily, did they demand blood? By his own tale, which instinct told her was the full truth, he had done nothing to provoke all custom and honor. She must watch, wait, and see what time itself would bring in answer. Kill—her fingernail bit into that last ominous notch. Though perhaps—with Shagga wrath so raised against him, he might welcome death rather than to fall into the hands of the priests.

Priests—it would seem that there were always priests to deal with. Her mouth twisted disdainfully as she thought of the Axe of Rou. But he, she believed, from what she had sensed of him was a relatively simple man—wily in a way, of course, but no match even for the Zacathan. He might well be brought to support them up to a point and right now they could use support.

She stretched. By the Flowers of Moon Valley, how she longed for a dip in one of the Three Pools with the comfort of an oil rub thereafter. Before this journeying was done with the Jewelbright might well be the Jeweldimmed and worth no second look from any man.

The Axe of Rou duly returned, at the first dim light of day, somewhat to the surprise of Jofre and Taynad though it would seem that Zurzal had been expecting him.

"You have taken council?" he greeted the priest.

"What do you offer?" countered the Axe.

"Let one of your own, one whom you trust, go with us— let him bring guards also if you will. What we find—the solid portion will be yours—we shall keep only the record of its finding."

"The trader U-Ky leaves today," the priest said. "It is true I shall be with him as it is necessary that I return to the Walls. And my Deves will bear me company. If you can bargain for transport with U-Ky—then let it be done."

It seemed that the Zacathan had very little trouble striking the bargain with the red-maned trader whom Jofre continued to watch narrowly. The fellow was a double for that alien who had been on Wayright though there was no way he could have made the journey back without their knowing it. It must be that there was such a strong

resemblance between members of his race that it was difficult for outsiders to differentiate between them. What Zurzal offered him was a packet of silver pieces, such an exchange allowed by Wok Bi, in whose presence the transaction was done—silver being, it appeared, in rare supply on Lochan.

Their bargaining obtained the use of four of the swing carrying monsters. Zurzal, with the scanner across his knees, occupied the left swing of the first, Jofre the right. Behind them came Taynad with the Jat, balanced by a selection of equal weight of their gear, and the final bearers transported the rest of their equipment.

The heat as they set out was intense but at least, perched on swings, they were above the insect swarms. Though the constant movement of those seats made the off-world riders a little giddy and queasy, inclined to hold on tightly wherever a good anchorage offered.

U-Ky's caravan was a fairly impressive command and he rode to its head. There was also the bearer who balanced the great weight of the Axe against a tall pile of bundles. Swinging along behind the priest were the robed Deves. Strung out behind came some of the maned people, only a few of them red-maned and the rest as yellow-backed as the tundra.

Their rate of progress was no faster than a ponderous walk; apparently the huge bearers kept to what was a steady pace for them and never displayed any change in gait. Under the climbing and burning sun this travel was misery for the off-worlders and Jofre had to fight to hold on to his patience.

The yellow tundra seemed to stretch forever and though the caravan headed confidently forward, there was

no trace of trail or road to be seen, nor any markers rising to guide the unknowing. It must be that the natives were like animals or birds on some of the other worlds which possessed ingrown direction skills.

They made no halt for nooning but as the sun shifted westward there began to show a line of dark marking the junction of sky and land ahead. It was toward that they continued doggedly even as the sun set and the quick dusk of Lochan closed in.

Still the caravan showed no signs of coming to a halt and the off-worlders were decidedly uncomfortable and tired. Then, out of the northern shadows, there shot a beam of light which flickered, Jofre decided after a moment's watching, in a distinct pattern. He was aware of movement on the right-hand swing of the bearer ahead of him; the rider there, one of the yellow manes, had raised what looked like a thick stick. From the tip of that flashed in turn an answer to that flare ahead.

So announced they swung on into what was an encampment, nearly as large as the caravan itself as to numbers. There were no sod buildings here, rather stretches of woven reed mats set to form very crude tentlike enclosures. While awaiting them were not only members of the maned race, and robed Deves, but a new type of Lochanian native. These were short in size, hardly larger than the Jat, and armored—or shelled—with dull green carapacelike body covering from which a wide, also shielded head and thin knobby jointed limbs projected. They did not mingle with those who crowded forward to greet the caravaners, rather held off in a party to themselves.

Jofre, catching good sight of one standing just beneath

one of the massed luminous moss torches of the camp, recognized this as a tribesman concerning which there had been a very short note in their scant study tapes. This was a Skrem, one of the nomads whose tribes drifted along the very edge of the Shattered land.

The off-worlders were glad to be able to slide down from their shaking conveyances and immediately sought the outer regions of the camp for relief. Even the issha training, Jofre decided, had not prepared him for such a journey as this had been. He drew a deep breath as he relatched his belt; even another fraction of a time mark might have been a disaster.

The small outlander party was left alone. Their luggage had been carelessly dumped as their bearers trudged mechanically away to the assembly of their own kind. There was no offer of any tent covering, but the three united in piling their equipment so that it gave a measure of shelter and they did not try to approach the low-burning fires which marked the fore of those misshapen tents. They had their trail rations and they selected small shares of those, knowing from the start they must take good care of the highly nourishing, if near-tasteless stuff, since living off the land might be impossible.

The caravaners apparently had a more robust meal to suit them. Joints of some unidentifiable meat were spitted over the fires and then portions sawed off with belt knives to please the diner. Bulging skins appeared also and were passed from hand to hand. The Lochanians, Jofre noted, were quite practiced in the tricky maneuver of throwing back the head and allowing a thick curl of liquid to flow from the lower bag end directly into their mouths.

This informal feasting was still in progress when a party of three approached the impromptu campsite of the off-worlders. Against the glow of one of the fires could be made out the unwieldy bulk of one who could only be the Axe of Rou, attended by one of the Deves, and scuttling along at his side one of the Skrem.

The three from off-world arose, the Jat pushing in behind Taynad, peering around her with timid curiosity.

"Well journeyed," Zurzal had the translator at ready. "What does the Axe desire of this company?"

For a moment or so after he came to a halt the priest merely puffed as if he had made the trip across camp at some labor.

"Strangers, Rou frowns upon your travels."

"How so?"

"The season is late, we move too slowly, there is no entering the Shattered Land after the Wild Winds rise."

"Our pace is one set by you and your people, Axe of Rou. Can it be that Rou now requires that we prove ourselves by finding a faster way to satisfy *His* bidding in this matter?"

"There is one." The priest paused as if he were undecided about this, as if he were being forced against his will to come to a decision he distrusted. "The Skrem know another path. This is I'On." He indicated the strange native. There was little to be seen in the way of features on that one's face. The helmet (or the outgrowth of natural skull) reached forward in a visor shape which fully shadowed the eyes. Below those half-hidden pits the face narrowed to a sharp point of chin, the nose joined to that in a beaklike extension.

I'On made no move nor sound to acknowledge the introduction. Instead he stepped ahead of the priest to stand directly before the Zacathan, his head moving slowly up and then down, as if he measured the much taller lizard man from head to foot and back again.

Zurzal could not speak any greeting since the other's speech had not been picked up to be read by the translator.

From the Zacathan, the Skrem turned to Jofre, favored him with the same scrutiny, passed on to Taynad, and last of all shot his head a little forward as if to get a better look at the Jat, which had squeaked and withdrawn nearly behind the girl.

Having submitted them all to some form of his own measurement, the Skrem returned to the Zacathan.

What issued from the beak mouth was a chittering sound not unlike that Jofre had heard the hive man give back on Wayright.

"Why hunt you ghosts?" sputtered the translator.

"To learn," Zurzal returned briefly.

"To learn what?"

"The ways of the past."

"Those of the silences are eaters of men. Would you fill their pots joyfully?"

"I would learn of them—"

"There are always fools in the world." The contempt of that pushed even through the translator. "Well, what have you to offer, fool, to be taken to meet the results of your folly?"

"What do you ask, I'On?"

The Skrem did not answer at once. Rather he turned his head slowly as if to inspect all the pile of their

belongings. Then of a sudden, so suddenly, that it brought
Jofre to a crouch and ready to defend himself, he turned to
the guard.

"This one goes also?"

"He goes," Zurzal assured him.

"He will have a service to offer—when the time is
ready. Let him be also ready."

"What service?"

"It shall reveal itself. So be it. The Shattered Land shall
be a gate opened to you, fools. We shall claim our price
when it is right. Be ready to move out at first light."

He turned and left them, brushing past the Deves and
leaving the priest to stare after him before the Axe looked,
his big eyes a little narrowed, at the Zacathan, and on to
Jofre.

"What does he mean? What service can such as you
offer the drifting ones?"

"You heard, Axe, what we heard. It would seem that we
have now an open-ended bargain. But it will have to
suffice."

For a moment it seemed as if the priest was going to
protest further and then he turned away, but not before he
shot another look at Jofre which was both speculative and
unpleasant.

"Why me?" Jofre actually voiced that question when
they were alone again.

He heard Taynad laugh. "Did he not speak of ghosts
who want man flesh for their pots? Perhaps he would herd
a particularly toothsome dish in their direction. But I
think—Learned One," she said slowly, "that Skrem—he
has a strong inner sense—he sought. Us he could not

touch—but the little one," she stooped and gathered up the trembling Jat, holding its body close, "it knew and feared. I think that we had best be doubly on guard."

"As if we can be anything else," Zurzal returned. "This is indeed perhaps folly, yet I cannot—I cannot stray from what I would do here!"

# ✳ CHAPTER 27 ✳

**WHAT I'ON HAD TO OFFER** on his part they learned the next morning. Though the caravan moved on its way, the off-worlders remained with the Skrem. Two of the Deves also relinquished their traveling swings, though the Axe had gone with the others. It was apparent that the priest fully intended to have his own sources of information—or control—accompanying the Zacathan's party.

The stamping march of the bearers was well away from the overnight campsite when the Skrem went to work. He scrabbled in the mosscarpet some distance away from the trampled ground and came up with three rods which he fitted together—much like the tripod on which the scanner rested. But what was then affixed on top was a round of what appeared to be crystal, backed with an interweaving of the same material as the rods.

As the off-worlders remained by the pile of their gear, the Skrem affixed the platter to the tripod and wriggled it back and forth. Jofre recognized something from the Lair

days—their mountain sentries had used burnished mirrors for the flashing of messages overland. This must be a similar form of communication.

Swiftly the Skrem tilted his signal back and forth. Then from the northeast there came a flicker of light in return. Methodically the Skrem set about dismantling the apparatus and then reburied it, pulling the moss back over it,

How long must they wait? Taynad leaned back against a box of supplies. It seemed to her now that her wits certainly must have been astray when she had joined up with this muddle-headed Zacathan. Jofre was oathed to him, she was not—save by word alone. The mission to Tssek had been her first big one and it had fallen apart through no fault of her own. She had been given those orders—why did she continue to question them this way? She could only return in thought to those moments when she, Jofre, and Yan had been one—as if at that time there had been forged something as strong as a blood oath. It was almost as if her own will had been weakened, that she had been drawn along as one sometimes was in ill dreams when one struggled against an invisible threatening power.

"Power—strong—big—" She had a mind vision of a fire raging up into the sky, heat which was not from any sun, even one as hot as this one. Yan crouched against her. The Jat's paw hand rested over her hand and its large eyes were turned up to view her face. "Power—" Yes, that had sprung from Yan's thinking, not her own. She shot a glance in Jofre's direction.

He was watching the actions of the Skrem with complete absorption as if he expected some trouble to

burst from a gesture or action on the part of the alien. No, Jofre must not have been touched by that half-message.

Taynad closed her hand gently about the Jat's. "Power?" She struggled to give all the strength she could to make that word a question.

What she received in return did not altogether surprise her. A wavering, oddly slanted face flashed into her mind—Jofre—as Yan must see him.

"Power?" she asked again in thought.

Flames—shooting flames bursting outward as if a dozen lasers were firing at a single target. She instinctively cringed. Yan was very sure.

The flames were, of course, merely a picturing of punishing force, of that she was certain. The guard could have not smuggled in any weapon that would reveal itself so. In fact she was very sure that she knew exactly the number and style of every piece of armament he had hidden about his person.

There were tales that the Shagga could produce strange effects—bemuse minds—make one see what was not there—even as the issha could protect themselves for short periods of time. But Jofre was not Shagga—to them he was the enemy who must be erased—one way or another.

Why did they want him prisoner, that was a small puzzle—better dead—off-world dead where he would be no problem. Why prisoner—and only dead at the last resort as the instructions passed to her? Or—her thought took another small leap—were those twigs and their messages counterfeit? The Guild was supposed to possess infinite knowledge. She knew that Zarn had been charged with certain delicate negotiations with the Guild. Suppose it was

the Guild who wanted Jofre—alive—or dead by her hand?

Her eyes lowered to that hand curved to comfort the Jat. Shadow did not slay Shadow. She must have better reason—Which came back to—

The Jat squirmed closer to her. Another mind picture—blurred—so distorted she could make nothing of it. Except that she was certain that it was an object—something which Jofre owned, or controlled, or—

"They are coming!" Zurzal was on his feet, looking out over the tundra in the direction which that flash had marked. There was certainly movement there and at a speed far transcending the plod of the bearers. As they plowed on through the moss the new party revealed themselves, however, as grotesquely alien to the off-worlders as U-Ky and his caravaners had been.

There were four mounted figures, each leading a line of four-footed creatures but apparently by no lines or reins, the mounts being followed without urging by six of their own kind, in a line behind each of the riders.

They were of the same musty yellow as the tundra, their legs long and thin, their bodies apparently hairless and also nearly skeleton-slender. They held their heads on a straight line with their bodies as they came, and the muzzles ended in sharp points. Those heads were small in proportion to a spread of horns, bending sharply backward, which were flat and shovellike in appearance.

As the runners came pounding up to the deserted campsite Jofre saw that their feet were long and narrow, the fore ones sprouting claws which apparently were not retractable. The Skrem who brought them rode well forward on those slim backs, their hands gripping the edges

of the shovel horns.

In height they were close to the size of a small horse such as Jofre had seen used for pleasure riding on Wayright, and on the backs of those without riders there were weavings of odd-looking harness. But there were no saddles; apparently one was to perch like the Skrem, hold on to the horns, and hope for the best.

The Skrem made no move to aid in the loading of the extra mounts, gathering in a knot around I'On and chittering loudly. Fortunately the animals they had brought did not seem to resent the actions of the three in dividing up their gear and stowing it into the baggage nets. Jofre wondered if what they had to haul would not be too heavy a load but the creatures, except for a grunt or two, made no complaint.

At length it was time for they themselves to scramble up, finding that their seats on those ridge-boned backs were not comfortable—but, as with the swings, had to be endured. The riders were back in place, and I'On mounted behind one of those. At some signal the off-worlders did not catch the party wheeled in parade order and headed out, northeast, in the same style as they had arrived, lining up behind the four leaders.

It was a rough jolting, and the hold on the creatures' horns did little to steady one. But at least they went at a good speed and the animals, ridden or laden, apparently were ready to keep to that pace. Within a short time there loomed before them a rise in the land like a wall. The grey stones of it pierced the moss. The Deves, who had done nothing to help with the luggage, and both bestrode one of the animals, uttered a call which blended both of their

voices. This was the Var, a natural walling as far as the Lochanians knew, separating the plains from the highlands. It was also a cut across which a bridge had been strung—an exceedingly fragile-looking bridge—by the approaches to which there were both maned men and Deves stationed. However, at the sight of the two Deves with the Skrem party these fell back and the first of the riders was out on the bridge.

At least here their mounts slowed to a walk and ventured out on the swinging support at well separated intervals, so there was a wait on the far side for their party to again assemble. Also here their path led through gullies and there were rising hills. The vegetation changed to a sharp degree. The yellow moss of the tundra was gone. Here were skeleton-thin, branched shrubs, around the roots of which clustered patches of indigo blue, an eye-aching green, and a bloody red growth which put forth bristles, not unlike thorns, and attracted a great many flying things.

Back and forth they wove through these gullies, sometimes seeming even to turn completely around. Ahead, against the sky, there was a rise of taller hills, mountains. As on the tundra Jofre could distinguish no path or road, or even markings, yet their leader did not falter and those who followed showed no lack of confidence in him.

Once in such a land, Jofre thought, how did one win free again? And from what little they had been able to gather the Shattered Land was even more chaotic.

They came to a halt at last, the off-worlders bone-shaken. Zurzal, because of his greater height, must have

found it even a tougher ordeal, though he made no complaint. Here was a spring where water rippled through a crevice in the rocks and threaded down into a pool, which in turn fed a stream. There were gauzy winged things dancing over the water, prismatic colors glinting off their wings as if those were formed of fine lace set with tiny jewels.

That rider who had shared his perch with I'On did not dismount as all the rest swung down. Once the other mounts were free they clustered around that leader which ambled at a much slower pace down the stream, leaving the rest of the party behind. The Skrem paid no attention to the off-worlders, rather gathered in a group about I'On, producing bags in which they rummaged to bring forth what looked like handfuls of dried grass. Two of their number went on hands and knees to the stream side and busied themselves flipping over the water-moistened rocks, now and then scooping up what looked like a pallid wriggling grub which they tossed over their shoulders, their finds eagerly pounced upon by their fellows. It would seem that this was a time to eat.

Jofre had had enough training in living off the countryside on Asborgan to have tasted—without any pleasure but most stoically—insects and rough gathered herbs. But he was glad that for now they had their own trail rations.

The mounts were being watered downstream and then turned to foraging on the most purplish of the bristle growth, chewing it vigorously until dark, slimy juice dribbled from their jaws. With a compressed meat biscuit in one hand Zurzal produced with the foreshortened other

a square of nearly transparent stuff which had been folded into very tight compress but shook out into a wide strip which Jofre identified as that mapping of the ways on which the Zacathan had worked many hours from time to time ever since he had obtained from the dying spacer the coordinates the other had brought back from his ordeal on Lochan. But that Zurzal could make any sense of what was marked there was a wonder to the guard. This up-and-down land might present landmarks by the thousands to the educated eye, but those would exist for a native, and he doubted whether the spacer had been in a position to sight many.

The Zacathan's head came up and he was staring now at the north line of heights, which were like broken teeth gnawing at the sky. They seemed to be paralleling that line rather than heading directly towards it. But was it the boundary of the Shattered Land? Jofre was sure that even Zurzal could not tell.

He got to his feet and walked up and down, to stretch muscles, battling the various aches and pains their riding had produced. His inner thighs felt raw, chafed by the constant pressure he had had to keep to hold his place. But if it were so for him, what had it been for Taynad?

The girl sat with her back to a lichen-crusted stone. Her eyes were closed and there was that masklike quietude in her face which he could understand. One hand, holding a barely nibbled journey square, lay laxly across her knee and the other rested on Yan's head.

"Eat!" Jofre moved to stand so that his shadow fell across her and hid her from the rest of their company. "Without food, strength goes." Even in his own ears his voice sounded rough and he must rouse her into seeking

inner strength, for there could be no falling behind. He did not believe that the Skrem would in any way suit their form of travel to those in their company. While any Sister to Shadows had to be issha-tough, her own training had differed in places from his—and he did not know, could not judge how much. Why had she agreed to Zurzal's offer? So far her communication skills had not been put to any testing. He stood in hesitation—there was a wish to somehow lend her strength now as he had when she had brought the Jat out of its catatonic seizure, yet he was at a loss how to do that. He knew very little of women—that was a subject on which none of the Masters ever dwelt, and before a boy gained puberty he was drilled and disciplined into control over the body's desires.

An issha who had well served on the missions, proved himself worthy to have his bloodline carried on, could be assigned to a mating by selection. Then he passed into another category of fighter, became a trainer, or an advisor. But otherwise women played no part in his life.

It had been growing on him that there was indeed a difference between them, issha-trained though they were. She would have been as disciplined to meet him as a battle comrade only had they been on a double oathing. As a Jewelbright she was a warrior of an entirely different breed. He felt rough-handed, as unskilled as a boy at his first mustering in the arms court.

However, he slipped down beside her now. The Jat stirred and looked at him. Reaching across the girl, who had not moved, Yan caught at Jofre's hand, keeping its own grip also on Taynad.

Heat, first a warmth and then a flame against his ribs.

The stone from Qaw-en-itter—he knew it too well now to doubt that it was so making known its presence. Power? Jofre's free hand slipped inside his girdle, his fingers closed on that source of warmth.

Power—strength—his thought fastened on that. Flow of strength—he fought to draw upon it even as he had in the battle to win the Jat. And it was coming—up his arm—across his body—into that other hand—the paw which held him in such a grip. And beyond—though he could not trace it any further than Yan, he was sure that the Jat was channeling it into Taynad.

Her eyes opened and focused on him. There was the faintest trace of a frown troubling the mask of her face.

"Draw—" He spoke that single word as an order.

The flow was continuing, not as heavy as it had been before, but steady. Then her hand jerked away from the Jat, breaking the chain.

"Who—what are you?" She demanded that sharply, straightening her shoulders, pulling herself away from the rock support.

"Issha feeds issha when there is need," he returned, drawing his hand away from his girdle. Why would he not share the secret of his find with her? He could not tell except there seemed to be a guard on his tongue, a shutter in his mind when he thought of it.

"It is well." Once more she showed him the mask. "It seems I am too far, too long from the Lair." He thought he could detect a measure of resentment in her speech and she was using the language of the Lair which had many inflections and subtle shadings. Yes, she could well resent the fact that she had displayed signs of fatigue.

"It is always well to give." He used the formal speech of an instructor. "Is it not written so in the Laws of Kale?"

What answer she might have made to that he was not to know, for Zurzal roused from the studying of his flimsy map and there was the clatter of feet on gravel as their mounts headed back upstream in their direction.

Remounted, their leader swung them on along the stream for a space and then there was a scramble up a slope and for the first time the dim marks of a true trail—which turned and twisted up into the heights beyond. This was far harder riding than even the gully wandering had been and the holds they must keep on the horns of their mounts in order not to slip from their seats crooked their fingers with aching cramps. Jofre concentrated on looking only at those horns and making sure that his hold was the best he could grip. To look out into the empty air, down, or even at the length of the slope ahead was disheartening.

They hit at last what seemed to be a pass and on either side the rock walls towered. There was a searching wind, as chill as the tundra plain had been hot. Yet there was life of a sort clinging here, for both walls were festooned with weblike binding and Jofre, daring for the moment to look beyond his hands, saw a shaking of those lines. Climbing down was a ball-like body, hardly to be distinguished from the rocks in color, legs as thin and apparently as supple as the webbing sprouting from under the round of its body.

Jofre caught the sudden action of the Skrem bestriding the lead mount. Both he and I'On, seated behind, made throwing gestures. The ball thing gave a convulsive leap which left it dangling from the webbing by only two of its legs, the rest jerking frenziedly in the air. Protruding from

the round back Jofre sighted two small shafts. Then the ball lost its last hold, fell squashily and was sent farther on by a kick from his own mount which nearly unseated him.

There appeared to be no further danger as they won through the pass to the northern end. There their line of mounts halted, only those bearing riders gathering closer to the downward grade as if they consciously wished those they carried to see what lay ahead.

What did was such a frozen convulsion of nature that Jofre, though he had somewhat been prepared for such a sight by the tapes, thought could hardly exist on any world.

They called this the Shattered Land and they were very right in that description. It was all sharp ridges of rock, looking knife-sharp from above, with dark drops between. As if one of the Storm Gods of the old days had taken a sword half as wide as the sky and deliberately cut and recut the earth, turning soil where that weapon touched into the traps of blade-edged lava.

How could any man find a way through such a country? The expedition which had come to grief here had been borne by flitter—though Jofre wondered about the downdrafts and wind changes over such a territory. But on foot? This was one of those impossible tasks given to the Older Heroes in order for them to achieve immortality. One could perhaps achieve a measure of that, to be sure, in another way, by simply dying here, Jofre thought.

The mount bearing I'On as one rider had edged up beside the Zacathan.

"Here is the country you seek, stranger. Now what do you seek in it?"

Zurzal was busy with one of the belongings taken from

his belt, a small oval into which he now most carefully inserted a pellet. He held it out towards that riven world.

A moment later, to be heard even above the strange echoing cries of the wind through those broken vales below, came a small sharp sound. The Zacathan turned his hand slowly, with infinite care, and the signal strengthened.

"What we seek lies there." He pointed to the north.

Though they could not see the Skrem's eyes, Jofre thought that the alien might be staring at Zurzal's instrument with surprise. He chittered and was answered by his fellow rider. Then he turned to Zurzal with another question.

"How far?"

"That we must learn for ourselves," the Zacathan replied, "but the signal is strong. We cannot be too far."

One of the Deves joined them now, having dismounted. The wind whipped his cloak about, fluttering his head comb.

"No one enters this." He spoke the trade tongue but so heavily accented that it was difficult to understand.

The Skrem shifted around on his mount. It seemed that the heavy head covering kept him from turning his head easily. He chittered and Zurzal's com picked up his speech even though that was not directed to the off-worlders.

"The Skrem ride where they will. We would see what this one seeks. If it is of value—so shall it be valued."

And without another word the rider seated before I'On pressed down on the horns of his beast and the creature took the first step down the line of broken ledges leading into the Shattered Land.

# ✴ CHAPTER 28 ✴

**WHAT MIGHT BE THE NATURE** of Zurzal's guide Jofre could not guess but certainly the attitude of the Zacathan would lead anyone to believe that he trusted in it implicitly. The guard thought back to that meeting with the dying man on Asborgan. Had what he had passed to Zurzal then come to lead them now?

However, this was no country into which to venture as that night was drawing in. The broken, knife-edged lava remains formed a constant threat. From what Jofre could see bubbles must have formed in the molten rock, to burst, leaving jagged teeth to threaten any unwary step.

Apparently the Skrem were well aware of this danger. Once they had reached the end of the downslope, they clustered on a semilevel space, making no move to enter the broken maze even though the signal Zurzal carried sent forth its constant assertion that what was to be sought did lie ahead.

It was a cramped and uncomfortable camp they set up. The rugged lava flow provided some small shelter and once again the party separated naturally into three. While the

off-worlders worked at getting their gear free from the baggage beasts they were left alone, each animal as it was unloaded moving away to join its fellows. The Skrem hunkered down without looking to their mounts, gathering in a knot about a spot of fire the Zacathan could have covered with his two hands.

Between the Skrem and the off-worlders the two Deves found a resting place. They made no move toward any fire, only bundled their robes more tightly about them, and Jofre noted that they drew hoods from the folds of those robes over their heads as they settled back-to-back, one facing the Skrem gathering, one Zurzal's party, as if they fully intended to keep full watch on all those they companied with.

Zurzal himself moved around restlessly for a space, the instrument in his hand not only clicking in a broken rhythm as he turned this way and that, but giving forth a glow which grew the brighter as the daylight failed.

At last he dropped down between Jofre and Taynad. "We must be closer than I reckoned." He was hissing as he did when excited and the stir of his neck frill was constant, as if being ruffled by some wind.

"This is bad land to cross." Jofre had made his own close inspection of the edge of the way in which that guide would send them. To transverse those glasslike splinters would take time and very careful study of any path ahead.

"But—there are flowers!" Taynad pointed.

Indeed there was life here. That bristly growth which had covered the ground on the other side of the pass had changed to another kind of vegetation, closer in some ways to the tundra moss, yet with a characteristic very much its

own. This did sprout thread-thin stems, hardly as long as a finger, so lifting high small white stars of flowers which seemed to lose no color in the closing dusk but rather to glow.

Beyond a clump of these there appeared to emerge from rock itself tiny lacy fringed leaves of a faintly reddish hue. While above this display there winged minute flutterers that moved from one star flower to another, as might the night spirits of the oldest legends.

Yan was entranced, moving away from Taynad and squatting down, now and then tentatively advancing a paw hand but never quite touching the display. Jofre picked up the faint touch of wonder which the Jat emitted. Then to the guard's surprise Yan reached up and caught at his own dangling hand, while the tall-eared head moved up and right as if that pushed-in, wrinkled nose was picking up some scent. Yan scrambled up, not losing touch with Jofre, and pattered on along the rock. They came to a place where the lava wall was taller and there Yan halted and pointed with the free paw.

Whatever attracted its attention must be above. Jofre moved closer to the surface of the wall, intent on a search for any such disastrous surprises as a webbing inhabited by the round ball bodies. But there was none to be seen.

He loosed his hand from Yan's grip and pulled himself up, to discover that he was now on the edge of a cup ringed about with the star flowers in thick profusion, so thick that he was aware of a delicate scent. And they were clustered about a bowl-sized pool of what appeared to be water though there was no sign of a spring, nor could there be in this land, he thought.

They had filled their water canteens at the spring over the mountain, and he would not disturb this small pocket—nor could they be sure it might not be tainted by some mineral. But to look down upon it was like looking into a miniature garden, to his eyes nearly as beautiful as that exotic lounging place the Holder had kept.

"Come," he called softly but he need not have done so, for Yan's summons must have reached her before his and Taynad was already at the base of the wall finding a way to join him.

A moment later her shoulder brushed against his. "It—is like the Moon Garden!" she exclaimed. "Perfect—as only the things made by the true spirit can be perfect. A thing to be fixed in memory forever!"

Jofre had reached down and pulled up Yan, settling the small furred body against his as the Jat leaned forward in his hold and made a soft crooning sound which blended with what they looked upon and became a perfect part of it.

"Food, explorers—" Zurzal's hiss from below brought them back into the world of here and now and they returned to the rough base camp.

They were careful with their supplies, rationing themselves strictly, being doubly saving of the water. The Skrem had not stirred far from their own chosen places and the two Deves still sat back-to-back. If they had eaten, it was in the shadow of their cloaks, a secret business.

The off-worlders followed their now set pattern of dividing the night into thirds, one to keep watch during each. Zurzal took the first watch since he said he wished to check on both the scanner (which he would have to do by touch in this lack of light) and keep an eye on the guide.

Jofre rolled in his covering, watching the shadowy movements of the Zacathan until sleep hit and he was caught in an ever-thickening darkness.

However, there was no mindless rest awaiting him. There was a stirring—first of memories which became oddly distorted dreams and then suddenly cleared into a real pattern. Once more he lay among mountain rocks and there crept upon him an unseen enemy. He fought to still his body, to seem the soundly sleeping one until that skulker came within hand's reach—There came a fumbling at his girdle—knife—

Jofre was awake with the speed of a threatened issha in enemy territory. His left hand had shot out to tighten on the one who had come like a thief, tightened with a crushing force, and in instant reply there was a scream of pain which sounded not only in his ears but in his head.

Sharp teeth scored his flesh. He had just time to deflect the knife blow delivered by his own hand so that that blade was not buried in the small body now squirming half across his middle. Yan! But why—?

"What are you doing?" Taynad was at him now, and her long nails cut skin below his eye.

"What is this one doing?" Jofre spat in return. He was reaching his knees now and had warded off a second attack from Taynad with force enough to send her back against the astounded Zacathan.

Jofre loosed his hold on Yan with a lightning-fast move, transferring it from the Jat's wrist to the nape of its neck so that he was able to hold it away from him. But what caught his attention first was the paw he had just released, for the whole of it was now aglow—so lit that

one could see bones within the skin and flesh. And that paw was fast gripped about—

The stone! The Jat had somehow attempted to steal his secret! Why? There was one answer—Jofre glanced for only a second toward Taynad. There was more light now— he had slept past the twin moon rise and even the lava appeared to reflect some of that downward glow.

Jofre's lips flattened across his set teeth. The Jat—so in tune with this issha-trained—she must have set Yan on him.

"Give." His hand closed over that of Yan.

The Jat whimpered, shivered as if whipped around by a bitter wind, but it obeyed, releasing the stone into Jofre's grip. Some of the radiance died during that exchange, but enough was left to make it certain that what the guard now held was nothing ordinary.

"So you would have the creature thieve?" Jofre said slowly, trying to make his contempt edge each word. "What else have the Shagga ordered to be done? Am I now fair game for any Shadow?"

She brushed her hand across her mouth. Above that her eyes seemed very large and empty as if she had raised a strong barrier. He might well know that he would have no truth out of her—unless such was pertinent to the game she had been set to play. He had thought from the first that what he had found at the ancient Lair was indeed powerful, but he had not suspected that he would be hunted off-world for it.

"What is it?" The hissing of the Zacathan's voice was pronounced. He had put out an arm and steadied the girl against his body. Now he added, in a lower tone, "There are other eyes and ears here."

Jofre swallowed, called on control for the stifling of rage and, yes, the odd sense of betrayal. In all his life he had trusted very few, and the last to have his full allegiance was the dead Master. Yan whimpered again and tried to pull away and Jofre freed him but did not yet hide the stone. Why should he? They had seen it. Taynad must know very well what he carried and had been given her orders. But why had she waited so long? On Wayright she must have had countless chances for the Jat to despoil him and then she could have disappeared out of their lives, or else passed her loot on so that she would not be suspected.

"Power—warm—" The thought kindled a picture of flames in his mind; it must have done the same to Taynad. But it was to the Jat that he aimed and steadied his answering thought.

"Why—take—" He wanted to scream that demand; he had to school himself to shape it in mind, to throttle himself into set control so that the Jat's fear would lessen enough to allow him contact. He certainly had no desire to send the small one back into the locking nonlife which had gripped it on Tssek.

"Power—" It seemed that the creature found it impossible to advance beyond that thought. Zurzal took a hand now.

"What do you have?"

Jofre tensed but the Zacathan had every right to ask that. With the issha oath-bound to him there could be no concealment. But what did he have? He could not honestly say. Now he tried to sort out his thoughts in some form. There might well be the chance that Taynad knew more about this than he did—what would happen if it fell into

her hands and she did know how to put it to use? It heightened issha powers—it had kept him alive during his early captivity on the Tssekian ship. He felt warm, good, confident when he held it. But what was it?

"I do not know," he responded with the exact truth. "It is a finding, brought to me by chance, as I once told you. I only know that it sharpens issha powers—it is perhaps a protection of sorts."

"Where did it come from?"

"Out of Qaw-en-itter—a dead Lair—just as I said." Again Jofre gave him the truth. "I nighted there through a mountain storm—and found it by chance—"

He had heard the sharp inhale of breath from Taynad. The names of all the dead Lairs were commonly known and he had doubly damned himself by admitting he had sheltered within such disaster-darkened walls.

Now the Zacathan looked toward the girl. "What is it?"

Jofre awaited her answer eagerly. He believed he could separate false from true if she tried to evade a flat answer.

"It—it seems a Lair stone—or a part of one," she answered in a strange voice, as if she inwardly did doubt the truth of her own words. "It—is Assha—"

Jofre's hand jerked, almost the glowing stone slipped between his fingers. If she spoke the truth, and surely she did as she saw it, then—then what was he? All knew that Assha power was a fortune-gift and that it came after long searching. When a Lair Master died and the stone of that still lived it was the stone itself that selected the next Master—the one it warmed to would be its voice. But that was also a dangerous trial—would-be Assha had been known to be blasted, fire-seared, when they assayed that chance.

This could only be a fraction of the Lair stone that had been. Perhaps its power was lessened by the lack of size, the fact it was not properly set in place. Yet he could not truthfully deny to himself now that what he felt when he held it was a welcoming, not condemnation of some reckless and overambitious action.

"May I?" Zurzal held out his one hand.

For a moment Jofre hesitated. It was as if the thing clung to him. But he allowed it to slip from his hold into the Zacathan's. The glow which it had shown faded as might fire sinking into ash. Zurzal held it closer to his eyes. His frill lifted and his dark tongue flickered out almost as if he wished to taste what he held.

"Radiation, yes." He turned it around slowly. "Of what kind—who can tell? Part of a Lair stone—"

"Part of a Lair stone," Jofre repeated firmly and glanced again at Taynad. "Did they lay oath on you—against me—to bring that back? The Shagga are jealous of the stones—they cannot use them—only the Masters can—and no Shagga can be assha—they walk another road. I do not claim to be a Master—nor Assha. But, see you!" He plucked the stone away from Zurzal and it glowed again. "Would you?"

Now he deliberately held it out to Taynad. She shook her head. "It is a thing of ill fortune out of a place accursed. I do not know why it should answer to any true issha—"

"Ah, but if you have listened to the Shagga, to the story I myself told you, Shadow Sister, you would know that I am not deemed true issha—my rights have been stripped from me—"

He had spread his palm, the stone resting flat upon it.

It was as if the heart of its dull red there held a sturdy core of fire—not blazing as it had when the Jat laid paw on it, but alive as it had not been in the Zacathan's hold.

"What task have they laid on you?" Jofre swept swiftly back to his original demand. "My death—the taking of this? And this little one—Yan is your tool?"

"No!" She shook her head and that tightly braided hair loosened somewhat. "I did not set Yan on you this night! It tried to tell me that you have some power; I think it wished to prove it to me. Yes, the Shagga would hunt you down. They have out their nets." She raised one hand and pulled at the fore of her braid loop, freeing the twigs. "They have given orders—"

Jofre stepped back a pace. He crooked his finger and Yan obeyed. Into the Jat's forepaws he dropped the stone.

"I take no advantage," he said. "What would you? Knives by choice?"

It had come so suddenly—though, yes, he had had his suspicions of her. But somehow he had never guessed that it would end in blade against blade. They were probably evenly matched enough—since they must keep to the single weapon agreed upon—and she was issha-trained. Also the knife was the first weapon for the Sisters, even as the sword or spear might be for the Brothers.

"Stop!" Zurzal was between them. "You are oathed to me," he added sharply to Jofre. "While that oath holds you are not allowed to seek a private quarrel. Is that not part of the oathing?"

"For issha—yes," Jofre returned slowly. "But now it is said I am not issha—otherwise the Sister would not take mission against me."

"I refuse to accept such a quibble," Zurzal hissed. His frill, flushing darkly, was a fan behind his head. "You are my oathed. And you," he looked now to Taynad, "I did not oath you but you accepted a bargain—were you already then playing another game? Had you taken oath to bring down this man?"

Slowly the girl shook her head. "No, Learned One, when I said I would come with you they had not sent any message to me. It was only afterward—"

"I have heard much of issha honor on Asborgan," Zurzal continued. "No, I did not formally oath you to my service, Taynad. But you accepted my offer freely. Does one need a ritual to keep full faith?"

Jofre saw her tongue tip show between her set lips. The heavy lids nearly veiled her eyes and for a moment she was silent as one who weighs one matter against another.

"Learned One, what I accepted I shall keep to for as long as this venture lasts—"

Jofre's hand moved away from the hilt of his knife. So until another day this would go unsettled. But he also knew well that issha word was unbending; she would hold only to a truce and that for the time the Zacathan would set.

"We had better settle down," Zurzal said, "before some of our companions grow interested and come to see what we are doing. I think none of us would want them to know about that." And he pointed to what blazed brightly in the Jat's hold. Swiftly Jofre recovered his treasure and tucked it away into hiding.

"I take the watch," he said, knowing that he could not sleep now, not until he had thought, weighed, and decided all he could about the days ahead.

# ✳ CHAPTER 29 ✳

**HOWEVER,** morning light found him with no true decision. What he could foresee was only what concerned his own actions; he could not know what Taynad might think or do. Realizing this, Jofre forced the whole matter to the back of his mind. What lay before them now was another kind of action. He had mistrusted this ragged land from the start and to work their way across it might well be beyond what any living thing—without wings—could do.

The Skrem broke their own camp and herded their beasts down to be packed by the off-worlders, the Deves still holding themselves apart, though keeping a close eye, Jofre noted, on both parties. There was a suggestion in this that they were not altogether ready to play trail comrades with the Skrem.

Though Zurzal's guide pointed out into those knife-edged ridges, he did not lead in that direction, rather paced a little south, pausing often to check on the com he held. Perhaps with other knowledge he had not shared with them he had some idea there was a way into this stark

country which could be taken on foot. Though Jofre remembered that the party whose directions they now depended upon had come by flitter and so had not had to face that impossible terrain.

The ranges of massed lava about them took on color as the sun arose. Those patches of small growth on them were in vivid contrast, but the small flowers which had greeted the night seemed now to be tightly closed. It was indeed a weird country, for the rock in places seemed to have been worked into faces which grinned, or grimaced, or gaped widely at passersby.

Out of their whole company the Jat seemed the most at ease for some reason. Its usual timidity had vanished and from where it rode perched before Taynad it made eager gestures and murmurs which sometimes sounded like small muted cries. Jofre began to wonder about the world from which Yan had been stolen—had it borne some resemblance to this riven countryside so that the Jat felt it had come home?

Suddenly the Zacathan brought his mount to a halt with a jerk on its horns, swung it around to face into the lava stretch. The com was giving forth a sharp series of notes, so close together they almost formed a kind of scream.

"Here—we strike cross-country here."

He said that as if he were suggesting no more than they cross one of the thoroughfares of Wayright. But there was certainly no road ahead—only a round wall which rose well above their heads. Zurzal swung off the beast, which snorted as if registering a strong protest to what it now faced.

"A foot march—over there? We cannot push the beasts into it!" Jofre moved up beside him.

"No other way. Let's take a look." He slipped the cord attached to one end of the com over his head and started to climb. Jofre was prompt to follow. Taynad had moved in at their backs, and, for now, he believed he could depend upon her to see that none of the natives would interfere without warning.

The porous material over which they scrambled had hand and footholds enough, but they had to be very wary of the cutting edges of broken-off pieces. Luckily it was not a long ordeal and when Jofre pulled up beside the already standing Zacathan he stared out on something he had not expected.

Through some ancient level of the land here the flow of the lava had narrowed into a river. Beyond that was another kind of rock, darker in color, not showing the threat of the broken edges. The distance between them and that island was not too wide to be spanned, though they would have to take great care in their going, perhaps somehow fashioning extra covers for hands and feet, or provide an advance guard to chop out the worst of the edges. It could be done, and for the first time Jofre saw that Zurzal was not totally brain-twisted by his desire to reach that goal.

On returning to the edge of the flow below they reported to Skrem and Deves what they had discovered.

"This you search for—it lies there?" I'On demanded.

In answer Zurzal had simply held forward the com, so that they could all catch its chatter, which was now steady.

"The ochs cannot go." The Skrem indicated their mounts.

"That is so. We must go on foot, carrying with us what is needful. But what we would find is not in the fields of

broken rock, it is on firm and older land." The Zacathan spoke with the authority of one who might well have seen exactly what he was describing.

"We think—" I'On made a gesture and withdrew, the rest of the Skrem close with him. They squatted in a circle some distance away, and Jofre could hear no sound from them. However, he did not doubt they were in debate over Zurzal's plan for the venture on foot.

It was one of the robed Deves who came up to the Zacathan now.

"Only the mad walk the Shattered Land." His shrill voice formed words via the translator. "Why do you urge death on us—take it upon yourself?"

Zurzal waved his hand toward the wall of the flow. "Climb and see. There are islands in the flow—it is not all as you see it before you here."

For a moment it looked as if the Deve would do just that—climb to see for himself. But then he wheeled quickly and swung up on the mount his fellow, already on his own beast, had herded toward him.

Without any other answer the two started away. The knot of Skrem broke apart and scrambled toward their own beasts, as if fearing the creatures might follow the two which the Deves bestrode. Their chittering reached the height of screams as they swung up to follow the runaways.

"That," commented Zurzal after a moment, "seems to be that. At least we still have the supplies."

Jofre wondered what good the small amount they had brought with them would do if they were left without transportation. On the other hand it might well be that

I'On and his fellows would catch the Deves and return. There was no way they, the three of them, could aid or hinder that chase at present. And he fell to checking over the woven containers which held all the equipment they had been able to assemble.

They made up three packs of the main essentials. Zurzal had used a knife and cut from his suit the half-empty sleeve covering his regrowing left arm. It was in length now a little past the elbow of his right one and the fingers of the hand on that side, when he flexed them, seemed to be as ready for work as those of his right. It was that miniature left hand which steadied the scanner in its web carrier.

Jofre had taken as much of the foodstuff and concentrates as he could crowd in his pack and knew he could shoulder. And Taynad worked with him putting together a burden of her own. His last addition was a roll of sleep coverings which he knotted into a rope, the other end of which he could tie to his weapons belt and carry up with him.

The Jat jumped to the side of the Zacathan as they began their climb—there had been no sign nor sound of the return of their fellow travelers. And it was Yan who had a ready paw to steady the scanner and aid the heavily laden Zurzal to make the top.

Once there Jofre jerked up the bundle of coverings and they all three set to work slitting them into strips and binding them thickly, not only around their own feet but around those of the Jat also, for with their other burdens they could not hope to carry Yan across that strip of lava flow ready and waiting to saw to pieces any flesh unaware enough to trust foot to it.

It was taking them a long time; the sun was well along towards setting. Jofre wanted to make that rock point which offered all the safety they could hope for before darkness closed in. Moonlight—under the two moons of Lochan, which whirled in orbit around each other as they passed—would not be enough to lighten all the pitfalls.

They selected what they believed was the narrowest of that anciently frozen flow and started their wavering path, for they could not keep to a straight line across it. As it was, the extra covering shredded from their feet, and they had to keep their pace to a crawl.

But there comes an end to every trial, Jofre thought thankfully, when at last he could put out a hand and touch the rock of the spur the flow had not engulfed. Again they must climb, first squatting to loose the tattered coverings from their feet and making sure that their packs were roped well together to be lifted once they had reached the top.

The Jat took the lead, again flapping its large ears and uttering cries as if it recognized the place, something of its exuberance urging them on. Then they were safely aloft and looking out into a stretch of country where the Shattered Land was not what it had been called.

They had reached a height and that widened out into a vast plateau where the fury of the mountain fire had not left any such scars as it had below. To the north, a little aslant of what might be the center of this open stretch of rock, gravelly sand, and a few stubborn patches of the yellow tundra grass, was a hill, the crown of which had been flattened off except for some humps here and there. It had a different look to it than the other heights around—as if it

had not come directly from the shaping of nature by wind and time.

The sound of the Zacathan's trail guide was now a steady drone and he headed out towards that hillock with the certain stride of someone knowing exactly where he was going. Nor had they been led astray, for, as they neared the truncated cone, they saw that the tundra grass had withered patches, that there were small heaps of the turf which had been peeled back so that the ground below could be trenched and trenched it had been, in narrow ditches. These no longer stood out clearly, for it was plain that they had been exposed to the weather for some time, but Jofre recognized the site as it had appeared on one dim tape. This was the doomed camp of the expedition which had made the first discovery.

It was only seconds later that they were fully shown what had happened. There were a series of rocks placed in a half circle about the edges of those ditches and mounted on each rough base formed by one of those was a skull. And they seemed to grin with a ghastly promise as the off-worlders drew near.

There were no other signs of any visitors—no remains of any camp structure if there had been such. Nor, as Jofre discovered as he circled the eerie site, any other signs of other bones. But not far beyond the ditches with their ghostly guardians there was a sinking of the plain which occurred abruptly and could not be sighted until one was almost on it.

Where the rest of the plateau stretching so far about them suggested a desert country, this slash in the rock allowed them to gaze down into a narrow file as different

from the land above as one planet might differ from another.

There was a thick growth of fleshy-leaved plants, large near their first rooting at the foot of the rise, dwindling in size as they climbed. The leaves each grew in a rosette which was centered by a thick red stem—the leaves being a sickly yellow-green. And on the stem was a trumpet-shaped growth which might be a bloom yet certainly gave no pleasure to the eye.

What was more important was that these plant beds bordered a stream of dark water—at least it seemed to flow like water, if a little sluggishly. Though, Jofre decided, they would hold off testing it as long as possible. There was something about this dank seam in the earth which repelled.

Dusk would soon be upon them and they must establish some type of camp. The threat of the skulls was ominous enough to make them sure they should select a site which they could defend—against what—or whom—they could not be sure.

They found the best cover the countryside had to offer farther on towards the cone hill where there were small bumps in the ground and Jofre, with a scout's trained eye, picked out three such which could form a rough triangle, their pack gear and stones dragged up to give some seeming of walls, low as those had to be.

Even Yan helped with the dragging of stones, and pawed up sods of the tundra grass to plaster between the loose rocks. They worked as fast as they could, though they tried to make certain they did not scant any loophole. A small fire, set in a hollow scooped in their rude for-tress,

could not be sighted across the plain top—though it would be visible from the hillock but to that he had no answer.

However, the night winds were chill enough that they must have a measure of heat. To keep that cup of flame alive during the night would be one of the duties of the sentry. And they carried to pile against one of their shelter rocks dried vines which crisscrossed the tundra growth and were thick enough to be broken into respectable sticks.

Once more they ate their limited rations slowly. Zurzal sat with the scanner between his outstretched legs, his good hand more occupied with examining that than by conveying the ration strips to his mouth. Jofre chewed as he squatted by another of their chosen boulders, staring out across that ill-omened stretch of trenches and the guardian skulls, back across the country they had come.

If the Skrem and the Deves, he thought with a resigned logic, really wanted to be rid of them, all they need do was to leave them marooned here. There was no way he could see that they would ever be able to make a return journey. Twice he was nearly moved to say that aloud but then decided that his own dire predictions must indeed be shared by all of them since they possessed the intelligence of sentient beings—even the Jat must feel that they must have indeed come to the end of the trail.

Still Yan had the perkiness of one at home with the surroundings. Earlier it had surveyed the skulls round-eyed and Jofre had been able to pick up a glimmer of disgust from the creature's mind. But there was no shadow of fear.

"Tomorrow"—Zurzal gave the scanner a final pat as if it were a pet animal ready to offer good service—"we need wait no longer. Tomorrow!" There was exultation in his

voice and his frill waved and stiffened, dark color flooding up through its ribbing.

Neither Jofre nor Taynad made answer. They were concerned with more than just tomorrow—the time which stretched beyond that. It might serve Zurzal completely that he prove for all time his contention was right—the ancient and unknown past might be made clear, recorded for the reading of others—but they were still engaged in living and preparing to continue that state.

Jofre took first watch. The Zacathan did not seem prepared to either settle down to rest or put himself to camp routine. He had edged out into the night as Jofre crouched tensely trying to follow his movements, as well as pick up any threat which might lie hid. Back and forth along those trenches Zurzal had strode, the com in his hand, until at last he seemed to find some point he had been hunting and stood there for some time.

There was something about that hillock which was now a backdrop for their own camp which kept nudging at Jofre. He had absorbed enough of the time scanted instructions the Zacathan had given on Wayright and during their flight to Lochan to believe that that rise might indeed hide ruins, part of a city or a single fortress. Yet those who had come here had not delved there but rather dug their trenches at its foot.

It was a place which could be defended—against anything but an air attack. Between quick glances at the Zacathan to make sure that he was safe, the guard began to set himself the problem of how that rise might be made to serve them best should those who collected skulls come to see what stirred here now.

Zurzal had returned when Jofre reached over to touch Taynad's shoulder, signal her for second guard duty. The double moons gave strange light to this barren country—it was wholly alien and more to be mistrusted for that.

"There is a watcher," she whispered. "Yan knows. See."

Her gritty fingers touched the back of the hand Jofre had reached to awaken her. And he did understand. The sending was very dim, but it was there. They were indeed under observation.

"Yan will know," she said. "Rest while you can."

Mistrust rippled in his mind and he repelled it. With her promise to the Zacathan she meant no ill, nor would she deliver any attack until she formally ended that courtesy tie. He could rely that she and the Jat would do just as he had been doing—stand guard.

So they won through to day again. Taynad reported that the watcher had withdrawn sometime in the early predawn and that the Jat had shown no fear concerning it.

They had to insist that Zurzal eat—he was as a child before a feast day—so eager to be at what he would do that nothing else mattered. With Jofre's help the scanner was once more mounted and then there was a tedious space of waiting as the Zacathan applied measurements and adjustments, making sure that the instrument aimed directly down, not across the central one of those ditches.

# ✳ CHAPTER 30 ✳

**THEY WERE NOT PREPARED** for what came with less warning than a mountain storm. The sound tore through the brazen sky, something totally foreign to this place which had so been forgotten by time.

A shadow swept over the plateaus like a giant Kag preparing to dive on prey—though that airborne craft did not indeed skim as close to them as the sound suggested.

Jofre had thrown himself flat, taking Zurzal down with him, half covering the Zacathan's body with his own. He was prepared in one instant of recognition to feel the sear of laser fire catching them both.

But the flitter's occupants had not taken their advantage and the aircraft swept on, over the hump of the cone—northward. They had been such easy prey that Jofre could not believe for an instant or two that they seemed to have been ignored.

It was a screaming cry from the Jat which brought him up to his knees, half-slewed around. Yan was pulling at Taynad, striving to drag her from where she had prudently

gone prone at the passing of the flitter, toward them. Why became understandable almost immediately.

The edge of that cut which bisected the plateau suddenly had developed a series of humps along its edge, moving things which flowed up and over as if they were part of some giant flood imprisoned below and determined now to be free.

Sword-knife in one hand, the barbed length of chain in the other, Jofre tried to settle his weight evenly, be prepared to meet that dash. The Zacathan had drawn his stunner but against this wave that would be little good. Taynad moved in, the Jat leaping up and down at her side and screaming. It stooped to scrabble up an armload of stones, nursing those against its small body as potential weapons.

The creatures from the chasm resembled Skrem—but of a different kind than those who had companied with them earlier. These were larger; they did not ride but scuttled at a speed which hardly seemed possible toward the beleaguered off-worlders.

The Zacathan's weapon hissed and the first line of the charge twisted and went down, frozen in the cords of stass. However, that was only a portion of those arranged against them.

Jofre's eyes narrowed, he measured distances, the footing before him, and then with the ear-splitting, heart-stopping cry of the issha, he went into action, meeting the first three of those who had tramped over their kind with the whirling hooked chain. One of those hooks caught under the edge of the helmetlike head covering of the foremost, and the force of the swing whirled the native off his feet, smashing him into his closest fellow.

Jofre was back in a crouch. The tip of his knife had caught the third at the point where a human would have had a chin and sent it down as cleanly as the chain had taken the others.

A rock flew past Jofre to strike another Skrem flat on the head so it staggered and fell. Then another and another such projectile flew with skillful aim. It was not only Yan who was the marksman. Taynad had joined him, proving herself an expert with even such crude weapons. Still they came.

Zurzal had had time to thumb another charge into his hand weapon and this he now discharged, adding to the line of motionless bodies.

The Skrem had made no sound when they attacked; only Jofre's cry had broken the silence. Now they could hear again the beat of the flitter engine. Jofre's shoulders stiffened. They had them at their mercy, those in the flitter, for he was very sure that the crew of that was not coming to their rescue.

Yet, it would seem that he had been wrong. The Skrem milled around on the edge of the cut, now forming another attack line. Yan was screaming again, jumping up, trying to catch at the Zacathan's maimed arm, draw his attention. Zurzal attempted to fend off the Jat and still keep his weapon poised.

Once more the flitter banked, withdrew towards the hillock, and the wild Skrem gathered. How many charges they could hold off Jofre dared not try to guess. He believed he did know what those in the flitter had in mind—the wearing down, even the death of him and his companions, whereupon they could move in and take what

they wanted. Yet surely those aloft must have superior arms on board—why this cat-and-mouse play with them and the wild Skrem? Except perhaps that they needed Zurzal to operate the machine and so were willing to keep their attackers at bay for now lest they destroy the scanner.

The Jat turned away from Zurzal and threw itself at the scanner while Zacathan, with a hissing cry, his neck frill an engorged crimson, clutched vainly after him. But the maneuver of the Jat brought the Zacathan's hand down on the controls.

There was a sound which drowned out the flitter. Jofre saw that machine tremble in the air, dip sidewise, as if its equilibrium was disturbed. Color, sound burst from behind. Jofre, by the very weight of that blow on his ears, was pushed against one of the rocks which had been part of their shelter for the night. It took some seconds for his eyes to adjust to the flow of images, so merged one with the other that it was difficult to see any one clearly. There appeared to be beings mounted and riding. Someone dressed not unlike the Axe was haranguing a mob of people into which the mounted warriors flowed and comingled— then the whole scene began to flicker at the edges—

Jofre was half knocked from his place by the thud of a small body against him. He threw out an arm to fend the Jat off, still so bemused by that swirl of pictures before him that he did not defend himself fully against that scrabbling paw.

Yan was gone, swallowed up by the play of pictures in the air fanning out farther and farther from the center point of the cone hill which was no longer that, but a great, towered keep more imposing than the largest of the Lairs.

The—the stone—the stone was gone! Jofre stumbled away from the rock support. Yan had taken his stone. Then—

There was no more change, weaving, misting about what he was watching. Instead it steadied into a clear stretch of a different world. The mounted warriors charged the crowd gathered around the priest. People who resembled the maned natives of the present produced weapons from beneath their robes, cut at the mounts, dragged riders like the Skrem from their beasts.

It was so real! Jofre edged closer to the rock and felt a body beside him. Taynad's breath came fast against his cheek. Forgotten was the attack from the chasm beasts. There was certainly no flitter in the air over this battle which they watched rage back and forth across a city so long lost that there was not even a dim memory of it left.

From the towered citadel issued more troops—these on foot. They were real, three-dimensional. Jofre could see them as well as if he had been there on the day when all this had happened.

Footmen fought footmen; those who were the priest's followers showed such ferocity one could only believe that they had good reason to hate the fortress guard. There were leaders standing out among them now. The priest was swept from his command position by a red-maned warrior who was a woman! Jofre could hear ancient screams, echoing from so far down the corridors of time that they were but whispers.

On and on it went. Then there was the seeming of a curtain which dropped between them and that wild scene. Figures moved within that mist but not so violently, and it

seemed to Jofre that they did not war—that the struggle was perhaps now ended or else time had jumped and it had not yet begun.

There were clearings of that curtain now and then but only for very short periods of time, just enough to give hints of a city fallen into decay. Afterwards strangers unlike any Jofre had seen on Lochan moved through those crumbling ruins. Until at last there was a final flicker and once more they were in the ruins under the heavy sun.

Zurzal knelt by the scanner, his hand out to the machine, not quite touching it. His frill seemed made of iridescent color, as if one emotion mingled with another to set it so agleam. His eyes were on the stretch of country before him as if they still saw all which had swirled there.

"Sssssssseee, sssseee—" his voice was a jubilant hiss.

However, Jofre had pulled Taynad around so that they both faced, not the country across which that picture had brought life, but the edge of the chasm. Those Skrem who had been brought down, either by Zurzal's weapon or their own efforts, still lay there. One or two not locked into stass were crawling towards the tip of the cut. For the rest—they were gone even as if they had also been swept away by the winds of the past.

"It—it was the Lair stone—" Taynad's voice was uneven, she breathed as one who had been running. "Did you not see—Yan, the Lair stone—the Jat took it—put it in the scanner for power. How did it know what to do? Why the Lair stone?"

She looked to Jofre as might a child who needed some answer to an important question.

Yan squatted still by the scanner. As the Zacathan, the

Jat was staring out to the dregs of the past. Jofre had no answer for her. Yan had been fascinated by the stone, he had sensed it in Jofre's possession before he had ever tried to take it in the night. But why had the creature known that it must be fitted into the scanner? How much had Yan ever understood about their quest and what they wanted to do here?

"Yan knows more than we can tell. He has his own reasons—perhaps sometime he will share those with us—"

She had gotten only so far when they heard again the sound of the flitter beat—coming out of the north. To bring on them again the horde from the chasm?

Certainly those in the flitter had done nothing to help them ward off the attack from the chasm; therefore, they were not to be depended upon now.

"Down—take cover—" Jofre had just time to shout that warning when the Jat streaked at a speed they had never seen it produce before, straight for the guard. Yan leaped, aiming for his head and shoulders. This was an attack for which the man had in no way been prepared. At the same time he staggered backward, trying to claw with one hand to free himself from the furry body pressed close enough to blind him, the forepaws which enwrapped his neck, there came another blow.

Jofre whirled around, fighting to keep his feet, but his bones might have softened in an instant. He crumpled to the ground, half bouncing off a rock. But even that encounter failed to scrape the Jat away and its body was now a lump-load on his chest. The guard found it sheer agony to get a breath, and he realized that, for the second

time, he had taken a bolt from a stass stunner, leaving him easy prey for any attack.

He did not lose consciousness; though, for a period of time he could not measure, he strove somehow to shift the body of Yan, hoping that would let him breathe easier. The fact that he did have some small movement in his neck was a faint promise that he could do this. Had the Jat taken to itself part of the charge of that weapon, thus giving Jofre the slimmest of chances? But again, how did the creature—?

"Be still—not move—" the thought struck into his mind. Yan's head was squeezed a little down so that the Jat's forehead pressed against Jofre's. The contact—could it be what aided their transfer of thought?

He had managed to edge his head around a fraction, something he certainly could not have done had he taken the full force of the ray. Now he could breathe—and hear—

But he could not see, save for a hair-fringed, tiny slit of what was beyond. The Zacathan's boots were within that very limited range of vision and that was all. Now—he must fight in his own way, as he had aboard the Tssekian ship, call upon his inner strength. And this time he lacked the Lair stone to amplify what powers he could summon.

The drone of the flitter was very loud; the craft must be setting down somewhere near. They had not stassed Zurzal for some reason. Taynad—? Apparently the Jat was not unconscious. It might well be as locked as he into helplessness of body but its mind was alert. Could he somehow reach Taynad through that furry head resting against his own?

"Learned One," it was a strange voice, speaking trade tongue, "you are to be congratulated on a most impressive display from your invention—or discovery—or whatever you claim it to be. We were duly made aware of just what this discovery has to offer—for our purposes, of course."

Zurzal's boots had not moved in that narrow slit of sight allowed Jofre.

"One success does not make for a continued series of them—" the hissing note in the Zacathan's answer had the fury of a reptilian arousal. "You play games, let us come to the point. I take it you are Guild."

"But of course," the smooth voice returned. "We tried to discuss matters with you some time back but it appears that you are a very stubborn lizard, Learned One. It was then decided that, until we had real proof of what you were able to do, we would just wait and see. We even helped you along the way—Gosal's ship was ready when you needed transportation, and if you had not won out of Tssek through your own efforts, we had plans to assist you there also. Yes, we have a number of work hours tied up in you and your affairs, Learned One. Now it is time to collect payment."

"Take the scanner if you wish," Zurzal returned. Jofre could see a slight movement as if he shifted weight from one foot to the other. "It will do you no good. That summoning of the past you saw burned out the charge."

"Oh, but surely that can be easily corrected. You yourself, Learned One, will be only too glad to lend your full assistance."

"I hardly think so," Zurzal returned.

"You are a master of knowledge—or so you Zacathans claim. But do not underrate others. We have our sources

also. I think you will be most eager to give us any aid within your power. Opgor, let us have a demonstration of your marksmanship."

Jofre could not mistake the crackle of a blaster. He saw those two firmly planted feet tremble, totter out of his line of sight. And there was a smell—the smell of cooked meat.

A hissing like that of a snake about to strike.

"Excellent beam control, Opgor. Now, Learned One, you may not have the use of that right hand of yours, and your other is not much good. But you can direct others in providing the agile fingers needed. Also—understand this, we know very well that if you cannot be provided with the proper regeneration treatment in time you are NOT going to regrow that one. So your cooperation is necessary. It really is very simple, isn't it? We shall see that you have proper accommodations and tending just as long as you give us in exchange some of the vaunted knowledge of yours.

"And it will not be limited to just the use of your scanner. Oh, no, a chance such as this comes perhaps once in a being's lifetime. You will provide our information experts with the sites of suitable delvings for the future. You see, in the end, the game is ours."

"Is it?" Taynad—what was she doing using that voice, addressing this Guild leader as she would a lesser servant?

"We have not indeed forgotten you, my dear. Guild bargains hold. You have been dispatched to ensnare one of your own kind—though a traitor. He is freely yours and in such condition that you will not have to worry about any guards. You will be lifted from here, returned to the port with your catch. Gosal shall again obey orders and see that you and this lump of meat will be returned to Wayright.

What happens beyond that, I leave to your own people. We have done as we were paid to do."

"It would seem, Veep," the Taynad Jofre could not see answered, "that you have taken into consideration every point except one. Your knowledge may run deep but I do not think that it encompasses the oaths of the issha breed. I gave the Learned One my promise to be one with him until this adventure was finished—"

"It is finished." There was a note of impatience in that. "The lizard has done what he desired—proved the usefulness of this time reader of his. Therefore, you are now freed. We will proceed as planned—"

"The lizard—Lord Rang—he is dying!"

Those words were like a jolt—as sharp a jolt of fear and energy as any the Assha stone had ever delivered. Jofre reached for strength from the Center, and that responded. He knew he could move again, but how greatly would the stass hinder that movement? He could only test it by the swiftest action he could summon.

His arm swept under the Jat's flaccid body.

"No watch now—" Those three words fed Jofre's energy another, if shorter, jolt. They believed him entirely out of the picture. Well, they would discover what an issha could do to revenge his oath!

There was a babble of voices to which he closed his ears. That rock he had slid down against at the first attack gave him a solid base against which he shifted now. Then he flung aside the Jat and was up, his back to the stone. And he had been right! Their attackers were gathered some distance away about a body on the ground and one of them knelt beside it, an open medical kit to hand.

Taynad? She was in the midst of them, Zurzal's frilled head on her knee. But her eyes sought farther afield—found Jofre. He tensed—she would cry out—

He had already picked his man. By the clothing and the way orders sprouted from him, this was the leader. His back was to Jofre, whom they had totally dismissed from their minds.

The guard inched forward. Had he been able to throw off all the effects of the stass, he might well have gone into action. However, his arms and legs did not respond to the orders his raging mind gave. Rage—anger—it was fuel, it could burn away doubts, increase energy if it were so used. Jofre allowed, in a sudden snap of control, his rage to flare.

He was behind that Guild leader, the clawed chain out, about the man's throat, its hooks biting into the other's thick flesh.

"Now," Jofre said in a set, quiet voice, "there is a new payment, life for life. You die, brother of all evil."

# ✴ CHAPTER 31 ✴

**"BLOOD PRICE—"**
They had frozen as if a stass had taken them all, though
they did not collapse. Jofre tightened hold with his left
hand on the chain, though he was not yet ready to supply
the final twist. His right flashed around and gripped the
blaster in his captive's holster, flicking it out into the
open.

One of that group of four about the prone Zacathan
rolled and was on his feet, running towards the flitter. Jofre
fired. A scream which tore the air was his answer. That
would-be escape ended with a sobbing, screeching body
rolling on the earth, beating at smoldering clothing.

The man Jofre held jerked, and then uttered a cry of
his own as one of the hooks tore into his flesh. He who had
tried for the flitter now lay quiet.

"Blood price—" Jofre repeated and his voice seemed
battle shrill in the heavy silence.

Taynad moved, setting Zurzal's head gently aside. As
she pulled up to her feet her hand skimmed along the side

of the man beside her, neatly disarming him. Jofre waited.
He could kill now with one twist of his wrist and burn down
those others in a wide-armed sweep, but such would take
in Taynad.

She held her own weapon steady but did not try to aim
at Jofre. Perhaps she did not dare, for, even as she crisped
him, she would be destroying also the leader he held.

"Drop your weapons!" It was she who said that and the
blaster was on the other three.

Perhaps the precarious position of their leader might
not have brought such instant obedience, but the fact that
they, too, were now within range of a blast which could not
miss made them indeed draw their weapons and drop them
to the ground.

"Kick them—" Jofre took a quick hand in the game,
though he was not yet sure by which rules Taynad was
playing—"out!"

That man who had continued to kneel by the Zacathan
with the medical kit picked his sidearm up by the barrel
and hurled it in Jofre's direction. The other kicked as
ordered, sending his weapons in the same direction.

Taynad turned again to the man she had already
disarmed. Still holding the blaster at ready, her other hand
grabbed at his dangling arm, ran down the sleeve there and
now held a knife by the blade. This she tossed after the
blasters.

"There is no blood price yet." For the first time she
addressed Jofre directly. "The Learned One still lives—if
that one can keep life in his body." She nodded toward the
one with the medic's bag.

"Do so," Jofre snapped. At the same time he brought

the barrel of the blaster around behind the ear of the man he held in the chain noose. That one crumpled so suddenly that he nearly took Jofre down with him before the guard could loosen his grasp.

He stood over that unconscious prisoner for a moment, eyeing Taynad. But she was no longer looking in his direction; her attention was all for the two men she covered with her blaster.

Jofre dared believe that, at least for now, they were on the same side. He used the chain for another purpose, in spite of the cruelty of the embedded hooks, and fastened the wrists of his captive securely behind him before dragging them down so that the hooks on the other end could be caught firmly in the boots, leaving the other's body arched as a bow.

With that one as secure as he could make him, the guard rounded one of the rocks to the side of the man from whose sleeve Taynad had dislodged the hidden knife. A blow delivered with the edge of his hand sent that one sprawling and his own belt was used to truss him up.

That left the medic, but Taynad was standing over him now as he worked on the Zacathan. Jofre saw that charred stump and his breath hissed between his teeth as if he shared some of Zurzal's reptilian blood.

"I guard," he told the girl. "There is Yan—"

"Yes," she agreed but she did not put away the blaster. With that still swinging in one hand she hurried to that small brown form curled at the foot of the rock.

"You!" Jofre demanded attention from the medic who had been keeping his head down, working quickly and, Jofre thought, with practiced skill at the Zacathan's burn.

Perhaps, seeing who he companioned with, he had plenty of skill in such matters.

"Tell me," the guard demanded, "what can you do to bring the Jat out of stass?"

"For humanoids there is an injection," the man answered, though he did not look up. "Whether that will work for a Jat—who knows?" He shrugged.

"You for one had better," Jofre said. He watched the last of the elastic casing applied to Zurzal's wound and then he gestured to the Jat. "Be about your business there now."

Zurzal slowly opened his large eyes. They did not seem to focus on Jofre, but before him, straight up into the sky. "The legions rode—" he said and his frill fluttered, save for where the weight of his head pinned it to the ground. "The legions of the lost rode—we saw them."

Jofre went down on one knee. "We did, Learned One. No man can now say that you are a fool—for we have seen the past alive because of you." He did not know why he chose those words, only they seemed to come without summoning as what must be said now.

"What—I am—" His right arm trembled, raised, and he turned his head that he might look down the length of his body to survey that wound of horror.

"You are alive, Learned One. And they are prisoners."

"But—you were in stass—"

"The Jat—it put itself between—now—" Jofre looked beyond Zurzal to where Taynad held Yan within the crook of one arm while the medic readied an infusion punch against the furred upper limb now dropping so limply over Taynad's knee. "Now, that medic of theirs tries revival."

"Little one—" Not words of voice, words of mind—Taynad's mind.

Jofre moved again to the girl's side. He no longer had the Assha stone; did that mean that he could give no more aid? He could only try. But he laid the blaster well within reach as he took Taynad into his hold much as she had the Jat.

"Little one—" She was mind calling, and he added to that call as best he could. There was a passage of power between them, he could feel the flow of it. "Little one, come back to us—"

Jofre's lips shaped the same words as blazed now in his mind. His rage had been expended in the attack, so he did not have that fuel for the inner fire. But there were other emotions besides rage. Yan had offered himself for a life shield—that was the act not of any animal Jofre knew, but the action of a man. Therefore all the emotion which could pass between battle comrades could—must come—NOW!

"Yan—dark—Yan—lost—" A trail of thought so tenuous he might almost believe it a wisp of his own imagination. But he felt Taynad seize instantly upon it as one might seize upon a rope to pull to safety some climber who had lost footing on a treacherous slope.

"Yan! Come—come—!"

At first no answer and then—yes, that line was holding. Jofre poured what power he could into their linkage, and Taynad, Taynad was a very anchor of strength!

There was a little moaning cry and Yan's head turned against the girl's shoulder.

Jofre gently withdrew his support. He felt as if he had spent long hours in the arms court, tired to weakness, near

dizzy when he tried to turn his full sight on anyone. Yet—
there was much to be done.

Somehow he got on his feet and went back to Zurzal.
The Zacathan had managed to use his growing left arm and
hand to lever himself to a sitting position and now he
stretched that small fist of immature fingers toward the
scanner.

Jofre looked beyond. The man he had burned down lay
in a patch of charred tundra grass—the flitter near him.
They had three captives on their hands—perhaps it might
be well to put the medic in bonds too—and they had the
flitter.

But suppose they were to load their prisoners and
themselves on that? He was no flitter pilot, he doubted very
much that Taynad had such training—and certainly Zurzal,
even if he knew how to manage the controls, could not do
so now. Also, supposing that fortune was to favor them very
wildly, and they managed to make the flight back to the
port—that might well mean they would simply be walking
into a trap. On Lochan he could not help but believe that
they were without any friends.

Something dangerous and foolhardy might be done
using at least the leader of this expedition as a bargaining
point but at present Jofre could not see his way into such a
maze. He would have to know the value of his captive and
whom he was going to have to bargain with. Certainly none
of the prisoners would voluntarily supply him with that
information.

It was now the time to reckon up just what their
resources were. He looked to Taynad still cradling the
Jat, though he noted that she kept one hand near her

blaster and one eye on the medic, who appeared very busy fitting various things into the bag on the ground between them.

So sweeping was Jofre's gaze that he caught sight again of that wave of Skrem out of the chasm. Their bodies were still inert. But how they could handle the stass he could not tell. Perhaps, being of another species, they were dead when exposed to even the low wave Zurzal's weapon used.

Also he saw but four in the Guild squad. Certainly no one else had issued from the flitter to counter his attack, nor had a weapon set within the craft been used to burn him down. But that did not mean that there could not be some nasty surprise waiting there.

Jofre spoke to the girl. "Those Skrem—if they rise again—"

She nodded briskly. "I shall watch, Shadow. There is also the flitter—"

"Which I shall see to now." Jofre glanced to the Zacathan, who now sat with his back against one of the rocky mounds. It was plain Zurzal had reached that position with an effort which left him panting, but his eyes were open and aware.

The two in bonds still lay quiet. Now Jofre moved in on the medic. Best make sure.

"Hands behind," he ordered.

"You haven't a chance—" The other set his bag aside and did place his hands behind his back. "They are going to come looking for us. Praspar"—he jerked a nod towards the chained man—"is to broadcast in a measured time. If they don't hear from him—" He shrugged.

Jofre did not answer. He had sacrificed most of his

girdle to be torn into strips and he made use of those well. No one was going to slip out of those.

His first assay must be to the flitter. Taynad could watch the chasm and the fringe of bodies at the edge of that. Were there any stirring she would sound the alarm.

He approached the landed craft with all the expertise of a scout exploring enemy territory, fully expecting at any moment to have some surprise confront him. The door of the cabin had been left slid well open when the squad had disembarked. He could hear no sound from within. Nor, when he reached out with that other carefully honed sense, could he pick up any suggestion that there was someone in concealment there.

Blaster in hand he made a final short dash from an angle which exposed as little of his body as he could hope and then was within, his back against the cabin wall, quick to survey all which lay about.

The accommodations were of more generous size than one would gauge from the exterior of the craft. There were six seats and behind those a space left free—perhaps meant to transport gear, though there was nothing there now.

Aimed through a small port on the right side of the first pair of seats was a piece of armament which might be either a larger form of blaster or a stunner—he half guessed the latter—and it was this which must have brought him down when the flitter came in for a landing. He had seen enough of such weapons of a smaller size that he knew the procedure for disarming the thing, and with two swift movements he did just that, rolling between his fingers the cylinder which made it workable.

There was a chatter of noise which sent him again into

a fighting half-crouch, blaster ready. The sound came from a box mounted before the same seat that the gunner must have occupied. The com—if he could only give the answer! But that was beyond him and he knew that he could not trust the medic. This was like Tssek, like much of Wayright—the machines were highly evolved—this one might even be able to report back on its own that there were difficulties. He would take no risks, no matter how slight.

Jofre brought the butt of the blaster down on the box which returned a screeching cry, as if it had indeed a life of its own, and then puffed out choking smoke which drove him to the door of the flitter.

His problem was no closer to solution. He stood now in a form of transportation which could save them all—but he could not put it to use. And to retrace by foot the way they had come, Zurzal suffering from that maiming, three prisoners—the Jat—The issha were taught to act as individuals; their whole way of life made them first and foremost dependent upon themselves and wary of losing any of that independence. He shook his head as if to scatter out thoughts he could not arrange in the proper pattern.

At least he could see one thing—set against the wall of the flitter was a rack holding water flasks. Sighting those his thirst awoke. He worked free the nearest and forced himself to take only three sips, not enough to wash the gravelly dryness from his tongue and mouth. But with that and two others swinging on their slings from his shoulder he returned to the party by the rocks.

"The Skrem are dead," Taynad greeted him. "Yan says so—" The Jat was still snuggled against her but now it squeaked with some vigor.

"Well enough." But at the moment that was far down the list of Jofre's immediate concerns. He handed one of the water flasks to the girl and took another to where the Zacathan half sat, half lay.

Somehow Zurzal had managed to wriggle around to get a hold on the time scanner with his small hand. He was fumbling now at that part of the mechanism which held the power coil and, as Jofre came up, that yielded to his struggle. A wisp of smoke answered.

"Gone—burnt out—"

The Assha stone, Jofre thought. Power—it had given the power to hold that vivid return of life. But it was shattered into—he ran his finger into the small chamber of the coil—heat and dust—only dust—

"It needed only greater power!" The Zacathan was leaning away from his rock support. "Now we know!"

"And, Learned One, what good will that do us?" Jofre was going to make no pretense of covering the gloom of his own speculations concerning their future. "I am no pilot, you cannot handle the flitter. If I loose any one of these," he nodded towards the captives, "we cannot trust them to deliver us anywhere save the place they wish. And overland—" He gazed out over the plateau toward the breakage of the lava river, "we have no chance."

"You have no chance anyway, Slip-shadow," the leader of the squad rasped. "They will come when we do not report in. If you think to make a deal with me—with that lamebrain," he glanced toward the man Taynad had disarmed, "or Yager here—forget it. The Guild doesn't deal—they'll simply fly over and stass us all and then pick up what they want and leave the—"

"Jofre!" Taynad was on her feet, looking north, "They come—in the air—"

He caught it, too, the hum of another flitter. He could try—it was so small a chance but the only one he had—Jofre called upon his full energy and made for the cone hill. Fear as well as rage fed him now. He pulled and threw himself from hold to hold. Somehow he reached the crest and crouched, panting heavily behind one of those smaller mounds. But he was not too exhausted to steady the barrel of the blaster on the top of that mound, ready himself for the single small chance he might have for a beam at the flitter as it bore in to stass them as the squad leader had promised. He was not even sure that if the beam hit it would cause enough damage to bring the craft down; he could only hope.

The craft did not swoop in, but made a circle well above where he waited. Then it slipped sidewise and his fingers tightened until he willed them fiercely to relax. He had a single second to see that emblazoned sign on the side of the flitter, to depress the barrel of his weapon. The flare of fire shot across the cone crest, it did not touch that machine.

There was no return—either of stass beam or weapon fire. The flitter dipped where the others were, and then lifted for a space to set down near the other flitter. Jofre drew a ragged breath as he watched the uniformed passengers emerge, take evasive action.

The first of those silvered helms reached the Guild flitter. Then they were all past it. One halted briefly beside the body, but only for a moment. Jofre turned and started down the hill, his body still shaking from the stress of that

charge to reach the heights. He found it far more difficult going. No one appeared to notice him until he made the final drop to the level where the Patrol troopers had the three from the Guild in tangle cords and their officer was fronting Zurzal.

"—a good catch," the officer was saying.

The Zacathan's frill darkened, his eyes were coldly reptilian. "Bait, Captain? Then we were bait all the time? Well, that explains some incidents I wondered at."

"Bait?" returned the officer coolly. "You greatly desired this expedition, Learned One. You wished to prove something, I believe. We merely allowed you to fulfill what you desired. You did get the results you wanted, did you not? We have some video-casts which are certainly amazing. And I do not think that you need fear any more attentions from the Guild. They have lost a great deal—including an in-port that they were very eager to establish in secret. On the whole, a most successful operation, do you not agree?"

Zurzal lifted his maimed arm. "One well paid for," he returned.

The Patrol officer lost a little of his confident calm. "We have regenerative facilities, Learned One. Our command ship carries a medic with the techniques. You shall be given every attention. We are most indebted to you—"

Jofre felt drained. There was no longer any need for an oathed man. He had completed his service and in a very checkered fashion. It seemed to him now, and painfully, that he certainly had not shown well as an isshi—in many ways.

Issha—Taynad. At that moment he remembered what

the Guild leader had said. Taynad had been sent to take him captive and deliver him to the Shagga. Well, enough of the issha was left in him that he would not be so easily disposed of.

"Friend—friend—"

Something tugged at his sleeve and he looked down to see that Yan had him fast. But the Jat was still in Taynad's arms, she had moved that close to him. He tensed.

"Friend—" It was imperative—it was a demand for understanding.

Jofre looked to the girl. "But you are oathed—"

She stooped and allowed Yan to slide out of her hold. Her hands went to her braids and she pulled out the notched twigs, showing them clearly to him.

"They sent me these on Wayright. I was ordered—but I gave no oath before the High Altar."

"They will hold you to it anyway. I know the Shagga."

She looked at him proudly. "The Shagga may order; they do not oath."

"They will oath against you then, unless—" He started away from the rock against which he had been leaning, a new energy building in him. "Your sleeve knife, Sister— give it!" He held out his hand.

She stared at him, not understanding. Yan pulled at her other hand and looked up into her face, uttering one of those small coaxing mews.

Slowly Taynad drew that most precious, most intimate weapon and held it a little away from her. Jofre put out his hand and closed it about the bared blade.

"Pull!" he ordered and almost instinctively she answered. He felt that smart as its keen edge met his flesh

and cut. Then she was holding a bloodstained knife, looking from it to him in wonder, as he brought his own hand up to lick the blood welling in that cut.

"You have done as ordered," he said. "My blood dims your blade. So can you swear and no one, Lair Master or Shagga, can hold you wrong!"

The mask which she ever wore cracked. For the first time he saw more of the one who wore it than he ever thought he might.

"It is so—Shadow Brother," she said in a half whisper.

"It is so!" he told her firmly. "Shadow Sister."

"Jofre, Taynad!"

They awoke to the present and answered Zurzal's call.

"My coworkers. Captain," the Zacathan said. "It is thanks to them that the Guild did not put an end to these games you all have been playing before your somewhat late arrival Now, I think, we should be shown some of this gratitude which you mentioned is owed to us."

They were off Lochan, aboard the Patrol cruiser and in the sickbed where the Zacathan lay with his maimed arm under a roofing bubble which kept in the fine spray bathing the charred wrist, before they were together again in private.

"You were oathed to me for this venture now ended," Zurzal spoke first to Jofre. "I declare you have fulfilled your oath. Unless—"

"Unless?" Jofre asked.

"Unless you wish to make it a life burden?"

"Never a burden!" Since he had knelt to say farewell to the Lair Master in Ho-Le-Far he had not felt exactly like this. There was no question in him but what the Zacathan

offered him now was all he could wish.

"Taynad Jewelbright," Zurzal seemed to need no more words from Jofre but looked past him to her.

"Not Jewelbright." She shook her head. "I think there are other roads."

"There is one we may take together," Zurzal said. "What we did on Lochan is only the beginning—there are treasures out of time beyond all reckoning—it is up to us to find our share of them!"

Jofre's bandaged hand arose—his fingers shaped "Greeting to Shadow Comrade," which seldom, if ever, in his lifetime, an oathed issha could pattern.

Taynad's hand reached into his full sight—"So let it be." Her fingers gave assent.

"We deal then no more with the shadows of others," he spoke aloud, "only those which shall be our own."

And into his wounded hand slipped a paw—a paw for Taynad also. The last link closed tight.

# Andre Norton

**"The sky's no limit to Andre Norton's imagination...a superb storyteller." —The New York Times**

**Time Traders**                      0-671-31829-2 ★ $7.99 PB
"This is nothing less than class swashbuckling adventure—the very definition of space opera." —*Starlog*

**Time Traders II**                    0-671-31968-X ★ $19.00
Previously published in parts as *The Defiant Agents* and *Key Out of Time*.

**Janus**                              0-7434-7180-6 ★ $6.99 PB
Two novels. On the jungle world of Janus, one man seeks to find his alien heritage and joins a battle against aliens despoiling his world.

**Darkness & Dawn**                    0-7434-8831-8 ★ $7.99 PB
Two novels: *Daybreak: 2250* and *No Night Without Stars*.

**Gods & Androids**                    0-7434-8817-2 ★ $24.00 HC
Two novels: *Androids at Arms* and *Wraiths of Time*.

**Dark Companion**                     1-4165-2119-4 ★ $7.99 PB
Two complete novels of very different heroes fighting to protect the helpless in worlds wondrous, terrifying, and utterly alien.

**Star Soldiers**                      0-7434-3554-0 ★ $6.99 PB
Two novels: *Star Guard* and *Star Rangers*.

**Moonsinger**                         1-4165-5517-X ★ $7.99 PB
Two novels: *Moon of Three Rings* and *Exiles of the Stars*.

**From the Sea to the Stars**          1-4165-2122-4 ★ $15.00 TPB
Two novels: *Star Gate* and *Sea Siege*.

**Star Flight**                        1-4165-5506-4 ★ $7.99 PB
Two novels: *The Stars Are Ours* and *Star Born*.

**Crosstime**                          1-4165-5529-3 ★ $23.00 HC
Two novels: *The Crossroads of Time* and *Quest Crosstime*.

**Deadly Dreams**                      978-1-4391-3444-3 ★ $7.99 PB
Two novels: *Knave of Dreams* and *Perilous Dreams*.

---